Shades of Love . . .

Vijay Mohan

GenNext Publication

ISBN: 978-93-8022-284-4

Price: ₹ 290/-

First Published, 2016

Published by

GenNext Publications
5, Ansari Road, Daryaganj
New Delhi - 110002
Ph. 23242060, 23261060
E-mail: gennext@hotmail.com

Cataloging In Publication Data–DK

Courtesy: D.K. Agencies (P) Ltd. <docinfo@dkagencies.com>

Mohan, Vijay, author.

Shades of love / Vijay Mohan.

pages cm

Short stories.

ISBN 9789380222844

1. Love stories, Indic (English). 2. Suspense fiction, Indic (English). 3. Short stories, Indic (English). I. Title.

DDC 823.92 23

Shades of Love . . .

Contents

A

TRIBUTE

To

My Dear Friend

(My Brother-in-law)

A Noble Soul

Captain Premvir Singh
(Skinners Horse Regiment)
(6 June, 1942-15 Jan, 2015)

No farewell words were spoken,
No time to say good bye...
He lived in style – He left in style

Author

Homage

I take it as an honour to dedicate this book firstly to my parents; my father Mehta Lok Nath Mohan, my mother Mrs Shyam Mohan and aunt Mrs Raj Bali.

My father had a passion for poetry and my mother had a flair for writing. My aunt more than a mother to me, was an Epitome of Bliss.

I wish I had finished this book during their life time!

This book is my humble homage to them.

I also dedicate this book to my wife Rekha Mohan and son Vikas Mohan for they lauded my intentions of publishing the present literature as well as contributed their might in making the project a success.

And all my sisters , specially Neelam Datta, our courageous sister as well as our cousin Reena Singh.

Any body else in their situation would have broken down to the ordeals they encountered.

Author

Acknowledgements

Dear Readers,

I would like to share with you something which, so far I have kept it to myself.

I was released from the Army in 1967. I was looking for other options. One of my uncle's, who was a film director, suggested me to join the film industry. My mother on the other hand advised me to persue the career of a writer as she was very confident of my writing skills. *But I listened to my..... heart and joined the Border Security Force.*

I couldn't tell her, Why? But now at the twilight of my life, I realise that I should have listened and acknowledged the advice and sentiments of my mother.

Well, coming back to the actual subject.

I have ventured into publishing this book of my short stories in English for those readers who are not comfortable with reading the books written in Hindi.

I may mention here that this book contains short stories which are very simple and translated in very simple English. So, they neednot consult a dictionary/reference book.

The credit for publishing of this book goes to my dear friend, Mr Jawahar Lal Malhotra and his wife, Mrs Savita Malhotra. Both of them prompted and motivated me to undertake this work.

I then motivated myself to accomplish this mission.

And then Reena Singh and Rajiv Saini (USA) came to my rescue in assisting me in translation of my stories from my

Hindi book *'Teri Meri Kahani'* into English. I must admit they both gave impetus to my assignment. And also Dr Pradaman Bhalla

And a special mention of Vivek Gupta for his computer back- up, which was of immense help to me in subsequent editing and correction of my script.

Master Vansh Malhotra of Spring Dales School, Pusa Road, New Delhi, a budding writer, has contributed two very meaningful stories in this book. Please do laud his efforts.

Thanks to GenNext Publications and its entire team and the editors.

Family : Usha Bajaj, Veena Mohindru, Pamila Singh, Neelam Datta, Manju and Satish Sagar, Rita Singh, PJ Singh and Amita, Kamlesh (USA), Anupam and Manu Singh, Nidhi Sagar and Manisha, Payal (Kinoo), Dr Namita, Col Giriraj, Reena Singh, Rajiv Saini (USA), Shelly and Molina

Friends : Rajinder Nath 'Rehbar', Dr Ramanendra Singh, R.N. Sharma, Dharam Pal Dewan, Sudershan Rana (Canada) Ved Sharma, Col. Radheysham Gupta, L.P. Singh, Sakshi Chauhan, Prabha Nadkarni and Shubh Chadha.

Extended Family : Lovely people who are in contact with me.

Army : Brig G.S. Gosal, Gen R.S. Nagra, Gen S.S. Sandhu, Maj B.S. Sahota, Col U.S. Rana, Col B.P.S. Bains, Col Ashok Misra, Col Nikhil Apte and Col R.C. Chadha.

BSF : R.S. Mehta (IG), V.K. Gaur (IG), K. Verma (Comdt), Y. Bannerji (Comdt), B.R. Chadha (Comdt), Dr G.P. Bhatnagar (IG). S.P.S. Tanwar (DIG).

Air Force: Air Marshal D.R. Nadkarni.

I have tried to present many interesting and captivating stories to my readers and want the book to reach the maximum audience.

Flaws teach you to be cautious in future. So, ignore my flaws and appreciate what you have liked.

In the end, I would just say, "I love you all who have been the part of my journey of life."

Vijay Mohan

Foreword

About The Shades of Love ....

The art of short story writing is diminishing because of proliferation of TV serials and electronics. Age old tradition of bed time story telling by Granny and Aunts is now unheard of. Print media hardly encourages writers because modern generation don't read stories. 'Shades of Love...' stories by Vijay Mohan herald a pleasant surprise. His web of 29 stories cover half a century wide canvass against the back drop of Army, BSF, Indo-Pak border and metropolitan towns of North India is captivating indeed.

He is poet by birth, soldier by profession, stage and film actor by passion and could not careless by style. His personality traits repeatedly emerge in his long and short stories. His multi faceted characters are replica of social surroundings he lived in. His personality is vocal at most places. The stories are a queer mixture of suspense, humour, romance and adventure. He presents his stories in three dimensions.

I met him nearly five decades ago on the lawns of India Gate soon after 1965 Indo- Pak war. He narrated stories at length laughing and giggling and adding tinge of his Urdu poetry. He said, "Borders can divide nations but they cannot divide love between two individuals."

He is all the time poetic, assertive and wades though rough weather of events and human fate cheerfully.

He has a simple and lucid style of presentation. Stories are absorbing and leave lasting imprint on memory.

Shashi Gaur and Virendra Kumar Gaur

Preface

I was listening to my favourite FM Rainbow channel. Jainendra Singh during his discussion with Dharampal Dewan, an author, he asked him to read the preface of his book. Upon hearing this I remembered that I had also to write the preface my latest book. I immediately switched off the radio and sat down to write the present preface.

Basically, I have been writing my stories in Urdu. On insistence of one of my dear friends, Mr Jawaharlal Malhotra, I had translated and published them in Hindi language.

But every day at the crossings; I used to find hawkers selling books written in English. And one of them one day told me that the customers preferred books written in English.

So, based on the abovesaid notion to reach to a larger audience, I decided to translate my book in English.

In fact, I wrote the stories published in this book over a period of last six decades. Some of them got published in reputed magazines; some of them were read by me on AIR Jammu long ago and some were lying idle on the shelves.

When I decided, I should publish a book of my short stories, I did not have an inkling that I had written so many stories during all these years. On going through my manuscripts, I observed that every second day, I had penned one story or the other.

Love is an integral part of life. And they are inseparable. Thus, to justify this, I have kept the title of the book as "Shades of Love . . ." Since I have travelled far and wide during my service tenure in Army and BSF, so the glimpses of those areas of my postings are bound to intervane in these stories. A couple of love stories have characters from military/para-military forces.

You will be surprised to note that in these love stories, rarely much dialogues of love between the lovers are exchanged. There are a few simple stories depicting the day to day incidents of our life. And all of you will easily connect yourself with those stories. Some of them are real stories blended with an element of fiction.

Now, I share with you the themes of my stories.

1. **A Girl from Lahore (The Beginning of an End)** is an intense story of love between a girl 'Roshan Ara' from Lahore and her love affair with an Indian Army officer. I have very well depicted a true picture of how the activities take place along the border. The sacrifice she made in choosing this decision and all what happened...? She is tough girl from Pathan tribe. We can divide the countries but we cannot divide the hearts.
2. In **The Blood Stains:** I have very well depicted the character of Gul Sher Khan, a BSF Commandant, a Pathan with a heart of gold. He is always remorseful as he could not fulfill the promise he made with Diljeet Kaur. The agony of her blood stains on his hands, always haunts him. And this time hearing the story from his wife, his friends avoided his . . . !
3. **The Story of a Crow and a Frog :** A tale of meaningful story of friendship between a crow and a frog, brings us the moral that 'a friend in need is friend indeed.'
4. **The Art of Handicraft :** This is the story of an old women doing an embroidery work. The work which the son does not appreciate. But when his mill owner sees that, he is thrilled. And offers to open handicraft centre in the village and buy all the stuff produced.

5. **Pushpa and Her Spects:** It is an emotional tale of a simple teacher from Kangra (Himachal Pradesh) and his playful wife. Her main identity was a pair of her spects, around which the story of the said 'Master ji' is crafted. She was a terrific sport's girl who even outplayed the boys, the men, in race as well as in horse riding. People had started calling her' Pushpa Chashme Wali' One day a calamity occurred. Her spects got misplace and then...! It is a very emotional situation, you discover it yourself.
6. **The Other Side of the Hedge:** It is very very simple and emotional story of a father and a son, narrated in simple words. It is about the human relationship. It shows how the father takes care of his son and how his son tries to pay off his father's debt. But is the present generation prepared for this gesture?
7. **The Sinners :** Sharda Devi is crazy for a grandson.When a girl is born, that cruel woman tells her son to bury the newly-born girl. When the grandson is born, she arranges grand festivity. But her plans fall like a pack of cards. A young woman lawyer comes to her rescue. Sharda Devi is amazed to notice that a young girl can also be so effective.
8. **The Final Decision :** It is the story of a tussle between a couple for a sibling for their son. Rajan wants to have; wife disagrees. But when wife agrees, circumstances revolt.
9. **A Smart Girl** is the story of a callgirl having good principles. She is clever enough even to out smart and dodge the police department. Her planning and sequence of her actions are worth appreciation. Please read it yourself and assess.
10. **Reshma–A Love Story,** of intimacy between a Kashmiri girl and an army officer. Here, I have very vividly portrayed the scenario of white and black sheep grazing in the grassland on the mountains of Kashmir valley and the young girls coming to collect dry twigs of the trees, and their chirping in a very mesmerising manner.

    And Javed, a villain, arrives on the scene and upsets the apple cart.

11. **A Gentleman :** A village girl while catching butterflies goes deep into the jungle. When she looks up, she finds herself surrounded by four vagabonds. A hunter saves her from disgrace. And drops her at her house.

12. **Beware of the Evildoers :** Is the story of a forest officer, his wife, their cute son 'Munna' and Riaz an artist. He happens to be staying close to area where Pervez and Shabana reside. Every time while pinching the cheeks of her pretty son, he would often caution Shabana to be careful from the Evildoers. His assignment got completed. Before departure, Riaz presented Shabana a book, which looked so real, though. There were no words inscribed on the book. She enquired from Riaz as to why it was so. He said a few words and went away.

    A few years later, they both bumped into each other. And then at the grave yard...!

13. **The Last Flight :** Julie had been personal assistant of Prof Dutt for the last so many years. She had developed a soft corner for him.But the circumstances do not support her.

14. **The Radish Leaves :** What story can there be about Radish Leaves? But why not? Read the story as narrated by Colonel Sandhu to Major Tony Madhukar and you will be astonished to hear it. Of course, the story gives the Major a shock of his life.

15. **From Heaven to the Earth :** Since he had good track record in heaven, so, Almighty sent Bhagat Ram in his *'Udan Khatola'* to visit earth to see his son. There he noticed his friend perching on a tree who cunningly got hold of his foot.

    And for this, Almighty admonishes *Yamraj* for this situation.

16. **A Girl with a Dog :** Is, in fact, the story of our professor friend, who invariably meets some girl, somewhere with a dog. Thus, the story between the Professor Paul and Rosie originated. Professor, though a retired simpleton, does not understand, why he is enchanted by that blooming beauty of a lass? He is astonished...! She entirely transforms him.

17. **After Ten Years :** Is the story of a love affair between a young girl and a boy. They are made to suffer, because of financial disparity. This story is amongst my first stories published in my college magazine in the year 1958.
18. **A Clever Twist :** Neeraj's wife is very religious, whereas he is atheist. His promotion is held up. To ward of the bad effects, his wife takes him to a 'hermit' for his blessings. He gets special blessings but they don't suit him. But why?
19. **The Test :** It is the story of a conflict in the mind of an ex student about his teacher. The teacher had been his mentor; teaching honesty. Can his teacher do this? He is in a affix.
20. **A Long Wait :** Is the eternal story of wait and sacrifice of soldier's wife. A story of love of two women with army officers, the first one waiting for the return of her husband and the other, waits for her boyfriend gone missing from the battle field. Well, life is like that. They both go to attend the ceremony of conferring of the gallantry medals.

    What happens afterwards? You guess...!
21. **The Beggar Women :** Is the story of common beggar women (carrying her child) whom you encounter and spot everyday, almost on all the road crossings. And there is nothing new. But then there certainly is something unique. People throw their lustful glances. Read and experience the new experience.
22. **A Spark of Fire :** A tragedy of circumstances in Sudhir's life, ultimately gets solved. But at what cost, when the spark has already burnt his house?
23. **Delusion :** Prashant had come home after many days. His wife playfully tells him that he has gone old. He just looks at her and closes his eyes. Why? Read for yourself.
24. **The Last Union :** It is story of the union of a girl and a boy, happening time and again. But it can happen only for seven births.
25. **A Crazy Heart :** Is the tale of an unsaid expression of love between a woman and a doctor; *of* a conspiracy, wherein

one of the planners herself becomes a prey. They go to the movies. They go for evening ride. They go to attend a marriage party and to a hotel to take part in a dance competition. And the end is... soulful.

26. **The Search :** Every day Akhtar watches a man from his window, searching for something on the track. One day, he asks the man. The reply that man gives to him, makes Akhter speechless.

27. **The Fourth Angle of a Triangle :** Is a very strange title. It is the story which I dreamt, with its title, characters as well as the end. And I just wrote it.. Either I am confused or I want to confuse the readers. Anyway it is an interesting story of Major Chatterjee and his three friends. And of course one of them is a charming girl.

28. **Sofia: A Girl from North-east :** Is the story of a bold, beautiful Manipuri damsel. She is fearless and comes to North to accomplish her mission. She is a heart-throb and the life line of the restaurant. Customers come there to have a glance of her hour glass-figure and not to eat.

    And then of course, entices Major Nagra for her mission.

29. **Ruby in Bell Bottom :** Is a satirical-comedy; Wherein in the Prayer Meet you find many pretty woman who had gathered there showering praises for the departed soul. Even the wife of deceased did not know her husband was so talented. Ruby with her 36-26-36 figure, wearing a white shawl looked an idol of grief. After the 'Prayer Meet' was over, people rushed to the refreshment counter like grey hounds.

    In the 'Party Meet' you read the efficient arrangement of the party, managed by a Captain Sher Singh. He is from an armed regiment and a seasoned player in this field. Many generals seek his advice in this matter. What happens in the 'Party Meet' I cannot disclose any thing as you will lose the element of surprise.

And it is this in nutshell all, what I have to say about my book 'Shades of Love . . .'

Vijay Mohan

1

A Girl from Lahore (The Beginning of an End)

I am a story teller.

For the past so many years, I have been telling you the stories of love, affection, and hatred, real and unreal, close to reality and away from reality. But ultimately my aim has been to entertain you and create a sense of awareness in your minds.

One day, I got a call from Rita Singh. She said, "You have been telling us stories about various subjects, but so far you have not written anything about the borders. This time do write a story about somebody across the border."

I went into perplexity as I did not make out what to write. Moreover I was not in mood to pen down anything. It was nothing else but just being very lethargic.

One day, I read the news about the sad demise of film actor 'Farookh Sheikh'. I had known him from close quarters. Instantly, I was reminded of 'Roshan Ara Sheikh', a pretty damsel from Lahore. I am surprised how her sad story had been lying buried in my mind for so many years. Or perhaps I had been afraid to share her story with others. Maybe, it is just a story similar to mine. I can't say... I am not very sure. I am in a fix.

I am still very hesitant to share it with others. But I feel compelled as I have to fulfill a promise I had made with Rita Singh.

There is turmoil in me. I now feel that my heart will explode if I withhold this story any further. Since I don't have the courage to narrate it myself, I let the hero of the story, Roshan, tell you everything himself, in his own words.

Borders can divide nations but they cannot divide love between two individuals.

Who was Roshan Ara Sheikh and where she came from and.... ?

We had met a number of times. Every year during vacations she would come from Lahore to Amritsar to visit her aunt. She was very fair, tall, and slim, with long tresses. She had pinkish oval face, blue eyes like the water of the sea, red lips and rosy cheeks.

I feel I have not been able to do full justice to her beauty. You may add any thing additional if you wish to, to create your own beauty in the direction of your imagination. . .

She would not come alone, but was always accompanied by her younger sister. Her sister was equally charming.

It was perchance that I happened to meet them. One day, my sister wanted to visit her friend Tavinder living near the Mall Road. She requested me to go along with her. As we entered Tavinder's house, we saw her lounging in her living room.

She told us that she was expecting her friends. Before she could elaborate further, the door of the drawing room opened. Aah... what was that? ... A whiff of sweet fragrance filled the atmosphere. Was the fragrance from the bouquet of the flowers she was holding in her hands or did it radiate out of her elegant body, I cannot say...

The girl was wearing a *salwar-kameez* with matching *dupatta*. She had an amazing sense of colour combination which we only see once in a blue moon. The cut and design of the dress was very peculiar, one which we rarely come across.

I was spellbound. It was as if a *'Taj Mahal'* had entered the room. Shah Jahan was a maniac. He got the hands of those artisans chopped off who sculpted this monument of love. What a farce! How could he do that?

I wouldn't dare chop off the hands of 'The Creator' of such a magnificent piece of art and beauty in pure flesh and blood.

You know thoughts can travel infinite distances in no time. And then I was back to myself. My poetic expression about her vanished. We had an eye contact. I felt as if magnetic waves of passion were emerging from her. She became conscious of my glance and just to overcome her feeling of shyness, she started fiddling with her *dupatta*.

Then I noticed a girl behind her. She had to be her younger sister, and quite charming herself.

Immediately on their entry, Tavinder first introduced Gagan to them. But at the time when I was introduced as Roshan, then I noticed a mild streak of mischievous smile on her face. Being very good in observing people I could not miss that. I later on understood the reason of that.

Later, they were introduced to us as *Ara* and *Rani*. In my first meeting I was very apprehensive about them. Their way of speaking, talking and body language was some what different than ours. It looked awkward to my sixth sense.

Anyway my doubts weren't unfounded and got cleared later.

We came to know that they were Pakistani girls and their real names were Roshan Ara Sheikh and Rubina Sheikh. And to conceal their real identity and to avoid the glare and stare of Indian people, they had been given Hindu/Indian names. Roshan Ara was addressed as Ara and Rubina as Rani.

In fact, it was due the similarity in our names that had brought a smile on her pretty face. I was 'Roshan' and she was 'Roshan Ara'.

We had, till now, not disclosed the identity of the Lahore sisters, as we were apprehensive about the reaction from our mother. We were sure that on knowing the facts she would tear us apart. To our surprise, however, the scene was absolutely reverse. Our mother was very thrilled to know about their real identity.

She herself was from Lahore. Her ancestors belonged to Peshawar but from there they had migrated to Lahore long back. She, too, was born and brought up there, and had all her schooling there. She had studied in Lady Harding College. She travelled down the memory lane back to that era.

In the evening, when both the sisters did not come, my mother became restless and told me go and bring them. The moment I brought them, there was radiance on my mother's face.

And without uttering a single word she hugged both of them very tightly.

She had not hugged us ever so tightly, as far as I remember.

Both the girls were puzzled. We were equally dumbfounded at the behavior of our mother.

My mother then took them aside and made lot of inquiries about the place of her birth.

To remove their curiosity I briefed them both about the background of this entire episode.

From then onwards, we noticed that our mother had developed a soft corner for them and had started paying special attention to them.

She would even cook special dishes for them.

All this continued till the time of their departure to Lahore. Even for their return journey, she would specially make *chicken birayani* for Roshan Ara and *'gajar ka halwa'* for Rubina.

In our few meetings I felt she had a crush on me. But she did not express that to me. I don't know what to say about that... I would have responded, had she uttered something. Till now, it was a one-sided affair.

We know for a fact that you can't clap with just one hand. If she had put her hand forward then I would have reciprocated and there would have been a clap.

So, that clap didn't happen and she ultimately left for Pakistan after spending her holidays.

Both the sisters were very fond of shopping and since our house was in the main *bazaar*, they would often drop in. And thus, our acquaintance grew. Every second day we had a party or a card session. Then all of us would go for a movie, or a picnic.

We went around the city and visited 'Jalian wala bagh', 'Golden Temple' and the 'Beating the Retreat' ceremony at Wagha Border.

In the evening all of us would play badminton and I then realised, what a terrific player she was! In doubles, she would always opt to be my partner. And in singles, she would even defeat me.

Then they both started visiting Amritsar very frequently.

This time she was a little more free and frank. Whenever conversing she would throw a smile off and on. It was then that for the first time I realised how enchanting and charismatic her smile was. During her laugh her snow-white teeth looked no less than a string of pearl necklace.

Alas, the day of their return was here, again... While sitting in the compartment of Lahore train she said, "This time my stay ended very fast. I do not know how the time flew?"

Then carrying on in a gloomy tone she said, "I will perhaps be not able to come here again." She had tears rolling down her eyes. She slowly murmured, "I am being engaged and will be married soon."

"Will you ...will you remember me?" she unexpectedly threw a question staring at me. What could have been my reply? I was quite confused to utter anything. I kept silent. I kept mum.

"Please do come to Lahore... to marry me." She said so many words and I merely stared ... mute.

She didn't have the nerve to raise her hand to say goodbye. I realised later that the least I could have done was, to have waved, but my hands didn't move. I don't know why?

And then the train started... slowly... and slowly, drifting towards Lahore.

The moment the train left; there was turmoil in my heart. I became restless... almost crazy. It became impossible for me to pass time in her absence.

The very next year, there was the Chinese attack on India. The government had declared an Emergency. The army went for a massive recruitment, and I was selected. I was sent to IMA (Indian Military Academy) for officers' training course. After passing out from the academy, I was posted to one of the unit's in Ambala Cantonment.

Life began to move at a comfortable pace. But Ara perhaps was never out of my mind. Even during the stress and strains of training, I did not let her thought get off my mind.

As luck would have it, I met Wing Comdr Anderson's niece Angelina in the Sirhind Club. She had come from Lahore to spend a few days with her uncle's family. During the conversation, I happened to mention to her about Roshan Ara. And it was a mere coincidence that she knew Roshan Ara very well.

On her return to Lahore, she told Roshan Ara about me. After a week I got a letter from Roshan Ara. She had written a very infatuated letter. I was on cloud nine to receive a letter from her. She had written that olden friends are golden friends. I wish you could come here to marry me. However, her words were very mysterious?

Tension arose between the two countries. In the process, movement of letters from both the sides got suspended.

I was helpless. I wondered what would be Roshan Ara's state of mind. It must have been very agonising for her.

As I had done couple of courses in foreign languages like Pushto, Chinese, Japanese and others, so I was attached with an interrogation centre close to Akhnoor Border (in Jammu area). I had the independent charge with one junior officer and five very well-trained *jawans*. I had to directly report to the Brigade Headquarters.

I had been provided with a barrack for us to stay, as well one bunker, some distance away from the border in view of unprovoked firing by Pakistan troops. I mostly stayed in the bunker. In case any need arose, the bunker could also be used as a safe house.

We were all permitted to move in civil dress and we could move about anywhere along the border. We had been granted blanket permission for this. We could cross over to other side of the border in exceptional situation by taking all necessary precautions.

One evening, my *jawans* caught a Pakistani officer roaming inside the Indian territory. They brought him to the bunker. I looked at the officer. He was extremely smart and somewhat senior to me in age. The strange thing about him was that he was in civil attire.

My *jawans* placed the weapon recovered from him in front of me. I noticed that it was not a service weapon but a 12-bore gun used for hunting birds and animals. They also recovered a bag containing a few cartridges. Apparently, he appeared to be on a hunting mission. But in these circumstances, when there is tension between both the countries, I decided to interrogate him to find out his purpose of entering our territory.

All this while, he was very cool. He disclosed that he was a major in Pakistan army. While hunting for rabbits and birds, he had inadvertently crossed the unmarked border with a tall wild grass on both sides of the border.

He seemed to have no nefarious intentions. He had narrated his side of the story very calmly in one go without my askance.

My instincts said he was telling the truth. Since I had been a hunter myself, I had twice crossed the border unintentionally chasing the wild boar. Once in Rajasthan and second time here in Samba border area. However, I still wanted to be certain and did not want to be callous in my sense of duty just because of my gut feeling.

I ordered my *jawans* to search him throughly. My *jawans* meticulously searched him and placed all the items recovered from his possession on my table. There were a few letters and his wallet. While going through the documents, I was convinced about his unknowingly crossing over to our side.

But a photograph in his wallet stunned me. There was a sudden gush of some past memories of my good old days and they started swirling in front of my eyes.

That photograph was of Roshan Ara. It seemed to have angered me and I enquired harshly, "Whose photograph is this?"

"My *fiancée,*" he replied without any hesitation. "Why? What's the matter?"

On hearing this, I lost my cool and felt like shooting him. But then better sense prevailed. I thought to myself, 'What's his fault in this?'

I asked my *jawans* to leave us alone and wait for my further instructions.

Then I told him that I could free him to go back provided he takes me along to Pakistan through the route he crossed over to our side. He was stunned to hear my offer.

"But why? What a ridiculous thought that is!" The *bizarre* idea perplexed, rather perturbed him.

I replied, "I want to meet Roshan Ara. " That confused him even more.

I then narrated our unfinished tale of love.

He agreed to my offer. After all, that was his only means of returning home in an uncomplicated way, and well, life is precious to all and who doesn't want to live...? Moreover, the better of all this was that he was not interested in marrying Roshan Ara. I, on the other hand, had started to see a possibility of being together with her. A thought I had given up.

In fact, it was his parents who had pressurised him to give his consent.

He took me to Pakistan through the same route he had entered India. Then he helped me to meet Roshan Ara. She embraced me very hard and wept bitterly.

On watching us, he became very sentimental. He said, "you have spared my life and in return of that I am prepared to help you crossing the border along with Roshan Ara." I was stunned at his courageous offer.

Then he asked Roshan Ara, "Do you want to go with him? It is very bold step for a girl. You will have to leave your parents and all other relations. Will you be able to bear their separation? And it is not easy to settle in a foreign country with different upbringing. You are a Muslim and they are Hindus. Think it over very seriously. It is not an easy decision.

For Captain Roshan, it does not matter much. He is a man and then he is just going to be in his own country, with his relations. But greatest risk for him is crossing over to Pakistan, and taking a Pakistani girl to India illegally. Abandoning and absenting place of his duty without permission. These are very serious offences and as per Army act if found guilty can be courtmarshalled.

The aim of my telling you all this is not to discourage or scare you", he said, "but to make you aware of the realities and hazards you are going to encounter later on in life."

He left both of us alone to seriously ponder over our decision of staying together in India.

On his return, we both told him that we were very firm in our resolution of staying and living together.

Then he told Roshan Ara that he was extremely happy that she was going with me. He did not harbour any malice towards her.

In fact during his college days, he had been in love with Shahida. Both of them wanted to marry, but his parents wanted him to marry Roshan Ara and he did not want to go against their wishes.

He was a Pathan and, true to his promise. He kept both of us hidden in his house. He had taken such a great hazard for us!

The very next night, he put us in his jeep and took us to the border. After dropping us he went back to his border outpost and stayed there for the night.

As I knew the location of the ambush parties, I had no difficulty in reaching my post. I had spoken to the junior officer and my confidant about my arrival. He had tackled the situation very well in my absence. Also, since it was dark, Roshan Ara couldn't have been recognised being in male attire.

Even the junior officer could not make out that the person with me was a woman. I kept Roshan Ara with me in the bunker. My main concern was to hide her in some safe place.

The next day, I locked the door of my bunker to ensure that Roshan Ara's presence doesn't get discovered. I carried out my official work from my barrack office. I requested my Brigade Major for 15 days of leave, which was granted without any questions. I handed over the charge to my junior and asked him to drop me at Jammu railway station in the evening.

In the evening, he brought the jeep to my bunker. On some pretext, I sent him to my office to bring a file and in the meantime put Ara in the rear seat of the jeep. At the Jammu railway station I kept him occupied in such a manner that he was not able to see Roshan Ara. I told him to hurry back as it was already very late.

Talking to my mother was out of question. But I did take my sister into confidence and told her everything on the phone. To my surprise, she was thrilled and asked me to bring Ara to our house in Amritsar.

"Have you gone insane? Mother will never tolerate this, "I said, my tone, agitated."

"*Bhaiya,* I have not gone mad. The happy news is that mother has gone to Bhutan to stay with father for two months since father's deputation has been extended."

"You mean to say that mother has left you all by yourself in the house." I asked.

"No, not alone, exactly. She has asked Shakuntla aunty to stay with me. Aunty has already met Roshan Ara, during her earlier visits, so there is no risk involved. Bring Roshan Ara here fast without any misgivings," she said anxiously.

Actually, I had been very worried about where to make arrangements of her stay. She was a tough girl. She appeared a bit quiet, little nervous but didn't exhibit any anxiety.

To make the journey comfortable, I hired a taxi and took her to my house. My sister Gagan was anxiously awaiting our arrival. The moment we reached she tightly hugged Roshan Ara. I do not know why Roshan Ara started sobbing.

Maybe, she had started missing her family. My sister consoled her. She offered her a glass of water and then went inside to get tea and snacks for us.

"Do you feel sorry for coming with me? Do you want to go back?" Staring at her I asked her.

She immediately put her arms around me and said, "No. It is not so." And tears continued to flow.

At that very moment, Gagan entered the room, seeing her Roshan Ara quickly separated herself from me. On watching this, Gagan gave a smile but out of shyness, Roshan Ara bent her head down.

For next a few days, both of us had a wonderful time. On the last day, when I was going back to the unit, Roshan Ara was in tears. I consoled her saying that I would be back soon.

In the morning, I reached my headquarters.

The moment my senior officer saw me, he called me to his office and apprised me about the firing on the border between both the sides. He further said, "There is flag meeting of senior officers of both the sides tomorrow at 10 am. You come prepared with your points."After that I went to my interrogation centre.

Next day. there was a delegation of officers present at the meeting to discuss the border issues.

And I was excited to see Kabir Khan? We both were very eager to know as to happened after he left both Roshan Ara and me at the border?

During the break, tea and snacks were served as had been customary and we both got a chance to be close with each other.

I quickly told him about all what had happened at my end. But the situation on his side had turned serious.

When till night Roshan Ara did not turn up, her parents got very worried and they started making enquiries at the places where her friends lived. They also checked up with there close relatives. But nobody had any clue.

Since it was matter of disgrace and their honour was at stake, they made hushed enquiries. When even after a week they were not able to trace her, her family members decided to spread a rumour that they had sent Roshan Ara to USA for higher studies.

And after a few days, they informed his parents that on the insistence of Roshan Ara to pursue her higher studies, they had sent her to USA. In these cirmstances, they should find another girl for him. And now his marriage has been fixed with Shahida. They are getting married next week. I congratulated him for his marriage with Shahida.

The meeting was over. We shook hands though we wanted to hug as we had developed a kind of affinity with each other but kept our feelings to ourselves. This would have sent a wrong message to our seniors. Our eyes were moist. He uttered only one thing. "Take care of Roshan Ara. Don't let me down." We both departed.

As luck would have it, I was called to my headquarters and was informed that being a member of skiing team as well as a linguist I was attached to a monitoring station at Simla, was relieved the same day.

Next day, I was back in Amritsar.

The main door of the house was open. I quietly tiptoed and went inside. Roshan Ara and Gagan were busy in playing cards. The moment Roshan Ara saw me, she threw the cards aside and came running and passionately encircled me in her arms. She was so thrilled to see me that she forgot that Gagan was also present in the room.

She had tears of happiness trickling down her rosy cheeks. It appeared as if the dew drops were falling on the rose petals.

I told them about my posting to Simla. They were both very pleased about this turn of events. I had a couple of days of joining time. After availing that I along with Roshan Ara reached Simla. My friend Captain V.K. Gaur had got me permission to stay outside the army area and he had managed to arrange a good house.

It was a comfortable house and was fully furnished. Except for the items of grocery, we had to buy nothing. She was happy preparing the best mutton dishes for me. It was then I realised what a cook she was! She was very good in culinary art.

Captain Gaur was very dear friend of mine, so I bared all facts about Roshan Ara to him. On learning the facts about Roshan Ara, he was extremely perturbed. "Do you know the magnitude of what you have done?"

For the next two days, he did not meet me. I could make out that he was very upset and worried over this episode. He wanted to solve my riddle but was in a fix, not sure how to go about it. On the third day, he came to my office during lunch time. "Roshan, what you have done cannot be undone?"

The first thing for you to do is, to marry her. Not a soul here knows about the background of Roshan Ara. To cover up everything he would arrange for a Christian wedding." He told me that a Father of the church was very closely known to him.

A year ago there was a fire in church and nearly 200 people had got entrapped in it. It was then that he got his troops, rescued the people and saved the church building. Since then the Father holds him in great esteem.

He requested the Father to organise our wedding. And ultimately the Father agreed to solemnise our wedding.

Captain Gaur made all necessary arrangements. The last hitch was to fix the date and for that he wanted to consult my parents. It was a herculean task. I knew they wouldn't agree.

He decided to go and convince them for their participation. My father told him point blank that he would never be a party to my wrong doings. He had also been on a foreign mission and he knew the complications and repercussions of this episode.

My mother did not want to hurt the feelings of my father and thus backed out. They, however, agreed that if my sister wanted she could attend the marriage function. Captain Gaur was able to convince my sister and brought her along. Roshan Ara was very pleased to see my sister and hugged her.

Both of them got very emotional and tears started rolling out of their eyes. They had met each other after a long time and in a tricky situation.

The marriage function was very simple and went on very well. It was attended by a few army officers and their wives.

My sister stayed with us for a couple of days and then went back home. When she reached home, our mother was alone as our father was away to the market. My mother, all these days, was anxiously awaiting my sister's return. My sister narrated everything to her in detail and all the while mother had tears in her eyes.

We were happily married.

In Simla, life was beginning to feel like pure joy... We were attending parties, watching movies and visiting various picnic spots. Since Roshan Ara was very good in sports, she took part in skiing, ice skating and roller skating competitions. To my amazement, she bagged prizes in almost in all sports that she played.

But yes! She had a passion for badminton. So every day, we would play the game with other officers and their wives. In singles, she defeated almost all the women. She became very popular among the women folk.

She was very happy and we were happily enjoying our life. She had almost forgotten her past and more or less left it behind.

There used to be summer festivals and carnivals in Simla. This time there was a proposal of Himachal Pradesh Government organising the function at national level.

The function stared with gusto. We attended all the ceremonies and enjoyed the function.

At the end of the function, there were matches of different games. Roshan Ara enjoyed them a lot as we all know by now, how crazy she was about sports.

On the last day of the festival, there were badminton matches. All national players had come to participate. In the single's category, Ms Nita Bagchi crushed her rival Ms Sameera, a former No.1, in straight two games.

There was a big applause from the spectators. They were all thrilled.

The chairman of the badminton association, Gen Chibber, was sitting and watching the game. He himself was a national player during his hay days.

While clapping, he said, "Is there anybody amongst the crowd who wants to try her hand against Ms Bagchi?"

Before I could anticipate I found Roshan Ara standing there. When the spectators noticed a girl challenging Ms Bagchi, they were thrilled and there was a big applause. I tried my best to call her back but she did not hear me because of a loud clapping from the crowd.

Finding her there, Gen. Chibber called her to come close to him and asked, "What's your name?"

This question of the General took my wits out. I did not know what reply she would give as everybody had known her as Ara.

She replied, "Sir, my name is Ara."

"And what's your surname?" he asked.

Now on this question of the General, I got more perplexed. But she kept her wits under control and said, "I am Ara Captain."

At this, the General gave a startled look and said. "Heard this surname for first time."

She kept her cool and shot back, 'Sir! If there can be a John Major in America and a family of a poet in India using poet's pen name 'Azmi' as their surname, then why can't I use the rank Captain of my husband as my surname? So, I am Ara Captain."

General was speechless before her this curt reply. He did not know what to say?

Anyway, the match started and in the first game Ms Bagchi comfortably defeated Roshan Ara. There was pindrop silence in the crowd. I got panicky. She felt hurt.

Her ancestors once belonged to an Afghan tribe. I had a strong notion that the tribal blood in her veins is bound to revolt and she would bounce back.

My gut feeling came out to be true and she defeated Ms Bagchi in next two games. Watching this happen, there was a big roar in the crowd. All the spectators stood up with excitement.

There was a rush of media people to have a picture of the girl, an *amateur* player who had outplayed Ms. Bagchi yet to be crowned the winner at national level.

There was a chaos; members of the badminton association got very jittery. They did not know how to react.

Gen Chibber was himself very amazed at this turn of events. In fact, he had said all this in a lighter vein, for anybody to come and play with national player. He did not expect that a girl will emerge from nowhere from amongst the crowd and overshadow the national winner.

Anyway Ara wasn't the official entry and this match was played as a sidekick. At the time of prize distribution ceremony Gen Chibber called Ara and told her to stand alongwith Ms Bagchi for the photograph.

And look at the greatness of Ms Bagchi, she removed the medal from her neck and put it on Roshan Ara. The spectators all stood up and gave a standing ovation to Ms Bagchi, for this gesture of her sportsmanship.

All the officers and their wives were very thrilled as well as proud of Roshan Ara's feat. We had a good celebration in the club.

Roshan Ara was on cloud nine. She was never so blissful. There was an extra glow on her already radiant face. That was the happiest phase of our life.

The very next day, her photograph alongwith Ms Bagchi with a caption *'An Amateur Defeats National Badminton Champion'* was splashed in all the leading papers across the country.

...And that was the beginning of an end.

Her photograph was recognised by her relations who in turn informed her parents. On the third day, some people from Pak Embassy alongwith senior Indian officers took us to Delhi. It was all a big shock for both of us. Nobody was prepared to listen to us.

This news was splashed all over the world by television channels. Kabir khan had been promoted as a colonel by then. He also saw this and got perturbed because even hardened criminals break and cannot withhold any information from the interrogators. Everyday he expected that there would be an arrest warrant against him for his abetment in the case. But no such thing happened.

He was all praise for the courage of Roshan Ara and Roshan for not mentioning his name before the interrogators.

Army authorities took us both alongwith them and handed over Roshan Ara to Pak diplomats who sent her back to Pakistan.

In Pakistan, her parents disowned her and the fanatic boobooed her.

One day Shahida asked Kabir, "I know why you remain so serious these days? Tell me what is hurting you?" Kabir remained tensed and did not utter a single word. And then continuing her conversation said, "Roshan Ara was once your *fiancée*. How can you be so heartless? Go and help her and it is no use sitting and brooding?"

Ultimately he broke his silence and said, "Shahida, do you know I am responsible for all her problems. Had I not helped her to elope with Roshan..." his voice trailed off.

Shahida cut his conversation short in-between and said, "I know everything. Long time back you had told me everything when on our wedding night you got drunk. So, go and rescue her from this humiliation. She has already been tortured a lot."

"But how can I help her?" he asked for Shahida's suggestion. Shahida was very practical as well as a compassionate women. What she suggested shocked Kabir?

"Go Marry her." This was a bolt from the blue. Kabir at least never expected this kind of solution to the problem.

"Have you gone mad? Do you want me to leave you?" he said in a state of shock.

"Who said that? We both will stay with you."

They had lot of argument regarding this. Ultimately, he agreed to her proposal but said, "Do you think Roshan Ara will agree to this kind of abnormal proposal?"

"You leave it to me. I will try to convince her."

Roshan Ara was shocked to hear Shahida's proposal. "Shahida, you know that I am already married."

"This marriage is only for your convenience. You will have a decent place to stay and live. You will not be a wife to Kabir but a friend of us both. Otherwise people won't let you live in peace." Shahida said.

Ultimately with a great persuasion, Roshan Ara hesitantly agreed to be part of this arrangement.

It was planned to have a quiet *'nikah'* ceremony during the next holy week. Everything was well-planned.

In the meantime, there was a marriage of Kabir's friend in Karachi. Since time was short, all the members of the party chartered a plane, but while returning there was big storm and the plane crashed.

And all the plans of Shahida and Kabir to rehabilitate Roshan Ara crashed.

After that, there was no information about her. Whether she was dead or alive, nobody had any inkling.

Of course, I was courtmarshalled.

It is more than 40 years now. I have lost my memory, though at times I happen to remember some past events.

But what actually happened to Roshan Ara? I am not aware of. I will just ring up my sister and enquire from her about Roshan Ara.

At that very moment, a nurse entered the room and said in an irritated manner, "Sir, doctor has come for your check up and you also have to be administered an injection. " She did not wait for any response and took him in his wheel-chair to his ward.

"Mr story-teller, you keep Rita Singh occupied. I will be back soon", Nurse said.

After a while, the nurse returned and said, "The patient has been given an injection. Doctor has advised him rest. I will bring him to the waiting room after two hours. In the meantime, you may go to the canteen and can have tea/coffee and snacks."

"Mr story-teller, what is the ailment he is suffering from?"

"I will tell you all, what he has missed and what he knows not.

After they were apprehended from Simla, they both were subjected to very harsh treatment. Army authorities wanted to know how he brought Roshan Ara to India and who helped them from Pakistan side. Both of them did not utter a word about Major Kabir Khan.

Secondly, army authorities wanted to make sure, that he was not passing on secrets about Indian army operational plans. Since Roshan was not involved in such activities, he did not admit it. He was tortured physically and mentally. He was tough enough to bear all this.

But taking away of Roshan Ara from him shocked and disturbed him mentally. He could not bear the separation of Roshan Ara. He went mad. It affected his memory and his health was the worst affected. He could not walk on his own and used a wheel-chair to move around."

Then nurse came and told us to come to the waiting room. We reached there and in next ten minutes she brought Roshan on the wheel-chair.

"Yes, I was telling you that I will just find out from my sister about Roshan Ara." He was breathing fast and appeared quite fatigued.

"Hello Gagan! I am your brother speaking. Can you tell me where is Roshan Ara these days?"

"*Bhai sahib*! I have told you number of times, you are so forgetful. She died in great distress 10 years ago."

"I do not know what rubbish Gagan is uttering! I am totally confused. Mr story-teller, I am very tired now. Let me sleep...!" Roshan said.

After listening to the story Rita Singh enquired, "My dear story-teller, when will he get back from his slumber?"

"It is his last sleep. He won't get up now. Let us not disturb him. Let him have his eternal peace." Saying these words the story teller vanished.

2

The Blood Stains

Soft like a flower and brave like a lion, this was the image of Gul Sherkhan's life. After promoted to the rank of a commandant BSF, he decided to pay a surprise visit to the border out-posts of his area.

He was a daredevil. He did not take guards with him. He just went alone all by himself.

There was no dearth of wild animals at the border area of Punjab and Gul Sherkhan was very fond of hunting. That is why he did not forget to bring his twelve-bore gun while coming from his house. He was very well familiar with this area, because he was posted here as an inspector twenty years back.

It was late at night. He was unconcerned about the world and was driving his jeep towards his goal. On both sides of the road were dense bushes. On one side were clump of trees while on other side were lakes. Suddenly, with no idea, from where, a deer came and crossed the road and vanished into bushes. Gul Sherkhan quickly picked up his gun and fired a shot.

A slight murmur came from the bushes and he... heard somebody moaning.

Gul Sherkhan, holding his torch in one hand and the gun in other, dashed towards the bushes. In front of him was a girl in red outfit, badly injured and writhing in pain. Girl's face was covered with a veil.

You... You... a woman, what the hell are you doing in this forest...? Gul Sherkhan said surprised.

"*Jee* I... I... But do not worry, my end is near," the girl said moaning.

"Don't worry, have faith in me, I will save you. I now...!" The words were stuck in his mouth.

And the veil which had up till now covered her face, slipped.

Beautiful face, arresting eyes and face...and he was taken aback and was reminded of his past. He had seen this girl a few years back. There was not much change in her complexion and beauty, though many years had elapsed. Same heavy dark eye lashes, same heavy tresses, same arresting face and...!"

"Yes! I have recognised you." This was Gul Sherkhan's voice.

"*Saheb*, I am grateful that you still remember me. I have been trying to locate you for the past so many years. Do you remember, you had promised...but my Darshan Singh did not turn up at the time of my marriage...! I wish you had not promised me..." She started sobbing.

All the past events started revolving one by one in front of his eyes.

Those days, he was posted at Shahpur police post. A BSF *jawan* from the same post was in love with a girl from the nearby village. Darshan Singh was a handsome young boy and Diljeet Kaur was like a blooming flower. Parents from both sides had agreed to their alliance. There were signs of war before the date of their marriage. Leave of all the *jawans* were cancelled.

One day, he was sitting in his office at night. The moment he raised his eyes, he saw a young and beautiful girl standing in front of him. The presence of such a dazzling beauty at this hour of the night shook him. He got up instantly from his chair.

"Who are you?" He asked her in an a imposing voice.

Sir! I am... I am Diljeet Kaur... He could not hear anything after that.

Diljeet Kaur's words got engraved in Gul Sherkhan's heart.

He said, unconscious of his atmosphere "Diljeet! You are really *Dil-Jeet* i.e., the one who could win somebody's heart. Yes, you are really a girl who could win anybody's heart. How appropriate is your name... long heavy hair, pink face like Kashmiri apple. And the rays emenating from it give relief to heart...!"

"*Saheb*... What are you saying? I had come to you for an important job. But I do not know what rubbish you are uttering?"

Gul Sherkan felt as if shaken from a dream with a jolt. He was continuously looking at her with wide eyes.

"*Saheb*, Darshan Singh and I are getting married day after tomorrow. I will be grateful if you could send him on leave tomorrow only."

He started feeling jealous of Darshan Singh's good luck. "*Saheb*, please do send my Darshan Singh tomorrow," and she...!

"Definitely, I promise you. Whatever may happen... I will surely send Darshan Singh on leave. But not tomorrow. Your Darshan Singh will reach you day after tomorrow morning. It is a question of one day... just... one day only."

Hearing such words, Diljeet Kaur stared at him with her smiling eyes, slowly lowering her eyes and thanking him, left.

Suddenly, Gul Sherkhan got orders to move to Delhi. On the second day while giving his charge to new inspector, he specifically told him, "Make sure that you send Darshan Singh on leave tomorrow as I have already made a promise with his *fiancée*. Mind it, it is a promise of a Pathan".

It was almost twenty years now and Sherkhan had more or less forgotten everything. But today because of this incident... Diljeet Kaur was injured at his hands... He saw that lot of blood had flown, she was continuously crying and was telling him, "*Saheb ji*, you did not send my Darshan Singh on leave"

"What are you saying Diljeet? I had given special instructions to the officer concerned to send Darshan Singh...!" Gul Sherkhan realised that Diljeet Kaur was finding it difficult to breath. He tried to make her lie down on the front seat with the help of the *jawan*.

"*Saheb,* please let me lie down at the back seat next to your *jawan*", she said murmuring.

Gul Sherkhan agreed, and with the help of the *jawan,* he made her lie down at the back seat. His hands were fully soaked with blood while doing so. He wiped his hands with his handkerchief and started driving towards next border-post Shahpur. There, one of his old subordinates Havildar Mela Ram, now an inspector, was posted there.

He wanted to reach there at the earliest and was keen to know what were the reasons, that Darshan Singh was not sent on leave.

On reaching the border-post, Gul Sherkhan stopped the jeep and ordered the sentry to call inspector Mela Ram at once.

"Sir! You are here and at this time?" This was Mela Ram's voice.

"Yes, I..."Gul Sherkhan could say only this much.

"Sir! I have just returned from leave in the evening and learnt that you have been posted here as our commandant."

"It is ok. Mela Ram. But at the moment I am in a big fix. You must be remembering that almost twenty years back a *jawan* named Darshan Singh was on duty at this check-post."

"Yes sir! He was...!"

"While leaving, I had given instruction to inspector Sharma to send positively Darshan Singh on leave. But I had to cut a sorry figure today as my promise was not fulfilled."

"What can I say sir! The day you left, the same night some *jawans* were sent on patrolling duty and Darshan Singh was one of them. Patrolling party was surrounded by enemies. Firing took place from both sides and poor Darshan Singh was..." Rest of the sentence, he could not complete.

"That means... You mean to say, Darshan Singh was killed. What are you saying? What am I hearing? Oh my God..." He felt that the bullet had not hit Darshan Singh, but hit him.

"How will I face that unfortunate girl?" He murmured.

"Sir! Of whom you are talking about?" enquired Mela Ram.

"Diljeet Kaur... and whom? The one who is in my jeep in an injured condition." And then, he narrated the whole story to Mela Ram.

"Sir!, there is some misunderstanding. Nobody is there in your jeep. Perhaps Diljeet Kaur has also played a trick on you. She invariably.... . !"

"What nonsense you are talking about?" Saying this, Gul Sherkhan looked inside the jeep. But, there was no trace of Diljeet Kaur. "Where can she go? She? I myself had put her in the jeep in an injured condition. Then, one of the *jawan* was sitting next to her. Perhaps...", he kept quiet.

"Sir! This has become her habit... Sometimes she enters my room and at other times she visits barracks of *jawans* and enquires, 'When will my Darshan Singh come on leave?'

"Mela Ram, you know how strict I am about discipline. It is against rules to allow a woman to either enter office or barracks. It is also against the discipline of force. "

Mela Ram was about to say something, but Gul Sherkhan snubbed him.

"Come, sit quickly in the jeep, I have to get her treated." During journey also, Gul Sherkhan did not allow Mela Ram to speak a single word and then said, "Mela Ram, if a female starts visiting the unit lines then how will the unit look after the security of the country?"

Now, the jeep had reached the place of the accident.

"See, this is the place where I had made Diljeet Kaur to lie down in the jeep. But where can Diljeet Kaur and the jawan go? There is no place of shelter, nor any hospital close by. "Then Gul Sherkhan turned the search-light of the jeep, but the result...!"

"Sir! I have already explained to you that you have been made fool of... by...!"

"Mela Ram, I myself picked her up from that very place and there was so much of blood. If you do not believe me then let me take you to that place and show you."

When they reached that spot, Gul Sherkhan examined that place thoroughly and tried to locate stains of blood, but couldn't find any blood.

"I had taken a *jawan* from the last check-post and with his help, I had put her on the back seat of the jeep," he said.

"Sir! Let's go there and checkup from them."

The moment the jeep entered the post, the check-post in-charge came running and after saluting him said, "Sir! Perhaps you were in a hurry and thus you left the *jawan* here." Hearing this, Gul Sherkhan casually looked at Mela Ram.

"And that jawan picked her up not once, but twice," said Sherkhan irritatingly.

"Sir! I can bet, that the *jawan* who was with you was none other than Durshan Singh. I mean to say that was the soul of Darshan Singh and none other. Now, I am very certain that that was Diljeet Kaur, s...!"

"Mela Ram, this is the same handkerchief with which I cleaned my blood-soaked hands", Gul Sherkhan said while taking out his handkerchief from his overcoat pocket.

Mela Ram looked at the handkerchief very carefully, but observed there was no trace of blood stains.

Mela Ram could not utter even a single word, but kept on looking at the handkerchief with his eyes wide open

Gul Sherkhan was happy that at least Mela Ram had believed what he had said. But the moment Gul Sherkhan was going to keep his handkerchief in his pocket after folding it, he saw there were no stains of blood. And it looked as if it has just come from the washerman.

Despite it being cold, his forehead was full of perspiration. He looked towards Mela Ram with helpless looks.

"Sir, this is what I have been trying to make you understand that on that day when Darshan Singh could not reach his home for his marriage... On hearing the death of Darshan Singh, Diljeet kaur committed suicide by jumping into a well. Now it is only her soul which keeps on wandering here and there and asking people about Darshan Singh...! How restless is she to meet him but how helpless....!"

On hearing Mela Ram, Gul Sherkhan was completely shaken and tears could be seen in his eyes. "Oh... My God, I wish, I had sent Darshan Singh on leave the same day." He felt as if his hand got drenched in blood once again.

Taking a deep breath, after completing this story, she said to Tony and Vinod,

"After this incident, Khan *Saheb* has developed a strange kind of *phobia*. He has a misconception. Whenever he would go to wash his hands, he would apply soap again and again as if trying to remove the blood stains from his hands.

I have also tried to explain to him time and again, but...That is why I was trying to dissuade him from washing his hands.

Vinod looked at his watch. Khan *Saheb* had taken full twenty five minutes to wash his hands.

"Please forgive me, my friends, I took a little extra time to wash my hands. Actually, I was in a fix...!"

Vinod and Tony would have asked Khan *Saheb* as to the kind of the problem he got into... if Sultana had not narrated the whole incident. But they kept quiet. And while getting up said, "Ok Khan *Saheb*! We take your leave. As it is we are already very late."

Sultana and Khan came to the door to see them off. Vinod and Tony were feeling little uneasy to shake hands with him. When they turned to go, Khan said stopping them, "Friends, will you not today shake hands with me while departing?"

Next moment their hands were in Sherkhan's hands and they were feeling as if the stains of blood which were on Gul Sherkhan's hand have been transferred to their hands.

3

The Story of a Crow and a Frog

Vansh Malhotra

There was a tree near a pond and a crow lived there. He used to drink water from the pond every day. There lived a frog in the pond. He would watch the activities of the crow but always stayed away from him as he was afraid of him.

One day the crow said, "I see you everyday. Why don't you come near me?"

"I am afraid of your long beak. You will hurt me with that," frog replied.

By and by, slowly began their friendship. They would sit together, eat small insects and play with water. It so happened that one day the crow did not turn up. The frog's anxiety started to grow as he waited for the crow.

When the crow did not visit the pond for couple of days, the frog got very worried. The frog then decided to go near the tree where the crow lived, to find out about his whereabouts.

He was shocked to see the crow lying injured on the ground. The crow had injuries on his feet and wings. He was very weak, too.

He told the frog that it had happened because of a fight with a falcon. The frog went back to the pond and came back with wet soil of the pond and applied it on his injured parts. Then he went back again and this time brought some insects and water for the crow.

Thus by his care, the crow recovered soon and was able to fly.

After some time, there was a drought in the area and all the vegetation dried. There was nothing left to eat. The crow then told the frog that due to drought and lack of food, he and all his other friends have decided to shift to a place where they can get plenty of food to eat. Then the crow along with others migrated to a better place.

After a few days, the pond also got dried and no water was left for drinking and insects for eating. The situation was such that the frog was on the verge of dying due to starvation.

One day, the crow thought of visiting his friend. He was shocked to see the condition of the frog. Due to non-availability of food, the frog was on the verge of dying. He had become very very lean and thin due to starvation.

He thought of a plan and picked up the frog in his beak. He then took him to an area which had a pond with lot of water and insects.

Thus, he saved the life of his friend.

A friend in need is ....!

4

The Art of Handicraft

Vansh Malhotra

Jeevan's father had died due to some prolonged illness. His mother was very proficient in embroidery work, which she had inherited from her granny and that was the only source of her income. She worked day and night to earn enough money for educating her son.

He studied hard and became a manager in Bhagwan Dass Cloth Mills. He got married and started living in the city but his mother did not agree to leave her native place.

Once she fell ill and Jeevan brought her to the city for her treatment. It took her long time to recover, so she carried on with her embroidery work to pass her time.

One day, Jeevan invited his owner for the dinner and at the same time he did not want his owner to see his uneducated mother with a village background. He left her at the village.

His owner arrived in his house and visited each of his rooms. When he went to the room where his mother stayed; he was very much impressed with a piece of embroidery made by his mother. She had left that piece in a hurry.

He desired to meet her immediately. They all went to the village and he offered a big amount of salary and a high post to his mother.

He offered his mother to start a handicraft centre in the village and that all the items produced will be purchased by Bhagwan Dass Mills. He also offered the office car to his mother for visiting the mill every day and for that she would be paid double the amount than what was being paid to Jeevan.

"You know, this ancient art of embroidery is in great demand in foreign countries."

Jeevan and his wife were surprised to hear all this. They had not so far given any importance to the embroidery work being done by his mother. They thought it to be waste of time.

At last Bhagwan Dass said, "Your mother is a real gem. I wish somebody had earlier appreciated her art of needle work."

"

5

Pushpa and Her Spects

It was yesterday afternoon; I was feeling drowsy after having had a heavy lunch, when my wife, *Rekha* said - "Were you looking for your spectacles?" As soon as I set eyes on my spectacles, I was reminded of my mother's spectacles.

It had been a long time since her passing - 13 years. I tried to close my eyes and go to sleep but the vision of my mother's spectacles kept coming before my eyes. After all these years, I had no idea where her spectacles might be. I got lost in thought; as I kept thinking about her spectacles, I started to get agitated.

A thought occurred to me that I would feel better if I looked at an image of my mother wearing her spectacles. Then I remembered that I did not have any picture or photograph of my mother with her spectacles.

I got so agitated that I went out of the bedroom and called my sister, *Pamela Singh*. It was close to 3 pm; she usually takes a nap after lunch, around 2:30 pm. However, she was awake and she picked up the phone.

She recognised my voice and said: 'What's the matter?'

"*Pam* - do have any photograph of Beeji (mother) with her spectacles?"

She said that she probably had one but she would have to look for it.

"Ok, if you come across one, please let me know."

Even after speaking to her, I was still agitated. So right away, I rang up my sister *Guga* (Neelam) in Manimajra, and asked her about the photograph. She said she had a wedding photograph of our parents in which my mother had her spectacles on.

'So please make a copy and send it to me tomorrow.'

Shortly thereafter, I got a call from my niece, *Kinoo* (Payal)- "Uncle, I have a very old photograph of grandma, from many years back, when she had attended *Mallika*'s birthday. She is wearing her spectacles in that photograph." Right away, she took my email address and emailed me the photograph.

Now, another problem arose; my computer was on the second floor, I had a pacemaker implanted in my heart and my doctor had strictly forbidden me from climbing stairs. Neither did I have a printer; nor was there anybody around to help me with that.

Night had fallen by this time, but it became difficult for me to get through the night. As the hours dragged by, the pages of my past story started coming before me.

Then I remembered *Ram Lal*, my former classmate. He was with me in my journey from the 10th grade to college. He was very hardworking, upcoming and always got a scholarship in every class.

He was a resident of Himachal Pradesh and had come to Pathankot just for his education. Later on, he got his B.Ed. degree and went back to his district, Kangra, and took up a job as a teacher.

Later on, I came to know that he used to come to Kangra only for two months. He was actually posted to a distant, isolated place, to which there was no easy means of transportation. Walking was the only way to get from one point to another. It would take one day to get there and one day to get back. When the seasonal snow fell on the mountains, he would come to Kangra for the winter break.

Despite these circumstances, he was content with his life. His passion was learning and teaching others. He would teach the school children and then would get wrapped up in the books that were to his liking.

After the break, when he would return to his place of his work, the major part of his luggage consisted of his books.

Although he used to say he lived in Kangra, but the actual location was about 25 to 30 miles away in the forest.

The name of the village was 'Samakara'; there were only a few houses in the village—about fifty.

There was a big room in the house in which all the inhabitants and their guests stayed, and there was a small room in which he stayed, whenever he came there. He had to pass through the big room to get to his room. There was a verandah outside, at one end of which there was a bathroom and a toilet at the other end.

The big room had an attached kitchen as it was very difficult to go out in the cold winters. There was no electricity, so they had to use a kerosene lamp.

You must have understood the layout of the house by now; so, whenever he came on his vacation, he would go through the big room, to his room which was full of books.

Two weeks before his winter vacation, there was a big storm in the area of the school where he taught; on the other hand, another big storm hit the area where his house was. This was a different type of storm.

What happened was his mother's distant cousin, Havildar Tomar, had sent his daughter Puspha (who had cleared her B. A.) to his mother's house. There were many reasons for this. Pushpa's brother went to military school for studies. Mother was not there and Havildar Tomar had to go for a course for 6 months. Pushpa could not stay alone in the house. He thought that Pushpa had seen a lot of city life, now she should at least have a taste of village life.

Even though Pushpa wore spectacles, she did not suffer from any inferiority complex. Alongwith being a good student, a good cook, and a good athlete, she was a crack shot.

As soon as she came into his house, she won over Ram Lal's mother, his sister Sheela, and his two younger brothers, Dev and Krishan. In fact, she became their ring leader and there was a lot of hustle and bustle in the house, way more than before her coming.

However, Ram Lal preferred a quiet and peaceful atmosphere, as he did not like too much noise and bustle. By the time he got home, Pushpa had already transformed the atmosphere of the place.

It took Ram Lal two days to get to his place, through all the snow and ice. When he reached the house in the afternoon, he was taken aback by all the noise emanating from the house. The thought flashed through his mind that never before had he heard so much noise in his house. As soon as he entered the house, his eyes opened wide—Pushpa was running, pursued by Sheela and her two brothers.

As soon as his mother laid eyes on Ram Lal, she spoke in a stern voice: 'Look, Ram Lal has come; cease shouting and stop this noise. I will not tolerate this anymore. All the children stopped, while Pushpa stood where she was with a confused expression on her face.

Ram Lal looked towards Pushpa; he saw a fair-complexioned girl wearing spectacles, with a confused look on her face. His gaze locked on her face. Normally, he avoided looking at other women but there was something special about this girl because of which he was unable to tear his eyes away from her face. Pushpa also kept staring at him in a surprised manner and then smiled and went outside.

Then Ram Lal came out of his daze and quickly went to his room.

While giving him dinner, his mother told him that the girl's name was Pushpa and gave him all the details about her. He quietly took in the information and then went for a walk into the village after dinner.

He was tired, so he came back quickly and went up to his room to sleep. However, as he was passing through the big room, he looked at all the beds to see which bed Pushpa slept in.

Pushpa was sitting on the first bed next to his room; the second was occupied by his sister, and his brothers, Dev and Krishan, were sitting on the third and fourth beds, while his mother was sitting on the last bed.

During the day, they would fold up the beds and put them in the verandah, spread a rug on the floor and play cards or some other game.

Ram Lal was tired so he woke up late; everybody had already eaten breakfast and were playing cards, after spreading the rug on the floor. They were speaking very quietly out of fear of Ram Lal. Ram Lal slowly opened the door of his room a little, and secretively started looking at Pushpa.

Long, attractive face... big eyes... pretty nose and rose-colored lips... and... He quickly closed the door as he was afraid that somebody would notice his activity. He could not understand what had happened to him. Why was he taking such an interest in this girl? Nothing like this had ever happened to him before. Anyway, bowing his head, he exited his room and went into the village.

The villagers were happy to see him because whenever he came in the village he would find some kind of solution to their problems. He was the only educated person in the village.

When he returned after a while he saw a crowd of people gathered in the village square. When he got there, he saw Pushpa was standing there and challenging the boys of the village to a race. Ram Lal got scared by this action of Pushpa, as no girl in the village had ever challenged any of the boys before.

He tried in vain to explain to Pushpa. She said: 'Masterji, please do not intervene.' Ram Lal felt like he had been hit by a bolt of lightning; he was shocked as to how she dared to call him 'Masterji'. She then started to say: "Masterji, I am Havildar Tomar's daughter. It is very easy for me to win this race."

She didn't listen to any of Ram Lal's entreaties and all the boys started to line up to race. Among those one of the boys went to his house and brought a whistle and he gave it to Masterji.

Pushpa also took her sash and tied it around her waist and started to say to Sheela: "Sheela please set my spectacles on my nose." This was her pet phrase. She would say these words in every game.

Ramlal blew the whistle and the race started. Pushpa was running like a deer; she left everyone behind and won the race. All the boys were very ashamed and all the girls and women were very happy at Pushpa's bravery.

Ramlal (*Pushpa's Masterji*) disappeared as soon as Pushpa won the race.

He was afraid that perhaps Pushpa might challenge him.

Sheela used to go to the city to study. One day she took Pushpa with her to the college on the occasion of the college's sports day. Many different types of competitions were going on. On Sheela's urging, Pushpa also participated in the competitions and did well in all of them. Everyone was very impressed by her. The officers of the education department started inviting her to every event of the Kangra District after seeing her impressive performance. Even the director of the education department issued an edict that a special vehicle should be sent to bring Pushpa to every event as she was an inspiration to all the other girls.

Brigadier Samyal was very happy to learn that Pushpa was Havildar Tomar's daughter as he knew that Havildar Tomar was among the well known equestrians of the army.

Pushpa was invited to watch a polo match. Sheela, Dev, Krishan, and the other villagers also came.

After the polo match finished, Brigadier Samyal made an announcement that there would be a horse race and those Jawans who wanted to participate in the race, could do so. Many army jawans came forward to participate. The entire ground was filled with army officers, jawans, their families and the villagers from the nearby villages.

But surprisingly Pushpa was also standing in the line. All the people in attendance were astounded to see her. Their interest grew tremendously when in the midst of the army soldiers, they saw a girl. One of the Colonels went over there and started to say, my dear girl! you may not be capable of taking part in this race. But she responded "Sir! I am Havildar Tomar's daughter. You do not know me."

When she did not yield, finally Brigadier Samyal came to reason with her. She still did not listen to him, she was very stubborn. Finally Brigadier Samyal pulled the Colonel aside and said to him: "Colonel! The girl is very stubborn. There is no point in trying to reason with her. Tell her that she can choose whichever horse she wants."

Pushpa chose the horse, tied her sash around her waist and said to the Colonel – "Sir! I am Havildar Tomar's daughter. You will not regret this decision."

Because the Colonel had the mike in his hand, everybody could hear whatever was being said. Some of them smiled while others laughed on hearing this exchange.

Before the race began Pushpa addressed Brig. Samyal-"Sir! If you don't mind, please adjust my spectacles. "On hearing this Brig. Samyal smiled and adjusted Pushpa's spectacles.

You must have already understood that this was Pushpa's pet dialogue before the start of any game. The race began.

Initially, for a small distance, she was behind the others but, after that her horse started to streak ahead and in a little bit she pulled ahead, leaving others far behind.

Everybody started clapping loudly on seeing her going ahead of everybody. Earlier the same people who initially derisively used to call her "Havildar Tomar's daughter, "now were cheering her on ("long live Pushpa, the bespectacled one") *Pushpa Chashmewali Zinda Bad.*)

Brig. Samyal taking the mike in his hand announced that Pushpa will be given a special prize for coming first in the race.

Pushpa came on the stage and took her prize. Officers wives came forward and shook hand with her. Everyone got themselves photographed which were publishd next day in the Newspapers.

Ramlal was not much interested in any thing apart from reading and going for morning walks. Though he went through all the news about Pushpa, but, he never gave much importance to it, as he was not very fond of games.

One morning when he returned from a walk, he saw that Pushpa was sleeping on the first bed. There was a half open book lying on her body and she was wearing her spectacles. He stood there and gazed at her. Every one else was sound asleep. He looked very intently at Pushpa. He slowly removed the book from her hands and her spectacles and then gently placing them on a nearby table, walked away. After doing this he thought to himself that he had never done anything like this before. He wondered as to how he became so bold today. Same thing happened the next day and he removed Pushpa's spectacles and put them on the table the next day.

This went on for quite a few days. Ultimately Pushpa began to suspect that some one was taking off her spectacles and putting them on the table... In vain she tried to discover who it was but her suspicion did not fall on any of the member of the family. One day she resolved that she would stay awake during the night, so she may discover the truth of the matter. However the night passed but no one came; she was in anticipation of catching the perpetrator but, as dawn broke, she gave in to sleep. When she awoke she discovered the spectacles on the table.

She again resolved come what may she would not sleep that day. But then all of sudden beads of sweat broke out on her forehead despite the extreme cold. She held her breath and peeping through her semi closed eyes, perceived that spectacle removing perpetrator was non other than Ramlal. For some time Ramlal gazed at her for a few moments and then left for his walk.

She continue to lay there, holding her breath with great difficulty. But neither did she tell Sheela nor did she let on to Ramlal that she knew everything. This chain of events continued for few days. Now she started to enjoys this game, although Ramlal was totally unaware that Pushpa had uncovered his secret.

Infact, Ramlal also started enjoying this or it would be more appropriate to say that both of them had started enjoying this game.

Both of them had started falling in love unknowingly.

This sequence of events continued for many days. Neither did Ramlal have the courage, nor did Pushpa open her eyes.

For many days Sheela had been watching this game between the two of them. She could not contain herself any longer. Finally one day, she asked Pushpa "Pushpa, have you fallen in love with my brother?" Pushpa was unable to say anything. She lowered her eyes and nodded her head.

Now it was Ramlal's turn. Sheela played a trick and one day when she was alone with Ramlal said "Brother! You will be happy to know that Pushpa's marriage has been finalised." On hearing this Ramlal's face ashen.

On seeing his reaction Sheeela burst in to loud laugh. Then she said, "if you love her, why don't you tell her? After all for how many days will you be removing Pushpa's spectacle and putting them on the table?" Infact he was a very shy person. He became tongue tied in front of Sheela, just smiled.

The very next day, Sheela took Pushpa and Ramlal to the market under the pretext of showing them around, leaving them their by themselves, and herself went to her friend's house. Before leaving she said, "Brother! I will meet two of you at this spot at six in the evening. Till then, the two of you can see the market."

And in this manner, Sheela finally helped start their romance.

On hearing the whole story from Sheela, her mother arranged for Ramlal and Pushpa's marriage.

The strongest bond of their love was Pushpa's, spectacles which she would still leave on and fall asleep and Master ji would never forget to take them off and put them on the table.

She would still call him Masterji when they were alone or even together.

After marrying Pushpa, on his mother's urging, Ramlal took Pushpa, with him, far away to the place where his job was. Pushpa had never seen a place like this before. Initially she liked it a lot, but, after a while, she started missing the whole family. She also mentioned this to her husband.

Before Ramlal could make any plans, they received some good news. He had been posted out to a school near his village. Pushpa was very happy to hear the good news.

They both returned to their village. Once they returned to their village, they did not notice any change in their family. Masterji slept in his small room as before, and Pushpa in the first bed. All other family members slept in their respective beds as before. His mother tried to reason with Ramlal that his room was very small. "We can take a room in the neighbouring house and you and Pushpa can sleep in there." But Ramlal did not listen. Some times Pushpa would surreptitious go to Masterji at night.

Time went by the members of the household kept on increasing and decreasing. They increased because Pushpa gave birth to a son and decreased because Sheela got married. Both of Ram Lal's brothers went to Pathankot to study.

They got jobs in one of the companies over there. After a few years, Pushpa gave birth to a daughter and a few years later, Ram Lal's mother passed away.

Pushpa, Master Ram Lal and the two children were the only occupants of the house.

But the sequence of events related to Pushpa's spectacles remained the same. She would get tired and go to sleep and would forget to take off her spectacles. Masterji would get up in the morning, remove her spectacles put them on the table and then go for his morning walk.

Both the children had become very naughty. They would tease their mother by removing her spectacles and running away and then Pushpa would get exasperated and complain to Masterji – "Masterji! Please tell these kids to return my spectacles." Masterji would affectionately call the children and take the spectacles and put them back on Pushpa's nose.

As time went by, circumstances changed. Both children were now grown up. They had jobs and also got married. Nobody realised how time flew by. The son got a job in Delhi and the daughter got married and went to her in-laws in Faridabad.

Ramlal's son requested his parents to move in with him on multiple occasions, but Masterji did not accept the invitation. He was retired. He did not have any problem with shifting to his son's house but was content in his village. He did not feel like leaving. He was content with helping the people of his village with their problems.

After a few days, however, Pushpa suddenly passed away after a long illness. Masterji was devastated by this loss. Still somehow, he was able to recover from this great tragedy of his life.

However, there was one thing he did without fail, every day he would set up the first bed for Pushpa. He would place Pushpa's spectacles on the pillow and would then go to bed in his own room. Every morning, he would pick up Pushpa's spectalces from the pillow, put them on the table, and would then go for his walk.

This sequence of events continued for a long time and eventually Masterji stopped feeling Pushpa's loss. Subconsciously, he thought that Pushpa was still with him.

But one day a storm descended on the house; when Masterji got up in the morning and went to Pushpa's bed, he saw that Pushpa's spectacles, which he had placed on the pillow the night before, were missing. He got very agigated.

He looked through the entire house, in every nook and cranny. The kitchen utensils, his own room, all the cupboards and books, he looked everywhere but the spectacles were nowhere to be found.

He had gone almost mad; he was losing his mental balance. As night fell, his mental state worsened. He was all alone in the house; if he wanted to talk to someone, who was there he could turn to? There was no one to console him or to share his grief.

Masterji did not go on his walk the next day; he did not eat anything, nor did he read any of his books.

The surprising thing was that nobody had come into the house all night. Where could the spectacles have gone? How could they have disappeared?

He started sitting in the verandah every morning; neither was he concerned with his own appearance nor with the state of his dress.

The entire village was concerned with his state of affairs. He was considered the saviour of the village. Everyone looked everywhere for the spectacles but they could not find them.

The news of the disappearance of Pushpa's spectacles was published in every local newspaper, because Pushpa was very well known in the Kangra district.

I was posted in Assam for many years; as soon as I reached Pathankot, I read about Pushpa, her spectacles, and Ramlal's grief-stricken story.

I had visited Ramlal in his village on several earlier occasions. I took one of my dear friends, Shakti Chawla, with me and went to Ramlal's village. By the time I reached Ramlal's house, the villagers gave me every detail of his story.

Ramlal was sitting listlessly in his chair on the verandah. As soon as he saw me, he seemed to come to life, and he wrapped his arms around my neck and started weeping copiously.

"Mohan, my Pushpa's spectacles have disappeared." I cannot accurately describe how distressed he was. Hair disheveled, dirty clothes and he was physically quite weak. He had not eaten for many days. He looked tired while talking and was absolutely shattered.

I tried to comfort him – "Have fortitude, Ramlal; where would a pair of spectacles go? Don't worry, it will be found."

At that time, one of the villagers who was dumb, came up and started making gestures with his hands; I asked the sarpanch – "What is he trying to say?"

The sarpanch said that he has been trying to say something for the last couple of days. The sarpanch said that he was unable to comprehend what the dumb was trying to say. The dumb man came up to me, grasped my hand and started to pull me away. I immediately went with him. A horde of villagers was following us.

On reaching the jungle, the dumb man threw a stone at a branch of one of the tall trees. I looked up and saw a shining object, and quickly realised that it may be Pushpa's spectacles.

In a matter of moments, a young man quickly climbed up the tree and brought down the shining object, which, in fact, turned out to be Pushpa's spectacles.

We quickly headed back towards Ramlal's house.

Perhaps, on the night that the spectacles disappeared, Ramlal may not have fully closed the window. The next day, a monkey may have entered the house through the window and taken away Pushpa's spectacles.

So this was the solution to the mystery of the disappearance of Pushpa's spectacles.

When we reached Ramlal's house, he was sitting in his chair the way we had left him.

I came up to him and placing Pushpa's spectacles in his hand, laughingly said: "Ramlal, rejoice; we have finally found Pushpa's spectacles. My friend, you were getting concerned for no reason."

But, what was this? The spectacles fell from his hand. Both the lenses of the spectacles shattered and Ramlal...?

He had stopped breathing. He was motionless.

6

The Other Side of the Hedge

Banta Singh's father had been in a foul temper all afternoon. Banta Singh had been quietly listening to his tirade since then. His father then said: '*Bantya*, you don't know how hard I have worked to care for you. You were a small child at that time. I used to eat dry bread with curry but made sure you had delicious meals. You have forgotten those days but I can never forget them.'

Then his father sighed and started up again: 'I have been observing for many years that before we eat, you get me take off my spectacles under the guise of telling me to wash my face and hands, so that I may not see that you take the best portions of the meal and leave me the leftovers. I have done so much for you; I suffered a lot of hardships, but made sure that you were well taken care of. I underwent many trials and tribulations, but never complained once. Don't think I don't understand what you are doing. You can never... repay that debt.'

Banta Singh had been silent during this harangue, listening quietly, at last spoke: '*Bapu*, you have always misunderstood me. I have been trying for many years to repay this debt of yours, with interest.' After saying this, Banta Singh put his father's spectacles back in his hand. His father put on his spectacles and turned and looked towards his son.

Banta Singh was sitting on the floor with his six children... All the children were eating dry bread from their plates and Banta Singh was just moving his hands around in his empty plate.

7

The Sinners

This story that I am going to narrate to you is not new. In today's world it has adopted a new form.

The same old story—a grandmother's craving for a grandson.

Sharda Devi had to get her son married because there was no grandson in their family. This is why she wished her son to marry a girl who would fulfill her desire for a grandson.

For this mission of hers, she seeked help from their family priest (astrologer). So, whichever offer for alliance she would get, she used to consult it with their horoscope to the astrologer.

At last, the priest read throughly a girl's horoscope and prophecied that if her son would marry that girl, she would bless them with a son.

Then, Sharda Devi decided to get her son, Jagbir, married to Gauri. But before putting this into action, she visited Gauri's house, called her separately and told her the reason why she was getting her married to her son. According to the priest, ...she will be blessed with a son.

Sharda Devi was pleased to hear from Gauri that even she too wanted a son. It is only a son..., who...!

Mother, son and daughter-in-law, all three of them were very anxious for the birth of a son. Jagbir was keen to have a son as once he would be grown up, he would be able to preceed his father, like Jagbir had done after the demise of his father.

Sharda Devi wanted to keep this affair secret untill the time the son was born. She wanted to give a surprise to all her village people on the birth of her grandson. For this, she made a plan that for her daughter-in- laws delivery, she will get the delivery done in a nursing home in some other town away from her village.

It was a big nursing home. Sharda Devi had ordered lots of sweets for distribution. She had also got woollen shawls and clothes for nurses and other employees.

The moment the delivery took place, Sharda Devi presented a heavy necklace of gold to her daughter-in-law. Woollens and sweets were distributed heartily amongst all the employees of the hospital.

Lord almighty had fulfilled her wishes.

Sharda Devi, her son and daughter-in-law all of them were very happy. But the cheery atmosphere soon turned into one of sorrow and mourning on hearing the voice of the nurse.

When the nurse declared that instead of son, a daughter had been born Sharda Devi's enthusiasm vanished in thin air. Hearing this, Sharda Devi, on the brink of becoming unconscious, fell into a chair with a loud thud. The same thing happened with Jagbir whereas the daughter-in-law looked so pale that it looked as if there was no blood left in her body.

All three of them kept on sitting silently. After some time, taking some decision, Sharda Devi started saying, "We will tell the village people that the child was born dead. Remember this, no one should know about this reality at all."

"What should we do about this girl?" Jagbir asked.

Mother started saying, "We will bury her somewhere on the way." She sternly told her daughter-in-law, "Remember, this fact should remain within all three of us. No one should get an inkling of it."

"Mother, even I never wanted a daughter. I don't want to see her ominous face. I am inclined to agree to whatever you decide."

It was evening when finally they left Gupta Nursing Home. All three of them sat in the car, they had wrapped the girl in a blanket.

The distance between their village and the nursing home was roughly about fifty kilometers. On the way, sometimes a jungle could be seen and even the road was deserted. Jagbir stopped the car at one side in front of a dense forest and quickly started digging a pit with a spade and buried the girl inside the pit.

Jagbir drove the car straight to his mansion. His account clerk came running. His face was full of gaiety. He was anxiously waiting for the good news.

When he saw their faces, he realised that something bad had happened. That was the reason that they all had dejected faces. Sharda Devi told the accountant that a girl was born but, even she was dead.

This news spread in the village like a wild fire. On hearing this news priest Devdutt lost his wits, Sharda Devi had got her son Jagbir married to Gauri because of his prediction. On hearing about the birth of a girl, he quickly packed his belongings, and before Sharda Devi's accountant could reach him, he fled from the village along with his family.

He was aware that Sharda Devi was a very cruel woman. She could do or get done anything when she was annoyed or angry. In fact, there was a rumour that one day when she had lost her temper, she had her husband... Nobody knows as to whether this news was a fact.

Yes! This is definitely a fact it that after that day her husband was not seen anywhere. When her old priest disappeared, Sharda Devi called a priest from Mathura and asked him to very carefully prepare a horoscope of her daughter-in-law.

That priest, Ram Prasad, told her that there was some mistake in reading of previous horoscope, and, that was the reason that her ex-priest could not calculate properly. Actually, it was the second child who was supposed to be a son.

The second time, a boy was born and the happy news was circulated in the whole village. The whole village was decorated like a bride. Sweets and new clothes were distributed lavishly. Sharda Devi spent money like water.

The boy was very upcoming and good in studies. After graduating, Sharda Devi sent him to America for doing MA.

After finishing his studies, when he returned from America, he was not alone. He had an American girl with him. Sylvania was his class fellow. Both had got married. But Kundan did not inform anybody about it.

On seeing an American girl with Kundan at the airport, Sharda Devi thought that perhaps she was a traveller. On reaching near his grandmother, when he introduced her as his wife, Sylvania, she felt as if she was on the verge of collapsing.

Sharda Devi had been dreaming that she would get her grandson married to a big businessman's daughter. Her dreams crumbled like a wall of sand, in one go.

She reluctantly agreed to the circumstances. She could tolerate anything except for meat, fish and liquor. Everything which Sharda Devi despised started entering her house at the arrival of that American girl. She was astonished to know that her granddson who had never touched these things, had got trapped in them.

In reality, the main reason of all this was Kundan's wife. While staying with her, he had started consuming these things. Sylvania also got fed up of these restrictions. The atmosphere in her house in America was entirely different, from what she experienced here.

Finally she got fed up and gave Kundan a choice that either he separates from his relatives, or, she would go back to her house in America. He got trapped in a mental dilema because of Sylvania's ultimatum. He was at a loss to decide what was the right thing to do. On one side was a well and on the other side was a ditch.

Everyday a fight used to break out in the house. Sylvania was a very cunning woman. She had planned it all in America. There, in America she had estimated the value of all the property, owned by him. Her plan was successful. Kundan did not want to annoy Sylvania. That is why he thought it better to have a separate business instead of going back to America. On the other hand, he did not wish to go away from his relatives.

He asked for his share of property as he wanted to start his business separately. But his family refused. In a fix, he agreed to Sylvania's suggestion and filed a case in the court. Sylvania was a law graduate. She prepared a very strong case for Kundan and Sharda Devi lost the case in the court.

Sharda Devi decided to appeal in a higher court. Sharda Devi decided to spend money on suits but she would not give even a single penny to Kundan and Sylvania.

She was also upset because after so much effort and prayers she had been blessed with a grandson and today, this was the result. She handed over the case to Devika Rani, a well-known advocate of India.

Devika Rani studied the case thoroughly. The case started. The case was argued for many days and the day of the final judgement drew closer.

Devika Rani was sixty years old, she was very active but she had a heart problem. Sharda Devi used to meet her in her house along with her son and daughter-in-law.

Devika Rani had installed a CCTV camera and a speaker in every room. If she had any work to be done she used to talk directly to the domestic helps, PA and her driver via the communication system.

She had installed such a system in her home because one day while in office, she had a heart attack and nobody was present there to come to her aid. All the servants, PA and driver were in their respective rooms. It was fortunate that one of the servants had come to ask her whether she would have a cup of tea. Seeing his madam's condition, he at once alarmed the PA and the driver and she was immediately provided with the necessary medical aid.

This was also to her advantage that her daughter was working as a doctor in a nearby hospital of the city. Hearing the news of her not feeling well, she had come running.

Because of the CCTV. camera, all the happenings in the house could be monitored and every room had an inter-com.

Two rooms were fitted with monitors. One was in Devika Rani's office and the other was present in her bedroom. Most of her work was done in those two rooms.

On the last hearing of the case, an unfortunate incident took place. Devika Rani suffered a major heart attack. Her daughter arrived to take care of her. But her condition was so bad that the cardiologist advised her not to move around.

On hearing this, Sharda Devi, along with her son and daughter-in-law, came to her place to enquire about her health. She was afraid that if something happened to Devika Rani, her chances of winning the case would be ruined. This was owing to the fact that Sylvania was a very crooked woman.

Sharda Devi enquired from Devika Rani that what will happen to their case? She won't be able to attend the court. Alas, who will fight her case? Devika Rani smiled and replied, "I'll put everything right. You must have noticed that during my illness, my daughter, Sadhana, has been sitting with me since past fifteen-twenty meetings. She is aware of all the details of the case. She will be able to handle the case nicely."

"But, she is a doctor, how will she....?" Sharda Devi asked.

Devika Rani laughingly said, "You don't know. Sadhana is a law graduate. Earlier she used to work under me and handle cases. But six years back when I had a heart attack, she insisted to become a doctor. She had science subjects. She ignored all my suggestions and did a medical course. She preferred medicine over law. She says that she prefers to save people's lives. I agreed with her."

All this was being said in Devika Rani's bedroom. They saw on the CCTV that Sadhana was busy studying.

Devika Rani said, "All the time she is reading something or the other." Then she summoned Sadhana through her inter-com, to her room.

Sharda Devi was astonished to hear what Devika Rani had just said; that even a girl can achieve so much.

She used to reckon that only a boy could ....

In the meantime, Sadhana entered the room. Devika Rani explained the intricacies of the case to her.

"Don't worry mother. I will handle the case. It is just like the case which you handled previously." Then looking towards Sharda Devi, "Please come. Let us go through the case again."

Sharda Devi's son and daughter-in -law accompanied Sadhana to the office.

Sadhana asked many complex questions in context to the case. She wanted to reach every nook and corner of the case. During this time, Devika Rani kept her CCTV on. After some time her condition started deteriorating. The nurse gave her a sleeping pill and told her to go to sleep. She put her CCTV on recording before going to sleep. She thought that in the morning she would see as to what went on between Sadhana and other people, and accordingly she would explain to her, the important points.

Sharda Devi was amazed to see Sadhana's intelligence and she asked her, "Daughter, you did law and medicine too, because of your mother's health, so that you can look after your mother. Really it is creditable. I used to think that girls..."

Hearing their conversation, she said nothing, and replied using brief answers by saying Yes or No. Then for some time, she left them in the office and went to her room. Perhaps she had some other work .

Once she left them, Sharda Devi kept on talking to her son and daughter-in-law. After some time, Sadhana returned and got some important papers signed from them and sent them back.

The case started after two days. Devika Rani was very worried. Though she had full confidence in Sadhana, but Devika Rani's reputation was at stake.

After hearing the arguments of both the sides, the judge said that he will give his judgement the next day at 11 am. Next day the court was overcrowded as one of the lawyer in this case was an American lady.

Judge gave the judgment in favour of Sharda Devi. On hearing this, Kundan and his American wife lost their wits. They were thinking of crores, and now they did not get even a single penny.

After some time, when Sadhana came to Sharda Devi, she embraced her and suddenly it came out from her mouth "I wish, you were my daughter".

"She is your daughter," Devika Rani, sitting in a wheelchair said from behind.

"I did not understand. Devika Rani, what are you saying?"said Sharda Devi.

"I am stating the truth. She is your daughter" repeated Devika Rani

"But she is your daughter..."

"No. I found her in a forest a long time back. I learnt yesterday that she is your, your granddaughter. I wanted to know, what all Sadhana asked you, that day. This case was very important for me. I was not feeling well, so, I took some tranquilisers and went to sleep.

Before going to sleep, I had put my CCTV on recording mode so that, later on I would be able to see what all had transpired between you and her. I saw her going to her room for some work, leaving you all behind. I was surprised to hear the conversation between the three of you.

I learnt from your conversation about Gupta Nursing Home episode and later on learnt about the jungle incident. You could never imagine how bad I felt that one woman can do such abhorring...?

I would not have fought your case, if I had known it earlier. The judge had already given his verdict before I reached the court."

"But what were you doing...?" asked Sharda Devi.

"I had gone to the hospital to get the death certificate of my husband and got delayed there. On the way, the driver suddenly stopped the vehicle, opened the door and went running towards one side. When he returned after some time, he had a new born girl who was wrapped in a torn blanket, covered with blood stains. He told me that wild animals were taking her. I immediately took her to a nearby hospital and got her treated.

I had no child of my own. I told everyone that she is my daughter. Now you must have realised Sharda Devi that daughters are more helpful than sons."

Sadhna, standing nearby, kept on listening with remorse. Tears were pouring from her eyes. She went forward and embraced Devika Rani and started saying, "Mother, I can never repay you."

Sharda Devi was feeling ashamed of herself because of her deed. Still, mustering courage, she asked, "Will you return our daughter to us?"

Before Devika Rani could utter a word Sadhna shouted, "Never. People want a mother, a sister, a wife, but why not a daughter... Are We the Sinners?"

8

The Final Decision

"Decision! Decision! Decision! How many times I have told you that this is my final decision. Please don't disturb me, I am already very..." leaving his talk unfinished, he said.

"This problem is of your own accord. You want to leave your wife just for such a small thing." She said.

"You women are all like this. You want to support one another in no time. You call this a small thing?" He said getting irritated.

Ranjana was aware that it was of no use discussing anything with Rajan.

It was a few years earlier when Ranjana was studying with Rajan in the same college. She had a soft corner for him. But she did not disclose her affection to him. Her friend Shobha was crazy after Rajan and somehow she was able to put it across to Rajan. They both got attracted to each other.

Ranjana kept quiet because of her friend. She was feeling torn, but somehow she controlled herself.

She would think, what is that love which is not selfless. Love does not mean getting together. One can still be in love by staying away from the loved one. She could bear any sorrow for the sake of Rajan's happiness.

Then both Rajan and Shobha got married. Next day, Rajan was going to the market to buy something. Ranjana's house was on the way. It struck him, why not meet Ranjana?

Ranjana was living alone there and earning her livelihood by giving tuitions. He has been visiting her house earlier also. So, in order to give her surprise, he quietly entered her room.

While entering her room, he witnessed that Ranjana was looking at some papers with her back towards the door. He quietly went near her and was startled to see the paper in her hand. Ranjana was holding his photo in her hand. Ranjana, at the same time turned and while hiding his photograph, said, "You! Oh... Rajan..."

She could not look at his eyes. She realised that the secret was out.

"Ranjana, I wish, you had given me the slightest hint. I have been always very fond of you, but looking at your ideals, from your talks, I always thought that you had somebody else as your idol. Not even once, you gave me a hint of your feelings." Rajan said feeling sorry.

"What hint could I give you? And I never wanted to be an obstacle on your way of love. Now you both are married and you should not think of anybody except your wife. Now, I have no right to keep your photograph with me. Take it. I am returning your photograph to you. " Saying this, she put forward her hand which was holding the photograph.

Rajan saw that Ranjana's hand was trembling. Ranjana's eyes were full of tears.

Rajan continued looking at her for some time and then said, "No, please keep my photograph with you. I have no right to keep this photograph with me."

Hearing this, Ranjana's eyes started shedding tears. She continued sobbing. Rajan consoled her.

"Now, we both have gone so far, it is impossible to return," he said.

"I have been controlling my feeling since long, but today...I don't believe in selfish love. Love should not be restricted to union. There is something more, more to it. If the feeling of love is true, one can love from a distance. Rajan, I will feel fortunate if ever I am able to help you in any way," Ranjana said.

Rajan was posted out to another place after a span of four years. Shobha was at a good post in a college, so, she requested Rajan that she will stay here and continue working in the college. During vacations they both will meet each other.

Finally, Rajan agreed to this Shobha's continued staying with her son.

During this period, Rajan had been continuously writing to Ranjana. Rajan's letters had been indicating a little conflict between husband and wife. But, she thought that time will heal every misunderstanding.

The main reason of this misunderstanding was the wish to have a second child. Rajan was very fond of children whereas Shoha was against them. This was the main cause of conflict between both of them. This had also become a prestige issue for both of them.

One day Ranjana received a letter from Rajan. Only a few words were written in it, "Now it is the time of your test. If possible, leave for this place at once, the moment you receive the letter."

She was in a great anxiety on receiving this letter. She was making her mind and thinking, will it be alright to go to Rajan's house? After thinking for some time, she decided and reached Rajan's house.

"I know, what is your problem? There is no such problem which has no solution. But a person has to make an effort to solve it. Rajan, one has to compromise somewhere on a few issues."

"Ranjana, I have told you so many times earlier and I am asking you for the last time today, will you stand by me? He said feeling miserable."

"Rajan! You have put me in a great turmoil."

"Ranjana! Because of your insistence, I have tried my level best to make Shobha understand the situation, but she did not heed to me." He continued saying," You have asked me one year's time to solve this problem and that time is about to come to an end, only few days are left."

Ranjana had no solution to this issue. In the end, she replied him in affirmative. But, once again she requested Rajan to try for the last time to talk to Shobha on this matter.

Rajan agreed to this request of hers.

Rajan and Ranjana reached Chandigarh by boarding night train. Ranjana made Rajan visit Shobha after coaxing him for some time. Ranjana still had a little hope that perhaps they both may reconcile.

Before leaving, he said to Ranjana to be ready, as he will be leaving by tonight's train.

"Okay! Okay! First you go to your house." Ranjana said pushing him slightly.

It was Sunday and Shobha was at home. Her son had gone out to play. Rajan had discussed this matter so many times with Shobha earlier also. He was ready to compromise, if Shobha could agree. He started to say, "Shobha, in this frame, on one side, is a photograph of our son along with us for so many years and the other side is empty. Is it not possible to...?" He left the sentence incomplete.

This is how the chain of conversation started.

She said feeling dejected, "Rajan, I cannot help you in this matter. I don't know how to convince you. I am scared of this and..."

Interrupting her, Rajan shouted, "This is a very beautiful excuse of yours which you keep on repeating every time. May I take it as your final decision?"

"Yes! Of course, take it to be my final decision," she replied feeling irritated.

Discussion continued till evening, but no result came out of it. In the end, Rajan gave an ultimatum to Shobha that from now onwards he will have no relations with her and that he was also taking Ranjana with him.

"Now regarding the question of Munna, neither I will keep him with me, nor you. I am taking him along with me. I will put him in some good hostel."

There was hardly any time left for the train to leave. He quickly packed his son's and his own clothes in a suitcase.

Shobha kept on watching everything silently. Once he finished packing, he went to the bathroom to get ready. During this time, Shobha got up and went to the other room and brought something wrapped inside of her *sari*. She quickly opened the suitcase of Rajan and put it inside the suitcase between his clothes.

Rajan, while coming out of the bathroom told her. "It will be better, if you don't accompany us to the station."

Shobha just nodded her head but could say nothing.

Shobha went inside the kitchen. She prepared the food and told the servant, "You serve the food to *Sahib* and Munna." I am going out and will return later.

Shobha had not returned till the time Rajan and his son left for the station. He straight away went to Ranjana's house. Ranjana was restlessly walking inside her room . There was still a ray of hope that...

She lost all the hope, seeing Munna on the shoulder of Rajan, and sat on the chair feeling dejected.

'Shobha will behave in such an immature way,' she thought.

"Ranjana, please hurry up and pack your baggage. There is no time left now," said he, entering the room.

Ranjana packed her stuff with a heavy heart. She had no relatives in this world. So, she locked her house and left with him.

The train was about to leave. They quickly entered the first class compartment. They were all alone in the compartment. Rajan put his son on the opposite seat.

Both were keeping quiet. Both were feeling sad. How the circumstances changed their destiny?

"What a beautiful child he is!" suddenly her attention was drawn to the child and thought, 'What is his mistake? He is getting separated from his parents.'

In the meantime, a ticket checker came in the compartment. He checked the tickets and informed them, "from the adjacent compartment, a lady will join you at the next station. After that, you can bolt your compartment." Saying this, he left for the next compartment.

It was quite warm. Ranjana went to the bathroom to have a bath and change her clothes.

Rajan opened the suitcase and as he took out Munna's night suit, he heard something falling on the floor with a bang.

He picked it up and was amazed to see that it was the same double frame in which there was a photograph of his, Shobha's and Munna's. And on the other side now, there was a smiling photograph of a cute child, cut from some calendar.

Looking at this, his joy knew no bound and he uttered loudly, 'So, Shobha, you have agreed at last.' He quickly closed the suitcase, picked up his child and was about to pull the chain, when suddenly he was startled at somebody's voice.

"Mr Rajan, you...!"

It was a woman's voice.

He turned back and saw Dr Minakshi was standing in front of him. Rajan's hand stopped.

"It is almost six months since I met you. I had also told Shobha to let me know when you visit her, as I had to discuss something important with you, but...!"

"Yes, I was unable to visit this place for the past six months because of some urgent official work. This time also, I had come here just for today only. I had come in the morning and now I am returning at night", and then said, "I am in a hurry. So, if you...!"

She said interrupting him, " But it is also very important for you to listen to me. You know it well that a few months back Shobha fell down from the stairs. It was her good luck that she survived, but...!"

"Dr Minakshi was looking outside at the lights far away, from the window. Rajan, holding his son on his shoulder was anxiously waiting for her to complete her sentence after the word 'but', so that he may be able to pull the chain and get out of the train.

Dr Minakshi was feeling uneasy as to how to complete her sentence.

"Shobha is not aware that now she will not be in a position to bear a child and you... you also will not be able..., you will never become a father again."

These words were ringing in his ears like as thuds of a hammer. He shouted loudly, "No, no! Dr Minakshi please don't say like this, please don't say...!"

It looked as if he lost all his strength. His hand which was eager to pull the chain fell aside like a broken tree.

He just sat down on the seat with a thud. Now, he was in a big confusion. Ranjana's heart got a big jolt.

She had been listening to what all the doctor said. She had thought that once they reach home, she will try again to make him understand, but Dr Minakshi spoiled everything. Now, she was in a doubt that in the present circumstances, Rajan may... with Shobha...!

After some time, the train stopped at the next station.

Platform was almost lonely and deserted.

The door of the first class compartment was opened and deciding something, he got down from the compartment holding his son with one hand and in other holding his suitcase.

When he looked up, he saw Shobha standing in front of him.

Ranjana was standing behind him with her eyes full of tears... of happiness!

9

A Smart Girl

It was Sunday.

Manohar got up late.

Initially, he shouted for his wife Shanti while still in bed. When despite shouting for her so many times, his wife did not respond, feeling irritated, he finally got up.

He then realised that his wife was away to her parents' place for the last seven days.

But who was there with him in his bed yesterday night? He looked at the door. He recollected that perhaps he had taken some extra drink and had forgotten to lock the door.

When he was going to take the glass of water from the close by table, his eyes fell on a piece of paper which was lying there. It was a letter, he started reading.

Mister...?

You will be very surprised to go through this letter of mine. I had come to Chander Dass, who resides in a flat next to yours. After finishing my work and getting one thousand as my wages for the services rendered, I was going away.

I was in dire need of some extra money, and thought, from where it will come? While passing by your flat, I heard you calling, 'Shanti come here, come near me.' I immediately stopped there only.

I peeped through your window and saw you murmuring in your sleep. I kept on thinking for some time and then made up my mind, opened the door slowly and came and lay down next to you in your bed.

You kept on imagining, I was Shanti and I continued behaving like Shanti and kept on lying peacefully. I have taken out a thousand rupee note from your heavy wallet as my compensation for the services rendered.

I do need more money but I don't charge more than what my fee is.

After all I do have my own principles.

Yours,

Call Girl."

Reading this Manohar got a big jolt. He had almost fifty thousand rupees in his wallet. He immediately opened his wallet and started counting money.

Only one red note of thousand rupees was missing. Although he was sorry to loose one thousand rupees, yet he could not help appreciate the professionalism of the girl.

It was a week ago, when Inspector Vinod had called *Havildar* Pandey to his office and giving him a red coloured file said, "Pandey ji, what is the colour of this file?"

"Sir red...." *Havildar* Pandey replied.

"That means that this file is very important and its reply has to be sent to the Commissionar *Saheb* within a week."

After giving the file to Pandey, Inspector Vinod said, "Pandey ji, I have gone through the file. You also go through this file properly. After reading, do let me know the important points of this file."

Pandey came back after an hour and said, "Sir, I have gone through the file properly. Code name of this file is *Smart Girl* and stopping in between, he said, "Sir, why the name of 'Smart' Girl, has been given to this file when the girl is a call girl?"

Inspector Vinod screamed at him and said, "Pandey ji, don't get involved in the name of *smart girl* or *call girl*. You better explain the case properly to me.

"It is okay, Sir! This call girl Chandni is missing from Mumbai. Mumbai police has suspicion that either this girl is in our area or is dead. Commissioner *Saheb* has himself written in red ink that if this girl is found, then she should be arrested at once. And whosoever arrests her, will be given out of turn promotion.

And if that girl is not in our area, then close the file.

The very next day after Manohar's episode, Pandey saw the same girl of the file, going in to a flat and coming out of the flat in the evening. It was about 7 pm almost dark.

Pande thought it was a good opportunity to catch her red handed.

Later, he changed his mind and thought that why not I follow her and see what is she up to?

Deciding this, he changed his plan of arresting her and started following her.

For some time Chandni kept on walking and then entering a dirty lane, she was lost.

Pandey, hiding at that place was patiently waiting for her re-emergence. After some time when she came out, she was in a different outfit.

Pandey noticed that neither she was putting on colourful expensive clothes, nor, was she holding a coloured purse. And she was without a make up, simple hair style and was wearing a simple old *sari*.

On observing her, for a moment Pandey was in a fix. This time she was giving a look of a simple indian woman.

Once again, Pandey, abandoned his plan of arresting her and decided to chase her to find what she was up to.

After some time she entered a nursing home and climbed the stairs. He also entered the nursing home without any hesitation. He was in civil clothes, so, nobody could suspect. He could easily be taken as a patient.

He noticed her going into the waiting room and saw her talking something to the peon in a hushed voice.

The peon said, "Doctor *Sahib* is on round to see one of his patient's and he will be here any moment. You better go inside the doctor 's room and wait for him." Chandni went inside the doctor's room.

Pandey had been listening to their conversation. He went and sat down at a place from where he could listen to Chandni and doctor's discussion properly.

Chandni got up when doctor entered the room and started talking to him in a hushed voice. In response Dr Buxi told her in a strong voice, "You know it very well that for the past four years, your husband is being given these injections. If the injection was not very expansive, I would have given it myself. Today you got very late in getting the money. If you were late by thirty minutes...! Well! Give me the money fast, I will get the injection and will administer it to him."

You have been bringing money daily for the injection. It is your strong will power that you are able to arrange the money in spite of this rising prices".

"Doctor *Saheb*, I do all sort of jobs. Whatever work I get.... ! I cannot see my husband dying." Chandni replied crying.

"All right, now, please keep quiet. There is no need to worry now." He said consoling her sympathetically.

After hearing the conversation between Chandni and doctor of the nursing home, Pandey felt very sad. Tears came into his eyes. He started praising her in his heart for the sacrifice she was making.

He thought that she may be a call girl, but she is doing a very noble work. If it were some other woman, she would have left her husband to die, but would not have done such a downgraded act.

After hearing the discussion between them, he straight away went to Inspector Vinod's office.

On entering office, he said, "Sir! You are still here? I was under the impression that you must have gone home?"

"Pandey ji, we both are working together for the past six years. Have I ever gone home without you? We are from the same place, our residences are close by. Our train that leaves for Gurgaon is invariably late.

It would not have even started from Delhi till now. The train will take almost one hour to reach here. Then remembering something, he asked, "Pandey ji, did you find the girl or have come empty-handed?"

"Sir! You are right, I have returned empty handed."

Then he explained the complete conversation which took place at nursing home in detail to Inspector Vinod.

"Sir! there is no doubt that Chandni is a call girl but to save her ailing husband... Sir, I do not want to go to hell by arresting her."

After saying this, he gave the file to Inspector Vinod and said, "Now sir! I know I will not get my promotion. But I am not interested in getting my promotion by arresting a devoted woman."

Inspestor Vinod took the file from Pandey's hand and put it on the table. He took out a cigarette from the pack of cigarette which was kept on the table. He lit it with the lighter and took a long drag.

He was occupied in his own thoughts and was roaming around in his office and making rings of smoke of cigarette.

Suddenly, he remembered that Pandey also smoked sometimes and he offered one cigarette to Pandey. Pandey took a matchbox from his pocket and lit his cigarette.

Now, both of them were smoking cigarettes, but appeared as if they both were in deep thoughts. They both were engrossed in some serious ideas.

After some time, Inspector Vinod went near his table and started turning the pages of the file. Suddenly, he got an idea, he lit his lighter and put the file on fire in one go.

He then threw the file in a dustbin.

"Pandey ji, you also wanted that we both should not go to hell? Now, as there will be no file as such we will not have to go hell."

Havildar Pandey was startled to witness the whole scene.

On the other hand, when Havilder Pandey left the nursing Home, he was not aware that he was being followed by the peon.

The peon standing in a corner in the dark had witnessed everything that conspired between them. He also witnessed the the file being burnt.

He went running to the nursing home.

Chandni and the doctor Buxi were still in the office, busy in some discussion.

While entering the office, he said merrily, "Madam, Congratulation, file pertaining to your case has been burnt. Now, you are free. All your difficulties are over."

He narrated whole of the incident to Chandni and doctor Buxi. Hearing this, she embraced the doctor with great enthusiasm and immediately she took out money and handed fifty thousand rupees to doctor and five thousand to the peon.

Then continued telling doctor Buxi, "I am very grateful to you for agreeing to my plan about my husband's illness........ You got me and my file freed from the clutches of police forever."

Doctor Buxi put his arms around Chandni's waist, and with affection pulled her towards him saying, "Police has kept the code name of your file '*Smart Girl*' very appropriate."

How you kept the track that the file has been dispatched to police department here, and how you entangled me and my peon in your net? You are really not a '*Call girl*' but a '*Smart girl*'.

10

Reshma—A Love Story

Capt. Aslam was sitting on a chair near his bunker and was enjoying sun shine. After many days, the sun had come out. All around, the velvet green-coloured sheet was spread. In front of him, was the breath taking scene with small boats floating on the water and sometimes the groups of water fowls flying amid the clouds. And a group of small hillocks on the right side of Watlab's rest house at the back ground, were creating ripples in his heart.

On the left side at the top was a chain of dense forests and then the snow clad mountains which could be seen from a distance, gave a look of a girl sculpted in white marble. On the side of the lower side of the mountain, small rivulets of thin snow on the slopes of the mountain, gave the impression of roots of an old tree of *bargad* which had come out of the earth and could be seen outside.

At the slopes of the mountain was a grazing field, where white and black herds of sheep, goats were grazing and people were gathering twigs of wood at nearby small mountains. Whenever they would make a noise because of some discussion, it would divert his attention. But he was enjoying this captivating music. He was fully engrossed in this scene. God knows from where groups of clouds floating on blue sea of sky came that side and within no time they covered the sunlight.

Even this scene was very attractive and he was feeling that he may continue enjoying this captivating scene, but he realised that the weather had become a little cold. Against his wishes, he went to his bunker to get his coat. When he came out after some time, he saw that it had started snowing on top of that hillock and it was proceeding towards the slopes.

Watching the snow falling, the girls and the children who had gone to the forest to gather twigs of wood, started running down the slopes, keeping the bundle of twigs on their heads. The shortcut path to their village had to pass through his bunker.

The wood collectors were scared of snow fall and they started running towards their homes. They all were looking like a group of 'ants' from a distance. Within a short time, they covered this long distance.

The weather was going from bad to worse. Aslam was thinking of going back to his bunker, suddenly his attention went towards the forest. He saw that at quite some distance away from the group, a young girl was walking slowly, holding a big bundle on her head.

At one place, she stopped, turned her head and looked at the long way and then deciding something, started following the shortcut path. While on that path, she lost her balance and fell down there. The bundle of twigs fell down from her head and started rolling towards the ditch. The girl was watching that helplessly.

Aslam was waiting eagerly for her to get up. But, when after a long time, she did not get up, he felt worried. He quickly made up his mind and started going towards her. He was wearing a hat. On nearing that girl, he found that she was in a semiconscious state. She was moaning in pain. The girl looked at him helplessly.

He asked the girl, where has she been hurt? He might be in a position to help her.

The girl did not utter a single word, but pointed towards her feet. Aslam looked at her feet and it did not take him much time to realise that the girl's foot was badly hurt and there was some quick swelling at her foot.

"Is it hurting too much?" he enquired from the girl.

In reply, she shook her head, but could say nothing. Tears started rolling from her eyes and she started sobbing. Aslam said. "Have courage. Don't worry, I will just..." He looked all around, but could not find a place where he could take the girl to save her from cold...!

It had started snowing very heavily. He helped the girl carefully to get up.

He put girl's left hand on his shoulder and his right hand around the waist of the girl. The girl was a little hesitant to stand with him despite being in terrible pain. She gave Aslam a distressed look.

He understood girl's hesitation and said, "What to do! There is no other way? I can understand, but... I am taking you to my bunker. Outside there is heavy snow and also it is very cold. On top of that, there is no treatment possible here. There at my place, I can get you treated by a doctor."

Hearing this she almost trembled. She tried her best to get away from Aslam. He understood girl's hesitation and said, "Don't' get scared. There is no danger. You will be completely safe. You have no reason to feel insecure. Our army has been deployed here for the past so many days and then everyone is not the same."

The girl looked at him desparately. "Have faith, nobody will harm you. You will leave for your house, like..." She had no other option but to trust him, she went with him with a palpitating heart.

Reaching his bunker, he made her lie down on his cot and covered her with a blanket. He lighted *'bukharee'* (*kerosine* heater) with the help of a matchstick. The girl felt somewhat comfortable with the heat of the *'bukharee'*

Her body was cold because of walking in the snow. Even now after so much had taken place, she was still feeling miserable. She was constantly looking towards the door. Door was fluttering due to blowing of fast wind.

There was a big sound at the back. He saw that the girl had thrown the blanket and forgetting her pain she wanted to rush out of the bunker. He caught her.

"Foolish girl, why are you increasing your problems? Lie down like before. "He shouted at her. Hearing his high pitched voice, the girl got scared and again lay down on the cot. He came forward and covered her with a blanket.

Doctor was not available, so Aslam explained everything to the Nursing Assistant. After some time somebody knocked at the door, he opened.

Nursing Assistant examined her foot thoroughly and after applying some gel, he said, "She will have to stop walking for a few days." Saying this, he looked at the girl, she moved her head slowly, as if she was saying that she has understood.

"Can she be sent to her house with a little help?"

"No Sir! It will be very harmful for her to walk in this situation." They both looked in the light of the lamp that hearing this, the girl looked very upset.

"Alright, go and arrange for a stretcher and a few men."

"Okay, sir! I will go and make some arrangement for it." Coming out of the bunker he said in a low voice, "Sir! Looks like she is dumb. She did not utter a single word while I was examinig her foot. Had it been somebody else, she would have ...! Well, I beg your leave."

Aslam was astonished at this. He thought that the Nursing Assistant Joshi had said rightly. He himself had not heard her talking for the last two hours. He felt pity for her.

He looked at that village girl attentively. She was a very good-looking girl. Fair complexion, heavy eyelashes and heavy long hair touching her waist. Suddenly while looking at her, words came out of his mouth, "What is your name?" Then suddenly realised his folly and talked to himself, "What a fool I am? I am posing this question to a dumb girl."

This last sentence, he said very slowly so that, the girl will not hear it. But despite his taking precaution, she heard him and felt like crying.

She was thinking, "I wish, I could reply him, but...!"

"Sir! I have made all the arrangements, but..." Aslam was startled. "But what?" Aslam looked at Joshi questioningly.

"Sir! from the border out-post, Doctor *Saheb* rang up and asked to bring some medicines. I will have to go there."

"Alright, I will take a few people and will leave her in her village myself." Aslam said, deciding something.

Girl was transferred to the stretcher very carefully. At slopes, he would say, "Go carefully." On reaching the slope, he told the girl to point the way to her house. After a while, they were at her house. The labourers explained everything to her parents in their Kashmiri language. They were grateful to Aslam for getting her treated and escorting her to her house.

Then Aslam had to go on leave for a few days.

x x x

Aslam had returned from leave that very night. He reached a day earlier in his unit because he got a direct flight from Chandigarh. Before going to bed he gave instrutions to his orderly, not to disturb him early in the morning as he wanted to sleep till late.

"Sir... Sir", when he did not get up even calling him so many times, the orderly shook him. "Man, he is not letting me sleep", he murmured under his blanket and shouting at him, "What is the matter? I had given you special instructions not to wake me up early in the morning. I will get up at my own!"

"Sir! Why are you admonishing me? I have already told her that if I wake sir up, he will be very annoyed with me. But...!"

"Very good, tell her that I am sleeping. Come later." Covering his face, again he went to sleep.

He said, while scratching his head, "Sir! I tried to explain to her, but what could I do? That girl is very stubborn." He took a long time to pronounce the word, 'Girl' so that Aslam may get some time to think. On hearing the word 'Girl, ' Aslam was startled and holding out his head from under the blanket said, "You are talking of which girl...?" Then thinking he said, "I hope she is not the same Kashmiri girl? If she is the same girl, then stop her. I will come out fast after having a wash."

When he came out after some time, sunshine was at full swing. Same girl was standing with her back, a little distance from the bunker. Hearing the noise of his footsteps, the girl turned herself in his direction, Aslam was looking towards her. The girl kept her eyes down cast. She was blushing. Her tresses were touching her cheeks. She was wearing multi-coloured clothes. The way the girl was standing on both her feet, it gave the impression that now the sprain at her foot was fully recovered.

Aslam heaved a heavy sigh. He thought, 'I wish, she was not a dumb girl...Wish she could talk.' He was constantly looking at her. After a while when he realised it, bringing a smile on his face, he was about to open his lips, when he was astonished by a sweet voice.

He was stunned. Girl's lips like flowers were moving. "*Saheb,* I am grateful to you that you came to my life like an angel, otherwise I would have been buried under the snow. Your favour...! I will be grateful to you forever and...!" She said leaving her sentence incomplete, keeping her eyes down cast and scratching the earth with the tip of her shoe. He was watching her in a confused manner. While watching the girls lips move he felt as if he had lost his strength of speech.

"*Saheb*, what are you looking at? Will you say something, or, will stand like a statue." There was a smile of fresh lotus on girl's face. Aslam got surprised, "You... can speak also. I was under the impression that you were a dumb girl." He could not believe the girl's voice. "That day, you did not utter even a single word."

The girl said smilingly, "That day, when did you give me an opportunity to speak? You, yourself were...!"

"Oh yes, "You are saying correctly."

Within a span of some time, they were talking as if they were familiar with each other for a long time.

"Did you not go to the forest today for collecting wood? Are you celebrating a holiday...?"

She laughed... and it seemed to Aslam as if the bells of the whole Kashmir valley had started ringing.

"Yes I, as well all others did not go to forest because there is a fair in the village."

"What is in this fair...?"

"Circus people have brought bear, lion and elephant." She was explaining this with the jesture of her hands. She was listing the names of all the animals very innocently.

"Are you not afraid of wild animals?" He said teasing her.

"I do get scared, but circus staff put all the spectators who come to see them in a cage, and then they take the animals out." Aslam started laughing loudly.

The girl was surprised as to why he was laughing nonstop? Her eyes were watching him continuously.

"What has happened *Saheb*? Why you are laughing so non stop?"

When after some time, he could control his laughter, he said, "Circus people do not put the visitors in a cage, but they put animals in big cages and show their tricks."

The girl kept on thinking for some time and then said grinning, "What you are saying is absolutely right. I have never thought of that." Now, she was continuously laughing at her own foolishness.

"What is your name?" On hearing this question from him, she at once stopped laughing as if somebody had switched off the switch. Now, she realised that in her first meeting, what all she has been talking to a stranger without any hesitation? She was looking down.

She spoke very softly, "Reshm .... Reshma!"

You got very nice name, but "Reshm .... Reshma! Such a long name." She looked up and said grinning, "In fact, my name is Reshma, but at home everyone calls me Resham".

Aslam said mischievously, "But I will call you, Reshma" and started laughing.

Reshma smiled and said feeling shy, "Alright, you can call me by any name you like." Then looking at the sky, she added, "Oh, I have stayed here for such a long time, Now I will leave." While saying this, she took out a packet from under her veil and putting it on a big stone, quickly ran towards the slopes. "Hello, what is... this packet?" Aslam kept on shouting.

He opened the packet. There were home-made sweets inside it.

He looked up and saw that the girl in multicoloured clothes flultering her veil, was running down the slopes with the speed of wind. And when she was out of sight, he took out a piece of sweet and said, "Stupid, it is sweet like her."

Now, she had started interacting with him often while coming and going towards forest. She would put down the bundle of woods near his bunker and would take some rest. During this *siesta*, she would enquire about Aslam's relations, service and what not?

Within no time, they learnt about each other quite a lot and she became his girlfriend. Who could stop the fragrance from spreading? In no time the fragrance of their love affair spread between boys and girls of the village.

Javed who was crazy about Reshma's beauty became jealous. One day, he cornered her and said, "Reshma, you leave your this habit. For how long you will save yourself from me?" Saying this, he tightened his arms around Reshma.

"Get aside from my way, you rascal!" She bit his arm with her teeth like an enraged tigress. She got herself freed from his arms. There were signs of tooth bite, but as if he was mad about her.

"*Meri Jaan*, why are you getting annoyed. Is that Army man so fascinating?" Then grinding his teeth, he said, "I will make sure to take my right. Of course, I am ready to forget my right. And will take you to that Army officer myself, if you fulfill my desire today. After all, I have waited for you to grow up." He had a devilish grin on his face. He jumped at her and she was under him like a helpless deer. It was a moment of life and death for her. She fell almost unconscious.

In the meantime, Aslam arrived. He had seen Javed following Reshma from a distance. Reshma had casually mentioned that one of the boy from the village had bad intention on her and once or twice, he had seen him following her.

That is why, he had understood Javed's intentions. First, he freed her and later thrashed him badly. It looked like as Aslam was out of his senses. Reshma got scared and she stopped him from hitting Javed. On Reshma's pleading, he spared him and took her along with him.

After some time, Javed got up and left for his village limping.

On the one hand, their love continued blossoming, and on the other hand, Javed's feeling of revenge continued increasing. He was waiting for a proper opportunity. Now, whenever Reshma would go out, instead of going alone, she would be accompanied by other girls. Even when she would go to meet Aslam, she will take her friend Jamila. Jamila was her friend of childhood and she had not kept any secret from her.

Javed usually would go out of the village for a few days. Jamila would find out Javed's programme from his sister and during that time Reshma would roam around freely like a free bird with Aslam. But due to the presence of Jamila, they would feel a little hesitant.

Both used to meet under the *'Chinar'* tree near a big waterfall. Their love was at peak.

The war started. He informed her sadly, "I have to go to Bangla Desh tomorrow."

"What are you saying? So soon...", said Reshma. She started weeping bitterly.

"We just received orders today. I have to go and get all the arrangements made."

"Your news has almost killed me. Now, what will happen to me?" She was crying, holding him.

"Have faith, Reshma, I was planning to speak to your parents at the earliest. But, this war has upset all my programme."

"Aslam, before leaving, please come and talk to my parents about me. I am very scared. It may not happen that our love may...!"

"What are you talking? Don't talk in such a way." The moment, leave is granted, I will meet you near this waterfall, taking you in my arms would say that nobody can separate Aslam and Reshma. We are one soul in two bodies. God has made us for each other. If it were not so, then, just imagine I belong to Aligarh and have come here all the way and met you. My love, this is the God's wish," he wiped Reshma's tears with his handkerchief. And after a few moments, he took Reshma in his arms and after planting a kiss on her sacred fore-head, departed.

Reshma had been regularly recieving letters from him and she had been replying to him. Now, she would roam around like a sad...! She was not as chirpy as she used to be!

Javed got a job in the forest department in Pahalgaam and thus she had no fears any more. Aslam felt very happy learning about it because Javed was the real danger for Reshma. Letters continued between Reshma and Aslam.

Jamila was the only one who knew her secrets. One day, Reshma gave a big hug to Jamila and kissing her said, "Jamila, I am very happy today. Aslam is coming." After such a long time, Jamila saw happiness on her face.

"Dear Reshma, when is your crazy man coming?"

"You shameless, You call him crazy?" and she informed her merrily, that he was coming after ten days. And had asked her to meet him on that day in the afternoon near the same waterfall." After some time, she was absorbed in her thoughts. She felt as if the ten days were over and she was in Aslam's arms. She closed her eyes and murmured, " Aslam! You do not know, how in your absence I spent these days, how I spent these nights?"

"Stupid, wake up. This is day and not the night," said Jamila.

"You call me stupid, Aslam. Only I know what I have gone through."

"I am not Aslam, I am Jamila...This is the limit. You have actually started day-dreaming today." Reshma was shaken from her reverie and she opened her eyes. Her pleasant dream was shattered and she started sobbing, "I wish, you had not broken my *Sheesh Mahal* for some time more." She again started crying.

"Reshma, have patience. It is question of few days and after that all the happiness will be in your lap." And teasing her she said, "Then you will not remember me?"

Reshma passed those day, feeling restless. And on the fixed day, wearing a beautiful dress, she left for the waterfall with a beating heart.

"May I accompany you," said Jamila teasing her.

Though she was feeling very nervous, but on this occasion, she never wanted to take anybody along. On hearing Jameela, she kept quiet and looked down.

"I understand, you foolish girl. Does anybody like to be accompanied by someone? Go, may *Allah* fulfill all your wishes."

Aslam had written to her to be there near the waterfall by 2 pm, but she reached there at 1 pm. She was anxiously waiting for him... Time kept passing. Even sun was setting, but Aslam did not turn up. She was feeling very dejected and she left for her house crying...!

Aslam's leave was suddenly cancelled and for three months, he could not come. Time was so less, that he could not inform her. During those three months, he wrote so many letters, but did not get any reply from her.

He was aware that Reshma must be very annoyed with him, for not reaching there on time. If he was in her place he would have probably behaved in the same manner. He understood, but still he felt helpless.

On getting leave, he reached the hills of Kashmir. He wanted to give surprise to her by his surprise visit. So, he never informed Reshma about his programme of reaching there.

It was raining heavily at the time he started from Srinagar. Roads and bridges, all were in shambles and the buses were stopped on the way. He started for Reshma's village on foot. It was a long way to her village, which was located on a small hill. The rivulets were in full spate. Aslam unconcerned about the circumstances, was moving forward. He was fully drenched. He reached that mountain before sunset.

The moment he put his foot at the peak of the mountain and looked at other side, he could not find any remnant of the village. He reached there walking fast. There were heaps of destroyed and fallen houses.

He looked at every heap. He cried in a very loud voice, 'Reshma... Reshma.' But every time, his own voice resonated in the hills. There was no trace of Reshma. He could not find trace of any living soul in that village. Not even a single village was seen at far and wide places. The whole night, he kept on roaming in that ruined village. He spent the whole night under a tree.

Because of cold, he was down with the fever.

Next day, mustering strength, he reached the waterfall, but there also…! Two... three and… many days passed. He kept on lying down under the *chinaar* near that big waterfall, without any food or water. Now, he was in a very bad shape and was disappointed with his life. Then, suddenly…hearing sound of footsteps of someone, he became conscious, though he was still more or less unconscious.

Tinkling of foot ornament was coming closer and closer. He sat upright mustering strength. He was so weak that he was not in a position to call anybody. The girl was having her back towards him. But of red dress and the foot ornament, he could recognise her. These two things he had presented to Reshma.

"Re... Re... Re... Resh... Reshma," his voice was so low as if someone was speaking from a very far off place...! The girl had heard his voice and she turned towards him. He shouted, looking at her "you... you…!"

The girl came running to him. "Jamila… you… Reshma. I am asking you, why Reshma has not come…? Where is she? Don't know from where he got the strength of shouting so loudly? Jamila did not take much time to assess his condition. She started crying. Aslam was looking at her with bewildered look.

"Please answer me. Why has not Reshma come?" And murmuring to himself, "But these clothes… these clothes...! Perhaps, it is some joke…!"

She replied, "Aslam, that day Reshma kept on waiting for you near this waterfall till evening. But when you did not turn up, feeling upset she left for her house weeping. It was her bad luck, that in the isolated jungle she encountered Javed. She begged Javed but…" And leaving her sentence incomplete, she, said while crying, "And her life was tarnished..."

"Oh, my God, what have you done…!" Aslam, in despair caught hold of his head in his hands. He kept on sitting in the same position for some time and then recovering and taking some decision said, "Doesn't matter, I will accept her under any circumstances. I will bury Javed alive. But that will be later on.

First you help me meeting Reshma...." Jamila gave the impression as if she had not heard him. She kept on saying, "That day looking at her torn clothes and hearing her story of sorrow, heads of everyone in the village bowed in shame." The whole night she kept on crying and saying, "Jamila, how will I face Aslam on his return? People of village called the *Panchayat* at that moment. At day break, the *Sarpanch* gave their verdict, "Javed has to get married to Reshma." After saying this, she kept quiet for some time.

"So, Reshma got married to that scoundrel. At least... but why have you stopped? Say further. My brain is torn with being upset. Then what happened... Did in reality Reshma...?" He started crying unconsolably.

"Aslam, that poor girl did not eat and drink for two days. She kept on crying. On the third day, when villagers got up early in the morning, they were astonished to hear from the people who had gone to the jungle to collect the woods..." Jameela said sobbingly, "Reshma had committed suiside under this tree of *chinaar*. Her dead body was found hanging with a rope and..."

Aslam shouted loudly, "Reshma, what have you done? You left me all alone in this world... Reshma... My Reshma..."

Then Jamila continued saying, "Before her death, Reshma left a letter for me. It was written in that, 'You are my best friend. I cannot show Aslam my soiled face. I wish he could come that day and this sorrowful tragedy of my life could have been averted. I am leaving my Aslam in your care. Look after him." "Don't worry, I will look after you." Tears were rolling from Jamila's eyes.

Aslam was lying unconscious. There was no moment in his body. Jamila tried to make him sit, but all in vein. He had stopped breathing.

Many years later, a girl from the mountains, after narrating this story to a young man kept quiet for a while. Atmosphere was sad and full of sorrow.

"*Babu*! This is a very old incident. The villagers have constructed the tombs of Reshma and Aslam underneath this *Chinaar* tree near the waterfall. Those who could not be united during their life, at least could stay together after their death."

Every year a big festival is organised under this tree. People come from far and wide to wish for their love. They fill up water from this waterfall. They place flowers on the tombs of Reshma and Aslam. On that day, villagers observe a fast and do not put on new clothes. As if they are mourning for the atrocities commited on her."

"But, what happened to Jamila?" Young man suddenly enquired.

"That old woman who keeps on cleaning the tombs all day and lights the small lamps, is Jamila." Saying this, the girl fell silent.

That young man looked up and saw that Jamila was busy lighting the earthen ware.

The village girl was also quiet...!

That young man was also quiet...!

After breaking the silence, that innocent girl asked the boy, "I hope, you will not leave me and go like Aslam!"

11

A Gentleman

While trying to catch butterflies, *Champa* had gone deep in to the *jungle*. When she looked up, she saw herself being surrounded by Chaman, Badlu, Kashi and Makhan. It did not take her much time to realise their intentions. She tried her level best to run away but could not escape from their clutches. Finding no other way she started shouting for help.

As luck would have it, a hunter with a gun in his hands was passing by that way. On hearing her cries, he came running to the spot. Before they could play with her modesty, he jumped between them. He gave a thrashing to two of them with the butt of his gun and rest of the two seeing the barrel of the gun pointed towards them took to their heels.

"Come; let me drop you at your house," he said.

In a short time, Champa was able to control her nervousness and said, "*Babu*! It is your gentlemanliness that I got saved today. Had there been another wolf in place of you, then all of them would have played hell with me.

"*Babu*! I can not pay you for your gratitude. Had that happened then I would have killed myself." She said with tears rolling from eyes.

"Now there is nothing for you to fear. Yes! Where is your house?"

"That house at the end of the village, there I reside." Pointing her hand in that direction she said.

In a short time, while talking they reached the house. The girl insisted that she will not let him go without having a cup of tea. The girl then opened the lock of the house and hurriedly started preparing tea and *pakoras* for the stranger.

To keep him occupied the *hunter* started strolling in the room and... before Champa could be aware of anything, he hastily bolted the room from inside.

12

Beware of the Evildoers

'Pervez, come fast. See, I was talking about that man only. Whenever I take our child for a walk to the woods, I find him staring at us. He stares like... useless man, has made my life hell, that overflowing beard, unkempt hair, strange bag on his shoulder. He roams around here and there, gives an impression of a lunatic, mad man or there may be a loose screw in his head.'

She continued saying all to her, 'Now look, he is going around that tree. What he is staring at? Perhaps, he is really a mad man.'

Giving a verdict to her, she said, "Definitely, he is a mad man. Surprisingly, why has he only chosen the place in front of our house for walks for the last three days, he has made us put an end to our walks. We have virtually become a prisoner."

Pervez had just returned from three day's tour, and during this short time, some mad man had come to his area. His looks and actions had made Shabana as if...!

She explained everything to Pervez, as soon as he returned from the tour. Pervez was also surprised that for the last three months, he had not seen any mad man in his area. He was working as DFO of forest department and for official work he was supposed to visit various areas of the forest.

Consoling Shabana he said, "Okay! I will call the forest guard and find out why an insane man keeps on roaming around our bungalow."

He had just entered the bathroom to have a shower, when he suddenly heard Shabana's voice from outside. She was asking him in a loud voice to come out of the bathroom immediately. Realising the gravity of the situation, he quickly came out of the bathroom, wrapping a towel around him.

"What is the matter? Shabana, I have not understood anything. The tap was running at full speed." He said.

"That mad man…You came very late. He is still behind the trees. Wait for some time, after taking a round, he will come here. Shabana told him pointing towards that side.

"Okay! I was having a bath. I just came out without putting on clothes. I just wrapped a towel around me because of your anxiety. Tell me, where is that mad man?" He started looking towards the direction in which Shabana was pointing at.

He also could see a part of a man, behind the cluster of the trees. That man was not visible clearly. Yes! He gave a look as if he was trying to hide himself.

"Do one thing, just keep an eye on that man. I will go and quickly put on clothes." Saying this, he went inside, and came out putting on a pant and a shirt.

"Come, let's see, who is he?" He said, taking Shabana along.

"Pervez, take your gun along. Don't know he…"

"What are you talking? What is the need for a gun? He is not an animal, who…"

"You must have heard that mad people have more strength than an ordinary man. He is no less than a wild animal."

"Yes! Your argument has some weight. Okay! I will go and get my double barrel gun."

Taking the gun in his hand, he, along with Shabana, approached the trees. Now, that man was lying there with his back towards them. They reached very close to him treading softly. Pervez was checking cartridge in his gun, when suddenly that man changed his side and his face was facing Pervez.

On seeing him, Pervez got into a fit of laughter. Even that man was startled hearing Pervez's laughter. Shabana got confused, simultaneously looking at Pervez as well as that mad man.

Shaking Pervez she said "Look Pervez, I was telling you about this mad man only... and you are...!"

Pervez was unable to control his laughter. That man was also looking bewilderingly at him. Tears came to his eyes while laughing. At last, he was able to control his laughter and said, "Well, he is not a mad man. He is a famous artist, Mr Riaz. He is not an ordinary man, but is four in one. Painting, sculpturing, writing poems and stories, all are his hobbies."

Then, Pervez and Shabana explained the whole incident to Riaz. "Oh, I am very-very sorry", she said slowly.

"Nothing to feel bad. It was my good luck that I was saved today. I am aware that Pervez *Sahib* is well known hunter. He has so many wild animals' trophies filled up with husk and kept in his drawing room. If, he had taken an aim at me, then I would have also been standing in one of the corner along with the other animals, instead of roaming around in this forest," he told Shabana, smilingly at her.

Shabana, felt very bad at today's incident. On hearing Riaz, she blushed and felt very embarrassed.

Pervez and Shabana's child was very good-looking. They used to call him by his nick name 'Munna'. While coming from the city, all of her relatives had cautioned her that her son is very good-looking, so, always try to save him from evil eyes. Someone had told her to tie a black thread around his arm, whereas another had said, put a black spot behind his ears. Since it was their first child, she had been following all their precautions. She would make him wear black clothes and black spot, etc.

In reality, Shabana herself was one in lakhs as well. She was extraordinarily beautiful. She had pink face, beautiful eyes, and very long hair, reaching up to her knees. So, it was nothing strange that her child was so good-looking.

After this incident, they all left for the city for a week. They stayed there for few days. When they returned, Shabana was very busy in the house hold work, and could not go to the forest for a walk.

Next day, when Pervez left for his office, she, along with her son, went for a walk to the forest. She would go far away in the forest during her walk. These forests were very safe. There were no wild animals. While returning, she met Riaz. When she saw him, she kept on staring at him. He had also understood her surprise.

"What is the matter? Why are you looking so surprised?"

"Actually, it is difficult to recognise you. Your long hair missing and...", she said.

Riaz interrupted her and said, "I got a haircut and got clean shaved and also changed my clothes. Madam, I don't want anybody following me with a gun and..." he said in a mischievous manner.

"I apologise for that incident. It all happened due to some misunderstanding."

"Nothing to feel bad, Mrs Pervez. I was just joking with you. Please do not take it seriously," and then giving his attention to the child, said, "you got very lovely and good-looking child. He resembles you in features and complexion."

On hearing this she blushed. It gave the impression that red colour of all the flowers had got accumulated on to her cheeks.

Continuing the talk, Riaz said, "Beware of the evildoers. If you care for my advice, take five red chillies and put them in fire after taking them around the head five times to ward off a spell. Do not forget it."

Shabana was thinking that one more work has been added. She has already been doing all the other...? Now, there is an addition of red chillies... She nodded her head slowly and after that they were busy talking about other things.

Like this, they had been meeting each other in some corner or the other in the forest. While playing with the child, looking towards her, he would remind her, "Do not forget that five chillies..."

Shabana had been addressing him as Mr Artist and he used to address her as Mrs Pervez.

While talking to him, Shabana learnt that he has come here to complete a novel. When he is not in a mood to write novel, he starts painting pictures.

Shabana would get her and her son's lunch in the jungle and all three of them would have their lunch together there . Riaz used to bring tea in a thermos and sandwiches.

Shabana stopped him from bringing all those things.

"Mr Artist, you are being formal with us. When the servant brings lunch for us both, then we can get a little extra food. Why do you bring cold food with you?

"Well, I cannot get in to argument with you because if I do, then I will be deprived of the delicious food made by you."

On hearing the appreciation about her culinary art, she would start blushing and her face would turn red.

He said all this while taking child's cheeks in his hand and looking towards her "Mrs Pervez! Don't forget to do...!"

Before he could complete his sentence, Shabana completed his sentence and both had a hearty laugh. .

In return of Shabana's this favour, he made a very beautiful painting of Shabana and her son and gave it to her.

How the time of six month went by, they never knew and he had completed the novel.

Pervz and Shabana had learnt about his programme of leaving that place.

A few days were left of his departure. On meeting Riaz in the forest, Shabana said, "Mr. Artist, we have seen the paintings done by you, and listened to the story/novel, but we didn't get an opportunity to see your sculpture."

He said laughingly, "Whatever you say, I will show you the sculpture made by me, before my departure, but it will be a normal sculpture." Saying this at that time, he was holding 'Munna's finger and kissing, and said, "I do hope, at reaching your house those red chillies...!"

Whenever she was reminded of this sentence, she would blush, because at that time, she was reminded of Riaz's words that 'Munna' has inherited her good looks and...

Next day, when she met Riaz in the woods, he took out a partially opened book and presented it to her.

"Is it your novel?" She said and took the book in her hand, only then, she realised that it was a book carved out of stone. It was exactly similar to the normal book. If she had not held that book in her hands, she would have not realised that it was carved out of the stone. He had carved it with such finery that all the pages could be seen.

"Mr. Artist, book is beautiful, but half-opened and nothing is written in it. Why is it so?" Shabana asked innocently.

"Reply to your first question, this book is incomplete like my life. And on the question of why nothing is written in this book, listen nothing has happened in my life which can be written in this book. When something is found worth writing, the words will automatically spring up." Saying this, he became somewhat sad.

Shabana also became quiet. She never wanted Riaz to rake about his life.

Parvez and Shabna received him, when he reached their house on Sunday. All three of them started talking on different subjects. Their discussion was continuing, when the phone rang and Parvez picked up the receiver.

On hearing the phone, he quickly put on his overcoat.

Riaz was astonished to see this and asked him, "What is the matter? Are you going somewhere?"

"Excuse me. I will have to go just now. Nearby jungle is on fire." Parvez said.

"Well, it is alright. Your job is such. Not like us...!" Riaz said smilingly.

"My friend! I feel jealous of your life. What a nice and comfortable life? No worries, no restrictions..." Pervrz said, taking a long breath.

"Brother, these are far-fledged things. You would have realised our difficulties if you were in our place," Riaz said laughingly. There was a pathos in his voice.

Pervez left after shaking hands and wished him good bye.

Lunch started. Shabana was serving food smilingly. "Mr Artist, you are being formal. Have something, from tomorrow onwards you have to eat cold sandwiches...", said Shabana.

"Yes! You are saying the truth. Actually, you have inculcated a bad habit in me. Now, I will not be able to enjoy meals for a few days." He replied feeling sad.

Lunch was over. While washing his hands he enquired "Has 'Munna' gone to sleep? "Yes, he goes to sleep early," Shabana replied.

"Very good-looking child..." he said.

Shabana was again reminded of what he had said earlier... and she blushed.

Then she heard Riaz's voice, "Do not forget five red chillies and throw them into fire after..."

"Okay! Mr Artist, I will do it always and will continue doing it," and both started laughing heartily.

After some time, Riaz left, wishing Shabana good bye.

Riaz was feeling sad and so was Shabana or you could say, both were feeling sad.

But it was not their last meeting. As luck would have it, he was given another assignment for writing two-three novels by the publisher. Riaz had been visiting these forests for three years in order to complete his novels. Like this, meetings between Shabana and Riaz continued.

Pervez mostly was on tour. Most of his time, Riaz used to spend with Shabana and they would have meals together. They had become quite close and informal with each other.

Then Pervez got posted to a far off place and that is how their meetings were few and far between.

After a long time, one day, while disembarking from the compartment, he dashed against a lady who was in the process of embarking the train. The lady recognised him. But, perhaps Riaz was in a hurry, so, he could not recognise her. But he was not in such a hurry, that he would not recognise her. He felt that this lady was somehow known to him and after recollecting for a few moments, he felt that of course she was Shabana. How could he forget her?

On looking at Riaz, she had a mild smile but perhaps that smile was not of cheerfulness, but of... sadness...!

Shabana had gone very weak and had also shed much weight.

There was sometime left in the departure of the train. Riaz made the porter stand near his luggage and went and sat next to Shabana. There was no other passenger in the compartment except for both of them.

"Mrs Pervez, I could not recognise you at all. What has happened to you?" Uttering these words, Riaz realised that perhaps some tragedy had taken place in her life. But he kept quiet.

"After some time of your leaving that place, I fell sick. I got all the possible treatment, but to no avail", she heaved a long sigh and continued talking.

"You are also looking very weak and very pulled down".

"Yes! It has been so because of two heart attacks."And then lightheartedly he said, "I feel that after my leaving that place, you forgot red chillies..." Shabana recollected everything on hearing that sentence of Riaz.

"Mr Artist, I have not forgotten.... that. However busy I was, I have been doing that chilli-thing on 'Munna' everyday...!" She said smilingly.

"What did you say? You have been doing on 'Munna'... He looked towards Shabana with startled eyes.

"But I told that... for you... And you have understood it for something else."

Hearing this, she was in a fix as what to reply him. She had been always thinking that Riaz was mentioning that for 'Munna' On hearing this from Riaz, even now she blushed the way she used to many years ago, despite her being so ill.

Guard blew the whistle. Both looked at each other. He got down from the train slowly and came near the window.

Train started moving very slowly from the station. But some body pulled the chain and it stopped.

Riaz unknowingly put his hand over her hand.

Suddenly, the words came out from his mouth, "Shabana! I will always be very worried about your health. Get yourself treated properly."

"Riaz, I will also be worried about you. You also get yourself treated properly."

"Now, what treatment I will have? I have already suffered two heart attacks and now, waiting for the third one." He said, completing his words.

But Shabana did not utter a single word. In fact, she wanted to tell him everything that Pervez got married again and her status in the house was not more than that of a maid servant. 'Munna' was in the hostel. She was all alone in this world, but..."

Then unconsciously, she put her other hand over the hand of Riaz and said smiling. "You have never recited any Urdu couplet.

He said smiling, "How can I refuse your wish? Now listen to what the *shaiyer* has said.

"Waqt-e-rukhsat, mein tham loon unka daman, uljhan mein ye khayal mujhko aaya hi nahi."

(At the time of departure, in confusion it never occurred to me that I should hold her hand).

Hearing this couplet Shabana started thinking, I wish! Riaz could hold my hand and Riaz also started thinking, if it was possible, he could hold Shabana's hand.

But it could not happen.

Train gradually started picking up speed. They both were waving their hands till the time train went out of their sight.

Don't know, why eyes of both of them were full of tears?

After a few years, Shabana was going to pay her respects on the tomb of one of her friends. Suddenly, she saw something and stood transfixed to the ground.

Her feet on their own went to that tomb and tears came rolling down from her eyes. In front of that tomb was the same book in one corner and now it was not unwritten. There were a few words embossed on it.

She went closer and started reading while sitting on the ground. These were the words on the book, "I dedicate this book to the person who gave me a name of 'Mr Artist'."

She lost all her strength. She kept on sitting under the duress of that grief. She was continuously crying.

When it was evening, she got up from there.

Pervez knew that Shabana had given the name of Mr Artist to Riaz. If he happened to read this then the secret would have been out. She was already very upset. She never wanted to add to her woes.

Shabana took out a sharp nail-file from her bag and tried to remove the word Mr Artist from that piece of stone, but while she was trying to remove that, the stone slid from its place and there was a piece of paper underneath it. Due to fast wind blowing, the piece of paper was fluttering. She swooped down at the paper and caught it.

Riaz had written on that piece of paper, "Shabana, I will miss you. This is the reply of your second question which you had posed that day, the day when I presented you the book".

Shabana had just turned after putting the piece of stone in her bag when a whiff of air came and she heard Riaz's soft voice.

"Shabana! Do not forget my five..." She still blushed like the olden times.

She quickly looked back. Nobody was there.

She started sobbing.

13

The Last Flight

A very good looking girl was sitting at the airport waiting eagerly for someone. Everyone was looking at her. On seeing the aeroplane coming, all the people started waiting for people to disembark. Everyone was concentrating on her.

Aeroplane landed on the track and passengers, holding their cabin luggage started deplaning from the plane. Friends and relatives were welcoming them by waving their hands.

At last, an old woman wearing a beautiful dress came down. The girl went running towards her and embraced her. She gave the impression that she was also very beautiful in her younger days.

"How are you Daisy?" The old woman said, putting her hand on girl's head.

"I am alright aunty! I had to wait for you for exactly one year. Last year also you came on the same day."

They came out of the airport while talking to each other. "Daisy, now you go and come back here at the same time. I will return by the night flight."

Daisy was keen to say so many things, but she knew her aunt's habits. It was useless to have any argument with her and bowing her head, she left without saying anything.

This is a very old story.

Miss D'souza was having her bath when her phone rang. She picked up the receiver while sitting in the bathing tub. She was surprised as to who has given a ring today? Nobody knew her in this city.

"Hello, Julie speaking."

Miss D'souza, what are you doing?" on the other end, Professor Dutt was speaking'.

"Yes ...Yes ...I..." Professor Dutt was her boss, and she was feeling awkward to say that she was in the bathroom. "I am having a bath in a bathing tub."

"Yes, sir! I am in my kitchen. Please tell me if there is any works."

"There is no official work. I was going to the club, thought that I may also ask you. Will you like to accompany me?"

Julie never expected this. She had been working with professor Dutt for the last two years but professor never asked such thing before.

"I will definitely accompany you."

"Okay! How long will you take?"

"Sir! just in five minutes...!" She said while keeping the sentence incomplete.

"It is alright, take your time. Get ready and come. I am waiting."

Perhaps professor Dutt had understood that Julie was in the bathroom, because she forgot to decrease the flow of the tap and noise of flowing water could be heard through the phone.

"Okay Sir!" Julie put the receiver back.

Julie had accompanied him to so many countries, but this visit was the first of Julie as a personal secretary and professor Dutt as a director.

Almost two months had passed since they had come to America. But they both had been busy in official work. They could not go to club even for a single day. Apart from them, nobody else was of an Indian origin in the office.

Professor Dutt was a professor in a college before joining this company. People used to address him as professor, out of respect for him. Professor Dutt had surpassed all the other experienced working staff even older to him. Because of these qualities, he was very popular in his company.

Smile was always a part of his face.

Julie was also no less in her work. She was also well respected in the company. She was only three-four years younger to professor Dutt. She was very good looking and was of stable nature.

Professor put down the receiver and started waiting for Julie. He lit a cigar, just to pass time and got engrossed in his thoughts.

Call bell rang and professor got startled.

"Please, come in," he said while still sitting in the chair.

The door opened and Julie was standing there in a beautiful dress. For a moment, even professor was also astonished.

Professor Dutt locked his room and left with Julie in his car.

Professor Dutt was driving very peacefully. In a short while. an other car overtook their car. The tyre of that car suddenly burst and that car overturned and resulted in a mishap.

Flames were coming out of the front side of the engine and the entrapped people were shouting for help. Professor Dutt at once stopped his car. He along with Julie ran towards that car. A couple in the car was very badly hurt. With great difficulty, they both helped the couple to come out of the car.

By that time an ambulance had also arrived.

Both the injured were taken to the hospital.

The couple who was injured in car accident was an American couple. Only both of them were in the car at the time of accident. As good luck would have, they both had left their children in the house and were going for a sight seeing.

Name of the man was Robert and woman's name was Margrate. Both belonged to a reasonable good family and Robert had a flourishing business. For many days they were in the hospital under treatment. Professor would spare some time and would go to find out as how they were.

Gradually, they became friendly and started visiting each other. There was not even a single party in which they were not invited.

He came very close to the American family and in a way, become a member of the family.

Seven year just passed by. During that period, Robert developed relation with a girl. It was their family matter. So, professor did not feel like interfering in Margrate and Robert's life.

One day, when he reached their house, he saw them shouting at each other on this subject, professor had to interfere, because they were talking of staying separately.

"Robert, though this is your family matter and I should not interfere, but because I am your family friend, I am compelled to interfere. You have a very charming and beautiful wife. You have two sweet children. Why you want to spoil your family life? Just for that girl, who loves you because of your business and also you are a rich person? God forbid, if tomorrow your business is lost and your money is also lost, she will not hesitate to leave you for somebody else. Your wife is beautiful and intelligent. Robert, why you are bent upon ruining your family life?"

Robert had actually made up his mind to separate from Margrate, he said, "Professor, the vehicle moves as long as both the wheels are of the same size. If one wheel is of car and the other one of the truck, then imagine what will be the condition of the vehicle? Yes! You Indians can manage the vehicle of life with different wheels, but not we Americans."

Margrate was sitting quietly and crying. But Robert was in a very hot temper. He forcefully pushed Margrate and if professor Dutt had not caught her by her arm, she would have definitely hit the wall.

Robert said irritatingly, "Professor, if you have so much sympathy with Margrate, then take her along." He laughed sarcastically.

Professor said, "You do not know what are you saying at the moment? You will repent one day, but the circumstances will not be the same."

"I am not those type of people, who will repent. What all I have said, is said. Do you feel ashamed, taking her along? Haven't you that much courage?" He said laughing loudly.

Though professor was of a serene nature, but hearing this he lost his temper. He got hold of her hand in his hand and said, "If it is your wish, then, I am taking her with me." It all happened so suddenly that Margerate could not understand anything and she accompanied professor Dutt. Margrate became Mrs Dutt.

After some time, professor Dutt was posted to some other country. Julie had to accompany him.

There professor Dutt was given a huge bungalow and apart from it at some distance away from the main bungalow, there was a small bungalow for the guests. Office was at some distance from the bungalow and flat for Julie was in the office building only.

Professor was in the habit that he never disclosed his return programme. He would say that the flights arrive late at night and why give trouble to people without any rhyme and reason. He would come straight from Airport to Julie's flat. Because his office was on the way and his house was after it. The moment he would reach Julie's flat, he would ask her about the office work. Julie would offer him a cup of tea. He would usually ask her laughingly:

"Miss D'Souza, now, why don't you get married?"

"Sir! In this country, whom should I get married to?"

And on pretext of putting the saucer, she would turn keeping her back at professor Dutt so that, he may not observe her tears.

Everyone in the office would address her by her name 'Julie' but despite so many years gone by, even now professor Dutt used to call her Ms D'Souza. Julie wished in her heart of hearts that for once at least professor Dutt may call her by her name 'Julie.' But it never happened.

The span of ten years just flew like that.

One day Julie was coming out of the shop after doing a few purchases, she suddenly saw Margrate at some distance. Margrate had also seen her. Margrate was accompanied by some man, whom she could not recognise from a distance. Margrate said something to him and he quickly entered a shop.

This time when professor Dutt returned from his tour, Julie casually mentioned him about that incident.

Professor kept on listening everything quietly. He wanted to investigate everything properly before taking any action... though he had full confidence in Julie.

He straight away went to his house. Margrate was not at home. He could not find anything in the house which could indicate the presence of any stranger. His feet carried him towards the guest house. There, he found Margrate and one man's clothes, scrambled inside the closet. He went through the complete bungalow, but there was nobody there.

"Perhaps Margrate has gone to seashore along with that stranger...!" Professor imagined in his heart.

Professor, standing there and thinking something kept on stratifying at setting sun for some time. And deciding something, he left for Julie's flat. Julie could understand that today professor is tense, but she kept quiet. She prepared a cup of tea for him. Professor said, while sipping tea: "Ms D'Souza, you told me correctly. Margrate, these days...! Well, Do one thing, you ring up New York. I just now want to speak to Robert."

Julie was upset...trying to get Robert on line. She was feeling scared, Why he wanted to talk to Robert after so many years. The servant informed that Robert was not at home. Professor told Julie to give his telephone number to the servant and tell him that Robert should talk to him immediately after returning home. But, the phone call never came.

Professor was not able to talk to Robert despite ringing him for six-seven days.

One day during the meeting in the office, there was a ring on Julie's phone. Julie picked up the receiver and on the other side was Margrate.

"Julie! Please send a car if possible. My car is stalled, and I have to go somewhere urgently."

"Okay! I will get a car sent." Julie replied in a low tone as meeting was going on.

Professor, who was sitting close by, heard everything. "You leave it. I will make arrangement," He said.

Today, professor wanted to reach at the bottom of this episode. He got up and went to the ground floor in a lift. He took out a new car of the company, so that Margrate may not be able to recognise it.

He purchased a new beard from the market. He stopped the car a little distance from his bungalow. He put on the beard, put his collar upside and put his cap towards front. He also switched off the car light which automatically switches on at the opening the car door, so that he is not recognised. After seeing that everything is in proper order, he entered with the car in bungalow.

Margrate was standing outside. She at once opened the door and sat inside.

"Please, drive to the airport..." She said perplexed.

She was scared that professor's meeting may not end before time and her plan may fail.

After driving for some time, she asked the driver to stop the car at a turning. The car was parked there for a minute. Then, someone opened the back door and sat inside.

Professor had never left his meeting half way. So, when he left the meeting in between, Julie was suspicious and started following him.

She had seen professor purchasing a beard. While nearing the airport, she stopped her car at quite a distance from the car which was ahead of her.

Margrate looked at her watch and said, "There is hardly any time left for the flight to be airborne."

Car stopped. Margrate quickly got down from the car along with that man. Professor was about to park his car, suddenly a truck came and hitting the car speeded away.

Professor's car collided with the front wall. He had been grievously injured in the accident.

Margrate and her companion suddenly stopped while leaving that place and came back. With great difficulty, they pulled out the driver.

The moment she saw him, she screamed, "Oh, It is you...?"

Professor's beard had fallen down. He changed his position and opened his eyes. He had recognised Margrate's companion, he was Robert.

Professor said moaning, "Robert you here... I have been trying to locate you for the last so many days. I rang you up so many times, but was told that you are on a tour. I wish, you could have met me earlier."

"Professor, how could I show you my face? That day, the way I behaved with you, called you all names, professor please. forgive me...please professor!" He implored and said.

By the time Julie had also reached there.

"What has happened, professor...?" She said sobbing. She put professor's head in her lap and with a handkerchief, started cleaning professor's face which was drenched with blood. She continued crying.

There was an announcement at the airport.

"Listen to an important announcement. Last flight is ready to take off. Passengers leaving for America are requested to board immediately."

Hearing this Robert looked at Margrate.

"Robert, you go... I cannot accompany you."

With great difficulty, professor said, "Margrate, what are you talking? Even after so many years, you want that Robert to go alone? Please, Margrate...go with him..."

"Go! Margrate, your children must be waiting for you. Robert, please take her with you. I have always treated her as your trust. I married her only...! Well, time is less Rabort, take her along, fast." Words were coming out of his mouth with great difficulty.

Robert and Margrate shook hand with the professor with a very heavy heart and left with tears in their eyes.

"Julie, I know what you wanted to say. But I was very helpless because of the circumstances. I was very helpless. I am telling you Julie...!"

Today, for the first time, Professor had addressed her by her name when he was at the corridors of death.

"Julie, you look after yourself." His head rolled down. His soul had taken the last flight.

Today, after fifteen years, an old woman was sitting there holding flower of respect in her hands.

I do not know why you have been visiting this place for the last fifteen years to pay your respect to whom? "Well...! Please hurry up..." standing close by, Daisy said. Perhaps that old woman was engrossed in her own thoughts. She did not reply Daisy.

"Aunty D'Souza, please hurry up and get up quickly. Now it is only the last flight left and there is not much time left for that also." Daisy said, shaking her.

But, what is this? Her body rolled down to one side.

And even her soul had taken the last flight.

14

The Radish Leaves

Major Tony Madhukar was extremely happy to hear about the posting of Colonel Sandhu. They both had served in the 92 Mountain Regiment a long time back.

Colonel Sandhu was posted as the commanding officer of Tony Madhukar's regiment. Unit was stationed at Gurdaspur in Punjab. Tony Madhukar went to Amritsar airport to receive him.

The flight was on time. He saluted Colonel Sandhu as per the protocol of the army and they both hugged each other. They were meeting almost after about five years.

Both got into the official staff car and were reminded of good olden days.

There were fields on both sides of the road. Mostly farmers had been growing radish. Usually farmers would take out radish from the fields and after breaking the extra leaves, would throw them. But, as the fields were close to the road, farmers would casually throw the leaves either near the side or even in the middle of the road. Two-wheelers like scooters, cycles, motorcycles had to drive very carefully while passing the margin of the road. But four-wheelers had no risk of slipping, perhaps because of this fact, the driver of the car did not bother to stay away from the leaves and continued driving on top of leaves, trampling them.

Colonel Sandhu and Major Tony Madhukar were engrossed in their talks. The moment Colonel Sandhu's attention went out of the car's side window, suddenly he shouted, "*Arai,* bloody fool, you are trampling leaves of radish? Can't you drive staying away from these?"

Major Tony Madhukar got a shock. He was surprised at Colonel Sandhu's behaviour; what big mistake the driver had committed. After all, they were not anything expensive, but simply radish leaves which farmers had thrown on the road.

The atmosphere had turned serious. You can say that Major Tony Madhukar kept quiet or you can say that he did not think it feasible to say anything.

The distance was not much, so, they reached their unit from airport in a short time and he dropped Colonel Sandhu in his room and came back.

They both met in the evening in the officer's mess. Major Tony Madhukar introduced Col Sandhu to all the junior officers and their families.

Whisky was being served and they both went and occupied a corner table. They started talking all about hither and thither. When they both had four pegs of whisky each, then thinking it as a proper opportunity, Major Tony Madhukar started talking about radish leaves. He finally asked him, that why Colonel Sandhu reacted in this fashion on watching radish leaves being trampled under the wheels of the car?

Colonel Sandhu heaved a long sigh and started saying, "I was aware that you will be eagerly waiting to know, and I was surprised that why you have not asked me about it so far? In fact, there is a long story behind this."

"Colonel Sandhu, what can be a story behind the leaves of radish? After all, leaves of radish are only radish leaves," Major Tony Madhukar started saying.

"No, Major Tony Madhukar, leaves of radish are not only leaves of radish, but they are much more than that. Now, I will narrate to you a true story about these leaves.

It goes a long long time back.

One Santa Singh along with his six children was continuing his life in a wornout hut in a village. After a day's hard work, whatever he would earn, with that money only, he would look after his children and himself. Though his daily earnings were meagre, not very much, but it was enough to keep for their subsistence.

The moment he would earn enough money to buy the necessary things, taking long steps, he would rush for his hut. He had to fill his children's stomach with those, otherwise they would remain hungry and he knew that all this time they would have been anxiously looking towards the door.

Coming out of his hut, unconsciously he would look at the pole at the corner of the street, where it was written, 'We two and our two' and he would heave a sigh and would think, 'I wish I also had a small family which I could look after properly.' Getting this feeling, he would at once turn back and would take all the children standing near the door in a big hug. They all were his dear sons, and were the remembrance of his wife Surjeet Kaur. He would curse himself as to how such a thought could come across his mind?

Surjeet Kaur, who had won his heart, passed away in a road accident...and he lost one leg.

Before closing her eyes. Surjeet Kaur had taken a promise from him that he will always look after them. And then she closed her eyes forever and left for other world leaving him in despair. Since then, he had been roaming here and there with the help of a cane.

All his assets were spent on the treatment of Surjeet Kaur and he also lost his job due to loss of his one leg.

This year because of sun eclipse, people did not come out of their houses. They were scared to loose their eyesight in case they venture out of their houses during eclipse. But they were unaware of this fact that if they do not come out of their houses, Santa Singh will not earn anything and his children would go hungry without food. On watching his children's sad faces because they had nothing to eat, he felt miserable and took his cane and made a programme to start for the market to earn a little money. Then he realised that the whole of the market was close. Who would employ him as a labourer? And if he loses his eyesight then who will look after his children? And, he felt dejected...!

He hugged his children. There were tears in his eyes. All the children had closed their eyes, sticking in his embrace. None of the children said anything about their hunger. Perhaps they had already understood his helplessness.

Somehow the night passed. The next day early in the morning, Santa Singh left for the job of a labourer. But that day also someone had spread the rumour that the effect of the eclipse will continue till evening. On hearing this, people who had come out of their houses started rushing back. Santa Singh kept on roaming in the market the whole day, but there was nobody in the market. There was no question of any labour.

When he asked those people who were running back to their houses about the labour, they took pity on him. Some one put a few coins in his hand which he returned. His self-respect did not allow him to accept the money.

He was returning home when suddenly he saw a coin of four annas on the track. He looked around to see if the owner of that money is around. But, all around, it was deserted. He removed that four annas coin from the dust with the help of his nails. Turning it on both the sides, he made sure if it was real. That piece of money was really real.

He fell into deep thinking. Whether this money was a part of alms? No, God has given him; he got it lying on the track. In fact, he was going home from this way to see if his children were alright and to give them solace. Holding this four annas, he ran towards market.

The door of one of the small restaurant (*dhaba*) was half open. He went inside and asked the owner to give *chapattis* for the said amount. That man handed him two *chapattis*. He thought for a moment, would these two *chapattis* be enough to fill his children's stomach? Thinking this, he returned the *chapattis* and got back his four *annas* and came out. The owner was looking at him with startled eyes. How he could understand Santa Singh's constrain?

Santa Singh was roaming in the market in the hope of getting something which will help to satisfy two days hunger of his children.

After some time, he saw a lone man sitting in vegetable market, in front of him was a pile of semi rotten radish. He enquired about the cost of it. The man casually replied, "One rupee." He took Santa Singh for a beggar on seeing his delicate condition.

Santa Singh hesistantly said, that he has four annas. The man said angrily, "Do you consider it as loot-free for all." And Santa Singh left the place without any discussion. The vegetable vender thought that all his friends had gone home after selling their vegetables. He was stuck there for the sake of these radish and deciding something, he called Santa Singh, "Ok, take all the radish in four annas."

Santa Singh tied all the radish in a torn cloth after paying four annas. He wanted to fly to his hut, but it was not possible. Now, he was running towards his hut.

He shouted for his children from a distance. On hearing his voice, five children came out of the hut. He got upset when he did not see his sixth child. He was aware that his youngest child was weak from the very beginning as he was deprived of his mother's affection and attention. Thinking about this, he murmured, "He may... No, No." And he shouted, "Where is *Chotu*?" He used to call him *Chotu* out of affection for him. On hearing his loud voice, all the children got scared. But, they were looking towards the tap of the street.

He also turned and saw for himself.

Chotu was standing next to the tap. He was drinking water in small quantity to satisfy his pangs of hunger. Santa Singh felt very miserable and thought, alas, God had to show him this day also!

Well, he washed all the radish with the tap water quickly. All the rotten leaves, he threw near the tap and taking his children under the shade of the tree nearby, breaking radish in to small pieces, he started feeding his children.

All the children were eating pieces of radish quickly. He thought who could be more poor and helpless in this world...!

He was thinking of this when suddenly he heard a voice of two children fighting behind him. He looked towards that direction.

He saw that two boys were fighting with each other to eat the same rotten leaves."

He kept quiet for a while and then... continuing, he said "Do you know Major Tony Madhukar, who was the elder boy of the two boys?

It was me.... !"

15

From Heaven to the Earth

God was very pleased with Bhagat Ram's behaviour and attitude. One day while serving God, he asked for such a boon that hearing it even God was startled for a few moments.

He wanted to have a look at that world which he had left twenty years back.

God never wanted to break his heart by declining his request. He tried to make him understand. He said, "The world is the same as you had left twenty years back."

"Sir! I had a son, I want to go and see him", He insisted.

"But it will take a lot of time to search for him," God replied.

"No sir! I will proceed directly to my village. There are not many people there. I will easily find him, Bhagat Ram said humbly.

"Remember one condition of mine."

"Sir! I will remember not to put my foot on earth, and am only allowed to talk to any person if in dire need and I will follow your instructions."

Taking permission from God, he started towards earth in a (*Udan Khatola)* flying throne. It was almost dark when he reached there.

On reaching the earth, he looked out of the flying throne, looked around but could not see anything.

He could see some movement on the tall trees. When he looked around attentively, he saw a few people perching on the tree.

It was a similar scene 20 years ago, when the Prime Minister had visited this village. He was also sitting on a big tree the whole night just to a have a glimpse of him from a close range.

After going a little further, he saw a big *baniyan* tree. He witnessed a group of people there also.

He asked his flying throne's driver to go towards other side. He again visualised a similar scene on the mango trees.

Now, Bhagat Ram wished to talk to somebody about it. Finally, he asked one man, "What is going on? Is some minister or Prime Minister is due for a visit here?"

On hearing Bhagat Ram, they all started laughing heartily. Bhagat Ram realised that he has asked something, which he should not have asked.

After going a little ahead, Bhagat Ram saw a huge *'Jamun'* tree and people sitting on the branches. He started talking to those people, "Are you sitting here to watch *Ramleela*?"

There also people made fun of him. But one of them said, "No, we are not gathered here to see *Ramleela*, but looks like, that you are new to this place."

"Oh yes! I left for heaven twenty years back. I have come here for a few hours today. Now, tell me why you all are sitting on trees, if neither there is *Ramleela* nor any Prime Minister is visiting this place?"

In the meanwhile, he heard a very familiar voice from a corner which had been addressed to him.

Bhagat Ram looked very carefully—he saw a man of bony structure, a weak person, sitting on a branch of a tree and was addressing him.

"*Bhagte Yaar*! You have not recognised me, I am your... Ram Lal, your Ramu...*Areey*, your friend Ramu."

Bhagat Ram tried to recollect him when that man said, "Oh yes, why will you recognise me, your old friend. Of course, it is not your fault. My body is...!"

A long sigh came out of his mouth and he continued talking, *Yaar*! You have not changed a bit. You are looking heathier. Same *noor* (glow) on the face...! Where were you all these days?"

"I was in heaven for twenty years, by the grace of God. I am having comfortable life over there." He looked towards the sky and said, I got very little time left, now, I will return. I will come here next time. I wanted to meet my son...!"

Ram Lal was looking at him with an unfulfilled desire. He thought for a moment... a good plan! He immediately asked.

"Bhagat Ram, one day while playing hockey, you had hurt your ankle bone. That time you cried a lot. The injury was, in fact, quite severe. Even now, I think it must be paining?"

"No, *yaar*! Now there is no pain. I am perfectly fit, but the scar is still there", replied Bhagat Ram.

Ram Lal said, "I don't agree. The injury was very severe, how is it possible that it may not hurt? Bhagat Ram, please put your foot towards me I will press it and see if it hurts. It is possible that while staying in heaven, you may have become young and that pain...!"

When Bhagat Ram heard about himself looking young, he felt very happy. He immediately put forward his injured foot towards Ram Lal.

Ram Lal was waiting for this golden opportunity. He at once caught hold of Ram Lal's foot with both the hands.

"*Arrey*, leave my foot. What are you doing Ram Lal?"

When, despite all efforts, Ram Lal did not leave his foot, he got scared and requested the driver of flying throne to take it up towards the sky.

As the flying throne went up, somebody else took hold of Ram Lal's foot and his foot was caught by somebody else and then like this chain of human beings continued... from heaven to earth.

On reaching heaven, Bhagat Ram came out of that flying throne with great difficulty, and dragging himself, went near

God and requested, "Please God, get me rid of this problem. These people will definitely break my foot."

God was busy conversing with Yamraj, god of death. He gestured Him on seeing this situation of Bhagat Ram.

He freed Bhagat Ram's foot from the clutches of Ram Lal. Now Yamraj, was holding Ram Lal's hands and all others were hanging from Ram Lal's foot... from sky to the earth.

Bhagat Ram quickly narrated his tale of woes to God.

"Bhagat Ram, I had already forbidden you not to go to the earth. But when you requested time and again, I did not feel like disappointing you." God said smilingly.

"God, there was neither any *Ramleela,* nor any minister was coming there, even then all of them were perching on the branches of trees like birds."

"*Arrey* Ram Lal, poulation has increased so much that there is no place on earth even to stand. If there was a place then, do you think you would have found them perching on the branches like birds?

Human beings are moving around earth like insects. . Population has increased so much, and nobody is paying serious attention to it."

Bhagat Ram was surprised to hear this from God and kept looking at him.

Yamraj then stared at Him enquiringly.

God admonished him saying, "You stay like this, holding the chain of all the human beings in the air.

This is your punishment. You have been also not performing your duty of keeping a check on the growth of population."

On hearing these words from God, Yamraj had drops of perspiration on his forehead.

16

A Girl with a Dog

Dev Pal had come to Bombay yesterday only. He was very happy in Delhi. With Jaiveer and Vikram, they all used to have good time.

Dev Pal had a circle of ten or twelve friends in Delhi. If I didn't mention about them, surely they will get annoyed. I would like to tell you that, whenever his friend, or it can be said that while their friend Sudershan Rana would visit Delhi from Canada, Jaiveer would invite everyone of his friends, namely, Radhey, Ved, Uppal, Nand Kishor...., for a get together, to a restaurant at Cannaught Place.

When all of them would gather there, atmosphere would turn something akin to college atmosphere. All old friends would meet and give a good hug to one another.

They would ask Rana in detail about various places in Canada. Vikram would ask him mischievously.

"*Yaar*, I have heard that girls in Canada are very advanced and bold..."

All the friends would look at him enquiringly. Rana would understand this enquiring vision and doing some sort of action, would smilingly say, "What do you understand about those girls... Friends, girls of that place don't mingle with everybody..." Everyone would laugh at his action.

Then non-veg joke would start amongst them. All the friends would narrate jokes better than the others.

One of their friends Kedarnath was a dejected soul. He was a poet, used to write poetry in English, and would narrate the poems in a sad tone.

"*Yaar*! I specially take leave from the office to come here. But here you all just don't do any useful work. You all don't do anything else except for non-veg jokes. In future, I will not come here." On hearing this from Kedar, all of his friends would laugh merrily.

Rana would make him understand, "*Yaar*! You have not changed a bit."

On hearing this, Vikram would say, "Rana, You don't understand him. He is a hypocrite. He used to sit with me on the same bench in the class. He would pull the veil of the girl sitting on the next bench slowly and when she would look behind, he would smile at her. Only I was aware of this."

"Now, listen Vikram, You are pulling my leg," Kedar would say irritatingly.

At this, all the friends would laugh merrily.

At the departure of Sudershan Rana to Canada, all the friends would stop meeting each other, except for Jaiveer, Vikram and Dev Pal. Jaiveer was very fond of inviting his friends. It gave the impression that perhaps he had an obsession of throwing parties for his friends. Sometimes, he would call Vikram and Dev Pal to 'Country Club' or 'Palm Court', or, 'Gymkhana Club' or 'Maurya Hotel'.

Maurya Hotel was next to Jaiveer's office, invariably they would gather there and Vikram would mostly sit in the chair facing the swimming pool.

Dev Pal would say, "*Yaar* Vikram, you always make me get up from that chair to occupy it."

On hearing this, Jaiveer would say, "You don't know, Dev Pal...Vikram doesn't know swimming. He enjoys swimming while watching those foreign ladies in their skimpy swim-suits, swim.

Vikram would say laughingly, "*Bhai* Jaiveer, You are correct. I am not a hypocrite. Whatever I like, I admit openly."

All the three friends would start laughing.

Yes! Dev Pal was not very happy staying away from such friends and in such an atmosphere. But what could he do?

He was forced to leave Delhi because his son and daughter-in-law Kewal and Kavita had been transferred to Bombay.

There was no other way but to come to Bombay with them.

His son and daughter-in-law were working in the same company. Both had studied in a English medium school and thus, were quite modern in their thinking. But while talking to their father, they would be very careful. They knew that their father was a very simple man.

His main interest was morning-evening walks, sometimes a visit to a temple and reading books. Books were perhaps the passion and soul of his life.

During his college days, he used to write Urdu poetry and paint romantic pictures. This they had heard from Dev Pal's old class fellows.

But they had not seen him writing or reciting Urdu poetry or paintings pictures during their early life.

It was his first day in Bombay. Juhu beach was very close to his house. The day he arrived, he left for the sea beach for a stroll. After walking for some time, he sat down on a close by bench and continued looking at the waves of the sea. High waves were moving in the sea. It was a very enchanting scene. He was engrossed in that scene.

He was watching the waves touching the sky and started thinking that there are so many sight seeing places in Delhi. But the scene of floating boats and the ships was entirely different and had its own grandeur.

He was engrossed in such thoughts when suddenly a small dog came running and started fawning at his feet.

He came out of his reverie, it was a small dog of '*Bhutani*' breed. If it was somebody else, he would have been scared but he had already reared up some dogs. He didn't feel scared at all. He looked all around but couldn't find his master anywhere.

For some time, he kept enjoying the fawning of the dog at his feet, then summoning his courage, slowly he started patting his head. On this, the dog started licking his hands.

Later on, he picked up the dog and put him in his lap. The dog gave the impression that it belonged to a rich master. He was a very clean dog and was smelling of *'Eud De Cologne'*.

He was thinking that if this dog was in Delhi, someone or other would have taken him along and disappeared with him.

He was engrossed in such thoughts till now, suddenly, he was brought back to reality by a sweet voice of a girl.

"Tommy, you are here and I have been looking for you at various places, she addressed the dog as if she was talking to a human being.

Dev Pal looked at her. She was a good looking, fair completioned girl of about twenty or twenty two years of age. She had a very pink complexion. Dev Pal was thinking that a lotus can bloom near a sea, but with a hue of hilly area..."

Till now, she had her attention fully on the dog, then, taking the dog from Dev Pal hands, "Sorry, Uncle, he must have bothered you a lot..."

"No, nothing at all. In fact, I am very fond of dogs, since my child hood," replied Dev Pal.

Yes, something was there, the touch of girl's soft hands generated an electric current in his body.

She sat on the bench next to him and started talking to him, but he was not paying much attention to the girl. He was appreciating her beauty in his mind... She had a slim body, pink lips, and blooming face. Youth was erupting from every part of her body.

Today after a long time, he got an opportunity to sit with a beautiful girl, whose beauty overwhelmed his brain.

In the meantime, the clock of the Church struck eight and he got up from the bench at once and without uttering a single word he left that place.

The girl was startled at this action of his and was thinking why this man has not said even a single word before leaving. Well! She was busy with her dog. The dog was sitting comfortably in her lap and she was talking to him on different things.

On the other hand, Dev Pal was thinking that today was the first day of the office of his son and daughter-in-law. He is suffering from diabetes and he had to have his breakfast at half past eight. Well! He reached his house walking fast. His daughter-in-law was already waiting for him to serve the breakfast. Kavita served the breakfast and said,

"I have kept your lunch in the fridge. Warm it up and please have it on time."

And soon after that, Kewal and Kavita left for their office.

Now, he was free for the whole day. After finishing his breakfast, he got the newspaper and started reading, but what is this? He was not able to concentrate on the newspaper. In reality, he had that girl on his mind. He was at his wit's end, he was wondering, what has happened to him. He had never felt like this before.

The whole day, he was entangled in the girl's image and thoughts. That girl was overarched on his mind. This was not the first time that he had met a girl with a dog.

There were so many times, when these accidents happened at different places. Somewhere or other, he would meet a girl with a dog. When he would tell his friends about it, they would tease him, "Brother! You had gone out this time. Did you happen to meet any girl with a dog?" Dev Pal would just feel abashed.

He would ask angrily, "*Yaar*, do you think, I am Vikram?" Actually, this type of pricks and pranks, he would get from Jaiveer.

In the evening, his son and daughter-in-law returned from the office. Everyone had meals together and went to their own rooms to sleep.

Dev Pal was not able to sleep properly the whole night and kept on shifting sides. That beautiful girl was still shining on his mind. He kept on thinking that even in the college his nature was not like this!

Well! He got up in the morning, went to Juhu beach and sat on the same bench. He was thinking why that dog has still not come, because if the dog comes, he will be accompanied by the girl. But he forgot that because of the dog, he came here an hour earlier.

Somehow he passed the time and it was his good luck, the dog came running alone and started fawning at his feet. He did not have to wait for long. The girl also came running after the dog.

She came and kept on talking some thing or other for some time. Dev Pal was busy looking at her and engrossed in some thoughts. When the girl realised that she is the only one who had been continuously talking nonstop and Dev Pal was sitting quietly and not uttering a single word, she got up saying, "Perhaps I am boring you. Okay! Now, I will make a move."

Hearing this, Dev Pal came into his senses, "No, I was thinking, how also today, the dog has come here."

"Normally, I have been coming here for a walk in the morning for some time and would bring Tommy along. Today also, I got delayed and like yesterday, he took his neck out from the collar and came running here. Otherwise, he is a very obedient dog. He always listens to me."

"What about the dog, even anybody else will listen to you." The words came out of Dev Pal's mouth softly, which that girl could not understand properly.

"Uncle, did you say something?" she said.

"No, not at all. I was appreciating your dog's cleanliness."

The girl was very happy that at least Dev Pal had appreciated her dog's cleanliness, she said, "I give him bath with a special soap and then apply *Eud De Cologne* on him, so that he may smell nice throughout the day."

Dev Pal again started thinking, 'What has happened to him? What all types of romantic ideas are emerging in his head? These types of naughty thoughts had been the forte of his friend Vikram', he thought.

Dev Pal was engrossed in such intracacies and on the other hand, that girl was chirping nonstop. "Oh yes! My name is..." Before she could say anything, the clock struck eight and saying 'excuse me', he left at once.

The girl again felt surprised as to why he runs away immediately soon after eight 'o' clock. The girl thought that she would ask uncle the secret of his running away at eight in the morning.

Next day, the girl came before hand and sat on the bench and started waiting for Dev Pal. But Dev Pal did not come that day.

The girl would come there daily and wait for some time feeling dejected, would go back to her house. Though she was not interested in him, but it looked strange to her that every time at eight 'o'clock, he would leave for his house immediately.

At last, one day, Dev Pal came to the beach and the girl was sitting there as usual on the bench, waiting for him. Dev Pal was looking a little weak and giving a look of a comic character in a loose pant and shirt.

Actually, Dev Pal did not give any consideration to the fitting of his clothes. Because of this habit, his classfellows in the college used to make fun of him. Yes! His shoes were very fashionable.

Actually, one of his friends Mahender Pental had been working as a part time employee in Bata Company. He was a very clever man. Either he will steal the shoes from the company, or, will get them discounted and being a good friend of Dev Pal, he would present them to him.

When the girl asked him the secret of eight 'o'clock, he explained to her that he was suffering from diabetes and that is the reason, he leaves at that time and have his breakfast in time. Because if he remains hungry, the level of sugar in the blood would decrease.

Due to this problem, he was not keeping well and thus he could not come for a walk. He told the girl, "That is why, today, I have brought my breakfast with me and will have it on time. There is no charm eating breakfast at home. If I sit here, I will enjoy the fresh air. My son and my daughter-in-law will come back in the evening around seven 'o'clock."

After some time, he took out breakfast from his bag, and started eating it. He offered the girl his breakfast, but she politely refused it.

When Dev Pal finished his breakfast, finding a suitable opportunity, she said, "Uncle, I have been staying here for so many years and come here for a walk every day. I have not seen you here before."

"Yes! I forgot to tell you my name. My name is Rosie. " Dev Pal smiled a little. He also told Rosie a few things about himself. He did not tell her that he had been a professor in the college.

Rosie kept on talking to him for a long time and whatever she knew about Bombay city, she told that to him. He thought that this girl is very talkative.

Rosie's house was nearby. One day when she insisted much, he agreed to go to her place. There were so many flats next to the sea. He was under the impression that Rosie must be living in some nearby flat.

But he was astonished when he reached there and saw that Rosie was standing in front of a big mansion and was saying,"Uncle, I stay here."

Dev Pal looked at her with wonder and time and again he looked at the mansion.

"Uncle, this mansion belongs to my forefathers." Rosie pressed the bell which was outside the door. After a few moments, an old man opened the gate. He wished Dev Pal with due respect and then said to Rosie, "Baby, you took a long time in returning, I was a little worried."

"George, I met this uncle on the beach and was talking to him while sitting over there."

"Your mother was also very fond of gossiping." He murmured.

"George, what did you say...?"

Nothing much. "But just like that..."

There were very big rooms inside that building. She took Dev Pal into a very well decorated room, which was a living room and full of expensive artifacts.

"George, please bring tea and also something to eat."

George shook his head and went away. Tea was brought. There were salty biscuits and cakes also.

George poured tea for both of them. Rosie told George, not to put sugar in Dev Pal's cup and told him to bring sugar -free for him. When Rosie offered cake to him, he said, that he does not take eggs and is vegetarian. While drinking tea, Dev Pal was thinking that no member from Rosie's household has come in the living room. Does this girl stay all alone by herself in this mansion? If so, then, what is the reason behind it? He was entangled in such thoughts when, suddenly he was surprised by Rosie's voice.

"Come, let me show you another room." When she opened the other room, he was taken aback. It was full of not thousand books, but lakhs of books, and the biggest thing was, that Dev Pal was very much interested in the books.

He immediately started looking at the books in the book rack. Rosie was surprised to see his interest in the books.

"Rosie these books are priceless. It is very difficult to find these in any library."

But how do you have so much knowledge about these books? These books are not meant for an ordinary person.

"Yes! What you say is correct. Actually, I have been a professor and I have done post graduation not only in one, but in three subjects."

"That means that from today onwards, I should call you Professor Dev Pal," she said smilingly. "This was a very old library. And people used to come from far and wide for those books which were not available anywhere and study them."

Before she could utter any other word, George came and announced, "Baby, lunch is ready."

While looking at the books, Dev Pal had forgotten that it was time for lunch.

"Rosie! I should leave now. Lunch is ready at home and..."

"Professor Pal, please have your lunch here today."

He kept on refusing, and Rosie continued insisting after all Rosie won and professor was forced to have lunch there.

Dev Pal was in the habit of taking a nap after lunch. So, soon after lunch, he came back home.

Now, they would have discussion on some subject or other, while sitting on the bench. Dev Pal realised that the girl is very intelligent and well read. But, time and again, he wanted to find out from Rosie, where are all the other members of the household? This part of Rosie's life was full of mystery.

One day, while Dev Pal was sitting all alone in the library, George brought tea for him. He realised that it was a good opportunity and at last he asked him.

"George, I do not understand, where are the other members of the family?"

"Professor *Saheb*. What can I say, some years back, Baby's all the relations had gone to south to celebrate 'New Year'. Baby was also supposed to accompany them, but could not do so as she had to take her examinations. And, she could not go with them. *'Tsunami'* came and all the family members were killed, not even a single member survived. We never discuss that incident. With great difficulty Baby recovered and..."

At that moment, Rosie entered the room and George left.

Rosie asked, "So, when should I start my studies?"

"Which studies," Dev Pal asked her surprisingly.

"Have you forgotten?" All my papers are next month and you had promised to coach me all my subjects.

"Oh yes! I now remember." He said astonishingly.

Now, he started taking afternoon *siesta* at her place and would go back before the arrival time of his son and daughter-in-law.

He would bring his lunch from his house. Rosie told him so many times not to bring his lunch, but Dev Pal said that his son and daughter-in-law would not appreciate it. Rosie agreed to this, but they would eat lunch together.

Yes! He informed them that the whole day, he spends in a library, and goes through the books and takes his lunch there.

He did not tell them about Rosie because he was a little hesitant.

Gradually, his thinking also underwent a sea change while staying with Rosie for a long time.

Now, Rosie would take him in her car to the market and the shopping malls. One day, she purchased a proper fitting pant shirt and tie, instead of loose fitting shirt and pant. He was a little hesitant initially, but finally, after a few days, he did put on that tight fitting dress.

Whereas Dev Pal was a vegetarian, his son and daughter-in-law were non-vegetarian, and while he would shun parties, his son and daughter-in-law were very fond of parties. Both would put on simple clothes while leaving their house, but would change into western dress while reaching the avenue of party. They were very well-known in their circle in their parties. Both of them were very good dancers.

So, when they saw father putting on tight dress, they were amused and started laughing heartily.

"Father, these tight clothes today..." They continued laughing.

Dev Pal got confused and could not disclose that at the insistence on the part of Rosie, he had to put on these clothes. Avoiding it he said, "In fact, there is a Christian friend of mine in the library, who gave me these clothes..." and he could not complete his sentence.

So, when Dev Pal started putting on tight clothes and also started colouring his hair then, both were surprised... for a while. But soon they forgot about this change in their father, because they themselves were very fond of western culture.

Later on, they realised that it doesn't make any difference, whatever type of clothes father wears? He spends from his own pension money, whatever he wants, he can buy.

Jaiveer and Vikram would ring up on every Sunday. But instead of Dev Pal, his son would talk to them. He told them about the changes which had taken place in his father. They both were surprised to learn that Dev Pal has started putting on tight dresses.

Yes! I forgot to tell you one thing, that is, whenever Dev Pal would go to a new town, he would invariably come across a girl with a dog and Jaiveer and Vikram would definitely ask about her.

"*Yaar* Dev Pal! Did you meet any girl with a dog...?"

Jaiveer had a publicity business. He told Vikram one day, "*Yaar*! I have one day's work in Bombay. You also come along with me. We will go by the morning flight and return by evening flight."

As soon as they reached Bombay, they rang up Dev Pal's son, who told them, they can meet him in a library.

They reached the library after finishing their work of the office at eleven 'o' clock. What a magnificent library it was? It dawned on them as if they have come to an old fort. Same library, like it used to be at the time of kings, big racks of books...!

The peon of the library escorted them to the director of the library. Dev Pal was sitting in the chair of the director, but they could not recognise him.

Yes! He was actually Dev Pal....! There was so much of change in his dress and hair, that if his son had not mentioned them about the changes in him, they would not have recognised him.

They both came forward, and hugged him. They were indulging in small talks when in the meantime, George entered the room. Dev Pal asked him to bring tea.

In the end, Vikram did ask him, "*Yaar*! Your complete style has undergone a sea change. You don't give the look of an old Dev Pal."

At that moment, George came with tea, biscuits and cakes. He offered cake to them, after handing over the cup of tea. Jaiveer and Vikram had one piece of cake each. But what is this? Even Dev Pal took a piece of cake and started eating. Both were astonished that Dev Pal, who had never touched eggs in his life, was eating a cake made out of eggs.

They both were still in a fix, when at that moment Rosie's dog entered and started fawning at Dev Pal's feet.

Jaiveer and Vikram looked at each other enquiringly.

They were still in the process of thinking, when in the meantime, Rosie entered the room and without paying any attention to both of them, she said, "Tommy, why have you come here?"

Suddenly, it came out of their mouth, "Here also, there is a girl with a dog..."

Well! Still Rosie did not pay any attention to them and kept on talking, "Professor Pal, you are not feeling well since yesterday and I had also told you that you should cover your body with a blanket, but you do not listen to me." Her voice had a little authority, tinkling of annoyance. And then coming a little forward, she put on a blanket on his shoulder.

Till now, she had not paid any attention to them and realising that there was somebody else also, said, "Sorry! I did not see you." And all this happened so fast that Dev Pal did not get an opportunity to tell her that they were his college friends.

She also sat with them and continued praising Professor Dev Pal like hell. She praised him so much that even they both were unaware that he was such an intellectual person.

They both realised that now the track of his train has changed. His way of walking and talking, everything had undergone a big change. He did not give an impression of a fifty-fifty five years old. He had now started looking a young man of forty, forty five years old.

They did not talk much in front of Rosie.

While on the way, Vikram said, "I wish, we also come across a girl with a dog. This Dev Pal is very lucky, he always comes across a girl with a dog in every city"

Jaiveer said laughingly, "No, Vikram! You can say that some how or the other he meets a dog in every city." And they both started laughing heartily.

Rosie and Dev Pal started coming closer to each other. Now she would address him 'Pal' instead of professor Pal. Now, the circumstances were such that whenever his son and daughter-in-law would go out for ten- fifteen days for some office work, then Rosie would bring him to her house and would leave him back to his house before the arrival of his son and daughter-in-law.

He would spend his days and nights with Rosie, till the time of their arrival.

Once when Jaiveer went to Bombay along with his family, he saw that both Rosie and Dev Pal were dancing together in a hotel's party. Sandeep, Jaiveer's son asked him, "Papa! He is perhaps Dev uncle. But his dress. And then... He did not know dance."

"No son, he is not Dev Pal, but somebody else." Although Jaiveer had immediately recognised Dev Pal.

But the way Rosie was glued to him while dancing, looking at them, he was greatly surprised.

What a change has come in Dev Pal. How much Rosie has changed him! Tight, branded clothes, stylish haircut, non-veg food, dance and the most of all was that whereas he could not drive even a scooter, today after the party, he was driving a Mercedes car.

It did not take him long to understand that a new phase of Dev Pal's life has started. Now, he was not an old Dev Pal. A storm has entered in his life from where it was difficult to return.

Suddenly, Dev's son and daughter-in-law were posted out to Singapur and they were accompanied by their father.

It happened so fast, that Dev Pal could not get time to recover and understand the situation. They suddenly left for Singapur.

Rosie was also away to Bangalore for two days. Dev Pal could not get the opportunity to inform Rosie. Actually, she wanted to take Dev Pal along with her, but he was unwell.

On returning from Bangalore, and learning everything, she almost became a maniac, and lost her senses. She shouted at George.

"Why did you not stop Professor Pal and why did you not give me a ring?"

Actually, Professor Pal had become a part of her life and it may not be wrong to say that both had become part and parcel of each other's life.

"What an attachment...what an attachment!" George also failed to understand.

Rosie could not find him as to where he has gone, despite so many efforts.

She would roam around in the building like a mad person. Pal's separation had started having effect on her mind. She went into depression. Everyday her condition became bad to worse.

One day when George was cleaning the library, he got hold of Jaiveer's visiting card. He at once, rang him up and explained everything to him.

When Jaiveer became aware of the situation from George, he immediately rang up Dev Pal and explained the complete situation to him.

On the other hand, Dev Pal was also not very happy. He was also very preturbed. After all, what could he do. He could not explain to his son everything in detail.

On learning all the facts from Jaiveer, he made a plan to visit Bombay. As the time went by, he became more tense. At last, he got the flight and went straight to Rosie.

On entering the mansion, Rosie's Doctor took him to one side and said, "I wanted to meet you earlier, but didn't get a chance. In fact, I wanted to explain to you about Rosie's medical history. You are not aware, that Rosie is a serious patient of depression."

When suddenly all of his relations got killed in *'Tsunami'*, she got into depression and was in depression for many years. Gradually, she started recovering. She was regaining her health slowly.

Then you met her near the sea shore. This was told to me by George. And that was turning of a new leaf in her life, there was a change in her. Even I reduced the dose of medicine.

It was strange, as it is very difficult for such type of patients to recover so fast. And that too, when such a big calamity had taken place in life at such a young age.

George had been giving me all the information about you both. It was because of George, that she was alive today. If after this incident, George had not looked after her, she would have passed away long time back. George has been taking care of her for the last twelve years. That is why Rosie has been listening to him and taking medicines.

But more than medicine, she recovered from her illness, because of you. She has been trying to find a saviour in you and then...!

I have tried many times to contact you, but somehow because of some problem or other could not do so.

And also I was quite sure that as long as you were there, she will fully recover. This was important for me that I should make you aware of Rosie's true condition. I wanted that you should know the complete medical history so that, now at least no such incident should happen in her life which should make her old wounds afresh. And she may not be lost in her past miseries.

But suddenly, you went somewhere and same thing happened, of which I was scared.

Looks like as if she has developed some kind of affection for you. After your leaving this place, she suddenly went into depression. I gave her solace, consoled her and at the same time gave her the required medicine. But that day you just disappeared without informing her and now...!

Doctor, standing close by, further said, "It is too late now. It is difficult for her to...!"

Hearing everything from the Doctor, he quickly went to Rosie.

On seeing him, hugging him she started crying and continued enquiring from him, "Pal, where had you disappeared leaving me alone? I cannot live without you, can't stay... can't stay...!"

Rosie's head was in Pal's lap. Professor's eyes were full of tears and he had been crying...!

"Rosie, I wish, I had not gone." He was talking all rubbish in his insanity.

Jaiveer and Vikram both had taken a flight to Bombay and were watching this sad scene.

At last Vikram said, "*Yaar* Jaiveer! What relation do they have with each other?"

Jaiveer kept quiet and uttered nothing, but kept on watching the rise and fall of waves at far—far away in the sea.

17

After Ten Years

"Arai, who is this mad man?" Radha was holding a cup of milk in her hand. Hearing this voice, she shouted.

"Beware if you call him a lunatic..." She could not complete her sentence. Her face turned into ashes and her forehead was covered with drops of sweat, tears falling from her eyes. Cup of milk had fallen down from her hand and rivulets of milk were running towards the shallow drain. She had uttered those words with such a force that her own ears tingled.

A man with a long flowing beard was sitting close by. Earlier, he was laughing like a kid. Hearing Radha's high pitched voice, he also kept quiet and looked around astonishingly.

Looking at his innocent act, Radha started weeping again and went running to her room.

Radha's friend Sanjana kept on standing like a dumb and was watching. She could not understand anything. Radha's shouting and crying. Everything looked strange to her. Radha had treated her like her own sister and she had never talked to her in this manner, but today her behaviour?

There is really something strange, realised Sanjana. She quickly went to Radha's room, inside Radha was sobbing. With great effort, she made her get over the bout of weeping.

"Listen Radha, I am unable to understand what is my fault? Please forgive me if I have committed any mistake." Black spot of tears on her cheeks were making her look more beautiful. Radha wiped those spots with her veil and said, "In fact, it is all my fault. I have not told you anything... "and she again started weeping. Sanjana was confused and wondering what is that she has not told me as normally, she would confide everything to me."

After a while, Radha was composed and started saying that I wanted to explain to you this so many times, but then I thought that what was the use of narrating past events?

"Now, I will explain to you everything. Without explanation you will not be able to understand my behaviour.

"It goes back ten years. I was doing my graduation those days. Shekhar used to visit us almost every day. We were very fond of each other. Usually, we would have our meals together and if he was delayed for some reason, then I used to also stay hungry and wait for him.

"Do you know that his eyes were full of tears whenever I had any problem. Perhaps he used to hate my problems. On those occasions, when he had tears in his, he put on sunglasses just to hide them from me.

"I was aware of his this habit. I used to ask him laughingly, to remove his glasses. At that, he used to say, 'Listen Radha, I cannot see you suffering. I wish God give me all your problems.'

I used to put my hand on his mouth before he could complete his statement. Then, I used to pretended to be annoyed with him. He used to try many tricks to make me feel happy, but I stayed annoyed just to tease him. When in the end, he got tired, he would say, 'Imagine I am a photographer and taking your picture. Now ready, one... two... and three.' I would laugh at his trick.

I still remember that evening of a winter. He was explaining something about 'Shelly'. I did not know why I was not in a mood to study. I said, 'Ok. Stop it now, rest of it you can explain to me later.' On hearing it, he got annoyed. Looking at his annoyed face, I started laughing.

He was very short-tempered and when he saw me laughing, it increased his anger many fold. He slapped me very hard on my cheek. All the fingers left their marks on my cheek. Watching this, his complete anger vanished.

He removed all the marks of the slap from my cheek by rubbing them continuously and asked me my pardon and said, 'See, I just got into fit of rage for nothing. I am really a very bad guy. How nice it will be, If I lose these hands who have hit you and the eyes which has seen this scene.'

'Shekhar, I will never talk to you if you talk like this. Many a time you may hit, but never again utter these words. After all, who I belong to? Telling you the truth, I have not minded anything of yours except that I have definitely not liked your this very dialogue.'

Our love for each other continued growing because of so many incidents like this. Perhaps you do not know that he had presented this ring to me on my birthday and I also gave him almost the same ring on his birthday. While putting on the ring on his finger, I jokingly said, 'Shekhar! I hope you will not loose this ring.'

'I will keep this ring with me till I die and will return it to you before my death. After all, where will this poor ring stay in ashes.' While uttering these words, I do not know why he became sad. His way of saying was such that, I could not utter anything.

At last, one day, somebody put hurdle in our happy love. A few people came to our house for my alliance, but my parents refused them.

"Now that the matter of my marriage had started, Shekher thought it wise that he should explain to my parents about us both. One day, finding a good opportunity, he talked to my father, but my father refused.

"He liked everything about him except the salary part, which was three hundred only. He wanted that the boy should be earning minimum five hundred. Shekhar tried to convince him that he will be promoted in due course of time and his salary will also increase, but all in vain.

"Though, my parent knew that we both are interested in each other, but still my father stuck to his decision. My feelings had no meaning for him

"If we wanted, we could get married on our own, but we did not like this. Finally, I was engaged to a boy who had two-three houses and was earning one thousand rupees. My love was sacrificed at the altar of money.

"It was a few days before my marriage. It was the bank of river. We used to sit and talk there for hours together. Now we both were standing quietly. Whole of the atmosphere as well as everything around was quiet. Waves of river which used to be full of life, were also quiet.

"On one hand was setting sun and its tired green-yellow rays. And on the other hand were the moths going around the electric lamp and falling dead. It was a strange scene. All around it was a silent scene of death. I got scared of that silence and I broke that atmosphere of silence.

My parents are taking undue advantage of my silence and if I want, I can break this silence. Now I repent and wish that I could have done it. If I could have done that in the past, I would not have seen these days.'

He kept on listening quietly. 'Only wish I have is that you should always look after yourself.!

"I was moved by those words of his. Tears flowed from my eyes, but this time he did not wipe my eyes. He quickly left without saying anything and I could not even ask, where he was going? When he was out of my vision, I came back home, tired.

"After this, for ten years, I did not see him. Oh yes! I got a letter from him before my marriage. He had written:

'My Radha,

I should have come to attend your marriage, but what could I do? I cannot see my life being ruined. I have no strength in me to witness that.

Only yours,

..................'

"I tried to locate him everywhere, but could not find him. Even his relations had no clue of him. From his office, it was learnt that he was on one month's leave and had gone to attend a marriage, but so far he had not joined his duty.

"I wished several time in my life that at least once, I may come across him and at last one day I met him, but...

"Yesterday, I was coming home by a bus. I was sitting engrossed in my own thoughts, when suddenly I was startled by a voice of a man sitting next to my seat. The voice was the same, but his face...I looked at him carefully. I would not have recognised him but for his voice. He had all grey hair. His beard was so long that he was looking wild. Cheeks which were pink, were now black and had wrinkles and now he had sunken cheeks.

"At that moment, he had put on his goggles. Exactly same goggles. He had recognised me and like his old habit, was trying to hide his tears. I was about to tell him to remove his goggles, but a man came between us and I kept quiet.

"When that man moved forward, I observed that he was wearing a chain and there was a ring in it, the same ring which I had presented him on his birthday. I started thinking, what is the point of putting a ring in the chain? It may be perhaps because of fear of losing it or . . .? The past started revolving in front of my eyes. I was shocked at the sound of brakes of the bus. I saw people quickly getting down the bus. I at once looked at the next seat, but Shekhar was not there.

"There was a big crowd outside. I also got down and looked for Shekhar, but there was no sign of him. When, I asked people, what is the matter, they said that a man had fallen down from the moving bus. Then from other side, a voice came from two people, 'Poor fellow, he is blind. His hands are also amputated'

"I was wonder struck on hearing this.

'He may not... No, it is not possible,' I thought and immediately reached in the centre. He was actually lying on the earth unconscious. Pieces of broken goggles had fallen next to him. He was wounded badly. Blood was coming out from his mouth. I came forward and cleaned the blood with the border of my *sari*. I called him many times, but all in vain, he was unconscious.

"When he regained his senses in the hospital, he started shouting.

"Doctors informed that he got a brain injury and has weak state of mind.

"Do you know Sanjana, who is this man? He is same man and I got him here in my house so that I can look after him. He has nobody in this world to look after."

"Very sad story this is. I do not know whether your parents will be happy or sad at his condition. But it is definite that they will regret," said Sanjana.

At that time, a servant came with a ring and said that the mad man had given that ring, saying, 'Give this ring to your mistress as a gift.' "Poor mad man! And one thing more, master has sent him to mental asylum. He was saying that he cannot tolerate this man's unnecessary nonsence and cannot afford his daily expenses."

"No, It is not possible. I will not allow him to go to that hell. I will just now go and get him back." Saying this, she went to the door immediately. The telephone was ringing outside in varandha. She quickly picked up the receiver.

"Radha speaking."

From the other side, a doctor was speaking:

"Mrs Radha, Your husband had sent some lunatic a few moments back. He was trying to run away from our escorts and has been run down by a car. Now there is no hope of his... survival...!"

She could not hear anything else. Receiver fell down from her hand...

18

A Clever Twist

"How can I manage in such a small salary? God has not gifted you with a better salary, since the time, I have married you." And then, she spoke in an angry tone, "It is due to your not paying proper respect to God till today. Sometimes, you address Him as stone idol, and at other time the pictures that I have kept at my place of worship, the imaginary pictures. . Because of this insulting attitude of yours, you did not get your promotion. Even for the last ten years, your annual increment has also been stopped. My luck is...," and she started crying bitterly.

Neeraj was so far quietly sitting and listening to everything but when Shanti started crying, he came and sat next to her and consoling her said, "Shanti, please keep quiet, you are crying for no reason. You know it very well that I have no faith in such things. This is not today, but since so many years. But have I ever stopped you from worshipping? You have been visiting temples day and night. Have I ever put any restrictions on you?"

At once Shanti replied, "You don't clap with one hand. Only my worshipping won't bring prosperity in our life.

You are to be promoted. It will be your salary which is going to increase. You do not worship, call these idols, pieces of stones. And if you do not have faith in them, then how do you expect our luck to change for better?" She once again started weeping.

Neeraj was getting late for his office. He tried to appease her. "If you have any feeling for me, you will have to accept one condition of mine." She said.

Neeraj wanted Shanti should somehow stop crying. Said, "I accept each and every condition of yours."

"Promise me that during these *Dussehra* vacations, you will take me for a pilgrimage," she said merrily and now her tears had vanished.

Neeraj thought what type of promise he has given her? Anyway, we will see when the time comes. He was getting late for office. He took the tiffin in his hand and left for office.

Now, Shanti gave a look of a very happy person. Neeraj had learnt the secret of her happiness fast. One day when he was leaving for his office, he saw that Shanti was packing delicious dishes in the tiffin. And apart from it she was also packing *halwa* made from *desi ghee* and on top of it she had put almond pieces. When he saw this, his mouth started watering.

He was tempted to have his lunch immediately, but somehow he controlled this urge.

"What is the matter? You have made very delicious lunch today." He could not resist the temptation and finally, asked her.

Shanti came close to him and adjusting his shirt's collar, said, "You forgot, you had only promised...!"

"What did I say?" he said as if trying to remember.

"Only this, that you will come with me for a pilgrimage during *Dussehra* holidays. You just do not remember anything."

On hearing this, Neeraj was at his wit's end. The food which he considered earlier as very delicious, now looked as if it was '*khichri*' (a dish normally advised to a patient).

But there was no other way. He took the tiffin and without saying anything, he left for his office. Throughout the journey, he was thinking, how to get rid of this riddle?

Dussehra holidays were starting from tomorrow. In the meantime, the bus arrived. He did not get any chance to ponder over this problem. On reaching office, he got engrossed in work.

But when it was lunch break, he felt very restless. He thought over again, but could not find a solution. In the end, he opened the tiffin and started eating.

He did not enjoy his delicious food today. *Halwa* made from *desi ghee* and decorated with almond also looked like as if he is swallowing uncooked flour.

In the evening, office was over and all the clerks were leaving for their respective homes happily. They had fifteen days vacations and everybody had made some plan or other to visit some hill station.

But he has to... He felt like crying.

He reached home. He was not successful in trying to make his wife change her mind.

Shanti had done her packing during the day. Every bit of luggage was packed and she had even procured railway tickets for the night train.

Neeraj's condition was just like a criminal who was due to be put on gallows......? He could not do anything and he boarded the train alongwith his wife.

They were going to a hilly area to see a hermit with a long beard. That hermit was very well known person. This was told to Shanti by a friend of hers. Her friend even told her that after visiting that hermit, her family prospered very much.

Finally, they reached the place of that hermit on a hilly area. It was a long way to the cave. Shanti wanted to cover that distance on foot, but Neeraj told her point blank that it is not possible for him to cover that distance on foot. He was willing to go to the location of the cave provided Shanti make an arrangement for him riding on a mule.

There were thousands of devotees waiting in front of the cave to pay their respects to him. A fat woman, who was wearing saffron dress like a hermit, was escorting devotees inside the cave in a group of fifty. After paying their respect to the hermit, she would bring them outside by the same route. This chain of action continued till 10 pm.

The devotees had collected some money out of respect for the hermit and got an iron gate fixed outside the cave. That fat woman would close the gate from inside at ten at night and put a lock on it so that the hermit could get some rest.

There was a big rush at the entrance of the cave. However, Shanti could manage to take Neeraj inside.

The cave was resonating inside by 'Baba ki jai'.

After walking for some distance inside the cave in a dim light, all the devotees saw that in front of them on a raised platform a lanky person was sitting there. All the devotees felt very happy.

'Baba Ram Bharose Kharka Dharka ki jai!' The cave reverberated. In return, the hermit pressed his hands on the head of the devotees and blessed them, but his eyes were closed.

Everyone was trying to offer oblation more than the other. Some would offer lots of currency notes while the other would offer ornaments of gold.

Next to hermit's feet, a spring of water was flowing. People were filling bottles with that water, thinking they will also make their relative's life happy by offering them this holy water.

Neeraj was standing there hypnotised and witnessed everything. Shanti realised that once again the atheist in him has awoken. She jolted him forcefully. Neeraj understood that like all other devotees, he was also supposed to bow his head in front of that hermit and drink that nectar.

When all the devotees had *darshan* of the hermit, Neeraj thinking something, came forward and caught hold of hermit's feet forcefully. People standing behind shouted, *"Baba Ram Bharose Kharka Dharka ki jai!"*

Neeraj was holding hermit's feet with such a force that the hermit could not control himself and feeling bewildered, he opened his eyes.

He was staring at Neeraj and Neeraj was staring at the hermit. They kept on staring at each other for quite some time. On seeing that he was taking so much time, that fat woman said, "Please be fast, so many people have to visit here."

Shanti also got scared that her husband may not leave without hermit's blessings. At this, the hermit started saying to that fat woman.

"Do one thing, take all the devotees outside. I want to talk to this person separately and also take this woman along. Bring next group after some time for our ambience."

Shanti was feeling happy that her luck is turning as the hermit had stopped her husband for his blessings.

The hermit and Neeraj kept quiet and stared at each other for some time. After satisfying himself properlyNeeraj said, "You ... you..., I hope I am not mistaken."

Arrey, speak slowly, the hermit said smilingly. "Neeraj you have not been... You have actually recognised me."

Both hugged each other. Sitting next to him. Neeraj asked impatiently, "But you were Kamal Dev... How come you have become a hermit?"

"Neeraj this is a long story..." After taking a deep breath, he narrated the whole story, how he became *Baba Kharka Dharka* from K.D. Nath. Kamal Dev gave the impression that he was feeling little uneasy and wanted to unburden himself. He wanted to narrate his whole story to someone. He started narrating his story.

"Neeraj, you were aware that I was a good student and wanted to continue my studies. But my relatives got me married against my wishes because of money. No one listened to me at all.

I inherited my father-in-law's business. I had no clue of business; all my partners deceived me and usurped all the business. We reached that stage that it became difficult even to cover my household expense. My wife Geeta...!" Then, remembering something, he said, "Yes, this woman who brings all the devotees to me, she is my wife."

"Oh I see," Said Neeraj. Kamal kept on talking, "My wife kept on accusing me all the time, since the day she got married to me. One day for my peace of mind, at night, I left Geeta forever.

For a long time, I was roaming around in forests. One day I started for this place of pilgrimage. I had to cover the entire distance on foot and it took me one month instead of seven days to cover this distance. On the way I had removed my clothes for having a bath, when suddenly rain water came in a gush. And all my clothes were washed away. I was sitting behind a big stone and weeping, when suddenly a hermit came that way.

I do not know if he saw my long beard or my weak body because of lack of nourishment or took me for an orphan or he considered me a better and bigger hermit than himself. He took out a *kurta* from his bag and gave it to me. I quickly put it on.

That hermit was a very tall man and that *kurta* was also very long one. It came upto my feet and was almost touching the earth. It gave the impression that someone has put an empty bag of flour on a bamboo pole.

Somehow, with great difficulty, I covered the distance. In front of the cave, thousands of followers were eagerly waiting to pay their ambience to that well-known hermit Ram Bharose.

Whole of the place was resonating with *Jai-Jai* of *Baba* Ram Bharose. I don't know from where I got the strength, I reached that cave after passing through all the hurdles. The cave was full of followers who were present there like sandwiches.

I kept on standing there for four hours. People were holding coconuts, dry fruits, almonds, bananas, apples, oranges, every type of fruits. I was hungry for so many days, and seeing these fruits, my hunger increased.

It started raining cats and dogs. Lightning also started along with thunder storm. Suddenly, a very strong gust of wind came and all the lamps in the cave, extinguished.

One could hear *Baba's* voice on mike, "Morning always succeed after a dark night. Children, have patience. Whenever a trouble comes on earth, God comes here in the guise of a man and solves all the problems of mankind."

Today *Baba* Ram Bharose was making this back ground for his son. He wanted his son should succeed him and thus, this place may be a family inheritance.

"Devotees! A man who comes here in a short while and bows his head at my feet will be my successor and he only will serve you people. He will solve your problems." There was a great hustle and bustle there. To see *Baba's* feet, so many people got crushed under the feet during the *melee.*

In the meantime, suddenly an earthquake came, and stones from the cave started tumbling down. People started running out of the cave. During this *melee,* while I was standing at the end of the crowd, I don't know, how I found myself at the top of the crowd. Stones were falling rapidly and people were coming under them. It was a strange scene. Whole of the atmosphere was resonating with the cries of people.

Finally, my head hit a stone and I became unconscious. When I regained my senses, I saw that the whole cave had disappeared; *Baba* Ram Bharose had also passed away as he also came under a big stone. Perhaps his son had also come under a stone and died. I also would not have survived if a big stone had not given me support. I do not know how long I was under the shelter of that big stone. I tried to come out, but in vain. Some rays of light were coming inside from a small opening.

I looked at *Baba's* feet. There was a heap of paper money and lots of jewellery of gold and silver. There was no dearth of fruits. I was hungry for the last so many days, so, I just started lavishing on fruits.

Days kept on passing and there were no count of days. I got upset, sitting inside the cave. I was feeling suffocated. It was a must that I should come out of that cave, but there was no way.

Because of this problem, I again fell unconscious. When I regained my senses, I found myself in a special ward of some big hospital. People standing outside the hospital felt happy on hearing about my recovery. All the renowned doctors touched my feet with respect.

"*Baba*, you are great." Everybody was saying.

"I am not a great man. This is..." Those devotees who were standing there did not give me any opportunity to speak further and they started saying, "All great men say like this...!"

When the stones were removed from the entrance of the cave, you were found unconscious near *Baba's* feet and it was his' saying 'that when the problems come, then...! You just explain that everybody else died except you, tell us how and why...?

Neeraj, there was no way out but to keep quiet. I thought it better to keep quiet, media people came to take my interview. When they asked my name, I got scared. At that time I heard the voice of people standing outside, "*Jai ho Baba Ram Bharoase.*" I immediately told them, 'It is just because of blessings of *Baba* Ram Bharose' and told them that 'my name is Baba Ram Bharose Kharka Dharka Nath.' And thus, I became Baba Ram Bharose Kharka Dharka Nath from Kamal Nath.

Within a few minutes the news of my name reached outside the hospital, the people standing outside started shouting, *'Baba Ram Bharose Kharka 'Dharka...ki jai!'*

Best of the doctors were treating me. Before I regained my health, my devotees collected some money and got the cave repaired again. They also got the iron gate installed.

A great festival was celebrated on my recouping.

Watching my photographs in the newspaper, my wife Geeta came here.

We both are staying in this cave since then.

Neeraj, if ever I want to leave this place, even then, I cannot do it. What will happen to the faith of so many people? I cannot betray their faith."

Kamal had just finished his talk, when voice of many followers chanting *'Baba...*! was heard and Neeraj bowed his head in front of *Baba's* feet. *Baba* put his hand on his head and Neeraj got up from there and left.

Shanti was very pleased that *Baba* had paid special attention to Neeraj. She had now, full faith that come what may, but now their good luck is going to take place.

After reaching Delhi, every day she continued expecting for Neeraj's promotion.

He participated in office strike and along with others, his services were terminated.

Shanti could not believe this news. When she verified the news of termination of his service, she started cursing Neeraj since he did not pay his respects to *Baba* properly. He surely must be thinking of something else. That is why they have suffered such a calamity. All those people who had paid their respect properly, now are flourishing.

He tried his best to reason it to her, but perhaps she was possessed by *Baba*. She did not listen to Neeraj at all and declared that she will visit that place again with Neeraj. "How it is possible that only we are tyrannised!?

We are not that unfortunate that... She left her talk between and started crying bitterly.

Neeraj started having pity on Shanti. He thought "What a simple woman she is! That she has faith in that Baba."

He never wanted to explain her the real facts about Baba.

To appease his wife and to avoid the hazardous journey to the cave, he gave his apology letter to his company. He was reinstated to the company. But in a new grade in which his salary was cut by one third.

Even then, Shanti did not budge from her resolution of visiting that cave. There... she wanted to ask *Baba* as to why...?! he has not showered his blessings on them.

Finally getting fed up of the circumstances, he explained all the facts about *Baba* Kharka Dharka to her. After listening to everything, she pondered over for some time, she said, "Now, I have developed more faith in him. There is certainly something in him, that God has made him sit at such a high position."

"Why all the other people of the cave died? Why only *Baba* survived? It was God's will that he survived...! Now, I will not listen to any excuse. You will have to accompany me...!"

He was helpless and was compelled to go. Taking leave without pay, he left for *Baba's* abode along with Shanti. They did not even have money for bearing the travel expenses. As such Shanti sold off her bangles.

They reached near the cave around nine at night. Neeraj advised Shanti to wait till 10 pm and they will enter the cave at the time of closing the gate. Shanti agreed to this.

They quickly entered the cave, when Geeta was about to close the gate, they both rushed to meet the *Baba*. Geeta tried to stop them, but Neeraj along with Shanti, quickly entered the cave and reached near *Baba* Ram Bharose.

Geeta was very annoyed with them on this activity of theirs. So far no devotee has behaved like this. She was running after them, when *Baba* said in a raised voice, "They are my special devotees. You go and lock the outer gate and come back."

Geeta was wondering that Kamal had not behaved like this in past. On her return, Geeta saw Kamal talking merrily to Neeraj and Shanti. Neeraj introduced Shanti and himself to Geeta. She smiled and met them affectionately.

She smiled sheepishly and said, "You were his friend. Why did you not meet me the last time you had come? Had I known the facts, I would have insisted your staying with us for a few days. It is nice that you have come again."

Neeraj explained to them, their whole problem. Everyone had a hearty laugh.

"If this is the problem, Shanti sister, you both come and stay with us. We will share whatever we get. We are also fed up of staying all alone by ourselves. If we have your company, then, we will have nice time. God has given everything like money, gold, silver, but human beings need company. Somebody has said rightly that man is a social animal."

Shanti was very happy in her heart on hearing Geeta's suggestion. But hearing this, Neeraj was disheartened. He imagined himself in the guise of a hermit and shuddered.

Now, Shanti and Neeraj had been staying there for some time. Shanti was very happy. There were all amenities of life, such as free boarding and lodging. There was no dearth of money.

But Neeraj was perplexed from the very beginning about the atmosphere. He tried to make Shanti understand that this is no place to stay permanently. But Shanti was not ready to leave that place at any cost. A few times, she insisted that Neeraj should also put on saffron clothes of hermit like his friend and serve people and earn name and fame.

One day finding Shanti alone, Geeta hesitantly said, "I never wanted to talk to you on this subject, Shanti *behan,* but what to do. I am helpless." It looked as if Geeta was finding it difficult to find words.

Plucking courage she said, "You have seen that my husband sits in the cave from morning till evening. When at night, he comes to his room, he is so tired that the moment he lies down in his bed, he goes to sleep and I... I ... am also a woman I have also some wishes,cravings. But it looks like that it is all beyond him. Well! You have got everything.

If you agree, we can make a deal... You stay with my husband from morning till evening and whatever money and ornaments come in the form of offerings, you keep all with you and... during that period of time, from morning till evening Neeraj can stay with me in this room..."

Hearing this Shanti was surprised and she could barely utter, "Behan Geeta, what are you saying ...? you and Neeraj..." She was not finding suitable words to say anything further.

Before her leaving that place, Geeta said, "I will give you one week to think. There is no hurry. Take your time." Saying this, she quickly went towards the cave.

Geeta's suggestion created upheaval, in her heart. The whole night, she could not have a wink of sleep. On one side was the money and all the luxuries of life, while on other side was her husband.

She was in a big fix as to what to do and what not to do? She was unable to decide anything.

She switched on the light. It was 4 am. Next to her Neeraj was sleeping peacefully. She kept on staring at him continuously. Then it appeared as if she had reached a final...!

She quickly got up from the bed. She suddenly woke up Neeraj and putting a shawl on his shoulder she said, " Come fast with me. He tried to enquire something from her, but Shanti did not reply. And tightly holding his hand, she quickly went down the hill.

At some places, the descent from the hill was so steep that, they almost fell down. But Shanti was not worried and kept on running down with Neeraj.

Neeraj was wondering, what a problem he has invited? If they had lost the balance then!. ?

Though Geeta was not very happy about this plan, but Neeraj was happy that the plan which he made with the help of Geeta was successful.

Because he knew that a woman can tolerate everything, except sharing her...!

19

The Test

Every year, students have been coming from far and wide to this town for taking examination. A few of the students used to opt for this centre as it was at an isolated place and good for studies.

But most of the student used to come here as this place gave them an opportunity to copy and indulge in cheating. Apart from it, there were a few candidates, who had to clear the examination for some better prospects or some promotion.

Nobody was prepared to come to a so far off forest area. Finding no alternative, the university had to appoint Ganga Das as superintendent for the centre.

Within last four years, Ganga Das had purchased land and had also constructed a big house and thus, this centre had become notorious. Rumour reached the Vice-Chancellor and professor Balraaj was sent as a superintendent. His record was unblemished. Nobody was as honest as him in whole of the university. He was full of courage, loved to put in hard work.

He was always indebted to his teacher Chauhan for this, because he had given him such an education. He was going ahead and progressing in his life, facing many difficulties with ease.

Off course! During this little time, his eyesight had deteriorated and he was supporting a long hair.

Before commencing the examination, he addressed all the participants, "I would request you all to check all your pockets and in case there is any piece of paper with you, please leave that outside. You may be expelled from the university for three years just because of a small mistake on your part.

One of my respected teachers used to say that 'By cheating... you are deceiving yourself. If you are not capable of something, achieving that by wrong method, you will not be successful in your life."

And continuing further, he said, "I don't know how much my other friends have followed this? But I have fully followed it. And I can say with pride I have been very successful."

All other candidates sitting in the adjoining room could not listen to this.

Examination started.

At the end of the examination, papers were collected. One of the supervisor, while collecting paper from a student, who was sitting in a corner, saw that a few tiny pieces of papers fell on the floor from that man's hand. Small hints, pertaining to the questions which were set in the paper, were written on them.

The supervisor collected all the pieces of paper from the floor and said, "*Bhai Sahib*! You are indulging in such an action while you are on the verge of having your grey hair grey."

At that time, Balraj was passing through the corridor of that room, hearing this, he also entered that room.

Supervisor told Balraj, showing him all tiny pieces of paper, "Sir! See his age and see what he indulged in."

Balraj looked at that person attentively.

He at once recognised that he was Chauhan. He bowed at his feet and said, "*Master ji*, you have done this.... How can I now...I used to treat you as...!"

He was at a loss to understand. He felt as if somebody had throttled his neck. He could not utter anything after this. There were two big tears in his eyes. He felt that today, God has put him at a big test.

20

A Long Wait

Rashtrapati Bhawan was full of brave *jawans*. Today, all of them, who had shown bravery in the battle field, had established an example of bravery, were to be decorated with medals. Out of them, those who were alive came themselves to be honoured, while rest of them were represented by their close relations.

All names were announced turn by turn.

"Colonel Megh Singh, who did not hesitate risking his life, went behind the enemy lines...!" Someone was announcing on the mike.

General Mehta, his daughter-in-law, Brigadier Bakshi and his daughter were also present in the hall. They all got engrossed in their past events.

Those days, General Mehta was posted at Jammu as Brigadier. His son, who was a Captain in army, had come on leave.

One day, when Brigadier Mehta returned from the office in the evening, he asked his orderly Prabhu, as to where was Narender? The orderly replied that he has gone to see a movie.

He started murmuring. "Has this boy come here to spend his vacations, or for watching movies?"

He was making a note of his habits for the last so many days.

"Okay! Let him return today, I will take him to task."

When Narender entered the bungalow at night on his scooter, Prabhu went running towards him and narrated the whole incident to him, explaining that the Brigadier *Saheb* is in a very foul mood. He had not eaten, or had any drink so far and is waiting for him in the dining room.

Narender was at his wits end. He realised that today it was difficult to get away from his father's ire. So, like a true *jawan,* he got prepared to face the problem and entered the room. His daddy was busy smoking cigar and twisting his big moustaches.

"Good evening, daddy," he wished him while still standing.

"Better to say Good Morning, son. It is now approaching dawn." He said while sitting on the chair.

"Daddy, in fact my scooter was giving some trouble..." He replied making a lame excuse. But his father ignored this.

"I am aware that at what time and where, all of my officers are working. Then, can I not have information about you?" He said seriously.

Narender was not in a position to understand as to what was the meaning of his daddy's saying and how should he reply? So, he thought that it was best to keep quiet. "Son, do you know who is the most important person in war to give information about the enemy?"

"Yes sir! Scouts." He spoke in a subdued voice. He was amazed about what relation scouts had with his coming late? He thought that perhaps his father had an extra peg of whisky. But then, he remembered that his father had neither eaten anything, nor he had anything to drink since the time he had returned from his office.

"Son, you have said correctly. These scouts send all the information at the back. But why they are two in number?" And he again asked another question. "It is so, that when one of them is in an action, the other can look after the first one, and like that!"

"Exactly", interrupting him, he said, "Like this, life is a war and if, instead of one, there are two partners, it is always better. Could you understand what I am suggesting?"

Narender was a little nervous on hearing his conversation. He could not understand anything and said, "Daddy! I could not understand you."

"Then listen, I will explain to you in simple words. The girl with whom you spend time till late in the evening, it will be better if you get married to her." His father gave a hearty laugh and Narender felt shy to answer anything.

Both Narender and Prabhu were confused at his serious acting.

"Son! Please let me know her address, and I will go tomorrow and will settle everything."

"Daddy! You don't have to talk to her, but to her daddy" He immediately corrected his sentence.

He said smiling, "Oh yes yes, you will talk to her yourself. Give me her father's address. First, you tell me her name."

"Kamini", he said quietly.

He said, "Yes!" and looking towards Prabhu, he asked, "How is she to look at?"

Prabhu who was not anticipating this question, got little confused, "Yes sir! What can I say?" he said confusingly.

"Tell me properly, otherwise..." He said.

"Sir, she is beautiful. But, ... I have seen her from a distance," feeling a little scared, he said.

Next day, when Narender narrated the whole episode to Kamini, she was very amused.

"You were very proud of becoming an officer. Now, you have come on the proper track" she said, ... mischievously.

"Jokes apart, just tell me when your Daddy is returning from his tour. So that, I may send my Daddy to your place..." He said hurriedly.

"Why are you so eager?" Kamini said in a playful mood..

"You do not know my daddy's' mood. If he changes his mind, then, things can go wrong. He is very short-tempered."

"Listen to me very carefully before you send your daddy to our house and please tell him that my daddy is a business man. To him, making such noise of clicking boots, having cigar in mouth, time and again twisting his moustaches...!"

"You have again come back to your nonstop nonsense. You have shifted your conversation from where to where..." He said in an annoyed tone, while interrupting her.

On this, Kamini became serious and told him, "Daddy is returning from tour today."

Very next day, Brigadier Mehta, putting on Golf cap, reached Kamini's father's house. He pressed the call-bell, when a voice came from inside, "Come in *Mahashey ji.*"

Brigadier Mehta, while entering, said, "Please forgive me! My name is not *Mahashey ji.*" He had cigar in his mouth and his hand was twisting his big moustaches.

"*Mahashey ji,* you took me wrong. I was..." A man, who looked like a skeleton, wearing *shervani* and a cap on his head, said.

Brigadier Mehta scanned at that fragile type of man from head to toe and then said angrily, "Mister, I have already told you that my name is not *Mahashey ji,* but..."

"Sir! You have not understood. I have studied in a gurukul and you..." He left his talk in between, feeling disappointed

Kamini was eagerly waiting for the arrival of Narender's father, but here the scenerio was entirely different.

She was wondering as to what had happened to her father? Why he was wearing an awkward dress and he was talking such rubbish?

Brigadier Mehta mistook the word *'Gurukul'* for *'Raghukul'* and said, "I have not come here to hear any *katha,* but...!"

Realising that the situation was getting out of hand, Kamini entered the room and tried to bring the situation under control and said. "Uncle, perhaps you have not understood. My father was saying, that...!"

He was surprised and said, "So, he is your father, you mean Krishan Kant Sharma."

"*Beti,* it was nice that you told me now." And laughingly he admitted that he was taking him for somebody else.

"What you mean", he said with an expression of annoyance and stammering this time.

Kamini who was getting fed up, finally said, "Ok! This is now up to both of you. I am going inside."

On her saying so, both Brigadier Mehta and Krishan Kant Sharma started laughing loudly.

Kamini was perplexed and could not understand a bit.

"*Beti,* Mehta is my classmate from the college. I knew that you were interested in his son..."

"So, you both were pulling my leg," she said feeling shy.

They both got married. Now, he got his rank of a Major and during this time, he was sent abroad for specialised training. There he worked day and night and was known as one of the best among the officers.

His daddy was promoted to the rank of a General.

War started. Narender's battalion came under General Mehta's command. Taking into consideration his abilities, he was given a specialised work. He could undoubtly handle any task extremely well.

Wherever he used to ambush the enemy, it used to result in fatal encounter. Now, as a result of that the enemy used to tremble at the mention of his name. There was also a rumour that the enemy had announced a prize of one lakh to capture him.

There was a special mission for which he was called to Divisional Headquarters and after explaining everything, General Mehta said, "Narender, I am proud of you. If you succeed in the mission which has been assigned to you, it will be mentioned as a wonder in the army history and your name will be written in golden letters."

And then, giving him instructions, he started saying, "Please keep me informed about your minute to minute activities. Make sure that your wireless set should not stop working even for a second. For communicating, the code word will be 'Black Bird'. Okay! I wish you best of luck."

After shaking hands with him, Major Narender went back.

After getting orders from Headquarters, he immediately left for his mission.

The mission was very dangerous. He reached his goal taking his *jawans* along and after destroying the ammunition dump of the enemy, he returned fast. On the way back throughout, he was in touch with the General.

"Operator, what is the problem? Why the voice on the set is very weak?" He whispered.

"Sir! Perhaps battery has gone weak, I will quickly change the battery, " said the operator. Narender's special party was surrounded in enemy ambush. During this period, firing had started from all sides.

"Hello... Hello... Hello...! Hello, Black Bird...!" General tried his best, but there was no response from other side.

Many patrolling parties were sent to rescue that commando party. Both sides were engaged in a very heavy firing, and it was impossible to reach or return safely from there...

The war was over. Major Narender did not return. He was given 'Param Vir Chakra' for his bravery.

At that time, Kamini and General had gone to receive the award.

Many years later. Now, Kamini's son had become a young boy and was smart like his father. He had also joined the army and was a Captain.

One day, Kamini was reading a book when Brigadier Bakshi came there.

"Kamini, what are you doing? I hope you are not engrossed in some special book. If so, write my name in the waiting list." He said grinning.

"Bakshi, you have not got over your habit of... reading naughty books!"

"Now, I suggest you better pay your attention at looking after your brigade." Kamini said.

"You do not know, reading such books help in keeping the morale high. And the work gets done with a speed." He said laughingly.

"Your habit of college of being talkative is still the same. Of course, you have got a streak of grey hairs, but your way of conversation has not changed a bit. You still have the same attitude towards life." She said smilingly.

"But your hair are the same as were during those college days and then there is no change in your figure", Bakshi said, while delving into the past. "Do you remember, all the students of the college used to call you Hirni (a doe)? Kamini, What a gait you had."

Kamini, reminding Bakshi and said, "Bakshi *Saheb,* please come out of your past dreams. Long time has gone by," she said grinning.

Continuing his conversation, he said, "I reached a little late, and Narender came before me. Otherwise instead of him getting married to you, I would have given an offer of marriage to you. And...!"

"Did you see your face...?" Kamini said smilingly.

"Kamini, tell me what is lacking in me? I am handsome, young and...!"

Kamini said laughing heartily, "You should say! You were handsome, young...!"

Bakshi, realising at the talk going haywire, said, "Ok, do you say 'yes' or I go to General Mehta......!" Even at this age, Kamini blushed, hearing such words.

Taking hold of her, "What nonsense you are talking? At least, have some consideration for your young daughter who is sitting next to you. You are..." She could not find words to say anything further.

"You also got confused. I had come here to have a talk with you for the alliance of my daughter with your son Mohinder." Bakshi said feeling amused.

His daughter Nimmi was aware of her daddy's habit. So, she kept on sitting there during his discussion with Kamini.

Hearing this discussion, she felt very shy and ran away inside the room. And on the way she just collided with Capt. Mohinder.

"What is the matter? You are looking very happy today." Mohinder asked her.

Nimmi explained everything in detail to him.

"You are also my *Morni (a peacock)*, he said while taking her into his arms.

Again there was a war. Capt Mohinder's battalion was under Brigadier Bakshi's brigade. This time, Capt Mohinder was sent for a special task in the enemy territory. He was no less than his father in bravery.

"Son! This task is entrusted to you because of your intelligence and courage. See the irony of fate. The place where you are being sent today is the same territory where long time back, your father was sent and he showed his bravery, got PVC. You know we were great pals and course mates. But it is sad that he did not return from there," said Brigadier Bakshi in a little pensive tone.

"Sir! You don't worry...I will surely come back," Capt Mohinder said with great confidence.

Brigadier Bakshi had a misconception and it came true.

Capt Mohinder could fulfill the task which was given to him, but could not return.

* * * *

"Sir! Will you accompany Kamini to *Rashterpati Bhavan* to receive Mohinder's medal?" Brigadier Bakshi inquired from General Mehta.

"I have already paid once for my deed. This time, you go alongwith her. You had only sent Capt Mohinder on the task." General Mehta said smilingly.

Brigadier Bakshi was thinking, what a strong heart this man has got. Even under these circumstances also, he is smiling.

Rashterpati Bhavan . . . . The names were being announced.

Everyone was busy in his thought. She was startled, hearing the voice of a person sitting next to her. Somebody was saying, "Mrs Kamini Mehta. Your name is being announced."

Someone was announcing at the mike, Mrs Kamini Mehta is such a brave women, who had received a gallantry award Param Vir Chakra in this hall for her husband long time back and once again, she is here in this hall to receive a gallantry award Param Vir Chakra for the bravery of her son."

Once the function was over and on insistence of General Mehta, Brigadier Bakshi and his daughter came along to have dinner with them.

On entering the bungalow, General Mehta noticed that it was all dark everywhere in the bungalow. Light was not seen anywhere. He called all the servants, but did not get any reply, response from anywhere. "Where have they vanished today!" He murmured.

The moment, he stretched his arm to switch on the light of verandah, somebody put a pistol on General Mehta's temple and a second pistol on Brigadier's.

"Beware, if any one of you tried to play a trick."

Kamini and Nimmi both got scared at this incident.

All of them entered the room at the order of that heavy voice and then suddenly they heard a fire. Everyone was scared thinking, who has been hurt. Simultaneously, all the lights were switched on at the sound of a bullet being fired. A man standing in front of them was laughing loudly.

Looking at him, everybody was surprised and became mad with happiness.

In front of them, stood Capt Mohinder smiling, "Are you not really surprised?" He said.

Capt Mohinder told them that enemy took him as a prisoner and offered him that he should get involved with them, and told him that they will not kill him. He will be bestowed with all the luxuries and wealth. When he refused, he was taken to a dirty underground room. One more war prisoner was imprisoned there in the next room.

One day, one of the officer of enemy unit came there and said, "This *jawan* also did not listen to us, that is why he is still in this prison for the last so many years. You will also meet the same fate. At least, have mercy on your youth. Your well-being depends on obeying our orders.

After a few days, I agreed to their proposal. I gave them a suggestion that if they put me together with the other prisoner in the same room, I will try to convince him to agree to their suggestion. Officers of the enemy agreed to this and thus I made him listen to the enemy. We both were put in the same room together. We were given good food, but outside there was very strict patrolling.

Our plan was successful. We were able to run away from there after a proper planning and thus, reached India.

All of them said in unison, "But who was the other prisoner and where is he?"

"That was I". Everyone looked at the source of the voice.

In front of them, Major Narender was standing.

Kamini felt as if the whole world was revolving in front of her eyes and...!

She would have fallen on the floor, if Major Narender, making a swift move, had not caught her in his arms.

21

The Beggar Woman

Dinesh was passing through the new market of the city, when he heard a recognised voice. He turned around and saw the same young beggar woman standing in front of him.

"*Babu*! What a surprise to see you here?"

"Yes, I have come in this city yesterday only. So, thesedays you have made your headquarters here. That is why I did not see you in my city. It appears people of this city here give you more alms" He said laughingly.

"No *babu*! It is not so," and while continuing her talk said, "*babu*! Pardon my saying, but the people of your city are hungry, extremely hungry."

"But, what is strange in this? In every city there are bound to be some hungry people". He said smilingly.

"No *babu*! I am not referring about that hunger. I am talking about the lust in their eyes. The best thing in this city is that the people here do not cast their evil eyes on any women whether married or unmarried. But in your city people while placing the money on the palm of a beggar woman, had there lustful eyes fixed on her youth."

On hearing this, Dinesh shifted his gaze from that beggar woman to somewhere else.

Continuing her talk she further said, "Yes, I certainly appreciate one thing of the people of your city and that is that while they did not shift their lustful gaze from an unmarried woman, at the same time they did not cast lustful eyes on a married woman.

That is why while begging in your city I had to carry the child with me."

"Oh yes! Now I remember. Where is your child, whom you used to hold while begging?"

"*Babu*! I am not yet married. That child was on hire."

22

A Spark of Fire

The train was moving at a very fast speed. It was still one hour's distance to Goregaon. Sudhir was sitting all alone in the AC compartment. Goregaon was not an unknown place for him. He had stayed here 20 years ago. At that time, it was less of a town, and more of a village.

Now he had come here as the chief of the company.

Today he was going through the past memories.

During those days, he was posted here as one of an ordinary officer of the company. Once it so happened that he had to go out of this place for one month on some official work of the company. But suddenly a four-days holiday was announced and he thought of visiting his home.

Every incident of that day was very vividly imprinted in his mind. That night of fire was just like an ulcer for him. That night of inferno had made his life hell. The incident of that day had turned his life into such a turmoil, which could not be solved till today.

That day after alighting from the train, he quickly went to the Station Master's room. He dialed his residence number. It kept on ringing for quite some time, but no body picked the telephone.

He was thinking where could Lata go at this hour of night at 11 'o' clock? After waiting for some time, he put the receiver down.

He came out of the station. There was no trace of any conveyance outside.

Usually, the *tongewales* would leave the station after the last train had passed. But today they left early because of the rain and storm. Outside the storm was raging furiously. Rain had just stopped. He put the collar of his coat up and pulled his hat down a little and taking out his torch in his hand, left for his house.

This was the only time when he had informed of his programme very late, and Lata had not come to the station to receive him. Otherwise she always used to receive him at the station along with his servant.

He saw that at some distance from the road, a few labourers were warming their hands around a fire. One of them was singing melodiously a folk song and all others were enjoying the song while suringing their heads. He paused there for a few moments and looking at the flames, he moved on.

Long long ago, when he was not married, while passing through this place, he saw a house on fire. All the occupants standing around it were shouting for help. On reaching there, he learnt that their daughter was sleeping in a top floor room. Taking courage, he entered the house and looked around. It was difficult to climb through the stairs as the fire had started from the bottom. He contemplated for a while, and went around the house. He could see a pipe going upward towards the top of the house. Since he was young, he quickly went up with the help of that pipe and entered her room. He helped the girl to get up and brought her down slowly saving her from the flames.

Her relatives thanked him. The girl was nobody else but Lata.

After that incident Sudhir started visiting that house frequently and later on, they both got married.

But that day, he was not aware of either cold or late hours. When he came out of reverie, he saw himself, standing in front of the gate of his small bungalow.

He was about to knock at the door, when suddenly his eyes fell on the adjoining bungalow. He saw from a distance that a bright light was emerging from Deevakar's room. He looked at the light of the flame attentively and something struck to his mind.

He ran towards Deevakar's house and started knocking with a bang. Door was closed from inside. He shouted for Deevakar, but got no response. He picked up a stone from the ground and broke the glass of the window. He put his hand inside and opened the latch and went towards Deevakar's room.

Doors of Deevakars' room were also closed. Sudhir pushed open the door. The room was full of smoke. He switched on the torch, yelled for Deevakar, but could not hear anything in response.

He tied a handkerchief on his face and entered his room quickly. Reaching near Deevakar's bed, he focussed the light at his face. He was stunned, what he witnessed there.

Lata was in Deevakar's arms and both were unconscious because of smoke. He felt very furious. He decided to let everything get burned. He stopped for a moment when he reached near the door. Fire was spreading very fast.

Somebody had said rightly, "Women, thy name is infidelity," he thought.

He had very loveable relations with 'Lata' and what he got in return?

'It will be very fine if the cause of my sorrow burns and turns into ashes.' He wanted to see the scene of both of them reducing to ashes in front of his eyes.

'I have been going out on tours for so many times that means that both of them in my absence... I am here for the last six years and even Deevakar is also here with me.' He thought.

When he returned from these thoughts, the flames were about to engulf both of them. He ran inside and within no time he shifted them in the outer room. He first lifted 'Lata' and brought her into their bedroom and later he picked up Deevakar and put him on his sofa. He quickly administered first aid to them. He put a bandage on Deevakar's head which was bleeding.

By the time, the villagers reached there to extinguish the flames, Sudhir had already turned for the station.

In the meantime, he was startled by the noise of brakes of the train.

His chain of past memories broke and he was back in the present.

He quickly took out a handkerchief from his pocket and wiped his tears. He saw that the Goregaon station which used to support only two rooms, had developed so big that it was difficult to recognise. Light was shining at every nook and corner. During these thirty years, he had changed so many companies and been to so many countries.

Today, he had not come to Goregaon as Sudhir, but was known as 'Mr Roy'. In fact, his real name was Sudhir Roy but at that time, he was known as Sudhir only. But after this incident, he made himself known as Mr Roy.

The train stopped. Company's Assistant Manager, along with a few men, was present there to receive him. The moment he got down the train everyone welcomed him.

"Sir, my name is Ravi," Assistant Manager introduced himself and then said, "sir, you have come alone? You are not accompanied with Mrs Roy and all other family members."

"No, I have no wife and no siblings. I lost them only here some thirty years ago." He said in a tone which was barely audible and quickly getting control of himself, he changed the subject.

"How is the work of the company carrying on?" Roy enquired.

"Sir, everything is running smoothly. I am running the company for the last one year. The company showed a profit of thirty Lakhs during this period. Now that you have joined, the work will definitely improve."

Roy was very impressed by Ravi. He recollected that when he had joined the company, he was also very young and had the same enthusiasm, vigour.

In the meantime, other employees of the company also reached there and Ravi made all the introductions.

After sometime, they both left for the company in a big car. Ravi was continuously talking whereas Sudhir was engulfed in his own thoughts. There was no change in this road. He thought, it was same, but his life had changed drastically.

His heart started palpitating faster as the car passed the small place???

There were the same small houses and the small water grindig mill. Making noise *'Gharr Gharrr'* on top of a small rivulet. There was no change in them.

He missed his heart beat what he witnessed. His old bangalow was still standing there. On looking at it, he had a great desire, that he should instruct the driver to turn the car towards that bungalow, but he controlled himself and questioned Ravi "Who stays in this accommodation?"

"Sir, I stay in this bungalow. Earlier, it was a small place/ accommodation. But now a few rooms have been added to this and made it big."

"Who else stays with you..." Asked Roy.

"My wife, children and my old mother stay with me," Ravi replied.

And then he continued, "Sir, the big bungalow, which you can see from here is earmarked for the chief and is for you to stay. Last year only, it was constructed for the chief."

The car entered the porch of the new accommodation. One servant came forward, opened the door and saluted both of them. Ravi, walking ahead took Roy inside a big hall.

There, they sat on a sofa and got busy discussing company's affair. After some time, servant brought tea and some snacks.

Later on, getting up from the sofa, Ravi said, "Sir, now you can have a little nap. You are having dinner with me tonight. I will come to accompany you."

"There is no necessity of this. I can have my dinner here only."

"No, sir, there is no formality in it," saying, this Ravi left.

Roy felt a little uncomfortable the moment Ravi left that place. He wanted to take a round of that place, where he had spent some cherished moments of his life. Those moments which were most valuable in his life.

He quickly got ready and came out. It was turning slightly dark outside. His steps automatically moved in the direction of his old bunglow where he had spent some years of his life.

He was about to open the gate of that bungalow and enter the house, when he suddenly heard a small dog barking. He stopped there. He realised that at present somebody else is occupying this house. He has no right to enter inside the house and also since he was coming over for dinner in the evening here. It will be better if he can wait for some time.

He left that place with a heavy heart and left for that *jungle* where he used to go with his wife 'Lata' for picnics. He covered quite a distance busy in these thoughts.

Out of the *jungle*, the huts were the same as they were during his time. Suddenly an idea came to his mind. His servant, Babu Lal, used to live here in one of the huts, too. Why not find out about him? And enquiring about him, he reached his hut. He knocked at the door, but nobody replied.

He was about to return, when he heard somebody coughing. Without bothering about anything, he pushed the door open and entered the hut. Inside a small earthen lamp was burning. In such a little light, he could only see an old man lying down on a wooden bed.

He was more of a skeleton than a man and coughing continuously. Sudhir went forward, drew water from the pitcher which was kept close by and made him drink it.

The old man stopped coughing for some time. Then he asked him, "*Baba*, one of my servant 'Babu Lal' used to live here. Where is he these days?"

The old man replied, "I am Babu Lal. But... who are you?"

"You didn't recognise me? Babu Lal, I am Sudhir... Sudhir."

"*Saheb*...! You have come after so many years, I could not recognise you." Tears came in to Babu Lal's eyes and he started crying loudly and he once more suffered a bout of coughing.

Even Sudhir could not control his tears.

Sudhir quickly took out some water from the pitcher and made him drink after helping him to sit. Once the cough stopped, he started saying, "*Saheb*, please bring my box which is kept in front of me." And then murmured, "Perhaps, God made me live till now for that very thing only."

Sudhir kept that box on his wooden bed. Babu Lal quickly started searching for something in that box. Perhaps, he was not able to find that thing which he was looking for. He pointed with a finger to Sudhir to bring the lamp a little closer and after searching fervently for a while, he could find that thing which he was searching for.

It was wrapped in a small piece of a cloth. He took it out and put it in Sudhir's hand. It was a torn, old piece of a paper. "What is this Babu Lal? Sudhir asked.

"*Saheb*! Go through this. I have kept it more safely than my life for the last thirty years."

Sudhir raised the wick of the lamp as high as it was possible. Now the words were clearly visible.

"This is Lata's writing," he said, and at once started going through.

As he was going through the letter, tears started flowing from his eyes. On seeing Sudhir crying, Babu Lal started crying, too.

It was written in that letter...!

"My Sudhir,

You have still not returned despite so many years have gone by. I don't know where have you disappeared... I don't know who has gobbled you up. That day I received your telegram very late. Babu Lal had already left for his house. I thought that I will take Deevakar's servant along and receive you at the station. When I reached Deevakar's house, I learnt that he had given leave to his servant for the day.

Deevkar said, 'Please sit down, I will make some arrangement.' Deevakar was drunk. I got frightened and got up quickly to go out, but he came forward and bolted the door from inside and started misbehaving with me.

I shouted and cried but it did not have any effect on him. He dragged me to his bedroom.

I tried to get rid from his clutches and during this struggle, the kerosene lamp which was kept on the table fell on the carpet and fire broke out. But Deevakar did not pay any heed to this and continued coming towards me.

I was almost on the verge of losing my senses because of being frightened and tired. Suddenly I saw a torch on the bed. I clutched it in my hand and hit Deevakar on his head. After that I fainted and he fell down on the bed with a shriek.

The complete house was reduced to ashes by the time people came from across the *jungle* to extinguish the fire.

When finally, I regained my senses, "I saw myself in our bedroom and Deevakar in our living room."

But, so far, it could not be known, who saved us from that inferno.

Life has become a torture without you.

I am leaving this letter with Babu Lal. It may happen that somehow, someday life may bring you back to Goregaon and this letter of mine may reach you. I do not know that till that time if I will be alive or dead.

Oh Yes! After some time of your leaving, a son was born.

I have named him Ravi.

Your own,

Lata."

23

Delusion

A long time had passed since they had gotten married. He had come home today, taking leave for a few days. It was the festival of Diwali. The sound of bursting of crackers was coming from outside. They both were unaware of the outside world. Rani was in his arms and...!

When they regained consciousness. Rani said while moving her fingers through his curly hair, "Prashant! You have a few grey hair, there are black circles under your eyes and wrinkles on your face, hands, and neck.

Your body is not very agile any more. Now you have grown old." She laughed heartily and her laughter resonated in the room. Rani's eyes were mischievous.

Hearing this, Prashant smiled and casually glanced at her face.

He noticed that there were a few grey hair in Rani's golden hair. There were a few wrinkles on her beautiful face. The shine in her eyes had become a little dull. Her youth was also declining.

And...!!

But he could not say anything to his wife, or, one could say that he had not the courage to say this to his wife.

He heaved a big sigh and closed his eyes. He never wanted this perception to break that his wife was still not as beautiful and youthful as she used to be.

24

The Last Union

A car was being driven at a very fast speed on a hilly track. A soft music was being played in the car. A newly wed bride in red outfit was sitting next to a young man.

It was the first night of Gautam's married life. It was his earnest desire to start his married life in a dak bungalow which was situated at the top of a hillock.

Same thing happened. Despite so many objections from all the relatives, he quietly left the house from the rear door of his room. He was holding his new bride's hand in one hand and in the other hand, he was holding a briefcase in which he had packed some important articles.

The bride dressed in red outfit, feeling scared, came and sat next to him. Her long veil was still covering her face. She was still waiting for Gautam to uplift her veil, but...!

Gautam was still engulfed in his own thoughts and driving, though the distance was hardly much. The sky was studded with stars at the time of his leaving the house, but now it was overcast with the clouds.

There was a flash of lightning and thundering of clouds...!

It started raining and...!

It changed in to heavy downpour. Gautam was finding driving difficult because of the inclement weather, hilly area and stones falling down at various places. At few places, he was forced to get out of the car to remove the stones, to make way for the drive. This distance, which he used to cover in few minutes, now, he was not able to cover it even in three hours.

Char... Char... Char! If Gautam had not applied the brakes, the car would have definitely collided with a big boulder. The car came to a halt with a sudden jerk. Newly wed, who was sitting in the car, with her eyes shut because of feeling tired, suddenly opened her eyes.

On the way, there was a very big stone fallen on the road and it was difficult to remove it from the road even with the help of many people. There was no way out. Storm was at full swing. The bride was feeling scared because of frequent lightning and thundering of the clouds. But she was keeping quiet because she was feeling shy.

Gautam could not think of any other way and thought of returning home. He was thinking of reversing the car, when, suddenly he heard a loud noise behind the car. He looked outside the car. A big boulder like a hillock had fallen behind the car blocking his way.

Gautam came out of the car and with the help of his torch took in to account the whole situation. In front of the car were stones, whereas at the back was a boulder. It was next to impossible to remove any of the two. He had no woollens or blankets and it was not easy to spend the whole night sitting in the car.

Though the bride was still covered with the veil, but she was aware of the whole situation.

"I will go and find out some suitable place to spend the night. It is impossible to spend the whole night here in this cold weather. Don't get frightened...! There is nothing to fear," he said while locking all the four doors.

Though she was scared, but still the bride acknowledged this by nodding her head. She could do nothing as even her veil was not uplifted as yet.

Gautam started climbing the hill, holding the torch in one hand. He saw a hut at some distance in the sudden flash of lightning. He quickly went towards that. Track was very bumpy because of the stones. Not worrying about the track, he reached there taking long steps.

On reaching near the hut, he tried to listen if there was any movement in the hut. He heard somebody coughing. He knocked at the door.

After some time, an old man opened the door. He was holding a lamp in one hand. His face was like a man from Rajasthan, sunken eyes, long nose and big moustaches, unkempt hair. It was a strange looking face. Gautam kept on looking at him with bewildered eyes. Finally, the old man broke the silence.

"Who are you…? And so late at night… at this time… What do you want…?" He asked so many questions in one go. He then looked at Gautam with questioning eyes. So far, he had not seen Gautam's face. He lifted the lamp a little, and the light of the lamp fell on Gautam's face.

The old man was baffled to see his face. "You… You. .! After so many years...! and that, too, at such time of the night?" He was watching him very attentively. Gautam could not understand the words spoken in a low voice by that old man and said, "*Baba,* I was travelling in a car when suddenly the road was blocked from front as well as from behind by stones falling on the road. If you are in a position to provide us with some shelter for the night, I will be very grateful… my wife is also accompanying me who is at the moment, sitting in the car by the road side."

The old man was astonished to hear this and mumbled, "So, finally you did get married… This had to happen…. Oh yes, it had to happen. I knew it… Well. Now, I will have to make some arrangement for you." Though he was talking to Gautam, but looking far away at a distance.

"I do not understand you," he told that old man, feeling surprised and confused.

"Well... ! Forget it. I do not have an ample space in my hut which can accommodate both of you. "And then remembering said, "Oh... yes, a little distance from here, at the back, there is a ruined palace. Nothing is intact there except for a room.

Time has ruined everything. I was waiting for that room also to fall apart. In the meanwhile, you came. Perhaps my duty will be over by now. It may be over for ever."

His non-sense was beyond Gautam's comprehension. He was astounded to hear the old man talking as such. Gautam was astonished to hear the incomplete sentences of the old man. But he was urgently trying to get a room ignoring everything what the old man was uttering.

"*Baba*, show me the room. Perhaps it may serve our purpose tonight."

"It will serve your purpose for today...!" Saying this, he went inside his hut. When he came out of his hut, he was holding a bunch of keys in his hand.

"Let's go," he said in a strange voice. "It has been locked for the last so many years."

He was going ahead. There were so many turns on the way but it looked as if he was familiar with these tracks. After walking for some time, they reached near a big heap of stones and a room was there amongst the stones. An old lock was dangling on the door. The door was covered with mud at various places and wild grass was growing there.

The old man went forward and cleared the grass from the lock. He fitted the key in the lock and the lock opened without any difficulty. Gautam was under the impression that there will be some problem in opening the lock as it was locked for so many years. But... It just opened without any difficulty.

The room presented a strange look. Everything was at its proper place. Room was spick and span. It gave the look as if someone has cleaned the room just now. There was a four poster bed in the centre of the room.

Gautam was at a loss to see this, though a fierce storm was blowing outside, but it had no effect on the inside of the room.

It gave an impression as if the fierce blowing wind was feeling scared to enter the room.

Gautam quickly looked around the room.

"*Baba,* you were saying that nobody has opened this room for the last so many years. But looking at the furniture and cleanliness it doesn't give...!"

The old man said ignoring his question, "Sir! Did you like the room?"

"Yes it is okay!" Gautam again repeated his question, "you were saying that nobody had opened this room for quite some time. Long time has elapsed since it was opened...but, everything... Who had been living in this room?"

"Now, what will you gain by finding out this." Without waiting for Gautam's reply, he continued saying, "A princess, as beautiful as fairy used to live here. She was no less than a rose flower... Come, let me show you her portrait." While walking, suddenly he stopped near a picture.

A portrait was hanging on the wall in a golden frame. "This picture is very beautiful." Words came out of Gautam's mouth suddenly.

"She was no less than it. I don't know, why she was punished and for what sin in life?"

"Why, what happened to her...?" Gautam looked at the old man enquiringly.

"You can ask as to what did not happen to her...? She was put in a prison by the king... She was in love with an ordinary boy. She was adamant that she will get married only to that boy. There was no dearth of alliances for her. She was beautiful, young. Has it ever happened that there will be a relationship between king and a common man?"

Gautam was completely absorbed in old man's story. He asked, "How it happened?"

"It was the destiny... *babu,* destiny. No one could avoid it. The princess was very fond of horse riding. One day as she was riding, the horse went out of control, kept on galloping... galloping. One young boy, not worried about his life, caught hold of the reins of the horse.

The princess looked up and kept on staring at the young man who had saved her from death.

That young man was not an ordinary looking boy. He was no less than a prince in appearance... How I am talking of old remembrances? Old remembrances impart nothing else, but sorrows." saying this, he looked away from Gautam.

"Say, what happened later?" This story gave the impression that the story engulfed him in a magic. On his insistence, the old man said, "What could have happened *babu*! The whole night, the soldiers of the king continued searching for the princess and the princess and the boy, both were sitting around a fire, in a cave immersed in each other. In the morning, that young man brought her back to her palace along with her horse." The old man kept on looking far away while moving his hand in his hair and continued saying, "after this incident, the princess started riding to the jungle and will meet that young man. The security man who used to go with her, kept his mouth shut as he received enough money for keeping it a secret. One day that particular horse rider was replaced by another rider as the old one fell ill. He understood everything. The king was made aware of it. The princess was put under strict vigilance.

It was a rumour that the young man was banished from the kingdom. When the princess tried to meet that young man, she was imprisoned by the king... This is the same room where she was imprisoned and the key of this lock was always held by the king. No one was allowed to meet or talk to the princess. Her meals and the necessities were given to her from a small window. This continued for quite some time.

The queen tried to make the princess understand for quite some time, but she did not agree. The frenzy of youth is no less than a storm... And one stormy night when the lock of this room was opened, the princess was nowhere to be found. Everyone was surprised as to how could the princess vanish from a locked room?

She was searched in every nook and corner, but she could not be traced anywhere." Old man's eyes were watering and his voice was choking. "Since that time, this room is kept locked like this ever.

On queen's insistence, the King made an announcement that whosoever finds the youngman will be rewarded one lakh gold coins. The queen had this feeling that the princess will re-emerg at the young man's entry in this room.

That young man could not be traced. How could he be traced? The greedy minister's soldiers had thrown him in the river and did not inform the king. After so many days, when the minister informed the king about it, king felt very happy to realise that the obstacle of his way has been removed forever. The king rewarded the minister.

"The king was very cruel. Was any clue of the princess found?" Gautam interrupted him.

"No! How could that fairy be traced, I wish...! We have lost the track of the time in this gossip. Now go, and bring your wife. In the meantime, I will light up the lamp."

When Gautam, still absorbed in this story, reached near his car, he saw that his wife was sleeping while waiting for him. He awoke his wife and took her inside the room.

The room was lit but, *Baba* had left.

He realised that his wife was shivering because of cold. He said, while touching her hands, "*Arrey*, your hands are numb. Okay! You quickly get into the bed." There were soft blankets on the bed. His wife got under the blanket. When he came near the bed, he saw that his wife was already asleep. He did not like to disturb her.

Perhaps it was the last quarter of the night. He was surprised to hear some girl crying. He at once got up and looked everywhere with the help of torch. Nobody was there.

"Then, from where this sound came," he thought.

He got the impression that either it is his imagination or some dream. And again got in to the bed.

After a little while, when he again heard somebody crying, he immediately got up. He tried to listen to that voice attentively. The voice was coming from under the bed. He tried to see with the help of the torch light under the bed while still sitting on the bed. But, no body was there.

'Perhaps there is some room under the bed...' With this idea in his head, he jumped from the bed.

It was not an easy thing to lift the bed. But the moment he extended his hand to uplift the bed, it automatically went up!

Gautam was watching everything with awe. There was a small piece of carpet of different colour under the bed. He quickly removed that piece from there. He found a wooden door with stairs going down.

Voice was coming from that side.

He started descending the stairs slowly. In front there was a turning. The moment he wanted to turn, he saw that there was a half opened door and a girl was sitting there with her back towards the door. He stopped there. The light coming from the room was dazzling his eyes. The doors of the cupboard got automatically opened at the pointing of her fingers. When the girl extended her hand, a beautiful dress came into her hand. Then, again she pointed her fingers and a towel got into her hand, and now...

Gautam was considering it, not less than a magic play.

The girl went to the next room taking everything with her and the door automatically closed. So far, he was not able to see the girl's face. He entered the girl's room treading softly.

He could hear the noise of a shower from the next room. The voice of the girl singing softly, was coming from the room.

He looked around the room. The walls were studded with precious stones. There was no lamp in the room. The room was shining because of the glare of the precious stones. Suddenly, he saw a locker at the corner of a wall. There was no place from where a key could be inserted. He tried his utmost to open the locker. Despite his best effort, he could not open the locker. Later on, he thought of applying the second method. When he pointed his finger towards the locker, the door of the locker automatically opened.

On opening the door, his eyes were dazzled. Inside there was a heap of diamonds and the jewellery. He took out the diamonds in his hand one by one. In one of the drawer, there was the most valuable necklace of diamonds. He was astonished to see the necklace. The princess was wearing the same necklace in the photograph. The necklace was studded with diamonds and jades and what not.

'How beautiful it was looking around the long neck of the princess! He started thinking about the photograph of the princess.'

'Does this necklace belong to the princess?' He was engossed in such thoughts when suddenly the necklace slipped from his hand and fell down on the ground. It created a loud sound.

Gautam felt as if somebody was doing some movement there. He reached there quickly. The noise of water falling, had stopped. He put his hand on the door and the door opened at once.

Room was vacant. There were drops of water on the floor. At one side towel and the clothes of the girl were scattered. It gave the impression that the occupant did not have enough time to pick up the clothes.

There was no door in the wall. Bathing tub was full of water.

"Where has the girl disappeared?" Feeling disappointed, he came back near the locker. Just to make sure, that the necklace of the photograph and the necklace of the locker were identical, he picked up the necklace from the floor and returned to his room by way of staircase. When he entered his room, the bed which was hanging in the air returned to its place.

He straight away went to the photograph. There was no difference between this necklace and the other necklace which was worn by the princess.

There was one question which was wandering in his mind as to who that girl was? He thought of going to that old man in order to solve this mystery.

He quickly changed his clothes and opening the door slowly, went out.

The storm was still blowing furiously.

He reached the old man's hut, holding the necklace in his hand. The door was closed. He called him many times, but did not find any response. Getting irritated, he pushed the door. The door fell to one side at the slight push. The hut was empty.

"Where can the old man go at this time?" He thought in his mind.

He kept on waiting for a long time, sitting on a broken wooden cot.

On hearing the noise of shepherds, he opened his eyes. He was not aware, at what time he went to sleep while sitting inside the hut. *Baba* had still not come.

He came out of the hut. The storm had stopped and the sky was clear. He enquired from the shepherds about the *baba,* an old man replied, "*Babu,* this hut is empty for the last so many years and no body stays here. Perhaps you have been mistaken."

"What are you saying? I myself talked to him yesterday night. He opened a room in the palace for me to spend the night and you say it is my delusion." Hearing his loud voice, the farmers working in nearby farms gathered there.

He narrated the whole story to all of them. The headman of the village was also present there. He also agreed with that old man's story. Hearing this, Gautam was mentally disturbed.

"You all come with me. I will show you the room where I spent the night...! Oh yes! my wife is still sleeping there." He left for the palace along with them.

On the way, his foot hit something. He saw that it was his briefcase.

"How it is here? I had left it in the room." He tried to remember, murmuring something.

He put the necklace in the pocket of the briefcase. And as soon as he looked in front, there was no palace. All over the place, there were ruins. He stood there for some time feeling bewildered and upset. He could not believe his eyes.

"Where has that room disappeared? My wife was in that room... and I have left her on that big bed and..." There was a strange pathos in his voice. People were watching him with suspicion as if....! He understood their feelings and said, "And now you all will say that I have no car either. And no stone fell on the road, no boulder fell down on the road... Come with me... and see with your own eyes...!"

His car was parked there in the same condition as he had left.

"Now you can believe, what I have been telling you... Ha... Ha..." His laughter was strange and wild, too.

But he suddenly stopped laughing. He was looking in front and back of the car. There were no big stones and the boulder on the road.

"*Babu,* nothing has fallen on the road. When I came in the morning, the road was clear. Of course, your car was parked here."

He was laughing loudly. He was behaving like a mad man.

"Oh yes! I have become mad." And he ran away towards the boulders. He kept on searching and calling for his wife. but all in vain. The whole day, he was sitting between the heap of stones. Now, the day had gradually turned in to evening.

When Gautam did not reach the house till afternoon, his relatives rang up the *dak bungalow* and learnt that he did not reach there.

They all started in search of him. They saw his car on the way. A man standing close by told them, "A young mad man is searching for his wife among those boulders." And he repeated the same story which Gautam had told him.

The relatives brought Gautam back home who was sitting in between the stones.

Next day at far off place in the jungle, police found out his wife's dead body. There were no marks of any injury on the body.

He got over his sorrow with the passage of time. His condition improved. In order to get over his sorrow, he kept himself busy most of the time.

* * * *

A few years passed.

Who is not fond of grand children? His relatives were forcing him to get married again, but he did not agree.

But one day, he was forced to agree to his parents' wishes.

"Whatever you say... I accept everything."

"But son, you select the girl."

"No, I will accept any girl, you choose."

The girl was selected. All preparations of marriage were in full swing. The near and far off relations reached home and there was lots of hustle and bustle in the house.

Father of the girl, Rai Bahadur had a big mansion. All the arrangements were made there. The marriage party was made to stay there only.

Rai Bahadur wanted to send his *Dewan,* outside on some business purpose. But the *Dewan* gave Rai Bahadur a suggestion- "*Rai Saheb,* it is a very important work. It will be proper if you go yourself."

Okay! *Dewan Saheb.* If you feel that I should go, then I will go myself. I will return tomorrow by air. Please look after all the arrangements of marriage properly. There should be no mismanagement."

"*Rai Saheb,* go with an easy mind. All the arrangements will be done properly."

"Oh yes! I need not worry when you are at the helm of the affairs." Rai Bahadur said by resting his head on the chair.

During next two days, there was such a fierce storm that all the flights were cancelled for two days. Telegrams and telephones went out of order.

The day of marriage approached but *Rai Bahadur* could not return. All of Gautam's relatives were upset that the time was approaching and...!

On realising their tension, *Dewan saheb* consoled them and said, "Why are you worried. Poonam is just like a daughter to me as she is *Rai Saheb's* daughter. If *Rai Saheb* is not able to reach here on time, I will perform all the ceremonies. You continue all the preparations."

Dewan saheb was extremely happy at the time of marriage and gave the impression as if Poonam was his real daughter.

As the seventh round of *saptsadi* was over a strange thing happened.

A necklace from the neck of the bride, fell down on the ground. Gautam was about to pick up the necklace, but suddenly he stopped.

"From where has this necklace come to you?" He was reminded of the princess's necklace and quickly he picked up the necklace and left for the room where he had kept his briefcase.

He took out all the things from his briefcase. The same necklace was shining there amongst the stuff taken out from the briefcase.

All the guests were astonished on Gautam's suddenly leaving the marriage place. Gautam's mother also followed him.

Dewan saheb, understanding the gravity of the situation said, "Please all of you go and sit at your chairs. I will go and bring back Gautam."

He went to see Gautam along with Poonam. Gautam was holding both the necklaces in his hand. He would look at that necklace which he had found in the room of the palace and other one which had fallen from Poonam's neck.

Looking at Poonam, he said, "From where did you get this necklace? This necklace belonged to that princess. Well! You don't know about it."

Poonam was quiet. She had no answer to Gautam's question.

"Okay! Say something... Why are you not replying?"

"I will tell you from where this necklace has come," said *Dewan sahib.*

Gautam looked upward and retraced one step feeling astonished. In front of him, the same old man who had opened the door of the palace for him, was standing. Same face, big eyes, big moustaches but today he was wearing very expensive clothes and his face was showing authority, but that night, his old torn clothes...

"You are here...?" Gautam asked him in a surprised tone. Gautam's mother who was standing nearby said, "Son, please talk to him with respect. He is *Dewan saheb.* And when Rai

Bahadur did not turn up then, he only performed all the ceremonies."

"Mother, you are not aware of him, I will explain to you."

When *Dewan saheb* realised that situation was getting out of control, he requested Gautam's mother to leave them alone as he wanted to talk to Gautam separately. He asked Poonam to stay there. When Gautam's mother left the room, he closed the room from inside.

"Okay! You ask me what you want to know? But before that you will have to listen to one story." Saying this, *Dewan saheb*, moved forward, uplifted the veil, from Poonam's face in one go.

Gautam got such a shock that he was about to fall. He sat down in a nearby chair at once. He could only utter, "Princess..."

"Oh Yes! Princess. She is the same princess. That day when you had come to the hut, I immediately recognised you, but you had forgotten me. "

"How could I forget you? How could I remember you?" Gautam said interrupting *Dewan saheb.*

"You are the same young man with whom princess was in love. In that life you both could not meet, but for the last so many lives I have been an instrument in getting you both united. See the irony of the situation, that, every time *Rai Saheb* had been her father and I have been his *Dewan*. Had he seen you, he must have recognised you. At the time of engagement ceremony also, you could not come and I showed him someone else's photograph. Even now I sent him away on the pretext of business since I was aware that the weather will be inclement for the next two-three days and it will be impossible for him to return." He said looking at horizon from the window.

Gautam was now looking at Poonam. Gradually, they were regaining their past life. She ran to him and was engulfed in his arms.

Dewan saheb continued saying, "I had no idea that you had taken the necklace from the locker of the princess that day. I tried to search the necklace everywhere but could not find it.

With great difficulty I was able to get the same type of necklace made, so that there was no difference between the original and the copied one. I was scared that if Padmavati found out that the original necklace has been misplaced then...It was Padmavati's great desire that she should get her daughter married while she was alive. When the princess was not traceable, she lost her will to live. One day when her health was really in bad condition, she called her brother and said, 'Brother, I have a few days left of my life. It was my earnest desire that I should solemnise my daughter's wedding myself. But, perhaps I was not destined to do so. If ever you come across the princess, please give this necklace to her, a present from my side.' After saying this, she removed the necklace from her neck and handed it over to her brother."

Gautam asked, "Who was her brother?"

"Who else he can be...? I am the brother of that poor lady, the one, who could not fulfil even her last wish. I looked for the princess everywhere but could not find her and with that sorrow of not finding the princess, *Rani Padmavati* left this world forever.

I have been an instrument in getting you both together in every life. But I could not meet Padmavati even once. I wish, I could find her, and her soul would have lived in peace seeing you both together. But it was not to be so in her fate...! Her soul must be meandering somewhere." *Dewan saheb* while wiping his eyes said in a sad voice "Do you know that day, what had happened to your wife? That night...!" But both Gautam and Poonam were engrossed in each other's thoughts as if they were recollecting the past remembrances. They were not listening to what *Dewan saheb* was saying.

After a gap of so many years...!

Gautam lying on a four-poster bed narrated this story to the lady who was sitting next to him and said, "Do you know Poonam... Remember. This is the story of both of us for so many lives. We have been meeting for many lives.

You had lost your memory in a car accident a few days back and I have lost my body. Now I have only few moments of my life, left. I will not be able to die peacefully till the time you recollect your past life and assure me that you will again meet me in our next life. How can we meet unless you recollect your past life before I take my last breath? Oh! I am going through so much of pain princess . . . Poonam, try to recollect."

It appeared as if Gautam was talking from a far of distance.

Poonam, sitting nearby, started crying bitterly. She was finding it difficult to control herself.

"Stop it Gautam... stop it. I remember every word. But looking at your serious condition, I had some apprehension that if I show that I remember everything, you may not leave me forever... Please don't go leaving me alone," and she once again continued crying bitterly.

"You little fool. If we have to meet again in our next life, then, why cry?"

"No Gautam, no. I will not be in a position to tolerate such a long separation...! The life after your leaving this world and till my death, again rebirth after death, from infancy to young age and from young age to the time till we meet again, such a long journey, I can't bear. Tell me how will I be in a position to get over such a long span of life?"

She kept on weeping holding Gautam in her arms. Her tears were falling on his face.

When she recovered a little, she wiped her tears from his face. There was a slight smile on Gautam's face, and two big tears were simmering at the corner of his eyes as if they were in honour of their union in the next life.

Poonam called Gautam, but the cruel hands of death had snatched him, closing his lips forever.

The old *Dewan* was standing near the door. Tears were flowing from his eyes.

He was feeling morose that they both were not aware of the fact that it was their 7th and the last union.

25

A Crazy Heart

When in the evening, Dr Sharma returned home, Seema was not at home. The house was open, so, he realised that she must be somewhere close by.

When after a while Seema returned, he asked her, "Where have you been?" She replied that she had gone to visit new neighbours who have occupied the opposite house as new tenants. "Both husband and wife are very nice. They got married two years back."

Before she could say anything else, he interrupted her laughingly, "But you had been saying, it is nice that the house at the front is not occupied for the last one year and should remain unoccupied. If it is occupied, then there will be no privacy left and now..."

"You have one track mind. It is correct that I had said something to that effect, but what is the harm if some decent neighbours occupy that house?" And remembering something, she said, "You made me forgot to tell you that I have called them for a cup of tea in the evening. You have a wash and get ready. They will be here any moment."

Dr Sharma said teasing her, "Now that, the new neighbours have come, you don't think my face is clean." Seema understood that he was in a mood to tease her.

"Okay! As you like." saying this, she went to the kitchen.

"*Arei* Seema, how forgetful you are!" he said. "What have I forgotten," she said from the kitchen.

"You have not mentioned me neighbour's name," he shouted from the living room.

"Can't you speak a little softly? They can hear everything from the living room. Yes! Their name is Mr and Mrs Mathur," she replied a little annoyed. Dr Sharma realised that if he utters something more, Seema will definitely loose her temper. He got up from there. He had a wash, combed his hair and returned to the living room. Seema was busy in the kitchen preparing eatables. Dr Sharma had nothing much to do, he lighted a cigar and started smoking.

After a while, Mr and Mrs Mathur arrived there. Seema had already met them. They were introduced to Dr Sharma. Dr Sharma said at once," Mr Mathur, if you had not come here now this moment, I would have gone to your place and..." Hearing this, Both Mr and Mrs Mathur started laughing heartily. Mr Mathur said, "Then what...?"

"In that case, the tea which you are having here, Mrs Mathur had to offer us there," and everyone started laughing.

One day while gossiping, they learnt that Dr Sharma was none other than a famous story writer, 'Kewal Sharma.' They both were very fond of his stories from the very beginning. Now, whenever they came across Dr Sharma, they would start discussing his stories. They would ask him about from where he got material for the stories and if he could add some extra scene, it could have been a better story. Like this, they became very close to a great extent and also became free with one another.

"Dr Sharma, Please do write some story on us."

"I will definitely write, but before that I will have to find some masala."

"Why you need a plot, just write some fiction?"

"No, it is not like that. For writing a story, one has to have some facts," said Dr Sharma.

In the meantime, Mrs Sharma entered and enquired, "What has been going on here with them?"

"It was something special, but..."

"Okay, do let me know, what was going on," she asked.

On this, Mrs Mathur said, "We have requested Dr Sharma to write a story on us, but he is harping on for some '*masala*' (idea)."

"Are you going to write on some bird, that you require some *masala* (spices)," said Mrs Sharma.

At this, all of them were amused and she said, "We have been married for the last seven years. I have been telling him time and again that you have been filling the papers by writing so many stories. Can you not write a single story on me? But every time he postpones. You may try getting him write a story perhaps you may be better off."

"The problem is of a theme. Let us join together and try to help him find out some theme," Mrs Mathur said smiling. Once more everybody had a hearty laugh.

"Please tell us, how you started writing stories? Earlier it may have been your hobby, and after that your hobby....", Mr Mathur said.

"Don't talk of his hobbies. His hobbies cover the length from Kashmir to Kanya Kumari." She said innocently.

Mathur said, "His hobbies may not be hobbies, but GT Road." Then everyone again smiled.

"Yes, it is something like this, that instead of one, I have many hobbies. Like going for hunting in Kashmir Valley to catching trouts and trying to catch fish in Beas river in Punjab and hunting patridges in Haryana..." Mathur interrupted Dr Sharma in between, "Yes, we have understood. You will take us to Kanya Kumari while hunting and there you will catch fish in the ocean." Again they all started grinning.

Mr Mathur went to Delhi for few days, on some tour. Saroj (Mrs Mathur) had just returned from the market when the phone rang.

She picked up the phone and said, "Mrs Mathur speaking." On the other side of the phone, Mathur said, "listen Saroj, I will be delayed for some time more...!"

"But we have to attend the marriage at Vermaji's house tomorrow. I recollect. That is why I rang you up. You attend the marriage alone and say sorry on my behalf."

"I can go alone but the route is very isolated and the distance..."

Do one thing, ask Sharma, he will be able to arrange something. Okay! Bye... bye and the phone got disconnected. She also put the receiver on the craddle.

Saroj went to Sharma's place. Dr Sharma opened the door. "Please come in Mrs Mathur. Come and sit."

"Actually thing is this, Just now...," she said while standing there.

"Surprise, what is the problem which you don't want to narrate while sitting," Dr Sharma said smilingly. She explained her problem to Dr Sharma and said, "I will take Mrs Sharma along, tomorrow."

"But she has left for Jallandhar today only."

"I am very surprised, she left without meeting me," said Saroj.

"No, it is not like that. Before leaving, she wanted to meet you, but you were away to the market and my brother-in-law is getting engaged tomorrow. His telegram was received today in your absence and Seema had to leave at once."

"Then you will have to accompany me," said Saroj.

"Okay! If I have your permission, can I offer you a cup of coffee now and I too can have," he said grinning.

"Where is the coffee?" asked Saroj.

"Water is on the gas. It must have boiled by now..."

"I have to purchase some present for Mr Verma. Why not, we have coffee there only?"

"But... water has boiled. Why not...?"

"What difference does it make? You get ready and in the meantime, I will go home and lock up the house, saying this, she left.

Reaching home, she took out a beautiful *sari* and *blouse* and put it on, then after combing her hair, she put a spray on her.

When Dr Sharma came out of his house, she was already there. He took out the keys from his pocket to start the scooter.

"Leave it. We will go in car. Do you have intention of freezing?" She started the car and he sat next to her.

Dim light of music panel was falling at Saroj. Dr Sharma saw that Saroj was looking very fascinating in that *sari* and the light smell of the perfume was pervading in the car.

"What are you thinking about...?" Hearing this, Dr Sharma was surprised and said, "Nothing, it was just...!"

Dr Sharma saw that a sweet smile adorned her face and lines of *'kajal'* were emerging out of the corner of her eyes. He asked changing the subject, "Why do you always use *'kajal* in your eyes'?"

"It is because nobody should cast an evil eye on me," she said grinning. Dr Sharma also laughed.

"But I am very confident that I have no danger from you...I am quite safe!"

"How beautiful your big eyes are...?" he was rehearsing that again and again in his mind.

Before, something more could be said, they reached the crossing of Canal Road. She got busy in maneuvering the car from a congested road and after a few moments, they reached Raghunath *Bazar*.

"First, let us go and buy a present, otherwise, the shops will close. After that, we will go to some good restaurant and have hot coffee," she said.

Both of them purchased a nice *sari* from 'Mona Lisa'.

"This blue *sari* will suit you," Said Dr Sharma pointing towards a *sari*.

"How can you say so....?" she enquired.

"Your fair complexion, this blue sari and on top of that, design of flowers...! Once upon a time, I was very fond of playing with colours."

"Surprisingly, you never mentioned earlier about you doing painting. I also used to scratch a few lines on the canvass myself during my college days," said Mrs Mathur.

"Then, why did you leave this hobby of yours. A person can spend whole life with colours."

"Sometimes, these colours can make life colourless. Mr Mathur was not interested in paintings. So, I stopped it."

During this period, the shopkeeper asked, "May I pack some other *sari*, Sir!"

"No, I had to purchase only one *sari*," she said.

Both of them came out of the shop. Saroj started the car and after a few moments, she parked the car in front of 'Cosmo Hotel'. Both of them entered the hotel and sat in a corner. In the meantime, waiter came.

"What would you have with coffee? It is late in the evening. I think, we can have dinner here," he said.

"No, I will only have coffee here. If I have to have something to eat, first I will have coffee and later on, I will have mutton chops and cutlets with *naan* at *dhaba*. I like it very much," said Saroj.

"Okay, then." Dr Sharma lighted his cigar and started smoking. After some time, coffee was served. Both of them started sipping coffee slowly.

In the meantime, there was an announcement, "Ladies and Gentlemen, you will be pleased to know that there will be a ballroom dance competition, day after tomorrow night. You all are invited. Thank you."

"You had so many hobbies. Was dancing one of your hobby?" asked Saroj.

"Oh yes! I do it sometimes *Kabhi kabhi paon patak leta hoon* I try to throw my steps here and there." Saroj could not help smiling on the word *'patakna'*. "So let us do the practice of 'Patakna' day after tomorrow." Both laughed.

After having coffee, they had chops, cutlets and *naan*. It was a little spicy. Dr Sharma took out a packet from his pocket and offered Saroj, "Oh! Here is a sweet dish for you."

Saroj putting her hand forward and breaking a big piece, said, "You do not know, chocolate is my favourite. Specially, whenever I undertake some journey, I will take four-five packets of chocolate with me."

"But I have never seen you eating chocolate during the span of two years."

"It is because Mr Mathur is not fond of chocolates." She said.

Suddenly, it started raining heavily. Both ran towards the car. Car was at a distance. They were fully drenched before they could reach the car.

Saroj started the car and they left. It was raining so heavily that despite using wipers, Saroj was finding it difficult to drive the car. The road at front was not visible. Once or twice, they avoided accident.

They had to stop the car when they reached the 'Canal Road'. There was a traffic *jam* ahead. They were finding it difficult to get down from the car and see what was wrong with the traffic?

"Looks like, you are feeling cold. Come! I will drive the car. You come and sit in my seat." They both exchanged their seats without coming out of the car. Dr Sharma removed his coat and put it on Saroj's shoulders and started saying, "Put it on. You are feeling very cold."

"Thank you" Saroj could utter only those words. She was really feeling very cold. She was feeling comfortable after wearing the coat.

Dr Sharma was driving slowly. Now, they both were talking. While talking, sometime, Saroj would come so close that it was difficult for Dr Sharma to drive. Sometimes, she would put her hand on his shoulder.

They reached their house. Dr Sharma parked the car and keeping the packet in her room, he said, "Okay! I will take your leave."

"Sit for some time," Saroj said. She was feeling very happy. After chatting for sometime, he said, "I have to submit some important papers tomorrow. Now, I will go and put them in order. Okay! Good Night!"

Next day, Saroj went to Mr Verma's house with Dr Sharma. On the way, she told Dr Sharma that Mrs Verma was her college friend.

"Mrs Mathur, you never disclosed as to who is getting married?"

"Oh! I am sorry! I forgot to tell you that Mr Verma's sister is getting married."

Reaching there, she introduced Dr Sharma to everybody and said that "Because of him, I could come to this marriage. If he had not escorted me, then..."

"*Arrey*! Who will not like to escort a beautiful lady like you?" Mrs Verma said, pinching Saroj.

Saroj blushed. "What nonsense are you uttering? So, finally you have come back to your real self. At least, have some control on your tongue.

It is her old habit to talk nonsense. She doesn't feel... unless she blurts some nonsense."

"I hope you have not minded? Dr Sharma" Mrs Verma asked.

"No, there is nothing to mind. I appreciate, the appreciation coming from a smart lady like you", he said, without any hesitation.

On hearing this, people standing close by laughed heartily.

After the marriage function was over, Saroj and Dr Sharma took leave from them and came out of the bungalow.

'Now, let's have a cup of coffee each.' Both of them said simultaneously and grinned.

One day as car was giving a little starting trouble, so, both decided to go on the scooter. It was late at night and was very cold. Dr Sharma started his scooter.

Saroj tied a scarf on her hair to save herself from the breeze and sat on the scooter's back seat. She took shelter of Dr Sharma's back, just to avoid cold flush of wind. Route was very bumpy and she was experiencing lot of uncomfort.

She was feeling scared of falling down because of unsteady drive, and she was holding the seat tightly. Once she got a big jolt and to avoid falling down, she put both her arms around Dr Sharma's waist.

"It is long since I have travelled by scooter. Either you take me in a taxi, or, ..." she said.

"Okay, You can sit whichever way you feel convenient."

As the distance was getting over, Saroj's arms around his waist tightened. Now, she was pressed very close to Dr Sharma's back.

Saroj continued saying, "Sometimes, I really like to roam around like this at night!"

"Okay! Then let's go for an outing near the bank of river!"

"No, it is very cold today. Let it be some other time." She said smilingly," though doctor and medicines are free, but health is my own."

On reaching home and opening the door, "We will make coffee here only." Saroj went inside and prepared the coffee and both of them had it together.

"Alright, now you go and sleep. It is already very late." Dr said.

"Don't you like my sitting here? You are saying time and again.... !"

"No, you are taking me all wrong. I was meaning that it is already very late and you also must be very tired."

After some time, she got up and left for her house.

Next day, when Dr Sharma returned from his work, he saw Saroj was already waiting for him.

"Have you forgotten that there is a dance competition in Hotel Cosmo," she reminded him.

Dr Sharma feigning ignorance said, "I totally forgot about it."

"Take this, I have brought a present for you", he said.

While opening the packet, Saroj asked, "I hope you are not doing any drama." Then, looking at the *sari* in the packet, she said, "Oh! This is the same *sari.* What was need for this?"

Now, Dr Sharma was wondering, why he has presented the *sari* to her, and what was their relation?

Looking downward, she asked Dr Sharma, "If Mr Mathur enquires from where I have purchased this *sari,* what reply can I give?"

On hearing this, he was perplexed and did not know what to say. "You think about it. Go, and get ready fast." Saroj left for her house to get ready and Dr Sharma went to his house.

On reaching his home, he lighted a cigar and was in deep thought. What relation I have with Saroj that I gave her...! At last, he shook his head and got busy in getting ready.

Saroj reached Dr Sharma's house after getting ready.

Dr Sharma said appreciating, "You are looking very pretty in this *sari...*"

"Thank you!" she said. "You are also looking no less in this blue suit."

He said laughingly, "I was thinking how to new pinch you?"

"Whatever the way, you may like," replied Saroj merrily.

"Well, let us forget it for now! At some other time?" said Dr Sharma.

Both of them entered Hotel Cosmo and sat on the chairs. There was a lot of crowd and dance had just begun.

In the meantime, the announcer taking the mike, announced, "Now, I will request Mrs and Dr Sharma to come to the dancing floor and give company to all."

They both got a shock on hearing this. Dr Sharma told Saroj, "I am sorry, perhaps there is someone known to me, but he doesn't know you...! I am very sorry."

At this, Saroj blushed and looking downward said, "It doesn't make any difference."

"By this time, the announcer reached them after making a way from the crowd..." Sharma, looking puzzled, said, "*Arrey*

Gandhi, you are here. I was also astonished as to who was there, who knew me? They both hugged each other tightly.

Gandhi was facing Saroj whereas Dr Sharma's back was towards Saroj. Gandhi, being very outspoken, "*Yaar* Sharma! You got a very pretty wife. Oh yes! Mrs Sharma, I am his useless friend. I..., instead of you, embraced him."

"What nonsense, you are speaking. you must at least think before you speak? She is Mrs Mathur, and your *bhabi* is away to...!"

Disengaging himself from Sharma, he said, "Please forgive me. I have not attended his marriage, so..."

Then he said smilingly, "Well! You make a nice dance couple. You will surpass everybody. You both will bag the first prize ..." Saying this, he came and sat down in the chair next to Saroj.

"Will you allow me to say something, or keep on talking nonstop. Mrs Mathur, he is my college collegue, Gandhi. He has almost same nature as your friend Mrs Verma and.... !"

Gandhi said amusingly, "Okay! You introduce me to Mrs Verma. I will manage with her only."

Addressing Mrs Mathur, Dr Sharma said, "Now, you have seen him..."!

"If you continue talking, dance competition will be over", Gandhi said while getting up.

Dr Sharma and Saroj got up and joined the dancers. A western tune was being played on the *orchestra*. Both were dancing on this tune least worried about any body around.

"You are keeping me at a distance as if we are doing *'keeklee'* (a kind of Punjabi folk dance) instead of ball room dance." Saroj said smiling. Sharma gave a simple nod and even not wanting...?

"Now, it was the last round of dance, somebody announced on the mike. At that moment, suddenly lights of the hall were switched off. Saroj came closer to Dr Sharma. Dance was in full swing. Roughly after approximately two minutes, lights were switched on and after that dance was over.

"According to the Judges, today's best dancing couple is Mr and Mrs, Sharma", was announced.

Everyone clapped heartily. Actually, Gandhi had got their name registered as Mr and Mrs Sharma and now only, he realised his mistake.

They both got up hesitantly and received their prize. When they both were returning from the dancing floor, they were surprised to see Mrs Sharma and Mr Mathur sitting there in the hall. Dr Sharma and Saroj felt very conscious.

Before Mr Mathur could utter, "Congratulations," Gandhi came from behind and said, "Please forgive me. I was not acquainted with Mrs Mathur. I, by mistake...!"

Dr Sharma interrupting, said, "Meet my wife and Mr Mathur." Gandhi wished Mrs Sharma with folded hands and shook hands with Mr Mathur.

Sharma asked Mr Mathur, "How you both happened to be here?"

"I took a morning bus from Delhi and on the way at Jallandhar, I met Mrs Sharma at the bus stand and thus, we came together. On reaching home, we saw both of you were missing. I was about to give a ring, suddenly I saw two tickets of booking at 'Hotel Cosmo' and so, I along with Mrs. Sharma came here."

Mrs Sharma smiled at Mr Mathur's clarification.

"When we reached here, you both were going towards the dance floor and we did not feel it proper to interfere," Mr Mathur said laughing, "Today, you both have excelled in dance."

Gandhi while getting up, said, "I have to reach the hotel! I beg leave of you."

'Good night', after that all of them got up. While sitting in the car, Mr Mathur looked at Mrs Sharma and smiled.

Now, Mr Mathur was driving the car and next to him Dr Sharma was sitting in co-driver's seat. Mrs Mathur and Mrs Sharma were sitting behind in the rear seat.

Everyone was sitting quietly in the car.

On reaching home, when Mr and Mrs Mathur were about to leave for their house, when Seema offered them coffee. She said, "Please come, let's have a hot cup of coffee."

Mr Mathur replied, "Okay! Let us have." Saroj left for her room, saying she will be back in a moment. After some time when she entered, she was wearing a different *sari*.

"Saroj, why did you change your *sari*? It was suiting you very much. But when did you purchase it?" asked Mathur.

Saroj said while trying to change the subject, "I have bought it long time back, but perhaps I forgot to tell you."

During this time, Seema brought coffee and everyone took a cup in their hands.

"Mrs Sharma, you prepare very nice coffee, Mathur said, praising her.

Mrs and Mr Mathur left for their house, after the coffee was over.

One evening, Mathur came scared and out of breath and said, "Sharma, Saroj is feeling very uneasy. Please come and examine her." Sharma took his bag and left.

Mathur was following him. Mathur turned and looked at the back. Mrs Sharma was also looking at that side. Both smiled.

"Please go inside the bedroom. I will bring the thermometer." Saying this, he went to another room.

Saroj was lying unconscious on the bed and was murmuring something. Dr Sharma put his bag on the table. He was about to feel her pulse, when suddenly, she caught hold of his hand tightly and again murmured, "Kewal, I... with you...", and uttered a few words which Sharma could not comprehend. But he got perturbed on Saroj's behaviour.

Mathur was standing at some distance, holding thermometer in his hand. Sharma freed his hand from Saroj with a jerk and taking out two tablets from his bag said, "Please bring a glass of water, we will make Mrs Mathur pop up these two tablets. Then everything will be alright."

Mathur said, "Give these pills to me. I will administer the tablets. Sharma handed over the tablets to Mr Mathur and left.

Mathur threw the tablets in the dustbin, the moment Sharma left and muttered, "This is the only remedy for her."

Saroj got up and got busy in household work, the moment Sharma departed.

"Now, everything is fine!" Mathur asked Saroj and she replied in positive by nodding her head.

A few days went by.

Somebody knocked at the door. Dr Sharma opened the door. Mathur said while entering the house, "I had purchased two tickets for a movie, but I have some urgent work in the office. So, I cannot accompany her to the movie."

Mrs Sharma was sitting nearby, Mathur requested her, "Please, you may accompany her."

But, she replied immediately, "Sorry, I will not be in a position to accompany her. My son is having his papers tomorrow and I have to help him in preparation for the examination.

"Then, Sharma, you go with her. I wouldn't have bothered you if Saroj had seen this movie earlier...! And this is a very nice picture." Sharma agreed to go with Mrs Mathur at Mr Mathur's request.

They had to go on the scooter, because Mathur was taking the car.

"Do you remember that, one day you had promised to take me to the bank of the river for an outing. Why don't we go for that outing today?" she said.

"But Mathur has sent me to go with you for a movie, and..."

On repeated request, Sharma took Saroj to the river bank. Throughout the journey, she was holding on to Sharma's waist very tightly.

Reaching near the river, Sharma parked the scooter at one side. Both went and sat at the bank. A slow and cold breeze was blowing. It was all quiet all around.

"This was just an excuse to come with you for an outing. Otherwise, I have already seen this movie. " Saroj said smiling.

"But...!"

"Let me finish, what I want to say, then you can say whatever you wish to.

It is a very old story. You were in the medical college those days, while I was a first year student in a nearby college.

You were a story writer and I was a big fan of yours. I would read all your stories. So many times, it occurred in my mind to meet you. When I got the courage to meet you, you had already left the college after finishing your studies. My desire of meeting you just remained unfullfilled."

"This is an old story. Now, Saroj you are Mrs Mathur...."

"Kewal, what is all this. All the time, you have been addressing me as Mrs Mathur. Can you never call me Saroj."

Dr Sharma realised that at the moment Saroj was getting very sentimental and there was no point getting in to argument with her.

He lighted his cigar and was lost in his own thoughts. Saroj also got lost in her olden days while reclining against his back.

"Let us leave, there is no point sitting here in cold," he said.

Saroj looked at her watch and said, "There is still time for the movie to finish. Let us go to some coffee shop and have something to eat and drink."

"And If we happen to run across Mr Mathur...?"

"He will have no free time at the moment. He will be very busy in his office work," Saroj replied.

Next to the coffee house, was a tailor's shop. Saroj got down from the scooter and entered the shop.

"This is not a coffee house..." Sharma said.

"I know it," she interrupted him.

After getting inside the shop, she said something to the tailor and he brought a light white coloured suit immediately... He looked at Sharma and said, "Sir, please come inside and have a try," and taking the suit, he went inside the trial room.

Sharma was surprised to hear the tailor master request. Saroj while allaying his amazement, said to him, "I had given this piece of cloth for your suit to the tailor master."

"But, from where did you get my measurements," Sharma enquired from her.

"The other day Mrs Sharma had asked me to bring back her *sari* and your suit from the drycleaner. I gave the measurement from that suit only."

"But, what was the necessity of it...?" Sharma said.

Saroj said, pushing him inside, "Go inside, tailor master is waiting for you. He may not put on the suit himself, if he loses his temper."

"Okay! As you wish..." he said.

After some time, master called Saroj. "Madam, you also come and see the fitting of the suit." He himself came out.

Saroj went inside and said, "It suits you very much." Then opening her purse, she took out a matching tie. Tying the tie, she said, "Now, look. How this suit matches the *sari* presented by you!"

Then Sharma realised that Saroj was wearing the same *sari*, which he had presented her.

"Well! Now, you go outside so that I may change this suit." Sharma said.

"No, keep putting on. It looks very nice on you." she said.

"In case Seema asks me, when I gave this suit for stitching, what will I say?"

"Tell her you had purchased this suit and given for stitching when she had gone to Jallandar."

Alright..., whatever you say...!

Then he said, "Let us move."

"Will you let me not new pinch you, " she said mischievously.

"Okay... Okay. You can do new pinch.... !"

"First you shut your eyes. Then I will do...!"

Sharma closed his eyes and Saroj getting closer put her lips...!

"May I come inside, Madam. Saroj was feeling irritated at him disturbing at this inappropriate moment.

Pulling and adjusting the coat from behind, master said, "The fitting is perfect. Madam, *Sahib's* suit is matching well with your *sari*." And continued saying, "Would you like to get it packed, or...!"

"No," she said at once, "he will go back wearing this suit."

"Now, you will have to leave the shop from the rear door, as it was already time for the shop to close. The front door has been closed."

They came out of the shop and went to have coffee.

"Let us hurry up and have coffee fast. It is time for the movie to be over." Sharma said.

After finishing coffee, they left for the house on the scooter. Enroute, they both were thinking, what excuses they have to make?

On reaching home, they observed Mathur and Seema in some discussion.

While looking at him, he said quickly, "Sharma did you get a prize in the picture hall?"

"I did not understand," Said Dr Sharma.

"Actually, we were early for the picture and there was sufficient time, so, I thought why not collect the suit which I had given for stitching some time back. Earlier, I did not find time to collect it."

Seema, who was sitting quiet till now, started saying, "It is suiting you very much."

And then paying attention to the tie said, "Did you buy this tie along with the suit?"

Sharma was getting scared of telling a lie every time.

Saroj said interrupting, "Of course, it was purchased alongwith it."

"I was not in a good mood. So, I thought why not have a chit chat with Mrs Sharma." said Mr Mathur.

"What happened", enquired Dr Sharma, lighting his cigar.

"Some time ago, I got a call from my GM that I have been posted to Poone. Now, you tell me. Is it not a reason to feel bad? We were here for less than three years, and now so soon they have posted...!"

Hearing this, Saroj was at the brink of crying, but with great difficulty, she controlled herself.

They had to leave for Poone within a week.

The day of departure arrived.

There was still time for the train to steam off. Seema left all three of them in the compartment to buy some magazine for herself from the book stall.

All three of them were fully engrossed in their conversation. Mathur while looking for something in his pocket, said, "My ration for the journey is about to finish. " He wanted to say about his cigarettes. He at once went to the stall to buy the cigarettes.

Now. there was nobody in the compartment except Dr Sharma and Saroj. Door of the compartment was shut.

Saroj said, "I have been here with you for the past two years. You, during this period, have been always addressing me as Mrs Mathur... Mrs Mathur. Can't you for once call me Saroj? Will you never fulfil my this wish at least for once, Kewal?"

While saying this, she had become very sentimental, and put her head on Dr Sharma's shoulder. Dr Sharma got very nervous at her action.

Cautioning her he said, "If now, either Mr Mathur or Seema come here, do you know what can be the consequence?"

Despite Dr Sharma's repeated warnings, she did not bother and kept on sitting in the same position and then said, "I care dam about the consequences. I am prepared for anything today."

Saroj's emotions were at her peak. Even Dr Sharma got scared.

"See Mrs Mathur, you are happily married to Mr Mathur and having a comfortable life. I am very happy with my wife Seema and have no dearth of anything in life. Then, what is the need for us to get involved like this? It is a sin for both of us."

"Yes, It is a sin. And a very beautiful sin and I feel like drowning myself in it," Saroj said.

Dr Sharma was in a fix. Unconsciously, his hands went towards Saroj, You could just say that, the distance between their arms was getting closer and closure...! They were in this position for a while, when suddenly they got a jolt during the shunting of the engine and... that brought them to their senses.

"You had mentioned that you are very fond of eating chocolates especially while travelling. I will just go and get some chocolates, for you," Said Dr Sharma. "In the meantime, you arrange your stuff."

Mathur and Seema were sitting on a bench of the platform. Seema was going through an article and Mathur was busy smoking a cigarette.

Mr Mathur and Seema would occasionally talk to each other. In the meantime, they saw Dr Sharma got down from the compartment fast.

"Are you going anywhere Sharma?" Mathur enquired. "I am just coming." Saying this, Sharma got lost in the crowd of the station.

Immediately after Sharma's departure, Mr Mathur said, "Mrs Sharma, let us go to Saroj. There, I will tell you something very interesting."

Both went inside and Mathur closed the door.

Saroj was busy sorting out her luggage.

And in the meantime, Sharma came back with chocolates. Dr Sharma had just opened the door a little when suddenly lights went off. He stood there waiting for the lights to come.

"Saroj, come, let us appraise Mrs Sharma of our conspiracy."

Dr Sharma also wanted to know about the conspiracy!

They were unaware of the fact that Sharma was standing at the door of the compartment and listening to their conspiracy plan.

Before Saroj could say anything, Mathur on his own started explaining everything to Mrs Sharma.

"When we learnt that Dr Sharma is the story writer, we requested him time and again that he should also write a story on us. But, every time he had been repeating the same sentence, 'I should have some *masala* to write a...!'

"Every time we would ask him, 'Did you get any idea about writing a story on us, And every time, he would say 'no' to it. One day, in order to give him some *masala*, I alongwith you also roped in Saroj. But I never disclosed it to you. In the beginning,

Saroj did not agree, but later on she agreed because of my insistence. You are not aware that Saroj had been a good actor of her times in the college."

For long, Saroj who was keeping quiet, and listening to everything, at last said, "It was not good on your part. You got me to this...!"

"But this was an act for giving Dr Sharma a plot for the story," Mathur justified.

"This is what you think", and then opened up saying, " Did I ever disclose to you that I knew Kewal Sharma from the college days? I was crazy after his stories. I had a crush on him.

On the first day when Seema introduced us to Dr Sharma, I recognised him. But I kept quiet. I kept this secret to myself.

I never wanted to relive my past feelings. But, You got me involved in your plan to make him write a story about us.

Do you know that the blue *sari* was given to me by Dr Sharma? Did I tell you that the suit which he is wearing today, I gave him?" Saroj kept on talking in a trembling voice.

All this conversation was going on in the darkness and Kewal Sharma was listening to all this.

Tears were flowing from Saroj's eyes.

At that moment, lights of the compartment switched on. Everyone looked at the door.

Kewal Sharma was standing there with his head down cast.

26

The Search

Akhtar was in the habit of going through the newspaper early in the morning. It was winter season. Akhtar peeped through the window glass. It was a little misty outside.

He witnessed a man with bent back and going at a distance with his eyes down cast. He gave the impression that perhaps he was looking for something which he had lost.

Akhtar kept on staring at him for some time and later on he got busy with his studies. Next day again, he could see the same man going through that small road. He saw that the man with bent back passing through the road, in the mist, and looking down, searching for something.

So many days went by like this. He had in his mind to go outside and enquire from that man, what he had been looking for, but every time his resolution of finding out, was changed because of exceptionally cold weather.

But this time, without worrying about the cold weather, he went out and reached that man. He was a very old man. Akhtar asked that man—

"Sir! I have been watching you for so many days, you have been passing through this small road, looking for something.

I got the impression that you have lost something very valuable and you are trying to find it."

That man with bent back, initially laughed heartily and then said, "Oh yes! My son, you have certainly guessed correctly. I am really looking for something which is very precious to me. I am trying to find that particular thing which I had lost fifty years earlier on this small road. I am searching for my youth that was lost here."

27

The Fourth Angle of a Triangle

Pawan Jamwal, Raman and Major Ashok Chatterji were very good friends. After all, their hobbies were the same. Their main hobby was Astrology. All three of them were taking an Astrology class.

Major Chatterji's mother lived in Calcutta. One day, she came to Delhi for some important work. She had to get some papers signed from him. Time was at a premium. She took a taxi from the airport and went straight to Major Chatterji's college. The principal invited her into his office and offered her a chair to sit; he, then, inquired of his peon," Do you know Major Chatterji?"

"Yes Sir! The same who is part of triangle... I mean to say ...triangle." The principal looked at him in a surprised manner and said, "I don't understand..."

The peon explained, "Sir! Major Chatterji and his friends are always together, whether it is in a class or at the market. That is why the entire class addresses them as triangle."

On hearing this, Major Chatterji's mother smiled. After this, whenever Major Chatterji's mother rang up to talk to him, she would tell the principal, "Please, call Major Chatterji of triangle on the phone."

The principal, on hearing her say the word 'triangle', would smile.

The first angle of a triangle, Pawan Jamwal, forty years old, slim and tall, always moved at fast pace and a gait like a leopard. His hair missing from the front of his head to a great extent. He was from Himachal Pradesh. He had picked up a job immediately after graduation. He always got to the bottom of whatever he was working on. He was always full of enthusiasm and looking for newer challenges. He was ready to work twenty-four hours a day.

However, he had a low opinion of the opposite sex. He would look at girls with suspicion. He would openly say that he never had any confidence in any girl. It seemed as if he had had a bad experience with a woman. Most of the time he would utter this line,"Woman, thy name is infidelity."

But he kept it a secret, the name of the girl who had deceived him.

Once there happened an interesting incident that will really amuse you. One of his friends, namely, Premnath, was in love with a girl. They were both planning to get married. They also had a live-in relationship.

One day, Pawan Jamwal started saying to his friend, "*Yaar*! You give me your friend's number and in a few days, I will prove to you that this girl is faithless. It is my bet with you."

On hearing him talk like this, Premnath started laughing and said, "Pawan, you don't know anything. We both have been staying together for the last three years. You will lose the bet. Malti is very much interested in me."

Finally, after Pawan's requesting him many times, Premnath gave him Malti's mobile number. The next day Pawan started his game. He started giving missed calls to Malti.

Finally, Malti gave Pawan a phone call after a few days and enquired, "Who are you?"

"I am very impressed by you. That is the reason I ring you up."

Malti thought, "What is the harm in giving a ring?"

That is how this chain of events started. After this, Pawan started talking to her on a daily basis. Pawan knew her name but still one day, when he found a good opportunity, he asked her, "You have still not told me your name. How should I address you?"

Initially, she was a little hesitant, but later on she told him her name.

"Do you stay all alone or...?"

What could Malti say? She could not even say that she was in a live-in relation.

She said, "I stay all alone."

"Then let us meet tomorrow at Sahara Mall." Pawan insisted so much that Malti could not refuse him. Malti thought that after all what is the harm in meeting?

Now, they started meeting quite often. Pawan had not told her anything about himself.

One day, after many days had gone by, finding the proper opportunity, Pawan described all the facts to his friend Prem. But Prem did not believe him.

The next day, Pawan purchased a ladies' suit and showing it to Prem, said, "Prem, I am going to gift it to Malti tomorrow."

Hearing this, Prem smiled. He had full confidence that Malti was not that type of girl. She would never accept a gift. But he definitely felt bad that so much water had flown under the bridge and even then, Malti had not confided in him.

The next day, Pawan gifted the suit to Malti and Malti accepted the suit cheerfully. But on reaching home, she hid the suit among the rest of her clothes.

When Pawan reported about the suit, Premnath quietly tried to look for the suit in every nook and corner of the house, but he was unable to find it.

"It looks like as if you have given the suit to some other girl, not to Malti."

"Prem, you keep on watching. Sooner or later, that suit will appear before you." Pawan said, smiling mischievously.

When Malti returned from the office in the evening, on seeing her wearing the suit, Prem started to lose his temper. However, he controlled his temper and asked, "Where has this suit come from?"

"*Arey yaar*, it has come from the market, where else could it come from? In fact, I had bought it a few days earlier and, perhaps, forgot to tell you about it."

When the secret was out, they had a big fight.

It is not clear whether Prem and Malti got married or not, but Pawan proved the truth behind his words, "Woman, thy name is infidelity."

Now, let us look at the second 'angle' of the story.

Second angle—Raman...around thirty years old. Fair complexion, average height and his gait and accent was somewhat like a Britisher and if he stood amongst the villagers, he would give the impression of being a villager.

He would dress himself as per situation. He was very fond of couplets (Urdu poetry) and expert in plays. He was very impressed with the couplets of 'Galib'. At every step, he would recite Galib's couplets and he was also passionate about theatre.

He had great expertise in interior designing and oratory, was very artistic and a very deep thinker. He would win people over with his sweet behaviour.

He had so much faith in his ability, that clients would get impressed by him and would give him advances to the tune of 10-20 lakhs even before the job was done. No doubt, he was an excellent actor.

He was in love with his childhood friend. Although that girl belonged to Bangalore and he was a Punjabi, he resolved to marry her. Raman's mother tried her level best to make him understand, as she was a very worldly wise woman. She, herself, was a director of a company. So, she tried to convince him to do otherwise, but Raman did not listen to her. Eventually, he married the Bangalore girl.

His mother was, after all, a mother; she could not do anything to change his mind and accepted the fact that her happiness depended on her son's happiness.

Initially, Raman's married life went well, but as time went by, the girl started to feel home-sick. She explained that to Raman and started saying, "Raman, please shift your interior decoration business to Bangalore."

But he didn't listen to her, as all his clients were in Delhi and the NCR and it was not easy to start afresh and find new clients in Bangalore. Finally, after a long discussion, his wife gave him an ultimatum that she would not stay here.

A few days later Raman gave a blank cheque to his wife and said, "Fill up whatever amount you want." But she tore the cheque and threw it away as she was not after money.

She was adamant that Raman should shift to Bangalore. But he did not listen to her. Finally, one day, she left him and went to Bangalore, where from she applied for divorce.

During this period, Raman got involved with another woman. She had a daughter who was six years old. She had also come to the same advocate (that Raman had hired) to file divorce papers against her husband.

Raman started taking interest in this woman. He felt sympathy for Shaloo, that woman.

After some time, he got divorced from his wife and Shaloo from her husband. Since they empathised with each other, one day they finally got married.

Laxmi Ma, Raman's mother this time objected a lot, tried to make him understand, but Raman did not agree. His friends and relatives also tried their best to make him understand, but to no avail.

After one year, he was blessed with a son. He was very happy. He used to come from his office, whenever he found some spare time.

Problems do not come informing. During second year, his second wife started showing her true colours.

On every second day, he had to go to the police station. Raman got fed up by bribing the police.

One day, she crossed all limits. He was sent to 'Tihar Jail' and had to spend one night there. Now, how long you could put wooden utensil, on the fire? Raman lost all his patience.

He took divorce from Shaloo.

Now, Pawan was a bachelor without marriage. And Raman was also a bachelor after divorcing his two wives.

Third angle of the triangle...

Major Ashok Chatterji... Well built, smart and very cultured and would talk in a well behaved manner.

He studied in Hindu College in Delhi. He appeared in a test for army and cleared it. He went to IMA in Dehradun for training.

His mother Maushmi Chatterji was the principal of Miranda College. His father expired, before he could complete his training. His mother had to go to Calcutta, leaving her job.

There, in fact, was plenty of land and property but nobody was there to look after it.

After his training, he was posted to Ambala and it was difficult to look after the land.

Many years passed and now he was promoted to the rank of a Major.

He met a girl in 'Sirhind Club' in Ambala. That girl was the soul of the Club. Ashok got trapped in her beauty, or you can say that the girl trapped him.

Both were fond of roaming around. Every thing went on well for two years. His wife took admission in a flying club in Delhi and shifted to Delhi.

Occasionally, she would come to Ambala to meet him and he would also visit Delhi to meet her. But this arrangement could not last for a long time.

A young boy from a very affluent family took admission in Delhi flying club. Boy was rich as well as smart. He would come to the club in not less than a Mercedes car. He became friendly and the intimacy in them grew.

Rama started reducing her visits to Ashok in Ambala. Earlier Ashok did not take notice of it.

Finally one day, he went to Delhi flying club, then, he came to know everything.

For some days, they both had some differences with each other, but...! she wanted to fly like a kite.

And the thread of the kite slipped out of Ashok's hand!

There was comfort and luxury with that rich boy, while here with Major Chatterji; it was the routine old-atmosphere, from which Rama had started getting bored. On the other hand, Major was a simple person, sticking to his principles.

Major Chatterji accepted this breakup because he was a couldn't careless type of a man and did not bother about it for a long time.

He was fond of Bengali plays and Rabindra Sangeet. He used to remain busy in these and would mostly visit Delhi to see them.

During war, he was wounded and was a prisoner of war. He was kept in the prison and was released from it after a gap of five years.

He served for some more time. He was about forty years old at that time. In fact, he had joined the army at the age of twenty and after serving for about twenty years, he took retirement.

He was having a reasonably good pension. He also got a plot of land from the army quota on which he had constructed a beautiful house. Otherwise also, he was from a well-to-do family and had no dearth of money.

In the morning, he would go to play golf, in the afternoon; he would visit the army club to play billiards.

In the evening, he would attend Astrology classes.

He would have his meals usually at home only. Sohan Singh would cook delicious meals for him. Sometimes, he would invite his friend to his home. He was very fond of throwing parties. Mostly Pawan and Raman were his guests. They had the same interests: to see plays, recite Urdu couplets and discuss Astrology.

The course timings were in the evening, he would take all his friends after the class was over, to his house. They would continue playing cards and have whisky till night. Sohan Singh would not leave any effort to make the dinner tasty.

There is a strange story of the cook Sohan Singh.

One day, Pawan and Raman had to go to Major Chaterji's house for some important work. They had to get some important documents attested. Without informing Major Chatterji, they came to his place.

Major Chatterji was having breakfast at that time on his dining table. When they both reached there, they saw a smart Sikh man in a pant, shirt and tie serving breakfast to Major Chatterji.

"Sohan Singh, please get some breakfast ready for both of them."

"Sir! I will just prepare for them and serve." Sohan Singh left.

Both got surprised. They could not understand anything.

Realising their confusion major, said, "I know what is going on in your minds. First you finish your breakfast peacefully, then, I will explain everything in detail to you both.

Sohan Singh quickly served them the breakfast. And looking towards Chatterji's face said, "Sir, I have to be in the office a bit earlier today. I have to appoint some new staff. The maid who comes to clean utensils will clear the table."

Chatterji replied, "Ok, you may leave." Sohan Singh wishing everybody, left for his work.

Once Sohan Singh left, Pawan started saying, "Sir! Do let us know quickly about Sohan Singh." "The story of Sohan Singh is very short and simple. Long time back when one of my cooks retired, he brought his son to me and started saying, 'Sir! My son is a very good cook. You keep him with you and let him study alongwith doing the work of a cook.'

"Sohan Singh has been staying with me, alongwith continuing his studies."

"But you had becomes prisoner of war. Then what happened to Sohan Singh," Raman added.

"Then, he went to Calcutta and stayed with my mother. When I was released from the prison and joined my Unit, my mother sent him here. He loves my mother dearly. She also treats him like her own child. He is also conversant with Bangla language. He speaks and understands it.

He did his BA and MBA, while staying with me. Now, he is a personal officer in a company. I have told him many times that I will keep somebody else for cooking, but he would just not listen.

'Why do you worry for me? You are otherwise very busy doing office work. Sohan Singh just would not agree and says that only I would cook for you and would not allow anybody else to do the cooking. My father had taken a promise from me that I would always look after your meals. He has prepared my lunch and in the evening, he would prepare my dinner after returning from his office. He is very persevering.

If he is delayed in the office, he would tell his GM that he would not stay in the office beyond six 'o' clock as after reaching home he has to prepare dinner for me.

Everyone in the office is aware of this fact that he does cooking for me and he tells everyone with pride. He has no complex about it. All the office staff respects him for that."

Astrology course was of six months duration. A girl took admission in the course after one month of the commencement of the course.

She was about twenty eight years old with wheatish complexion. She had very sharp features, eyes like fish, captivating face; spoke very sweetly as if honey is dripping from her tongue. Impressive gait, long hair reaching her waist level.

There was suddenly a commotion amongst the students when she entered the class. She was an MA, MPhil. On entering the class, she gave a glance around everywhere. There was only one seat on the bench which was vacant and that was next to Major Chatterji.

She gave a smile to him before sitting there and then she sat there without any hesitation. Major Chatterji also welcomed her by bowing his head.

When the class teacher entered the room, seeing a new student he said, "Madam. Will you introduce yourself?"

"Sir! I am Maithali. I am an MA, MPhil. I have interest in Astrology. That is why I have joined this course. Would you like to know anything more about me?"

On this question the teacher was a little nervous and said, "No, it is more than sufficient."

Major Chatterji told Maithali about himself that he is a retired army officer, after the class was over.

After this, Maithali without any hesitation, started conversing with Major Chatterji. Otherwise also Major gave her the impression of a very matured person.

It was Sunday the next day. It was a holiday for the class. Major and his two class-fellows, like every Sunday, went to army club, they played *'Tombola'* and after having beer have had lunch in the club.

Maithali had joined the class only previous day. The centre of talk was Maithali. They kept on talking about her in a casual way, like, from where she has come, she belonged to which place, and what all she does, etc...!

On Monday, when the class started, she saw a vacant place next to Pawan and sat there.

Major Chatterji was bewildered on seeing this. He was aware that Pawan was very peevish of women. He dreaded that Pawan might not say or do something annoying. Before sitting next to Pawan, she looked at him smilingly and sat down.

But Pawan neither replied her smile, nor gave her a smile.

During class, if there was some point which was beyond Maithali's understanding, as she had joined the class one month late, then she would ask Pawan. There were so many points of Astrology which she never knew.

Pawan had no recourse but to explain to her. He would clarify whichever question she asked.

Major was very happy to notice that at least Pawan had started talking to a girl.

When in the evening, after the class was over, Major Chatterji started saying, "Pawan, I am very happy with you".

"Major Chatterji, for what you are happy with me?"

"I am happy as you did not say anything unsavory to Maithali. Otherwise, I was little apprehensive that you may not make her run away because of your bitter words."

"Major *Saheb*! I did not like her sitting next to me. But what could I do? All the other seats were occupied. If there was any unoccupied seat, I would have certainly shifted. She was disturbing me time and again by asking various questions . I had to clarify to her all the answers of the questions which she posed to me."

Raman who was listening to the chit-chat at last could not stay quiet and smiling said, "Major Chatterji, Pawan may say anything now, but he was replying to Maithli very lovingly. "

Major Chatterji started laughingly heartily on hearing Raman's argument.

On the other hand, Pawan said seriously, "Only I know as to how I managed to spend two periods with her. To tell you the truth, I was feeling like running away from her. You know it very well, how I get irritated with girls? But I was helpless. What else I could do?"

Major Chatterji, while enjoying said, "My friend! You are a young boy...? Girl is beautiful and smart."

"No! you do not know these girls. You do not deal with them. I am very much aware of their traits."

Major Chatterji started saying, "Friends, I touch my ears. Even one woman has taken a breath out of me."

"Major Chatterji, you touch your ears once, where as I touch my ears twice because I have gone through this torture twice. Not one but I have left two wives."

Hearing this, the three friends started laughing heartily.

Maithali's incident of sitting with Pawan continued for a week. Pawan had opened up with Maithali a little and started conversation with her freely. Major Chatterji was happy that at least some change has taken place in Pawan's nature.

However, Pawan's ideas about the girls were same as ever. That is, "Woman, thy name is infidelity."

Pawan had to leave for Himachal Pradesh for some sort of feud relating to property. Before leaving for Himachal Pradesh, he explained everything to Major Chatterji and he conveyed the same to Raman.

In the evening, when Maithali enquired about Pawan, Major Chatterji told her that he had gone to his native place.

Next day, when Maithali could not understand a few things of Astrology, she went and sat with Raman.

The place near him was vacant, perhaps the boy who had been occupying that seat had not come that day. Raman was a different type of man. He used to speak very sweetly. Very cultured and a big 'actor.'

He used to explain everything to Maithali very politely, whatever questions she would ask. Maithali, because of this attitude was very impressed by him.

The time of one week passed very fast.

Since Raman had been bitten twice, so, he had been taking all the precautions. He also had no confidence in women. He was very careful about his actions.

Major Chatterji was happy for one thing that at least both Pawan and Raman had started talking to Maithali.

He had doubts that perhaps they both may not talk to her at all or boycott her.

The day Pawan returned from Himachal Pradesh, the class was divided into groups of four students each.

Members of Maithali's group were Major Chatterji, Pawan and Raman. Their group used to be to allotted projects and they would be the best (stood first). Maithali was very intelligent and she would solve every question in a jiffy.

Now, after the class, they would sit in the canteen and would continue chatting for a long time. Gradually, they learnt about one another. Major Chatterji's parties were mostly celebrated at his residence.

And the day *'Tambola'* was played; he would take all three of them with him to the officers, mess. All of them would play *'Tambola'* and mostly Maithali would win full house.

Since Major Chatterji had a car and mostly on the day of a holiday he would take them either to a restaurant or, to a movie.

Like this, since they both had come very close to Major Chatterji, he would tell them, "She is a good girl. One out of you two should propose to her...."

"Major Chatterji! Please give this suggestion to Pawan. He has not tasted this fruit. As far as I am concerned, I would stay away from it I touch my ears."

On hearing this, Pawan Jamwal would say, "Why, do you have some enemity with me? You want to put me in this trap. Let me be a free bird. Don't put me in a cage."

Major Chatterji would give a good laugh. Jokes like this continued for a long time. Major Chatterji kept on telling them that you will not be able to get such a nice girl.

Once there was a marriage of one of the relative of Major Chatterji. The programme was to last for four days. On Major Chatterjis insistence, Maithili also agreed to accompany him to Jaipur.

All four of them started from Delhi in Major Chatterji's car. They stayed in 'Diggi Palace' at Jaipur. It was an old building dating two hundred and fifty years old and was converted into a hotel. What a breath taking building it was!

For four days, all the four friends went around Jaipur, did shopping, and visited the forts there. During this visit, sometimes Major Chatterji felt that Maithali has become very friendly with Pawan and another time he felt that she has become more friendly with Raman.

On returning back from Jaipur, he called Pawan and Raman to his house and asked both of them directly, but none of them confessed that they had any such feelings for Maithali.

Some times when all four of them would go for a stroll, then Major Chatterji would purposely go for a walk towards one side so that, both of them may have some opportunity to sit with her.

Once they made a programme to visit Manali. When they reached the hotel, they were told that there were only two vacant rooms in the hotel. Now, they were in a fix as to what arrangement of sleeping should be made?

Major Chatterji used to snore very much and was not ready to share his room with anyone. Now, if he had taken one room for himself, then remaining all the three had to stay in the other room.

The biggest problem was as to what arrangement should be made for Maithali.

Major was reluctant to let anybody sleep in his room because of his snoring habit. On the other hand, Pawan and Raman were also not ready to let Maithali sleep in their room.

Finally, on making them understand, they were ready to let Maithali sleep in their room and otherwise also there was no other option.

They all had breakfast together the next day and then went for a stroll towards hills.

Major Chatterji was the oldest amongst all of them but very fit and was the fastest in climbing the hills, the other three were trailing behind him.

Major Chatterji was happy that like this, their friendship will increase and perhaps some result may come out of it. One of the two may develop some interest for Maithali.

When Pawan and Raman went to one side for gossiping, Maithali saw a good opportunity and went to Major Chatterji and point blank said, "I will not sleep in their room."

"Did something happen at night?"

'No, nothing happened at night. The thing is that both of them kept on shifting sides so often that I could not sleep peacefully."

Major Chatterji kept on listening to her but did not utter a word.

After some times, when Maithali went to the washroom, both of his friends came to Major and said, "Major Chatterji! We will not sleep with Maithali in the same room."

"Then where will she sleep?"

"That we don't know, we will not mind sleeping in the verandah. We could not get a wink of sleep in that room."

"Then what should we do with Maithali?" Major Chatterji questioned.

"We don't know, do something. Oh Yes! You can make her sleep in your room."

"*Arrey*! How is it possible? How can she sleep in my room? I am a big snorer. She will run away from my room within five minutes."

After listening to both the parties, they had only one solution and that was that Maithali will sleep in Major Chatterjis room.

Maithali was prepared for every proposal except that in any circumstances she was not ready to sleep with those two in their room.

It was Major Chatterji's turn to bear the brunt.

Maithali and Major Chatterji kept on having discussion on various subjects for a long time and later on they went to sleep. When he was certain that Maithali had gone to sleep, he then quietly picked up his blanket, opened the door slowly and went to sleep in the verandah.

And continued sleeping there only till morning. He went inside at the break of dawn and went to sleep on his bed before Maithali was awake.

Nobody was aware of this reality.

Pawan and Raman were very keen about it.

Maithali and Major Chatterji, both were behaving in a very normal way. They were quite surprised and wondering as to how could Maithali tolerate Major Chatterji's snoring?

The reason being that they both had already enjoyed Major Chatterji's snoring at the Jaipur trip.

Anyway! By staying for three days in Manali and staying together in the class, she had become very free with Pawan and Raman.

One day it was off. All three of them made a plan to visit Major Chatterji. It was around 8 am. They reached Major

Chatterji's bungalow and found him going through the newspaper sitting at a table.

Major Chatterji welcomed all of them and asked, "How did you raid my house so early in the morning?"

We were free, so, we came here suddenly, all three of them replied in unison.

The maid servant served tea and biscuits to them. He insisted that all three of them should have lunch there and briefing his maid said, "They all will have their lunch here."

Sohan Singh entered the drawing room around twelve 'o' clock. Both Pawan and Raman had already met him. Maithali had not the opportunity to meet him. He wished everyone 'Good Morning'.

"Sohan Singh – it is a holiday today, you then... !"

Sohan Singh interrupted Major Chatterji and said, "Sir! There was a special meeting in the office today and I had to go. Please don't worry; I will prepare lunch for all of you and in time. The maid had informed me on phone that you are having guests for the lunch.

In fact, my scooter didn't start in the morning. I was in a hurry to go so I took your car to my office and brought everything in the car."

Maithali could not understand anything. After all who was Sohan Singh? He was dressed up in pant, shirt and a tie and was talking about preparing meals.

He was still standing there when... he remembered something and started saying, "Mamma rang up from Calcutta and you know it, she rings you up daily. Why don't you tell her?"

"You know my mother very well. You have stayed with her for so many years. She will not listen to me."

"Sir! She is your mother after all. Every mother is always worried that her son should get married. Let a daughter-in-law come home and increase gaiety in the house. Either you tell her that you are not interested in a marriage or...!"

Major Chatterji said interrupting Sohan Singh, "Ok. I will tell her. First you go and get cold beer for all of them."

Sohan Singh went away.

Earlier also, Sohan Singh had told his mother that he has two friends and both of them find marriage, a burden. And she will have to do something in this regard.

Major Chatterjis' mother was very worried because of this. She had been thinking about as to what is the solution of this problem? She had been thinking that somehow she will have to break this 'triangle' but this 'triangle' was very strong.

Reason being that there was a very strong bond between the three of them and no solution was insight.

Maithali was astonished because she knew nothing about Sohan Singh. On watching her to be in a fix, Pawan and Raman told her whatever they knew about Sohan Singh.

Maithali used to write some stories and somehow she liked the character of Sohan Singh.

Sohan Sigh brought the beer and he served it to everyone.

She refused beer and said, "I don't take beer. If possible, then, bring mango juice for me." Sohan Singh immediately brought mango juice and after serving it to Maithali left.

One day, Maithali saw it as a good opportunity and came to Major Chatterji's house. Sohan Singh was alone there. He was surprised to see her there and said, "Madam! Major *Saheb* is away to the market along with his friends."

"Of course! I know it and that is why I have come here. I, purposely, did not go with them so that, I get an opportunity to talk to you alone and write something."

Anyway, Sohan Singh was an educated person, he explained in detail about Major Chatterji, his mother, his other relatives, house in Calcutta and about himself as how he stayed with Major's mother for ten years, he told her everything.

He also told Maithali that his mother has selected a girl for Major Chatterji. She is waiting for major's consent. If everything goes well, she will celebrate his marriage during the holidays of *'Durga Pooja.'*

"Madam, actually one sister of Major *Saheb* stays in America and she visits Calcutta to meet her mother during holidays of *'Durga Pooja'*. One of her friends also stays in America and his mother is very much influenced by her. She would love to have her son get married to her. She is also coming to Calcutta during *'Durga Pooja'* along with her sister. That is why his mother wants to celebrate this pious work done during that period."

Next day, when Maithali entered the class, Major Chatterji said laughingly, "Learnt from Sohan Singh that you are planning to write either some story or an article on Sohan Singh. Please write a story on all of us also."

Hearing this, Maithali said nothing but just smiled. Pawan and Raman started laughing, on hearing this.

During this period, Maithali had come more close and friendly to Pawan and Raman. Major Chatterji was confident that one of them will definitely purpose to her. The question is who will purpose her first, Pawan or Raman. It was a big riddle for Major Chatterji.

On the other hand, the days of *'Durga Pooja'* were drawing near and phones of Major Chatterji's mother were coming constantly one after other.

Sohan Singh would daily remind Major Chatterji that he may or may not get married, but must go to Calcutta. Otherwise also, it was quiet sometime that he had visited Calcutta. He used to go to Calcutta invariably in the vacations of *'Durga Pooja.'*

There were many students from Bengal, so, management decided that they will have three weeks holidays during *'Durga Pooja.'*

Vacations of *'Durga Pooja'* were declared, but Major Chatterji was not making up his mind to visit Calcutta. Since he did not go to Calcutta, all his friends Pawan, Raman and Maithali also stayed back and did not go to their respective homes.

Actually, Major Chatterji had purposely stopped them.

He was in a great fix. In fact, he was falling in love with Maithali and she also was aware of this. He was dreading from going to Calcutta. He was aware that once he visited Calcutta, his mother would get him married to the girl who had come from America.

How could he with the girl who was unknown to him?

Major Chatterji's sister had also reached Calcutta from America. According to Sohan Singh his sister's friend had also come with her. Everyone in Calcutta was anxiously waiting for him.

Sohan Singh was also worried because he had been visiting Calcutta on every *'Durga Pooja.'* Come what it may. But this time due to this course and...!

When Major Chatterji did not reach even after one week of vacations, then one day unexpectedly, his mother landed there without informing him.

At that time, Major Chatterji was busy with all three of his friends.

She took Sohan Singh alongwith her and ticking off Major Chatterji, she said, "Ashok, what type of son you are? You are not bothered about me. Almost one week of vacations are over, and you are still in Delhi. You immediately come with me. I have come in a taxi. Sohan Singh has packed your luggage and had put it in the taxi."

"Mamma, first get acquainted with my friends. We all are attending six months course, we meet daily... We had gone to Jaipur and Manali together. I just can't leave them like this." When nothing else struck to him he gave this lame excuse.

"Have they chained you that you could not go leaving them behind? You are not concerned about your mother but they should have some concern for their parents. They all should leave for their respective homes."

On hearing this from his mother, all of his friends bowed their heads in silence.

"Ok, introduce me to your friends."

All his friends touched her feet. Maithali was about to touch her feet, "I will not let a girl touch my feet." She embraced her and said, "You are a cultured and well behaved girl. You have a very pretty face." Sohan Singh had been telling me about Pawan and Raman. I have looked after him like a son. He also desires that I should get Ashok married at the earliest.

After this, I have to get Sohan Singh married. If Ashok does not get married then, how will Sohan Singh's turn come?" On hearing this from his mother, everyone started smiling.

Then she gave order to Sohan Singh in an army style, "Sohan Singh, you leave them in their homes in *Saheb's* car and then come to Calcutta by train. I am taking Ashok with me in the taxi to airport."

Once *'Mataji'* left, Sohan Singh took them in the car and left them whereever they wanted. Later on, everyone left for their homes.

One day before the course started, Sohan Singh rang all of them saying that he had come back and that Major *Saheb* was returning from Calcutta tomorrow. And also *'Mataji'* got Major Chatterji married... to the American friend of her daughter.

Major *Saheb* is throwing a party in view of his marriage in his house. You all are invited tomorrow by 8 pm. All three of you must come."

"But Sohan Singh, Maithali...." 'Pawan could hardly utter these words. The phone got disconnected.

"There is nothing to worry. Every body will come to attend the class. We will take Maithali from there and leave for Major Chatterji's. We may be a little late but it doesn't matter", Raman said.

Both the friends had put on their best suits. When after a long wait, Maithali did not turn up, they took a taxi and left for Major Chatterji's house.

Major Chatterji had also invited some of the VIP's of the city.

Sohan Singh received both of them and made them sit at a special table. Sohan Singh looked here and there... Pawan and Raman understood that he was looking for Maithali.

Anyway, they thought it best to be quiet for sometime. .

In the meantime, Major Chatterji came in his special Bengali dress and shook hand enthusiastically with them.

He was about to say or enquire something when Sohan Singh interrupted and asked, "*Saheb*! Which whisky I should bring?"

"*Arrey*! Is this to be asked? Go get *'Shivaz Regal'*, soda, ice and couple of snacks..."

In the meantime *'Mataji'* came there, Pawan and Raman touched her feet and they congratulated her on the marriage of her son.

Sohan Singh was just passing in front of her when she called him and said, "Go, bring Ashok's wife here."

Sohan Singh shook his head and went inside.

In a little while dressed in a typical red coloured Bengali *sari,* Mrs Chatterji came. She was covering her head in a veil.

'Mataji' put her hand lovingly on her shoulder and said laughingly, *"Bahu,* lift your veil up. They are not outsider, they are Ashok's special friends."

Bahu was a little hesitant. So, *'Mataji'* came forward and with one fast jerk put her veil up...!

The moment her *ghungat* went up... Pawan and Raman jumped from their respective chairs as if they had got a high voltage electric shock.

They were stunned. Maithali was standing in front of them. They could not believe their eyes.

'Mataji' was smiling while looking at their perplexed faces.

And said, "Since I had to get my son married, and your 'triangle' was very strong and a big hurdle in my way, so to break your triangle I planted Maithali to make the fourth angle of your triangle."

28

Sofia: A Girl from North-east

I have been a story writer for the last so many years, I have been amusing you with the stories of love and romance, real and fake—imaginary, facts and fictions. My main intention was to amuse you and bring new ideas in your life. Suddenly, I was surprised to see today's headlines in the paper. It was written, there had been a scuffle between the people of North and the North-east... Then I remembered Sofia. Suddenly, the words came out of my mouth, Sofia, "where are you?"

In response to my words, I heard the soft voice of Sofia. It was softer than the sound of dew falling on flowers. 'My story teller! Why are you so restless? I am with you from time immemorial!'

Sofia belonged to North-east and was a 23 years old girl. She was tall, fair complexioned, heavy dark brown hair were falling up to her shoulders, had dreamy eyes, pink lips and a figure which gave the impression as if God had moulded her with his own hands.

She met Shanker and Dayal in Greenland restaurant. Shanker was fond of visiting places, and he took Dayal to that restaurant, and there, they met Major Ranjit Nagra, an old acquaintance from their college days.

In their first meeting, Sofia astounded them. What a smile she had! It sent people, who were in their senses, in a trance.

She welcomed everybody with folded hands. This was in fact, the custom of the restaurant that they made the most beautiful girl stand at the entrance of the restaurant. She was looking like the fairy of 'Basara' (a city in Iraq). She was the pride and soul of the restaurant.

People were transfixed by her beauty when they entered the restaurant and often forgot what they had come to eat.

People sitting in the restaurant often used to steal glances at her. Perhaps it was their helplesness that they had to get up to fetch eatables, otherwise they could spend hours just looking at her.

As it is, she was a *'Tota.'*

You all must be wondering that from where has this word *'Tota'* emerged. One day, I was listening to a programme on an FM channel, on the radio. On it, a girl was giving a programme, she asked the listeners about the meaning of the word *'Tota'*. When nobody could answer her correctly, she told them that *'Tota'* is used for a beautiful girl in Punjabi language.

On hearing this from the announcer, I saw the face of Nandlal Puri, my college friend in front of my eyes. He was very jovial and often while looking at a girl, he used to remark, 'What a *Tota*' and I got lost in my past.

Well, Sofia really was a *'Tota'* and a *'Tota'* in real sense. People used to come there not for eating but to look at her. On entering the restaurant, they used to occupy the chair in full view of her. Flirts used to keep on drinking beer and enjoyed looking at her. Noticing this, the manager of the restaurant doubled the price of beer and eatables served on those tables.

This time when Shanker and Dayal arrived after a long interval at the restaurant, they saw that she was talking in a very friendly manner with Major Nagra.

She welcomed everyone with a smile and folded hands but she used to greet Major Nagra shaking hands with him affectionately. Everyone had started feeling jealous of Major Nagra because of this. Those people who were very fond of her, felt very annoyed at this in the heart of their hearts.

Whenever she put her soft hands in Major Nagra's, his happiness knew no bonds. Actually, it was not so but the onlookers used to feel it that.

Restaurant's manager Manish, a married man, used to feel jealous on seeing Sofia's affection towards Major Nagra. A couple of times he told him in a low voice, "You shake hands with her not only once but, so many times. Sofia can get some sort of infection. Her hands are very delicate, like velvet." When he said this he could feel Sofia's hands in his own hands.

Major Nagra ignored this suggestion of his and then he was not a fool that he would leave such a good opportunity.

It seemed that perhaps his relation with Sofia was limited only till shaking of hands.

Then one day, Manish, while talking causally told this to his employer, Sagar. Since there was lot of noise there, so, Sagar thought that perhaps the manager was talking about Dayal. He explained to him that if she shakes hands with Dayal, then it is good for us. She will stay here and then making his left eye wink, laughingly he said to him, "As it is, I feel Dayal has got no courage. He looks a harmless type of person. You are unnecessary worrying about him..."

Manish started saying in a serious tone, "Sir! You don't know him. God knows what all dry fruits he eats. You never know, he may surpass *Baba*...!"

Manish realised fast that Sagar has linked Major Nagra with Dayal. He at once told Sagar about Major Nagra.

Sagar started saying, "Manish, we have to see our business. Not what Sofia and Major Nagra do." Then remembering something he said, "it was you only who has been saying that Sofia is having an affair with a member of the staff."

"The relationship is going on between the two. And as it is the boy is young and...!" Manish replied.

Sagar interferingly cut between said, "It may be possible that she is indulging in passing time with Major Nagra."

Manish was in deep thought. He was in a fix. On one hand was a young boy and on the other hand elder to Sofia was a good looking and smart, army officer. He jerked his head and started thinking that what a fix he was in! He has a wife at home. She caters to all his needs. So, what will he gain by thinking about Sofia? For a few days, Manish had to go to his hometown for some urgent work. When he returned from his leave, his assistant Jagdish told him that Major Nagra now comes here daily in the afternoons and stays till the evenings. He leaves for his home when Sofia's shift gets over and Sofia leaves for her flat in Delhi by bus.

"But we cannot allow anybody sitting in the restaurant for free, Manish said in a raised voice. "Sir! He doesn't sit here for free, he has given one month's advance and Sofia has also booked the front table for him, on a daily basis for him." "And what happened to her boyfriend? Didn't he stop Sofia to see Major Nagra? asked Manish. "He stopped her but, when Major Nagra showed him his pistol outside on the road, he got so scared that he left his job here and ran away. Sofia is also aware about this incident."

"But Major Nagra is merely friendly with her. We learnt that he has no such feelings in his heart. Yes, he is jovial natured. Sofia's friend also said that he has told her to select a good boy for herself."

"Your boyfriend was useless, that is why I chased him away. It is time for you to get married. So, you should get married to a good boy from your society at the earliest."

Hearing this, she often used to laugh. "Ok uncle! I will find a good boy at the earliest. You don't get worried."

"What did you say? Do I look like your uncle?"

On hearing this, she used to laugh loudly, "You definitely have some... ideas in your heart."

Major could not make out, how he should react in context to Sofia's remark.

Then she laughed and said, "Say! You are neither my uncle, nor you wish to be my boyfriend. Then what are you to me?"

On hearing this, Major Nagra started thinking. After some time he said, "I am your guardian."

She said smilingly, "This relationship is very confusing. I don't agree to this. What relation can a good looking girl like me should have with a handsome person like you? It is an insult to my beauty."

Suddenly, Sofia had to go to Manipur for a month because of her mother's illness. Major Nagra went to the railway station with her to see her off. Sofia shook his hand affectionately as usual. She had tears in her eyes. But Major Nagra could not understand why there were tears in her eyes... He started thinking.

The guard waved green light. The train started moving... And she kept on holding onto Major's h and. But, till when! Then, on its own Major's hand slipped from her's. She kept on standing at the door and waving till the station disappeared from her eyes.

Major Nagra was reminded of the days of his youth, when he fell in love with a girl from his college. This... this affair continued for some time and when the time for marriage came, she ditched him. At that time, he vowed that never again he would think of marrying. His relatives also tried to convince him but all in vain.

Then he joined the Army. In the evening a visit to club and drinks were the routine. Life was going on very nicely. He stopped thinking of marriage.

Also, marriage brings lots of responsibilities like wife and children. It was better like this. Life was enjoyable. He had nothing whatsoever to worry about.

Perhaps there was a problem of network in Sofia's place. Thus, despite many efforts she could not converse with Major Nagra.

Almost a month had passed when, while returning from the North-east, she tried to interact with Major Nagra. Perhaps there was also a problem with the network even there, therefore, she was unable to contact him. And when for the second time she tried contacting him, she noticed that the bag in which she had put her mobile phone, was missing. Either it had been misplaced or somebody had stolen it. But thank God, the second bag in which she had her cash and railway ticket was intact.

After reaching Delhi, she straight away took a taxi for her restaurant, 'Greenland', reaching there, she learnt that Major

Nagra had not been visiting that place for some time. On learning this, she became very restless.

She also tried her best to locate Shanker and Dayal. Both of them had also not been visiting that place for some time. Perhaps, it being the end of the year, they were busy with income tax problems.

On the other hand, no body was aware of Major Nagra's mobile number. One day while conversing, Dayal had told Sofia that because of security reasons Nagra does not give his phone number to anyone. It was an exception that he had given his phone number to Sofia.

Now, Sofia had joined hotel 'Ocean Blue.' She had been feeling Major Nagra's absence very much. But, she was helpless. She had nothing but waiting.

Major Ranjit Nagra was suddenly sent away on some special mission by the army. On his return, he learnt that Sofia had joined hotel 'Ocean Blue.'

"Why did she leave your restaurant, 'Greenland'?" Major Nagra asked Manish.

"In fact, she got a higher salary in Ocean Blue, transportation from home to place of work, as well as a flat for living was given to her. On top of this, she was given the post of AGM.

On seeing Major Nagra in the restaurant, Sofia's friend informed her.

On learning this, she came running to him. She shook hands with Major Nagra and lovingly embraced him with a brief hug. He was very confused at Sofia's action.

"I have been waiting for you for the past so many days." Then holding his hand, she escorted him inside the hotel, Ocean Blue. She made him sit next to her and got a cup of coffee for him.

In hotel Ocean Blue, it was looking strange to Major Nagra. In restaurant 'Greenland', everybody knew him. Here, the members of staff, surrounding him, were new to him but Sofia was unaware of this, she was talking non-stop with Nagra. She was talking about her mother and her treatment.

After that, she introduced Major Nagra to her GM. He met him with due respect. As it is, before employing Sofia at 'Ocean Blue, he had investigated fully about her. He had also learnt that Major Nagra was the permanent customer of 'Greenland' and was very close to Sofia.

On Sofia's request, the GM gave special permission to her that Major could sit with her. Since her place of duty was inside the office, she kept on a steady flow of conversation while doing her official work.

One day, when Major Nagra did not turn up at the hotel, Sofia got very tense. His mobile phone was also switched off. She went to Major's house in her office car. Major was not feeling well so, she had requested her GM for a few day's leave.

"Sofia! There is no need for you to take leave. I will get you a flat on rent, next to Major's house. From there you will be in a position to look after the Major and do office work on your laptop at the same time. When Major recovers you can attend the office again and whenever required in between, I will call you for a short while."

She was the life of hotel 'Ocean Blue' and GM wanted to keep her happy at any cost. He gave Sofia a flat very near to Major's house. Sometimes she would visit Major's house ten times a day, just to find out his well-being. Everything was OK till now. Major's neighbours did not pay much attention to Sofia.

One day, she crossed the limit when Major's condition deteriorated, she shifted to his house with her bag and baggage.

Major tried to convince her that she was an unmarried girl and he...! but she did not agree.

When people used to come to find out about his welfare, she would call him 'uncle'. Otherwise she would address him as 'Sir' and gradually she started calling him by his real name, Ranjit.

Once Major recovered fully, even then, she refused to go back to her own flat. She would look after Major nicely. She would serve him fruit juice, soup and nourishing food.

Many days passed since she had started staying with Major. A girl from Sofia's village narrated all this to her parents.

They both came running. She was still at Major's house at that time.

They tried to convince her that it was not correct of Sofia to stay in Major's house. But she started to say that, "I will stay with uncle in this house."

"Daughter, how is it possible? Neither you, nor he is married...!"

Then she bluntly said, "Then I will get married to uncle."

Her parents as well Major were surprised to hear such a statement. She had just talked about marriage in a rage.

Sofia did not bother about anybody. Her parents kept on trying to explain things to her and she kept on saying 'yes' and 'no'.

At last, tired and beaten they returned to Manipur.

As it is, she was a very stubborn. She decided to come to Delhi after finishing her education. Everyone known to her objected.

Everyone said, 'It is a new and unknown place. People of Delhi...' Without listening to anyone, she boarded the train and came to Delhi. She was not acquainted with anybody. She was very bold and fearless girl. She was an expert in *judo* and *karate*. Though she gave an impression of being a very delicate girl.

After reaching Delhi, within two days she found a nice job for herself. She was full of confidence. She did not feel scared here.

Well! She continued staying with Major Nagra without worrying about people's opinions, though Major was a little hesitant while staying with her.

She would get ready and help Major to get ready and she will go to office and take Major along with her. The official car would come fifteen minutes earlier and they both would sit in it and leave for office.

Understanding Major's illness, GM gave a separate room to Sofia because he knew that she would like to look after better when she was near him.

Any other management would not have tolerated her coquetry behaviour if it was some other employee. But such was Sofia's personality. She was the lifeline of that hotel. Tourists used to come to that hotel because of Sofia's name.

She would receive every new tourist and accompany him to his room. Tourists used to become her fan just in such little time. Everyone had her phone number. They would book their room in the hotel beforehand.

The occupancy of the hotel had increased, since the time she had joined the hotel. Rooms of the hotel were always fully occupied.

Once it so happened that when she had gone on leave for seven days, the occupancy of the hotel came down to less than fifty per cent. She might work or might not, mere her presence was sufficient for the hotel.

She was very popular amongst the staff and also the tourists.

Within ten years, she was promoted to the post of GM. There in restaurant 'Greenland', Manish had also been given the post of GM. The two of them often met each other.

A big party was arranged when she was promoted to the post of GM. Sofia went herself to extend the invitation of the party to the owner of 'Greenland'. Though Sagar was annoyed because of her joining hotel 'Ocean Blue', but when she herself went there to invite him, he did not have the heart to refuse her.

Whatever it was, she was everyone's heart-throb. She got rid of all the misunderstanding between the owners of hotel and the restaurant. She helped them become friends.

Now sometimes, she used to go to restaurant 'Greenland' for a cup of coffee. A ray of happiness used to spread on the faces of the staff and the customers and gradually, she started visiting Greenland once a week. On that particular day, there used to be a huge crowd in 'Greenland.'

Often Manish would say to Sofia, "Dayal *Sahib* had told us that Sofia is the soul of 'Greenland.' Call her back but we never bothered about his words. Dayal *Saheb* has got an ability to judge people. On hearing this from Manish, she would laugh and blush.

It could not be found out whether Sofia married Major Nagra or not. But there was a rumour that their daughter was studying in Shimla. But nobody had seen her.

Then suddenly one day, she alongwith Major Nagra disappeared. Yes! Her resignation letter was found on Sofia's office table.

It proved to be great setback to hotel 'Ocean Blue' and restaurant 'Greenland.' Both gave a deserted look.

What happened was that Sofia had started missing her daughter. Before joining the army, Major Nagra was a professor in one of the colleges in Shimla. He had a house there which had been locked for years.

Sofia got that house renovated. They both used to roam around the hills. Their daughter would come in the evenings and they used to spent the rest of the time with her.

Sometimes, the tourists would try to recognise her and get themselves photographed. In the beginning, Sofia could not understand the reason for this, but later on, she learnt that both hotel 'Ocean Blue' and restaurant 'Greenland' had put a big cut out of her at their entrance.

After Sofia left them, one day Dayal advised them to put a big cutout of Sofia in front of their hotel and restaurant. It may be possible that, it may make some difference in their income.

Whether there was any difference in their income or not, but it definitely happened that they both put the life size cutout of Sofia. After so many years, it was still there.

Hotel 'Ocean Blue' and restaurant 'Greenland' both had their Silver Jubilee on 25th of December. They planned to celebrate it together. They both decided that they will put Sofia's name in front of the name of their hotel and restaurant keeping in mind her popularity. That would make the name of the hotel as 'Sofia Ocean Blue' and restaurant will become 'Sofia Greenland.'

This news was published in the newspaper. On reading this, Sofia and Major Nagra made a plan that they, alongwith their daughter, will attend the function. Sofia informed the directors of hotel and the restaurant about this.

Both the directors felt very happy on hearing this . The news of Sofia and her family coming to attend the function spread like a wild fire. Because of this, all the seats of the function of 25th December were reserved.

Shanker and Dayal were sent special invitation on Sofia's request.

It was the evening of 25th December. The whole crowd was sitting inside the hotel waiting for Sofia.

Outside the entrance the owners of hotel and the restaurant were anxiously waiting for Sofia. Shanker and Dayal were also with them.

In the meantime, a car came and stopped in front of the gate. Sofia, Major Nagra and their daughter, all three of them alighted from the car.

There was no change in Sofia. She was covering herself with a light shawl. She was as beautiful as ever. Like she used to be in the past. Oh yes! She had put on a little weight.

Major Nagra was also 'slim and trim' as like olden times, though there were a few streaks of grey hairs.

What was to be said about their daughter Sofiana. If not known, people would have taken her granted as Sofia. She was exactly like what Sofia looked during her prime days. She was like a moving idol made by some renowned sculptor.

After receiving them, they were escorted inside. They were welcomed inside the hall, by the crowd who gave them a round of cheery applaud and a bouquets of flowers. Sofia went to the people and shook hands with them as was her custom in the past.

The owners of hotel and restaurant described, in detail, about her and her achievements. Both of them concluded their speech by pointing out that Sofia was the soul and pride of the hotel and the restaurant and they will always feel sorry of her leaving them.

Everyone was holding glasses in their hands, some were having whisky, some were having *gin,* while others were drinking juice. But Shanker and Dayal were having mineral water, I don't know why. Anyway! the atmosphere was very reverberating.

After that for having dinner, people sat in their respective chairs. Then, there was a loud blast of firing from the front. It was aimed at Sofia.

Everyone was shocked. People saw that some security people had apprehended a man who had fired the bullet. Then the police came and arrested that man and whisked him away. Everything happened in a jiffy that people could not understand anything. People started talking amongst them about this incident.

Sofia took the mike and asked people to sit quietly and relax, and said that "What has just happened, forget it. Come, let us all enjoy the food together."

But now, people were just not interested in food anymore. They were very eager, restless to know about the firing. Understanding the situation, Sofia started saying that if people were so eager to know the happenings then, she would explain them all the facts.

"I came here from North-east on some mission a long time back. In fact at that time, I was an active member of North-east Peace Council. This is not a government organisation but a private one. The aim of this council was to enhance the feeling of brotherhood and to keep peace.

A few years earlier, when the news of conflicts between the people of North and North-east were published, then, our peace council was suspicious that some other country is at the back of it. That country does not want that we, from North-east should progress. They do not want that people from both the region live peacefully and with brotherhood. They want to create differences among us and they aim to destroy the peace and harmony with which we live.

So, the council decided that it should send one of its member to Delhi to investigate and to counter it. I was the most active and fit member of the council. That was the reason that I was selected and sent here. I was given three months training in *judo-karate* and firing and all types of weapons as well as gathering of the intelligence.

On coming here, I found a job in 'Greenland' within two days. After some time, I learnt that some mischievous people have made their headquarters in 'Ocean Blue' in Ghaziabad as security in Delhi was very tight. Then I started going to hotel 'Ocean Blue' on the pretext of having tea and coffee. I used to go to the hotel when it was time for the director to come and everything went according to my plans. The Director of the hotel spotted me. He enquired about me from his GM. GM told him that I was an employee of the restaurant 'Greenland.'

Then the very next day, I was offered a job in 'Greenland.' It was just what I wanted for my mission. I accepted their offer. They also increased my salary and apart from giving me a vehicle for coming and going, they gave me a place for living, too.

On the other hand, I made friends with Major Nagra. All this I did for accomplishement of my mission. I knew that he was from the security and worth confidence. He fell into my trap. Or you can say, gradually, I, too, fell into his trap.

When I told Major Nagra about my mission, he at once agreed to help me. I was given the post of GM and had a separate office in which I and Major Nagra together started keeping an eye on the suspicious people coming and going from the hotel.

We also got Colonel Chadha, a retired Security Expert known to us, take up a job in the security department. He was an expert in net-working. According to our plan all the rooms in the hotel were fitted with security systems and we started tapping and recording suspecious people.

Gradually, we learnt about those people and got them killed in one encounter or other. Then only one man was left. He was the ring leader of this gang. He was named as 'Dr Dorgi Wang.' This was an *alias* used by him. He used to adopt a new name in every new place. He was an expert in disguising himself. He knew the languages of many countries. No one ever came to know the country to which he belonged.

I was under the impression that he had been killed in our last encounter. But Major Nagra had a doubt, that he was still alive and also that both his legs had become useless in that encounter.

So, when the hotel people advertised in the paper about our coming here on the eve of 'Silver Jubilee' then Major Nagra became suspicious that if 'Dr Dorgi Wang' is alive then he will definitely attack me.

So, before coming here, after disguising himself, Major Nagra came here along with a few security people did *recee* of the hotel and he stationed security people at different places.

Rest you have all seen as to what happened. For killing me Dr Dorgi Wang fired at me. But, you do not know how I survived. Dr Dorgi Wang never misses his aim. Dayal has got a very sharp vision. If he had not pushed me slightly, the bullet would have pierced my chest. Now that I am safe and sound, my mission has been completed. Now nobody will be able to create differences between the people of North and the North-east.

Everybody congratulated her by applauding. Dinner had started. Major Nagra, Sofia, Sofiana, both the directors, Shanker and Dayal were eating at one table and were talking about this incident. They were also discussing as to what they had achieved during the years gone by.

Dinner was over and it was time to leave. At last, Sofia started saying, "Dayal, I am grateful to you, it is because of you that..." and coming forward she embraced Dayal suddenly. Due to her this action, Dayal was surprised and confused...!

So far he had seen Sofia putting her arms around Nagra, but just shaking hands with others.

(In hotel Greenland she had been addressing them both as Mr Dayal and Mr Shanker. But, later when they became friends, she started calling them Shanker and Dayal).

Sofia realised Dayal was in a fix and understanding his mental state started saying, "Dayal it has been your wish for quite some time that I greet you with a hug...!"

"How do you know?" suddenly the words stumbled out of his mouth and he was embarrassed by his own words.

Winking mischievously at him Sofia replied, "I am not that dumb. I understand everyone's intentions and Dayal, you are thinking rightly at the moment that I never greet anyone by hugging except Major Nagra and when did I hug you with my arms around your neck?"

He listened to this, his mouth wide open. "Sofia, I didn't understand you?"

"I'll explain it all to you." Saying this she slid off the shawl from her shoulder. Below it a bulletproof jacket was revealed. Everyone noted that Dr Dorgi Wang's bullet was stuck inside it.

"I have been trained never to take risks." Seeing this everyone started praising her.

"Dayal, even today when I embraced you with a hug, even then this jacket was between us. As it is, I recognise everyone's heartbeat. Did I say anything wrong?"

Hearing her little speech, everyone burst out laughing. At last, Dayal started speaking in a loud voice, "Sofia, you are truly a strong North-eastern girl." Sofia shot back, "Yes, I am Sofia, a girl from North-east!"

29

Ruby in Bell Bottom

(A Satirical - Comedy)

Prayer Meet

Alas! The thing that I dreaded lastly happened.

I had especially instructed her, rather forbidden her, not to hold Prayer meeting. I did not believe in such rituals. But she did not pay heed to my wish.

The very day all the rituals were over. She called our neighbour Sharmaji (Sorry! not ours. But hers (*as I had departed. I was no more*).

On hearing my wife's call, Sharmaji came running to the house. "Sharmaji, you know very well what type of mental attitude Mohan *Saheb* had? He was dead against the holding of this prayer meet. But what should be done? I after all have some social obligations. May God bless his soul. . . I am sure he will certainly forgive me for this act of mine."

"*Behanji,* please tell me what all is to be done? I will take care of every thing."

"Sharmaji, from beginning till end, you have to take care of the entire event. Whatever would be the expenditure, please keep on taking the money from me."

"*Behan* ji! Don't worry; I know everything about Mohan *Saheb.* He was fond of *dhoda, dhokla, coconut barfi* and *rasgulla... samosa, kachori, mathi...!* He was fond of Espresso Coffee and Tata Tea of Premier brand. In addition, I will also keep *Sugar Free* for those who are diabetic."

Saying this, Sharmaji left to perform his duties and responsibilities.

First of all he went to sector market and met Sanjay, of Samrat bakery. He had been running the bakery for the last many years. He had also been taking care of all such prayer meets. He supplied all the items of refreshment at very reasonable and competitive rates. Mostly the items demanded were Mathis, biscuits and tea.

Sanjay was very astonished and surprised to see the elaborate list of items handed over by Sharmaji. He read the list again and again. He could not believe his eyes, because during the last couple of years nobody had placed such a list of eatables for any prayer meet. This had happened for the first time in his life.

He was going to utter something about the list to Sharmaji when his elder brother Ballu, sensing something, intervened and said slowly, "Sanjay, we have to see our business. Do not get involved in 'whether such items have been demanded earlier or not!' You better take the list which Sharmaji is giving you and make arrangement of the items required".

Then Sharmaji remembered something and said, "You also have to make arrangement for tables and chairs. Of course the mattresses and mats are already available in the Prayer Hall."

From there Sharmaji went straight to the temple.

Shri Chandgi Ram, the *Surpanch* had got constructed 2 halls very close to the temple. He used to give these halls on rent for various functions.

Since the first hall was mostly used for temple's activities, Chandgi Ram had entrusted the responsibility of upkeep of this hall to *punditji.* The upkeep and care of the second hall was looked after by Chandgi Ram himself.

Both the halls had been fitted with lights and mikes. However, the responsibilities of lights and mike of both halls used to be of *punditji*'s.

However, there was a rumour, that *punditji* had taken the first hall on one year contract from Chandgi Ram. This was of course between the two of them. How far this was true, nobody can say. *Punditji* used to give first hall on rent as per his own sweet will.

So, Sharmaji went straight to contact *punditji*. He explained everything to him. The *punditji* was a seasoned man. The first thing he asked about was the refreshment to be served at the prayer meet. On reading the list handed over to him by Sharmaji, his mouth started watering. He thought how nice it would be, if other people also started following the same.

The fact is that 20% of the eatables offered in the temple used to be siphoned to his house. This also was the reason for increase in his weight which had gone up from 50 to 250 kgs during the last couple of years. Earlier he was very agile. But now even on walking some distance he would get breathless.

The doctor had tried his best to convince *punditji* to reduce his weight but his habit of being a glutton always prevailed. During *Shivratri* festival, at least seventy kgs of milk used to be smuggled to his house through the back door. He would sell that milk at half the rate to the dairies around the temple.

After all, so much milk could not be consumed. They were ten members of the family. Even if they wanted, how much could they have consumed? His fridge always used to be full with fruits and sweetmeats.

Anybody from his village, who had to improve health, would visit *punditji*'s house on some pretext and in few days he/she would…!

He had also bought software and had started making horoscopes. It is another thing that he has not been able to prepare a correct horoscope for himself.

He had also started reading of hands. Any person who came to him for reading his hand, he would immediately say, '*Beta*, there is tension in your house because of some woman in your family.' Well, it is common that in everybody's house there is one problem or the other due to some woman. People used to get highly impressed with *punditji*'s prediction.

Then, he would tell that around the age forty-five, he/she would become financially well off. In fact, at the age of forty-five, an average person would have put nearly twenty years of service and would have made sufficient bank balance.

In addition, he had also started a business of sale and purchase of cars. He would take the car from one of his followers and sell it off to some innocent person at higher price. In other words, he had become a successful and shrewd business man.

And about the Donation Chest—the less is said, the better. I think it is better if I keep my mouth shut. *(Er, did I say mouth? I have neither mouth nor body. I can only observe everything from above. Nobody can see or hear me.*)

Yes, Sharmaji told *pundit* Shatrupal to get the hall inspected.

Shatrupal—nobody knows as to how he got his name as *pundit* Shatrupal. Some people would say that his father was a great fan of film star Shatrughan Sinha. Some people had another theory. They said his father had lot of *shatrus* (enemies) and to ward off the spell and to defeat his enemies, he had done so.

However, one thing is certain. He had pilfered so much money from the donation chest that he had made lot of enemies.

I could see everything from top. And one day I heard many loud voices coming from the small room, behind the temple. Although the voices were low, they appeared loud to my soul. I looked left and right (*Sorry! I again forgot that I had no neck*).

I could observe everything from top. There were two women in *punditji*'s small room. They were saying, "*Punditji* we also have to get our daughters married and here you single-handedly polish off all the money from donation chest. And all the fruit, dry fruit-milk, you sell off to sweetmeat shops and milk dairies around the temple at half the rates.

"Madam! You have been certainly misinformed. You are mistaken. I also have to show my face to God. How I could do such misdeeds? I don't wish to go to hell."

"*Pundit* Shatrupalji", they said, "We have concrete proof of all your evil doings." *Punditji* shuddered on listening to all what they narrated. He started trembling. He realised that his job was at stake. He begged of them. "You both are like my sisters. Won't you pardon your brother for this fault of his?"

On hearing this, both the women went towards the corner. They discussed something and came back and said, "*Punditji* you better consider everything seriously."

"Tomorrow, we will send our husbands. You discuss every issue in detail and don't forget that it is we who can save you from your adversaries."

"Okay my sisters! I will accept all the terms your husbands will propose." To this both women simultaneously said, '*Public hai sab janti hai* (Public knows all).'

Next day, *punditji,* to defeat his adversaries, made friends with the President and Secretary of the temple management committee. Now they both started getting their share out of the booty, sorry, out of the public donations.

And now people started calling 'Shatrupal' as 'Mitrupal'. Out of fun people started addressing him as Pundit Mitrupal, of course, in private.

(I learnt of all these developments after I had departed from the world. Then I started hearing all such things with the murmuring of the air, as living beings could not).

Yes! *Punditji* was lost in the list of the items of refreshment. After some time, his attention was drawn back to Sharmaji. *Punditji* took Sharmaji to the hall and got everything inspected.

Sharmaji had served in the wireless department and he thoroughly inspected all the equipment. He even checked the battery terminals. He did not want to leave anything to chance.

While holding the mike, he noticed *ghee* stains all over the mike. On observing this, *Punditji* realised that if the *ghee* stains are not removed then Sharmaji may change the venue to some other place or may give the contract to somebody else. *Punditji* immediately removed the cloth hanging on his shoulder and started cleaning the mike. But how could the dirt of so many years vanish so soon?

On watching *punditji*'s helplessness, Sharmaji, giving a stern warning to him said, "Make sure that the mike is cleaned properly or otherwise...!"

Punditji cutting Sharmaji's conversation short, said, "Sir, don't worry. I will clean all the equipment with my own hands."

Punditji thought' it would be very unwise if he lets this golden opportunity of eating such delicious eatables slip out of his hands. Then Sharmaji took the mike in his hands. "Hello... one... two... three...!" Finally satisfied, he left for his home.

The day of prayer meet came.

Normally, not many people attend such prayer meets. Rather there are very few. Sharmaji remembered that in the last such prayer meet, which he had attended, there were hardly 100-150 people.

But in this prayer meet he had expected very thin attendance. The reason for this was, that Mohan *Saheb* was hardly seen in such prayer meets. And people believe in the policy of 'give and take'. Sharmaji did some mental calculations, thought it would be a blessing if even 50 people make their appearance.

But behold! What was this? A mob suddenly surged from no where, near Hall No. 1. It seemed as if people had come to join AAP (Aam Aadmi Party). Sharmaji hurriedly calculated the strength of the mob which could be around 400 in number.

There was a traffic *jam* in front of the temple. The police controlroom immediately relayed this information to the DIG (Deputy Inspector General) traffic, Rakhi Sawant. She came running to the spot on her Royal Enfield motorcycle instead of her official jeep. In minutes, she was at the location.

She assessed there was no cause of worry and left the place, after giving suitable instructions to the traffic inspector.

Sharmaji immediately asked Sanjay to increase the quantity of items of refreshment. But Sanjay's brother, Ballu was a big planner. It was he who had leaked the list of items of refreshment to all his friends, residing in Jacobpura, New Colony, Arjun Nagar, etc....!

And then all his friends and in turn their friends had flocked to the temple on scooters, motorcycles, cars ... and on whatever conveyance they could lay their hands on. The crowd was so huge that the number of people outside the hall was more than the number of the people who were inside.

Anyway, the chairs from the hall were removed to adjust the extra crowd. Moreover, Sharmaji had assured my wife that all arrangements will be done in a proper manner. And that is why, before adjusting all the people inside the hall, he had shifted all the items of refreshment to the dining room.

After Sharmaji was sure that all people had been adjusted inside and nobody is left out, then he called his friend Ahuja and briefing him said, "Now, lock the door from outside, and keep the key with you. In no circumstances you will give this key to anybody. When this prayer meet is over I will give you a ring and then you open the gate from outside."

As per the instruction of Sharmaji, Rishi locked the door. What a lock, it was a big factory lock.

Ahuja knew that the timing of prayer meet was from 6 pm to 8 pm and there was a sufficient time. He thought that during these two hours why should he not finish his various other pending works?

There were a few minutes left for the programme to start when *Pundit* Satrupal started arranging the mike and other stores lying around. On seeing Sharmaji, he immediately removed the cloth hanging on his right shoulder and started cleaning the mike. But there was certainly something strange that his mind and heart were not keen in performing the prayer meet.

In fact, his... for all the items of refreshment and their aroma was ....! While sitting on the stage, his concentration was always towards the items of refreshment in the rear, in the dining room.

His greed to eat the refreshment was troubling him. While sitting on the stage his attention was again and again being drawn towards the dining room or towards the tables laden with milk cakes, *mathis, kachories, biscuit, samosas* etc.

At last after taking final decision, he called his junior Pundit near him, as he thought he was the only junior pundit who was less greedy as compared to others.

That junior Pandit came to him. *Punditji* said something very slowly in to his ears, "Chandrabhan! It was your long cherished desire that you should also get an opportunity to do the prayer meet. So today, I am giving you this golden chance. But be careful. You should not commit any mistake. Also, I am sitting in the rear in the dining room. And yes, I will give you ten per cent of whatever the donations are. If you agree, then say so...!" But before *punditji* could complete his sentence, Chandrabhan nodded his head meaning 'yes'. Not once but number of times.

On hearing this, there was a glow on the face of Pundit Shatrupal. He moved his hand over his fat round belly. Controlling himself, he said, "Brothers and sisters, today I am not feeling well and my junior Pandit Chandrabhan will conduct the prayer meet. I will be sitting near the sweet meats... I mean... I will be in the dining room."

He cursed himself! Because of the greed of sweetmeats, he was almost about to give himself away!

He went straight to dinning room. In that room nobody except him was permitted to enter. Reaching there he quickly gulped two-three pieces of *kachories* and milk cakes.

The scene of the hall was something like this... On the stage, there was *Pundit* Chandrabhan and in the rear of the hall, *Pandit* Shatrupal. In front, people were sitting on *durries* and mattresses and on the sides; people were sitting with their backs reclining against the walls. Towards the rear, there were some chairs which were placed for the special guests, dignitaries and renowned doctors.

Sharmaji was very perturbed with the condition Mohan *Saheb* had laid on his wife. That if she ever planned to hold his prayer meet, it should only be between 6 and 8 pm.

Otherwise also people were surprised to hear about the said timing of prayer meet. Earlier, during such meets the timings of the prayer meet had been either between 3-4 or 4-5 pm, and this time...! But they did not know that I had told the timing to my wife after a great thought and consideration. During my life time, whatever few meetings I had attended I observed the timing chosen for prayer meet between 3-4 or 4-5 pm was absolutely cock-eyed (absurd). Because people have their lunch around 2 pm and the timing of three-four or 4-5 pm is of their afternoon *siesta.* And to fix these timings for prayer meet was absolutely unfair... more like a punishment for the attendees.

People do come but have you ever carefully observed them? Yes. Why not? You have certainly observed them. You are also part of them. Most of the people are.... drowsy. With great difficulty people try to keep their eyes from getting closed. 95% people are asleep. People act in such a way as if their eyes are open.

Let me try and explain...

I thought, as most of the people go to Huda Park in the evening, so instead of going there, they would not mind coming to the prayer meet. And otherwise also, they would get good variety of eatables....! (While *visualing, my mouth started watering... Arei yes!* I *remember. I have no mouth so how can my mouth start watering?).*

Sharmaji was very impressed with the quality and standard of the items. This was a very strange timing of the prayer meet. As the list of items of refreshment had leaked to the people so they thought that though the timing of the meet between 6-8 pm is late but does not matter, they will get plenty of delicious items to eat.

After getting signal from *pundit* Shatrupal, Chandrabhan started the programme. He was saying such good words about me that, even I did not know that I was such a great person (*I felt very ashamed on being showered such false praises*).

People were not able to grasp what *Pundit* Chandrabhan was saying or it would not be wrong to say that even Pundit Chandrabhan himself did not understand, what he was uttering. I am sorry, I said something incorrect. In fact, it was for the reason that his whole attention was concentrated on those items of refreshment. Moreover, he had observed *pundit* Shatrupal gulping *kachories* and pieces of *milk cake.*

Some of the people were sitting very patiently taking the support of the wall. Although Master Puran Chandra's attention seemed to be centred on *Pandit* Chandrabhan sermons, but he was thinking about what he has to teach his students on reaching home?

In the front was Gopi. He had a provision store and was worried whether his younger brother would be able to handle the sales during his absence properly or not. Because in the evening after office hours, lots of people rush to market to buy their essentials.

My student Yogesh Aggrawal was sitting in the front row. He appeared to be very gloomy. He had a lot of affection with me. Many a times I had advised to him to get tiles fixed on his office wall. But I am not sure whether he still has got it done or not. Yes, he did say that he had selected the tiles with a picture of horses on them. The poor fellow is so hardworking. Though his elder brothers make fun of him and always say he must be loitering around somewhere on road. Anyway! What can I say, these are their views.

My friend Maj B.S. Sahota before coming to the prayer meet had put fish and meat *tikkas* in the micro oven with timing of two hours. So, that when he goes back...! His mind was constantly occupied with this. He was worried, for any delay would cause the fish and mutton tikkas to get over-roasted.

Also before coming here, he had put the soda and beer bottles in the freezer and was afraid they may not burst due to...! Then he thought that as it is exceptionally cold, the moment he goes back he will have two large *Patiala* pegs of whisky with hot fish and mutton *tikkas* and try to get rid of boredom of such prayer meet.

Like this, all other people were also engrossed in their respective thoughts.

The attention of almost all people sitting there, was drawn to the *kachories, milkcake, mathies, dhoklla* and the sweet smell of the items of refreshment lying in the dinning room.

When there were nearly forty-five minutes left for the programme to conclude, then *pundit* Chandrabhan took the mike in his hand and glancing at the gathering said, 'In case any one of you wishes to say a few words about Mohan *Saheb*, you are most welcome.'

After listening to all praises people showered upon me, it felt as if they were not expressing their views about me, but of some other great man.

On hearing such tailor-made praises, my wife realised that she hardly knew anything about her husband i.e. me. If she had known this thing earlier, she would have certainly got my form to join (AAP) Aam Aadmi Party filled.

First of all, Sharmaji took the mike and said, *'Devieo aur Sajjano*! Mohan *Saheb* loved me a lot'. And as he said this, he thought, 'What the hell he loved me! Every month he would hand over his water and electricity bills to me for payment. And everytime seeing me he would call me and start reciting some *gazals* or poems. All the years of my life I had served in the communication department and except the radio frequency I did not have had any interest in any other subject. There was a great difference between the wave lengths of our frequencies. Just to please him I would shower praises on his poems. Then I would open the net and waste my time in trying to understand the meaning of his stanzas of poetry.'

Sharmaji had told his wife, that he did not have even a distant association with poetry. But laughingly he would say, 'what to do? He is very boring and a *'chipku'* kind of person. He will not understand this thing (*I came to know of these things when I had left the human attire. Had I known this earlier I would have…?).*

Sharmaji came out of his reverie and started saying, 'May God give peace to his departed soul'. And before Sharmaji could say anything further Dr Bhalla took, rather snatched, the mike from him and said, 'Brothers and sisters!' I was not only a personal doctor but a very close friend of Mohan *Saheb*. He would open his heart to me and he had even disclosed all his personal matters to me. So much so, with whom and what relations… Anyway, leave it here. Moreover Mohan *Saheb* won't like me to wash his dirty linen in and…!

You don't know what type of help and service he had rendered to medical science fraternity. But the most important thing was that he was not afraid of any kind of surgery. I came to know of this when he came to me…!

One day Mohan *Saheb*'s niece Dr Namita Singh called him to her clinic, she did his X-ray, MRI, Ultrasound, CT Scan, etc, and God knows what else. She made a horoscope of his body and handing that to him said, "Uncle, this contains history of your eyes, nose, ear, throat, lungs, liver, pancreas, etc. Now, you have a very short time left. Please go and consult a good surgeon and get your car, I mean, your body repaired. Otherwise there are chances of it, breaking down any time, anywhere."

Initially! he was very casual and did not take her advice seriously. When after passing long time he did not take any corrective steps and did not change his attitude, then one day her husband Col Giriraj told him little sternly, "Uncle, when Namita is saying then why don't you show your *'janampatri''* I mean your medical history to a capable surgeon?"

It was at this that Mohan *Saheb* became serious and visited the nearest Chikitsa Nursing' home. There he met Dr Bhalla. He was not only thin, lean but very social and jovial. During conversation he came to learn about Mohan *Saheb's* taste and passion about poetry. Dr Bhalla gave so much applause for his poetry that he became doctor's fan and very happily said, "Doctor Bhalla, you examine me and do any operation which you feel necessary."

Doctor enquired of him if he had got his medical insurance policy. On hearing 'yes', he was overwhelmed and went to his cabin. He rang up his wife and said, "Rupali! You were annoyed with me that I have neither given a *sari* nor a golden necklace in the last three months. Now rejoice a patient of mediclaim has come. In addition to sari and golden necklace, I will also give you a treat at hotel with roasted chicken."

After this doctor operated him for *hernia*. A few days later, some city doctors came to Dr Bhalla and told him that they were worried as they were not getting human body for their research projects.

Dr Bhalla told them to give him some time. After two days. he called all the city doctors and told them that he had one living human being available and they can do all sorts of experiment.

Those doctors were astonished and first of all did not believe this. Later on, he told them that one of his friend and patient, Mohan *Saheb* is such an amazing person who does not fear coming under the knife.

After a few days, he introduced them to Mohan *Saheb* but cautioned them to be very lavish in showering praises on each and every *gazal* and poem, he recites. Thus in this process of appreciation of his *shairi*, they bisected all his organs for experiments, which added to the treasure of medical history.

"Dear friends, for the service he did to the medical science we have made our plans to erect his statue in Jhandu Ram Park which would be taller than...!

We have requested state, central medical wing to allot us 51 lakhs for this purpose. (*Then Dr Bhalla thought that though we have asked for 51 lakhs, but we will only spend 31 lakhs and share the rest 20 lakhs amongst...! Thinking of this he had a mysterious smile on his face).*

And for the inaugural ceremony, we have decided to call the health minister.

One of the persons from the crowd got up and asked, "Doctor *Saheb*, will the minister be from Aam Admi Party (AAP)."

At this question, Dr Bhalla losing his cool shot back, "*Nahin mere BAAP ka hoga*" (No, he will be from my ...!). And he soon realised his mistake and controlling himself, politely, apologetically said, "*Mere bhai*, when we belong to Haryana, then why would we call health minister of other state."

And continuing his conversation said, "Without taking your further time, I would only like to say that Mohan *Saheb* was a person with a very far sight and believed in the service of humanity." One day while sitting he said, "Doctor, as a woman after her demise does not carry her ornaments with her, similarly I wish to leave my organs here. So after my demise, please take out my organs and keep them secure in your laboratory."

"But first of all I would like to make an offer to my very close and dear friends, those who need them the most."

Dr Bhalla said that according to his desire he wanted his eyes to be given to his friend Radhey Sham. Hearing this, his friend was on cloud nine. After all what a blind man wishes? Two eyes! He abruptly got up but went into...! He remembered that his friend had the tendency of winking right, left and centre and by getting his eyes transplanted, he may also get into the routine of...! And shuddered at the thought of facing the ire of the people and uttered 'no' so loudly that people around got astonished.

Then it was the turn of his heart, for this Dr Bhalla called the name of his friend Dharam Pal. Due to excitement he quickly stood up as the condition of his heart was deplorable. But he thought that his friend was a 'dil pheink' type of person. He may also imbibe this habit of his friend and face fury of the public.

And he declined the offer.

Then it was the turn of his lungs. Dr Bhalla announced the name of Uppal. Hearing this you could see radiance on uppal's face. But that appeared to be very shortlived. He was otherwise a *'yoga'* instructor, but one day due to excessive cold he got *bronchitis* and his lungs got severely affected.

He then realised that his friend had the bad habit of smoking. Every day he would consume ten-ten packs *of 'Chaar Minaar' cigarettes.* He wondered as to what would be left of his lungs... He thought. It will be full of nicotine—nicotine...!

He refused to take the offer.

And at the end, name of Ved Sharma was announced. He is the owner of a Video Channel. On coming to know of the prayer meet, had left his office-work in between and come running, especially to be in attendance. All of Mohan *Saheb's* friends knew that he may not take anything but would definitely give something to his friend.

Mohan had left his kidney for him. He felt very *ascetic*. The condition of his kidney was deplorable. Before saying 'yes', he thought for a moment. It occurred to him that his friend being an army officer, would all by himself consume ten bottles of monthly quota of army liquor allotted to him. So what would be left in his kidney?

A scrap dealer would not pay even Rs five for these second hand kidneys.

When all of his friends declined the offer of his organs, Dr Bhalla showing a sense of helplessness said, "Well, as you people wish! We will then distribute these organs among the poor and the needy or auction them. And in this process whatever the funds are raised, will be added to the money allocated by the Government. This would help us in making the statue even taller than Qutab Minar". Hearing this people started clapping.

"Yes, lastly, the condition of Mohan *Saheb's* ears was so bad that he could not hear anything from his right ear. That is why; when anybody would come to him for collecting payment then he would put his right ear forward.

Since he had a hearing problem, he would fight with his family members accusing them of organising a coup against him...! Because of this hearing problem he had changed his *'will'* six times."

At this juncture, Simrti Irani from the crowd stood up and enquired, 'Dr Bhalla, what happened to his pacemaker?'

Dr Bhalla said *barely in audible* voice, "I had got that implanted with my heart, even during his life time."

He had hardly completed his sentence when, Jimmy Walia snatched the mike from him and adjusting his hand started weeping bitterly. (*After seeing his love and affection for me I felt like crying. Even my closest relations had not wept so vociferously. Tears started flowing from my eyes. But then I remembered that, since I had no body; how come tears can start dripping?*).

Jimmy Walia started saying, 'Brothers and sisters, my tears communicate that how much love and affection I had for Mohan *Saheb*. Not only me but my other twelve friends also; we all have formed a fan club in his memory. We request you all to be very liberal in giving donations and with your contributions we will do some charitable work like...! While saying this Jimmy Walia got lost in his thoughts. He thought, "Who the hell is interested in charitable activities. Rather with the money collected we have to pay off, the money Mohan *Saheb* owes to various people."

Realising that he had nothing more to say, he handed over the mike to his neighbour Colonel Bains.

He said, 'Friends, Mohan was a very kind-hearted man. He did not love the human being so much as he...! He had kept five dogs and used to look after them, just like his children. He had hardly spoken these words, when Y. Bannerji sitting in the corner, lifted the edge of his trouser and looked at his ankle, which had been bitten by his five dogs. This had happened five years ago but the bite mark and the scar was as fresh as if it had happened just yesterday.

He spat a filthy abuse. *(On hearing that abuse I got a big jolt. I thought I had done a great research on abuses during my lifetime but I had never come across such a terrible and horrible Punjabi abuse. Anyway if, I ever get a life again then I will definitely add this abuse to upto date my dictionary of favourite Punjabi abuses.)*

After hearing about the attachment to dogs, Premvir Singh remembered that Mohan *Saheb* had kept those five dogs for his security but would every morning bring them in front of his house for defecating.

And Colonel Bains instantaneously gave the mike to Premvir Singh. He was not prepared for this and just said, 'He had lot of affection for me. Everyday he would bring all his loving dogs to say good morning to me.'

The truth, however, was that the moment Premvir Singh would see them coming towards him, he would immediately caution his doctor daughter, Payal, to keep the injection for *rabbies* ready. As there are lots of chances that Mohan *Saheb*'s dogs may...! *(Come to kiss him and he may need the injection. Yes, I remember many times my loving dogs made a futile effort to..... But...... they were not successful and my friend was spared of this agony.)*

As the attention of the people was drawn towards *kachories, dhokla, dhoda,* milk cake... so most of the people were not able to understand as to what nonsense was being spoken about me.

(While suspended in the sky, on reading the unsaid views of the mind of people, I felt very hurt. They had betrayed my trust.)

Every month they would come and finish, polish off my army quota of ten bottles of liquor. and that too with *kaju, pista* and... non-veg *tikkas*. And what sort of horrible thoughts about me... they had stabbed me in my back...! *(Then I realised that when I had no back how they could stab me... It is good that doctors were not successful in saving me. Moreover, I don't want to live with such set of selfish people... Yes, if ever I get a chance in my next birth then I will get them bitten by my five dogs not once but five times, so that they remember this, for their next seven lives.)*

Then *punditji* picked up the mike and said, '*Sajjano*, there is still some time left and if someone wants to say a few words about the departed soul he may do so.

But what is this? *Punditji* had hardly uttered these words when, ten-twelve women stood up. *(I got panicky..... nervous. I felt, I had perspiration on my forehead. Then I realised, when I had no forehead, how could there be perspiration on my forehead.)*

But I did not know those women. I started getting worried. God knows what rubbish they may blurt about me, I thought. I started praying that soon my prayer meet should get concluded and people should move forward towards refreshment....... !

By this time, one of those women quickly snatched the mike from *punditji*'s hand. *(I got panicky, not knowing as to what none-sense she may say. Then I laughed at myself because I was no more. The question of being tense did not arise.)*

She started saying, 'Brothers and sisters; he was a gentle man,' but she could not say that, I had special feelings for her. The necklace she was wearing had been presented to her by me and I had even promised her of gifting her a pair of earrings.

She touched her both ears and looking up slowly said, 'you are a great liar. You should have at least fulfilled your promise of getting me the earrings.'

She started crying very loudly. My wife was perplexed and thought even she had not wept so bitterly on my demise, as this woman... and then how does she know Mohan *Saheb* so well. And she was saying that Mohan *Saheb* was a very gentleman, when even after forty years I had had not been able to assess and judge whether he was a gentleman or...?

Then Ruby came out of the bevy of women and quickly took the mike in her right hand. She had covered, wrapped her fully with a snowwhite shawl. She was looking like a statue of grief as if a sculptor had chiseled her out of a white marble stone.

I thought perhaps she is in a great shock because of my sudden departure; that is why in such an attire. While I was engrossed in such thoughts, that with a jerk of the left hand she threw the shawl aside from her shoulders, which engulfed *pundit* Chandrabhan.

The moment the shawl was off from her body, the fragrance of the perfume spread all around. The hall was full of sweet fragrance. The moment her shawl fell, the eyes of people opened wide. I mean the ones that were open, opened more widely and those which were close opened.

Ruby had put on red top and blue bell bottom and watching her well-chiseled, hour glass figure of 36-26-36, many people missed their heart beats. On watching her well proportionate body all the young crowd stood up in gaze. And all the older ones clutched their hearts with their both hands. Even in such a cold weather, many people had beads of perspiration on their forehead.

All the ladies present their started getting envious of her figure, but my wife remained very cool, much unperturbed. She just looked at Ruby and gave a broad smile. I thought that during her youth she herself had been a *beauty queen* and then I was not a fool that I had married her.

I do not know how my wife was able to read this thought of mine. Probably her sixth sense had started functioning. My wife looked up and as a gesture of thanks waved her right hand.

Yes, seeing mike in Ruby's hand I did get jittery. I thought she is very outspoken lady and may not divulge something about me. Her personality was such that people would have blindly believed her.

She had held the mike in her left hand. She held the collar of her top, looked up as if saying that you had bought this from shopping mall for me.

Then her right hand went towards her *bell bottom but I had not chosen that for her*. She looked up and understood and in heart of her heart said that day if your wife had not arrived, then this would also had been of...! Anyway, it is you who had given me the money to buy it.

During this scenario of 36-26-36, a heart specialist of the *NCR* was also present there in the prayer meet. He got very worried and felt that if for some time more Ruby did not put her white shawl back on her shoulders, then the chances are these that white sheets may be needed for all patients with heart ailment.

The doctor immediately signaled her and Ruby instantly understood the language of his signal. She had, for some time, worked in the school of deaf and dumb children. She quickly removed her shawl with a jerk from *panditji* and put it back on her. And thus the city was saved from the biggest calamity.

Yes, I forgot to mention that I had my first meeting with her in *HUDA* Park of my 17-A sector. That day she immediately put forward her hand. How could I miss this golden opportunity and I quickly grasped her hand.

The moment I held her hand in mine, a current of 44,000 watts entered my body. And had I not been wearing shoes with rubber sole; I would have been turned into ash. By Ash I do not mean film star, Aishwarya Roy, as she is commonly called.

She kept on talking and I kept holding on to her hand. She had very soft and tender hands. After all for how long, a delicate damsel could bear it. When her hand started to pain she looked towards me with... a pitiable expression.

I understood what she intended to say. "Yes, Yes... sorry... sorry... I am very very... sorry. In fact while listening to you I had forgotten your hand...!" I said regretfully. But the truth was that I had been deliberately holding her hand.

During the week we would shake each others hand at least three to four times. And my drama of holding her hand... continued. The fact is that along with me, even she had started relishing my hand shake.

Yes. She looked up towards..., as if saying, 'Who would hold my hand now?' She wanted to say much more. But ... she could not. And not wanting to, she handed over the mike to other woman.

First of all, I did not recognise that woman but later on, I realised that she was the director of the company I served. She had a crush on me, I mean...!

Whenever I sat in her car, she would intentionally put her hand over mine, as if she had not done it deliberately. But I understood her game plan very well and I did not desire to get entangled in her trap.

Whenever I mentioned about this to my friend Vikram, he would sarcastically say, My friend, be bold when she is herself tempting you then...!

I would always reply, "*Yaar*! I cannot. My company pays me a monthly salary of Rs 70,000. Out of this amount I pay an EMI of Rs 50,000. If table turns turtle then would you be paying my EMI?"

The thought of this conversation I do not know how reached my director. She pointed her hand up towards my direction and slowly muttered, "Today my sixth sense has perhaps become operational and I am able to listen what had conspired between you and your friend. I wish you had just mentioned this thing even once to me, and then I would have doubled your salary. I am surprised as to what type of *fauji* you are? Don't commit this mistake again in your next birth."

Now, *punditji* suddenly snatched the mike from my director and announced that the time of prayer meet was over. And requested the congregation to proceed to the dining hall where all the items of refreshment were laid.

And lo..., what a scene! The attention of all the crowd was already focussed towards the sweet aroma of the eatables.

They ran and attacked the dinning room like hunting dogs chasing the rabbits and deers. And within minutes there was a big disorder, the place got turned into a big battle ground.

In the *melee,* 11 people sustained injuries, hands of two persons got fractured, four person sustained skull injuries and three persons sprained their ankles. But the best part was that no one died.

After observing this scene of scuffle, Sharmaji thought that in future if at all he has to organise such a meet then he would make sure that there is doctor in attendance to give first aid to the injured.

And in today's meet, 200 people gulped off the refreshment arranged for 400 people. Half the number of people was left hungry.

In future to overcome such a calamity, in the next meet people will be made to form a queue and every individual would be handed over one packet each.

Prayer Meet Concluded.

There was a big factory lock on Hall No 1. Sharmaji decided to tell Rishi to open the door. But the battery of his mobile phone had got discharged. There was no way to contact Rishi.

Now all people in the hall had virtually become prisoners. Although the mobile phones of other people were functional but they did not have had the mobile number of Rishi. The people of the prayer meet were very impatient to reach their respective homes. There was suddenly a lot of commotion.

Next to Hall No. 1, as I mentioned earlier, was the adjoining Hall No. 2. So, the only way to come out of Hall No. 1 was through Hall No. 2, but the door was closed from the other side.

On hearing a lot of uproar from the adjoining hall, the door between the halls opened. But what was this? There were four very robust security guards stationed on both the sides of the door. On seeing them the crowd got petrified. All the guards had pistols in their hands. The people understood that they would have to have a control over them.

Sufficient chairs had been laid in the second hall. The security guards told the crowd to sit on the chairs and also to behave themselves. The crowd had no option except to obey as ordered.

They sat on the chairs. They noticed that a huge stage had been erected and a big banner hung there. The banner had the words, *Welcome to Party Meet.*

I will explain to you the reason behind holding of the *Party Meet*.

Some days before going up...!

A few days earlier I called Praveen and Rishi in the evening for a peg of whisky. During the drinks, I told them that they should keep all the details to themselves. And they should not take it lightly.

I told them that I am giving them this task as I have complete trust on them. Both of them were intrigued as to what duty I was referring to.

I had met Praveen a couple of years ago during shooting of a feature film. Both of us, very often used to go for the auditions together. As I was mobile, I would take him along in my car. We had worked together in many films and our friendship increased so much that I decided to take him to the hospital along me for the implant of 'pace maker'. He would always come forward to render any help I wanted.

Before coming to the hospital he advised me very seriously that I did not require the implant at that moment. Your pace is already very fast. Even faster than *Milkha Singh.* If you get yourself implanted with pace maker then your speed will become so fast that you would even leave great *Milkha Singh* far behind.

Then light heartedly said, "Sir! I was just joking. But the fact is that no doctor undertakes any operation on Sundays."

"You drove yourself to the hospital in your car. It is obvious that there is no specific emergency. This doctor is implanting the pace maker just for the heck of it. *I had been medical representative............ I am aware of the tricks of these doctors. He is doing this operation just to have his 40 per cent commission. He is making you a scape goat."*

And that is what happened. After implanting pace maker, when the very next day the doctor did not come, I realised that I had been the very victim of his atrocity.

The nurse wanted to say that after the implantation of the pace maker the doctor had left his job. Because he was afraid that experiment done on you... can fail any time and in that case...Bhondsi, Tihar jail was not very far...! But the nurse did not muster the courage to say so.

I panicked. I immediately asked Praveen, "Please check whether doctor had really implanted the pace maker or not. And doctor may not have had implanted pace maker of Chinese make. Chinese products are not reliable or have no guarantee. I don't know for how long it functions."

Do you recollect that the *Chinese* wife of our dear friend Tej Pal Singh could only run for? "I mean to say survived for five years."

Then Praveen took a hand towel to remove beads of perspiration from my forehead, said. "Sir! If the doctor has not implanted the pace maker, then you are definitely going to live for more than 100 years."

On hearing these words of consolation, I was much relieved of my worries. It was more than six months since the implantation of pace maker. Whether Dr Zalim Singh had implanted it or not, whether it was *Chinese or of Mayapuri,* it has not yet been confirmed.

I had met Rishi during the programmes of *gazal* and dramas. We both were very fond of dramas and would often go to watch the plays. His grandfather was fan of Mirza Ghalib. So, he too had developed a liking for the poetry of Mirza Ghalib. Every now and then he would recite a couplet of the poet.

We all have had the same tastes and therefore, we all bonded well with each other.

And then clearing their bewilderness, I said, "See friends, as you very well know I am dead against this ritual of holding these prayers meets. So, if God forbid, my wife plans to hold such a meet, in that case to counter that, you have to organise a Party Meet."

The very first thing you have to do is to book the Hall No. 2. So that party meet could be celebrated there to remove the gloom and boredom of that prayer meet from people's mind. Coming and going is part of life. A person who has come has to go. It is not something unique. Anyway, whatever the questions you have about party meet, you may ask me about them later.

Both of you are very aware of what my tastes are. Or you may say, I am fond of only two things. The first is recitation of poems, songs, watching item songs and secondly is to have sessions of drinking.

Praveen, you will take care of programmes of poems, songs and item songs. You will also make arrangement of inviting top. most artists like Ghalib, Sahir, Jigger, Javed, Gulzar... etc. and for songs Lata, Asha, Runa Laila, Reshma... and for item songs...! You must have three item songs like *Muni Badnam hui, Sheela ki jawani, Jalebi Bai* and yes make sure there is a rain dance of Mallika Sehrawat. It is question of my reputation but make sure Mallika Sehrawat is fully clothed.

Rishi, you will help Praveen in execution of the duties assigned to him as well as taking care of drinks and snacks. You have good knowledge of snacks and drinks. With eyes closed by just smelling, you can tell as to what brand of whisky it is?

Yes, now you both ask me the questions you have."

Praveen said, "Sir! The biggest question is that why would such renowned poets, singers and item song artists come to such a small place?"

"Praveen, when we offer them the money they ask for, then why won't they come? They work in the films for the sake of money. And then why would they have any objection on coming to such a small village?"

And bring them here in a special plane. After the plane lands in Junta Park then ferry them to the Hall No. 2 in a helicopter.

Praveen said, "Sir! Even then, if they decline to come then? And moreover, it is long time since some of them passed."

"I have a solution for that also. I have an old friend *Chamatkari Baba* (An Illusionist), a drug addict who stays near Kalka ji Mandir. He is mostly intoxicated and if in mood can create amazing illusions that the onlooker gets puzzled, rather flabbergasted. With his *tantrik* knowledge, he can transform anybody into anything like Jigger, Ghalib...! Can turn a goat into Runa Laila or Munni and even Sheela... He can turn donkey...? And be careful, don't go in front of him lest he turns you into a donkey!" I said with hearty laugh.

Hearing this from me, they both grinned.

"Sir! It looks as if you are talking about the times of bygone era of *Hatim Tai* or *Chander Kanta.* But during the present era it is not possible." Rishi replied.

I told Rishi that only time will tell. You will know later on how much truth is there in my statement.

Rishi said, "Sir! This is true that I have a vast experience and knowledge about the liquors. But organising a drink and snacks party is not my cup of tea."

"Rishi you don't worry about that. For this you go and meet my dear friend Captain Natkhat Singh." I continued after a brief pause and said, "Praveen, you have a very bad and good as well, habit of asking questions. Now, your question as to why his name is Natkhat Singh? The answer to that is that he was very naughty during his childhood. Then one of the servants of his father just at random suggested, "Sir! Why not we name Chotta *Saheb* as Natkhat Singh."

First his father thought for a moment that this *'son of an owl'* was playing a very crude joke and then he realised that the suggestion of his servant Makhan Singh was very appropriate. The name fitted well on his son and so my friend was named as Natkhat Singh.

But later on, on the insistence of his mother his name was changed to Sher Singh. His mother said that there was no doubt that their son was very naughty but there is no denying the fact that he roars like a lion.

So basically it is only me, who is aware of this fact. And only I, out of affection address him by Natkhat."

I then advised Rishi to go and seek the help of Captain Singh. He was a very seasoned officer of Armoured Regiment and he had organised great parties during his service and retired life. Keeping his experience in mind, many senior Army Generals come to him to take his advice/suggestions.

"And he has so much knowledge about the liquors that with eyes closed and without touching, just smelling a sealed bottle he can tell what brand of a particular whisky that is?"

After my departure from the world, my both dear friends and you may say my students started to undertake the mission I had assigned them. Praveen told Rishi, "I am proceeding to make arrangement for *gazals*, songs, item songs etc. You better go to Captain Singh's house and learn the tricks of organising a snack and drink party. There should be no let downs in Mohan *Saheb*'s party meet."

Anyway when Rishi reached Captain Singh's house, he was having an argument with his wife over the payment of some EMI. She was saying, "I am fed up with paying your EMIs. Your EMIs will end with my life only."

By then she noticed Rishi standing at the door. She just signaled him that there was somebody standing outside at the door to meet him.

He immediately called Rishi to come inside. After listening to his problems, Captain Singh told him, Rishi, don't worry. I will take care of everything. You leave all the arrangements of security and service of snacks and liquor upon me.

My housekeeper 'Chhotu' and ex-serviceman, bar man Ranjit will be there to assist you. But you must ensure that there is a very tight cloth wrapped around his nose. Though a bar man, Ranjit did not drink, is a teetotaler but he gets intoxicated with the mere fumes of liquor."

And then continued saying, "Please also make sure that there is a tight cloth wrapped around the mouth of my house keeper."

"But! Sir why so?" Rishi enquired in surprise.

"This is for the reason that Chhotu is so expert and while serving liquor he quietly gulps couple of pegs through his throat. And the beauty is that he does not let anybody notice this. So if there is a tight cloth around his mouth he would not be able to do any *hanky panky*. This check upon him is very necessary."

And then carrying on his conversation said, "Yes! Rishi, in this party meet of some his relations would also be in attendance. Amongst them would be three of his very close relations and make sure there is no let up in their sevice. But make sure that Bakshi, Neeto Walia and Pad Singh are made to sit on a far off corner table. Make sure that neither water nor soda is taken to their table. By seeing both these items they all loose their balance of mind and they get mad. Their blood starts boiling."

"But sir, why so?" Rishi enquired.

"This is because they prefer taking liquor in its real form; I mean to say neat, on the rocks. Bakshi to whom I taught how to drink, has overtaken me and has become my *guru*. In 10 minutes he polishes off so many bottles that it becomes impossible for twelve people to control him.

He is six feet two inches tall. When his wife has to buy five kgs of potatoes, she just places his two hands in the other side of the balance. Like actor Sunny Deol, each of his hands weighs two and a half kilos.

And don't ask me about Pad Singh, in just 15 minutes he starts calling cats and dogs."

"Sir! I do not follow. What is the meaning of this?" Rishi enquired.

"Even his wife Amita has not been able to elucidate the meaning of this during her married life of 35 years. After getting fed up with this habit of her husband, she has also started drinking Old Monk. The result is that now both of them start fighting like cats and dogs amongst each other."

Seeing both of them fighting like cats and dogs with each other, their son Sunny, in a fit of stress helplessness clutches his own hair. And his wife Manu watching this laughs boisterously.

"It takes Neetu Walia just 10 minutes to get drunk. And in this situation he climbs the flag pole of Nehru Stadium. When in spite of repeated requests he does not climb down, then finding no other alternative, his wife uses her pet monkey to get him down. She then offers her pet monkey a chocolate as an incentive. Monkey getting signal from her immediately climbs the pole and to get Neetu on the ground, pulls his knickers down. So, getting afraid of loosing his knickers and becoming... he jumps down."

On hearing this. Rishi said, "Sir! All of them are very fascinating characters."

"Time is less, otherwise I would have narrated you even more mesmerising anecdotes," I replied.

All people finally settled on the chairs. At the same time, Captain Singh and Chamatkari Baba both had made themselves comfortable behind the stage. Captain *Saheb* had told *Chamatkari*

Baba that he will be called whenever required. At the moment he should sit relaxed and enjoy Old Monk with *tangri kebabs* and *mutton chops*.

Captain Singh thought, first of all the programme of drinks and snacks should be organised, as the people during the prayer meet had suffered a very harrowing experience.

Captain *Saheb* then picked up the mike and started saying, 'I welcome you all in the party meet.' We are well aware and apologise for the inconvenience that all of you just experienced. There half of the people were left hungry! They did not get anything to eat, but on the contrary, have got injuries and wounds.

But here in our party meet, you all will get very good eatables like *seekh kabab, mutton tikka, murg tikke, english whisky, gin* and *desi tharra*!

And all you vegetarian people will get *paneer tikke, roasted mushroom, spring rolls*... fruit juice, Limca, Pepsi and for ladies red wine...!

On hearing these mouth-watering details of the menu from Captain Singh, people were over joyed.

Then with his commanding voice he said, 'But first of all, we would like to administer first aid to all those who got injured during the prayer meet.

You would all be happy to know that Dr Namita Singh has agreed to take care of the people injured in the incident. Now, none of you have to worry about this aspect.'

I had given clear cut instruction to Rishi to serve only scotch whisky then how come, this bloody desi tharra has come in between? I looked towards Captain Singh from above. Perhaps his sixth sense had become active. He understood my objection about the serving of *desi tharra* and with the language of signs explained to me that the village people don't relish English whisky as much as they enjoy *desi thaara.* They get a kick only with *desi tharra*. Unless they get it, they don't feel satisfied. So, they would only be able to enjoy your party meet if they are served with their choicest drink.

In fact, we both had learned this language of signs during in IMA (Indian Military Academy, Dehradun). There we both had fallen in love with two deaf and dumb sisters and those two sisters taught us the language of signs.

The session of drinks and snacks started. Even those who had never touched liquor, those absolutely teetotalers after consuming liquor were swinging right and left and those habitual drinkers were in an uncontrollable stage. There was a big confusion everywhere. The cloth wrapped tightly around Ranjit had fallen. And after getting intoxicated with mere fumes of alcohol, he had fallen and was lying in one of the corners of the hall.

As per his habit, Chhotu had very cleverly managed to consume a bottle or two of his favourite brands of Old Monk rum and as repentance was rubbing his nose at the feet of Captain Singh.

Praveen had already briefed the gathering that in the first phase of programme, there would be *Dama dam mast kalander* song by Runa Laila and later on item songs like *'Munni badnam hue, Chikni Chamelli, Jalebi Bai* and then in this severe cold, rain dance of Mallika Sehrawat. And that, too, fully clothed. *(Hearing this, I started shivering. But it dawned upon me that since I do not have a body, How I could shiver.*)

One of the villagers of Sukhrali who had alcohol for the first time, in an inebriated state started shouting, "Fellows! why Mallika Sehrawat is putting on so many clothes?" Hearing this, there was a deafening laughter from the crowd.

On hearing about the injuries sustained by the people, most of the poets and singers felt it safe to run away from the venue. Praveen apprised Captain *Saheb* of these developments. He told Praveen not to worry and immediately summoned *Chamatkari Baba* and briefed *Baba* of the latest situation. *Baba* took charge of the stage and with his expertise in the field of creating illusions, he created Runa Laila, Reshma and many personalities like Mallika Sehrawat and did not let people know that all whatever they saw were just illusions but nothing else. None of the artist was real. Otherwise also people had consumed so much liquor that they wouldn't have bothered to have a look at the artists. Yes! All of them were definitely enjoying the rain dance of Mallika Sehrawat. The programme of drinks and snacks was in its full swing. People were drinking like fish. There was no count, who drank how much?

But this was certain that Master Puran Chand was dancing with the woman wearing *Jhumka* with their arms around each other. Dr and my director were dancing with Runa Laila and were singing *Dama dum mast kalander.*

Pandit Shatrupal had consumed more alcohol than he could handle and in his state of intoxication, also started dancing with Mallika Sehrawat. One person ringing the mandir bells and the other ringing the bells of her male fans and well wishers. It was an enchanting scene.

My friend Rana was holding the hand of Sharmaji and thinking it to be the hand of Ruby was on seventh sky. It had been a few days since Rana had arrived in India and he seemed to have got this golden opportunity of hugging and holding the hand of such a blonde after a long time.

He wished to definitely visit India again to celebrate *party meet* the next year. He looked up towards the sky and said, *'Long live Mohan'.*

Our friend Pal is a saintly person. I'd rather avoid saying anything about what he was doing after consuming alcohol. He was holding a garland of roses and trying to put that into the neck of an English teen.

Our friend Ved Parkash, a creative person that he was, was holding his handy cam and was looking for some good subject for his TV Channel am sure he must have got some good *Masala* for his channel.

Uppal, when drunk, realised he had nothing to do. So, he started teaching *asanas* of *yoga* to beautiful women. And looking at all that from above, reminded about the sculptors of *Khujrao* I wish I had been there. But how I could be that lucky? And had I been there, my wife would have locked me in the ladies washroom. Sorry, I mean in a normal washroom.

Our dear friend Sodhi had consumed quite a bit of whisky. He is a Jat Sikh and believes in taking whisky not by pegs, but gulps it straight from the bottles. He had recently come from UK. He thought, Alas! People of England also celebrate their *party meet* affairs like this.'

After watching Mallika Sehrawat's rain dance, even people started perspiring in such a cold weather.

It was 2 am but the function was so enthralling that people did not realise how the time had passed. There all the people were criticising payer meet, here the same people were appreciating the programme of party meet organised by Captain Singh.

And at the end, a man stood up and asked, "Captain *Saheb*, what is the date for this *party meet* next year? Captain *Saheb* was dumbstruck and couldn't reply.

Programme ended.

Captain Singh knew it was the wish of Mohan *Saheb* that he should celebrate his 75th birthday on seventh March with great pomp and show. It is something of an irony of fate that he has not been able to do it himself. But by organising his party meet on seventh March we have fulfilled his long cherished desire. We made sure that his quota of liquor of ten years which he had earmarked for this function was almost fully consumed.

All the people except Captain Singh, Rishi and my wife had left the venue. Rishi packed all the leftover scotch bottles in his bag and decided to leave. At this juncture, my wife enquired from Rishi as to what he was carrying in his bag?

"Madam, nothing. They are just left over bottles of whisky," Rishi replied.

Simultaneously, my wife and Captain *Saheb* said, "What about our share of whisky bottles?"

"But Captain *Saheb*, I believe you don't ..."! Rishi said with an expression of surprise.

"It is true that I don't drink myself but I do serve liquor to my guests." Captain Singh replied.

And then Rishi looked towards my wife and said, "Madam you also...?"

"Who says I do not drink. Whenever Mohan *Saheb* used to bring his quota of 10 bottles I...! His friend use to remark that Mohan *Saheb* even after a consumption of one bottle does not get drunk. And then how he could? The fact is that I used to take out half of whisky from each bottle and fill it with water. So, how could he get drunk?"

Both Captain Singh and Rishi listened to this with their mouth wide open in surprise and then they all started fighting and struggling among themselves over their share of whisky bottles. My wife pounced upon them like a tigress and captured the whole bag.

Watching this delicate situation, Captain Singh preferred to run away. Rishi also felt the situation to be very tricky. As he felt that my wife had consumed a good quantity of whisky and was very tipsy turvy.

Then my wife took a bottle from the bag and putting that against her mouth polished off the complete bottle in one go. She was in a great state of intoxication and was just about to fall, when I held her. And in this process I got a big jolt and opened my eyes.........

I opened my eyes and noticed my wife sleeping next to me in the bed. She had held my hand very tightly and was blurting in her sleep, 'I will not let you go. I will not let you go.'

I had a laugh and I said, 'Who is going to leave you?'

Perhaps she could not hear me as she was in deep slumber.

About Author (Newspaper Articles)

PAIGAM-E-MOHABBAT: CONCERT WITH GHAZAL MAESTRO PANKAJ UDHAS AT SIRI FORT AUDITORIUM.

AUGUST 22 · 6:30 P.M.

From armyman to reiki healer

Captain Vijay Mohan, a retired army officer has found his calling in reiki

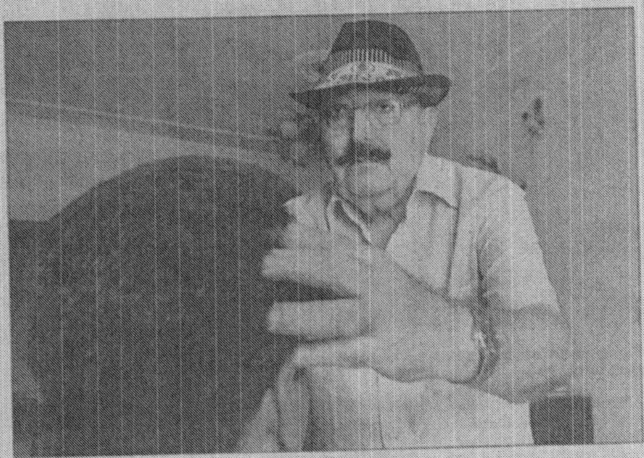

■ Captain Vijay Mohan indulges in his passion for healing patients through reiki. SANJEEV VERMA / HT PHOTO

profile

vijay mohan

Dhananjay Jha

■ dhananjay.jha@hindustantimes.com

Commissioned in the Army in June 1963, Captain Vijay Mohan was Commandant, Border Security Force, in January 1984, when he sought voluntary retirement.

Since then he has been living in Sector 17, Gurgaon, and has been indulging in his passion for healing patients through reiki.

He is very active and lively at 70 and very fond of poetry, short story writing and shayari. He also plays a small role in the Hindi film, Love Aaj Kal.

During his service, Mohan has served in Jammu & Kashmir, Kargil, Khemkaran, Assam, Rajasthan, Ambala and Cooch Behar.

During his early field appointment, he fought in the 1965 war.

VIJAY MOHAN IS VERY ACTIVE AND LIVELY AT 70 AND ALSO VERY FOND OF POETRY, SHORT STORY WRITING AND SHAYARI

Mohan has been fond of reiki, naturopathy, magneto therapy and astrology and learnt from pure experimentation. This led him to develop an interest in reiki. He has done his Masters in reiki and karuna reiki as well. Mohan has written short stories and composed thousands of couplets. He has also done a couple of programmes for All India Radio.

"I cannot forget the 1965 war. I just had spent two years in the Army and the battle at Khemkaran, near Amritsar, started. I served at high altitude of 13,000 ft at Gurez Valley," he says.

His only son lost his eyesight in his childhood; so he opted for voluntary retirement in 1984, deciding to settle down in Gurgaon.

"I found great solace in healing patients through reiki. So far, I have done it on thousands of patients. The government must recognise reiki. We raised the issue in a meeting at the Northeastern Council in Imphal last year," said Mohan.

One of the cartridges is from a Patton tank. SUSHIL KUMAR / HT PHOTO

Prized possessions from the 1965 war

Dhananjay Jha
dhananjay.jha@hindustantimes.com

Memories of the 1965 Indo-Pak war are still fresh in the mind of Captain (retd) Vijay Mohan, a resident of Sector 17. He relives it almost every day. When he left the battlefield, he collected some memorabilia. This is his most priced possession and, of course, invaluable.

"I can never forget the war. We won on the ground but lost many close friends," said Mohan. He added that as soon as the war got over, he collected the leftover articles from the battlefield.

"I collected three empty cartridges, one of which was from a Patton Tank, made in the USA. There were nearly 105 Patton Tanks and other tanks. They were seized and later destroyed by the Indian Army," he stated.

"Besides that, I also managed to bring home a war helmet and a compass, also made in the USA. It still functions very well," added the retired captain.

VIJAY MOHAN CAN NEVER FORGET THE WAR. HE SAYS THEY WON THE WAR ON THE GROUND BUT LOST MANY CLOSE FRIENDS.

The war began on September 6, 1965. There was a ceasefire on September 23, when the two governments agreed to settle the dispute amicably.

"These empty cartridges still bring back the thunder of the tanks and gun explosions. We did not know whose number was next. A friend of ours went to a well, hardly 50 yards from the camp for water. A shell fell on him and he died," said Mohan.

"We were in the Khemkaran sector, 30-35 km from Amritsar. It is then that we were asked to remain alert for a war," he added.

To advertise

GURGAON

Pizzas for children... page 3

Bollywood calling

Retired BSF commander Vijay Mohan and his wife Rekha are happy pursuing a career in the Hindi film industry

Vinod Rajput

ht.rajput@gmail.com

Age is just a number for Gurgaon residents Vijay Mohan, 71, and his wife Rekha Mohan, 68, and they are happy defying it. Instead of being satisfied playing with their grandchildren or enjoying post retirement bliss, this animated duo is busy carving out a career in Bollywood. After playing uncle aunty to Bollywood actor Imran Khan in Mere Brother Ki Dulhan, the duo is busy with another untitled film.

"Besides that, we have just auditioned for three more Hindi movies. We remain in constant touch with Delhi-based people who are in film production. We do not miss any audition which takes place in Delhi-N[illegible]," said retired BSF commander Mohan, who started his Bollywood career with Love Aaj Kal in 2008. Since then he has done more than half a dozen Bollywood movies and five advertisements.

Initially Mohan alone got suitable offers but his wife Rekha also used to accompany him to auditions and finally the duo got a chance to play husband-wife on screen. After Love Aaj Kal, Mohan played a corporator in Pankaj Kapoor starer, Office the movie. Then he worked with Abhay Deol and Sonam Kapoor in Aisha, No one Killed Jessica and Band Baja Baraat, before Mere Brother Ki Dulhan happened. "Now offers keep pouring in because those in the trade know us well and keep inviting us for the auditions," explains Mohan.

Why did this SD College, Shimla, graduate who retired as commandant from Border Security Force (BSF) think of standing in audition queues to become an actor at an age when most people prefer staying home? "I wanted to become an actor as a young boy but had to join the army after college in order to get married to my first love, Rekha. I had won the best actor award in college. But had I not joined the army at that point in time, Rekha's family would not have agreed to marriage," shares Mohan, who feels proud of having served in the army.

He is now happy to fulfill his dream of working in movies. Mohan humbly says that he could fulfill his dream because his wife Rekha encouraged and supported him in whatever he decided to do. And barring Saturday and Sunday, they do not mind standing in long queues amidst young crowd for film auditions. "It is fun even in a crowd if my better half is with me," says Mohan who also does photography. Meanwhile, his wife Rekha too does not mind the crowd or long queues if her husband accompanies. "We have stayed together at the Indo Pak border and in unsafe valleys for two decades. Standing together in audition queues is far easier," adds Rekha.

■ Vijay and Rekha Mohan have several films in hand. MANOJ KUMAR / HT PHOTO

> I had won the best actor award in college but joined the army. Now I am happy following my dreams and a lot of offers are coming my way.
>
> VIJAY MOHAN